Lyn Andrews is one of the UK's top one hundred bestselling authors, reaching No. 1 on the *Sunday Times* paperback bestseller list. Born and brought up in Liverpool, she is the daughter of a policeman and also married a policeman. After becoming the mother of triplets, she took some time off from her writing whilst she raised her children. Shortlisted for the RNA Romantic Novel of the Year Award in 1993, she has now written thirty-one hugely successful novels. Lyn Andrews now lives on the Isle of Man.

By Lyn Andrews and available from Headline

Maggie May
The Leaving Of Liverpool
Liverpool Lou
The Sisters O'Donnell
The White Empress
Ellan Vannin
Mist Over The Mersey
Mersey Blues
Liverpool Songbird
Liverpool Lamplight
Where The Mersey Flows
From This Day Forth
When Tomorrow Dawns
Angels Of Mercy
The Ties That Bind
Take These Broken Wings
My Sister's Child
The House On Lonely Street
Love And A Promise
A Wing And A Prayer
When Daylight Comes
Across A Summer Sea
A Mother's Love
Friends Forever
Every Mother's Son
Far From Home
Days Of Hope
A Daughter's Journey
A Secret In The Family
To Love And To Cherish
Beyond A Misty Shore

Lyn Andrews

Beyond
A Misty
Shore

headline

Copyright © 2011 Lyn Andrews

The right of Lyn Andrews to be identified as the Author of the
Work has been asserted by her in accordance with the
Copyright, Designs and Patents Act 1988.

First published in 2011
by HEADLINE PUBLISHING GROUP

First published in paperback in 2012
by HEADLINE PUBLISHING GROUP

4

Apart from any use permitted under UK copyright law, this publication
may only be reproduced, stored, or transmitted, in any form, or by
any means, with prior permission in writing of the publishers or,
in the case of reprographic production, in accordance with the terms
of licences issued by the Copyright Licensing Agency.

All characters in this publication are fictitious and any
resemblance to real persons, living or dead, is purely coincidental.

Cataloguing in Publication Data is available from the British Library

ISBN 978 0 7553 7186 0

Typeset in Janson by Avon DataSet Ltd, Bidford-on-Avon, Warwickshire

Printed and bound by CPI Group (UK) Ltd, Croydon, CR0 4YY

Headline's policy is to use papers that are natural, renewable and
recyclable products and made from wood grown in sustainable forests.
The logging and manufacturing processes are expected to conform
to the environmental regulations of the country of origin.

HEADLINE PUBLISHING GROUP
An Hachette UK Company
338 Euston Road
London NW1 3BH

www.headline.co.uk
www.hachette.co.uk

Dedication

For my treasured and only granddaughter Jemima Lyn Andrade – *meu pequeno anjo* – who is beautiful and a little poppet, although at times she can be like the 'little girl with the curl in the middle of her forehead' in the nursery rhyme! I have based Maria in the novel on you, Jemima – Maria's looks are typically Manx; you have inherited yours from Angela your Portuguese grandma – but I hope when you grow up you will have as happy, fulfilled and successful a life as Maria does – although probably by that time your Nanna Lyn will have 'shuffled off this mortal coil'.

Lyn Andrews
Isle of Man, 2011

Prologue

Peel, Isle of Man, May 1945

'IT'S OVER, LUV, IT'S finally over.' Sarah Kinnin's voice was low and hoarse with the emotions she was trying hard to control. Dressed for work in a dark grey skirt covered by a coarse but serviceable calico apron, a paisley print blouse and with her greying hair taken back into a neat bun, she had come straight from home to find her elder daughter. The auctioning of the day's catch was due to begin in an hour and she, as auctioneer, would have to discuss prices with the fishermen and then mark everything down in her book before she started the auction, but she had an idea that they would be very late in beginning today. She had known where Sophie would be, where she always came in the morning after she had seen her five-year-old daughter Bella into school. She would be down by the little harbour sheltered from the prevailing winds and weather by the grassy bulk of St Patrick's Isle.

Sophie never lingered at the school gate gossiping with the other young mothers, preferring to spend some time alone with her thoughts and memories. Bella always went off happily with her friends; she enjoyed school. But Sarah wondered if the children would all soon be sent home. They would be bursting with excitement at the news that was spreading like wildfire across the island – relayed by those who were fortunate enough to have a wireless set – and was now being heralded also by the church bells. Bells that had been silent for six long years. The war in Europe was finally and officially over. Germany had surrendered.

Sarah reached out and put her arms around the girl's shoulders and felt them shaking. 'Hush, luv. Hush now,' she soothed, but her own eyes were bright with unshed tears.

Sophie turned towards her and Sarah felt a stab of anguish as she looked into the brown eyes, which were full of pain and brimming with tears. Both her girls were attractive with dark eyes fringed with sooty lashes and the thick dark brown hair that denoted their Manx heritage, but at only twenty-four Sophie was a widow.

'Oh, Mam! Is it true?' Sophie asked, a sob in her voice.

Sarah managed a sad smile. 'That's why the bells are ringing, luv. Mr Churchill announced it on the wireless this hour past.'

Sophie nodded slowly, but then began to shake her head. 'Was it worth it, Mam? Was it all really worth it? Poor Pa lost off North Africa and . . . and my Andrew and . . . and all the other lads who left the island to fight . . . and my poor Bella left . . .' She couldn't go on.

Sarah gathered her daughter into her arms. 'I've been asking myself that same thing, luv, and the answer has to be "yes, it was". That evil man and his armies had to be stopped. There was nothing else we could do except fight for our freedom and our way of life.' She stared across the calm waters of Peel's harbour shimmering in the May sunlight, where the moored fishing boats bobbed gently up and down on the incoming tide. Both her husband and Andrew Teare, Sophie's husband, had been fishermen. John Kinnin had drowned when the *Tynwald* had been sunk and Andrew's boat had been dragged by its nets to the bottom of the Irish Sea by a U-boat three years ago. The entire crew had perished. Both she and Sophie had suffered devastating blows but at least she and John had had far longer together than Andrew and Sophie, she thought sadly.

As she tried to soothe her distraught daughter her gaze wandered across to the wide swathe of strand where the waves broke gently against the shore. Every beach, inlet and cliff top was festooned with barbed wire. Their little island was surrounded by a ring of cruel iron. All along the pretty leafy lanes that meandered through the glens and hills and villages signposts and names had been removed. Ugly concrete pillboxes had been built to house the guns that would have helped protect them from invasion, but despoiled the majestic coastline. Yet the blight of the paraphernalia of war was a small price to pay; they had not suffered the fate of the people of the Channel Islands, thank God.

Sophie was trying hard to control the emotions that were sweeping over her as she clung to her mother, knowing that she too had suffered the terrible grief of losing her husband and knowing too, deep in her heart, that Sarah was right. The evil that had swept across Europe had had to be stopped no matter what the cost and today neither she nor her mother would be alone in their grief.

'Come on, Sophie, luv. Pull yourself together. We've got to try to put it all behind us and think of the future, not the past. You have to think of Bella now,' Sarah urged.

Sophie dashed away her tears with the back of her hand. She had to make an effort for her daughter. It would upset and confuse the child to see her like this. 'I know, Mam.' She looked around. 'I suppose they'll send them all home from school now.'

Sarah smiled. 'I expect they will give them the rest of the day off. They'll be too excited to concentrate on lessons. People are already talking about organising parties to celebrate.'

Sophie squared her slim shoulders and tucked her arm through Sarah's. 'You're right, Mam – whatever we are feeling, we can't spoil today for Bella.'

Sarah nodded her agreement. 'Maybe Maria will bake one of her special cakes for us when she gets home. I'm sure I've got enough ingredients.'

A look of concern crossed Sophie's face as she wondered how her younger sister would take the news. Maria was a Land Girl and worked on the Sayles' farm, a seven-day-a-week job. She would have heard of the end of hostilities by now too for the Sayles had a wireless, and of course she would have heard the bells. She also knew of her sister's growing affection for Hans Bonhoeffer, a young Austrian internee from the Peveril Camp, who also worked for the Sayles. 'Mam, what will happen now to all the people in the camps?' she asked tentatively as they made their way up the narrow cobbled street lined with fishermen's cottages.

Sarah frowned. 'I don't know, luv. I suppose they'll be sent back to wherever it is they came from in the first place. It's all over now so they're no longer a threat, although from what we've seen and heard most of them weren't much of a threat to begin with. Except of course the few *real* prisoners of war and I expect even they will be glad to go home to their families.'

Sophie nodded; it made sense. This tiny island couldn't support the numbers of internees indefinitely. There was very little work for the Manx people themselves and she began to wonder what both she and her sister would do now, for obviously the Women's Land Army would be disbanded. She hadn't officially been a part of it but she had helped out at Sayles' whenever she could, and she had done other jobs too to support both herself and Bella. Sarah couldn't keep them all; with Pa dead she only had the small income from her work as an auctioneer, selling off the catches the fishing fleet brought back. Sophie sighed inwardly. There really didn't seem to be very much to celebrate at all today but she had to keep her spirits up for Bella's sake.

Maria had twisted her thick dark curly hair up into a knot beneath the turban she wore. The sun was now high in the sky and although it was only May the weather for the past two weeks had been very warm, and swinging the scythe as she helped cut the meadow grass for hay was hard work. Beads of perspiration stood out on her forehead and she grimaced. She must look very unappealing and unattractive, she thought, glancing across to where the tall, lithe figure of Hans worked seemingly effortlessly. He grinned at her and she smiled back, her heart skipping a beat as it always did. He was so handsome: his blond hair lightened by the sun; his skin tanned by working outdoors in all weathers; his eyes as deep a blue as the sea. She had liked him from the first moment she'd met him, the day he'd come with two other young men from the camp to work on the farm some miles inland from Peel. He'd been a little shy with her at first but she'd put that down to the fact that he felt very unsure of his position.

As the days had turned to weeks she'd got to know him better and he had relaxed more in her company; eventually they'd become friends. That friendship had blossomed into affection and now she was certain that she had fallen in love with him. She blushed slightly as she remembered the day a week ago when they'd found themselves alone in the barn.

He'd taken her in his arms and kissed her and told her he had never felt so deeply about anyone before.

'I know now what is in my heart. I love you, my Maria. I will love you for ever.'

She had clung tightly to him and had murmured 'I love you too, Hans, and we'll find a way to be together when . . . when all this is over.'

Now he called across to her: 'Don't worry, Maria, soon it will be time for us to eat and then you can rest.' He knew working on the land was hard for a girl and especially for one as slim as her.

'Thank goodness, my arms and shoulders feel as if they're on fire and I must look such a fright,' she called back, looking forward to sitting close to him under the shade of one of the trees that bounded the field as they ate whatever Maude Sayle would provide for lunch. They always chose to sit apart from the other workers because he had to return to the camp each night which meant they could only see each other during working hours. Their breaks were the only real time they had alone, apart from the odd snatched moments in a barn or the shippen.

'You never look "a fright", as you say it. To me you are always beautiful, Maria.'

She was about to ask him laughingly how anyone could look 'beautiful' in the uniform of the Land Army – boots, overalls and turban – when she caught sight of the small, stout figure of Maude Sayle hurrying across the field towards them, waving her arms wildly in the air. 'What on earth is wrong with her? It's not dinnertime yet and why is she running?'

Hans looked concerned. 'Perhaps something is wrong for Mr Sayle.'

They both dropped their scythes and started to run towards the farmer's wife but then Maria stopped dead and looked around in alarm. 'Oh, my God! Hans! Hans, listen! Bells! Church bells!'

Instantly he was by her side, his arm protectively around her. 'What is it? What is it that is happening?'

She clutched his arm tightly, upset and confused. 'I don't know. They are only supposed to ring the bells to warn us that . . . but it *can't* be, not now! The war is nearly over, Hans, we can't be being *invaded*!'

Maude had reached the little cluster of workers but was fighting for her breath.

'Mrs Sayle, what's wrong? Is it the invasion?' Maria cried, still clinging to Hans.

'No! No . . . it's . . . it's over! Let me get my breath, girl,' Maude puffed, holding her side, her round face flushed. 'We've just heard it on the wireless and I ran to tell you all. It's over! The war is over in Europe – they've surrendered!'

Maria threw her arms around Hans's neck and began to laugh with pure relief. For a few horrible moments she had thought the invasion that had threatened them for six years had come.

Hans hugged her and felt a wave of relief surge through

him. Now they no longer had anything to fear from Herr Hitler and his murdering hordes.

Maude beamed at them all. 'Come on back to the house with me, all of you. This calls for a drink to celebrate, even though it's a working day.'

With his arm still around Maria Hans led the little group across the field toward the farmhouse as Maude brought up the rear, still puffing a little from her unaccustomed exertions.

Edward Sayle was waiting in the kitchen, his weather-beaten face wreathed for once in smiles, a bottle of whisky and another of sherry already on the table.

'Come on in, all of you! Isn't it the best news of all? It's finally over, we've nothing more to worry about,' he cried, pouring generous measures for everyone.

He raised his glass. 'A toast! To peace and to freedom!'

The unaccustomed spirits burned the back of Hans's throat and he spluttered. Maria laughed and banged him on the back, caught up in the euphoria of the moment.

Maude smiled at them. They made a handsome couple, she thought. He was a decent lad who worked hard and she'd known Maria all her life; Sarah had been a childhood friend. She'd watched their growing closeness and had wondered if it would last but now a thought suddenly struck her. What implications did this news have for them? In time he and his family would be sent back to Austria from where they'd fled the Nazi advance; would the girl go with him? She doubted it for Maria Kinnin, like so many other people she knew, had never been off the island in her entire life. Her mother Sarah probably wouldn't allow her to go. Perhaps being parted would be for the best anyway, she mused, sipping her sherry slowly, but it was not really her concern. Let them have these few hours of happiness for who knew what the future held for them – for any of them.

When at last the celebrations had died down life began to get back to what passed for normal. The authorities started dismantling the coastal defences and closing the camps, and Sophie began to think hard about the future. There was still a little work for her at Sayles' for the summer months were always busy but she knew that once the harvest was in she could expect little more, and neither could Maria. Sophie was good at dressmaking but there was very little call here for her skills. There were professional seamstresses in both Peel and Ramsey and good shops in Douglas. Apart from housework there was little else she could do; the days when the women of Peel and the surrounding areas worked in their dozens gutting and salting the herrings were firmly in the past. Before the war Douglas, Port Erin and Port St Mary had always been crowded in summer with holidaymakers and no doubt they would soon return, but not many had come to Peel, so there was no work to be found in hotels and guest houses, of which there were few anyway.

She decided to discuss the matter with her mother one evening in September, the day after they had found out that

Hans and his family were to be repatriated to their country of origin the following week, news that had upset Maria terribly. She was still upstairs, lying on her bed sobbing.

'Oh, Mam, I feel so sorry for her. She really is very fond of him and she says he is heart-broken too,' Sophie said as she sat down opposite Sarah at the table.

'I know, but she has known for a while that the time would come when he'd have to leave. He's no choice, times are still very . . . troubled. She's very young, she's only just turned eighteen; she'll get over him and find someone else. But I, too, hate to see her so upset.'

Sophie twisted her hands together. 'Mam, what's going to happen to us all? Maria, Bella and me? There's no work and without that there's no hope of a decent future. I . . . I've been worrying about it for a while now. I'd like to be a dress-maker – professionally, that is – it's the only thing I'm good at but it would take time and money to get started up . . .' Her voice trailed off and she bit her lip.

Sarah put down the knife she'd been using to peel the vegetables and pushed the bowl to one side. She could see how anxious Sophie was. She sighed heavily. It was a dilemma that many families had faced and would continue to face and there was only one solution to this problem. 'Your only chance of making that dream come true is to leave the island, Sophie. Oh, it was something I never thought I'd have to deal with, my children having to leave to find work. Both your pa and Andrew had steady work – it didn't pay a great deal though we managed – but . . . but . . . the good Lord decided to take them and we have to carry on living as best we can. We both have to think of Bella's future too.'

Sophie nodded slowly. It was a decision she had been seriously considering. She would have to make a new life for herself and her child, away from the island. 'Where can I go, Mam?'

'Across to Liverpool, luv. That's the logical place. I know they've taken a terrible battering over there these last years but things will be starting to get better now, you'll find work and I'm sure your Uncle Jim and Aunty Lizzie will be happy to have you stay with them until you get on your feet. He is my older brother, after all.'

Sophie nodded her agreement. 'I'd be grateful. Will you write to them, Mam, please?' She reached across the table and clasped Sarah's hand tightly. 'I don't really want to have to go, Mam. I'll miss you terribly, but . . . but . . .'

Sarah smiled ruefully. 'But there is nothing else you can do, Sophie. You are still a young woman, you have to make a new life for yourself. There are too many painful memories here, luv. Every time you go down to the harbour or walk along the quay you'll be remembering that day. The day he didn't come back. No, in some ways it's the best thing you can do.' She paused, frowing. 'I think it might be a good idea if you take Maria with you. She'll find it hard to get work and once that lad has gone she'll be as miserable as sin. A fresh start would benefit her too. She'll meet new people, make new friends, maybe even find a lad to replace Hans Bonhoeffer in her affections.'

'Mam! Both of us and Bella? You'll be here alone! I can't leave you on your own!' Sophie cried.

'I won't be on my own. I was born here, I grew up here, I know everyone. I have friends. Isn't Andrew's mam, Fenella Teare, one of my closest friends? I have my work, too. Wouldn't I be a very selfish woman to force you to stay here just to keep me company? No, Sophie, I want you both to go to Jim and Lizzie and make a new life for yourselves, and Liverpool isn't *that* far away – just a couple of hours by ferry. I've made up my mind. I'll write in the morning.'

Sophie reluctantly nodded her agreement. Mam did have many friends, her widowed mother-in-law amongst them, and Liverpool wasn't that far away but to people such as her mam, Maria and herself, who had never been off the island before, it seemed like a great distance and not just in miles.

'I'll have to break the news to Bella and then try to scrape together as much money as I can for our fares and to pay my way until I get a job.'

Sarah picked up the paring knife again. 'I'll try to help out too, luv. It will be for the best.'

Sophie smiled. 'All we have to do now is convince Maria and I don't think that's going to be easy. Perhaps we should wait until Hans Bonhoeffer and his family have left.'

Sarah nodded and resumed her task. She knew in her heart that she was doing the right thing for her girls, but she could not help feeling more than a little depressed and bereft already.

Chapter One

'IN THE NAME OF heaven, Sophie, what have you brought us to?' Maria Kinnin's dark eyes were full of shock and disbelief as she stared through the murky October morning at the sight that was gradually becoming clearer the closer the Isle of Man Steam Packet ship, the *Lady of Man*, drew to the Liverpool Landing Stage. A thin veil of mist hung over the turgid waters of the Mersey and the ships they had passed had left wakes that resembled ribbons of dull, mottled pewter. There wasn't a breath of wind, the surface of the river was flat and the sky above was a uniform mass of gunmetal cloud.

She had come up on deck with her elder sister when they had passed the lighthouse on Perch Rock, eager to catch her first sight of the city that was to be her new home. Now that sight filled her with utter dismay. Was this what she'd left Peel for, she thought desperately? She'd been persuaded to give up all her hopes and dreams to come here; her ma and Sophie had said it would be a fresh start, a new life full of great opportunities and excitement but the scene of total devastation that met her eyes offered little prospect of either. They'd come on a wild-goose chase, she thought bitterly.

Sophie clutched her little daughter's hand tightly and shook her head in horror at the sight that met her eyes. The three majestic buildings that graced the waterfront were intact, although blackened over the decades by the soot from thousands of chimneys, both industrial and domestic, but beyond them was a total wasteland of rubble and burned-out buildings. St Nicholas's Church – the sailors' church her pa had called it – was a pile of broken, scorched stones and charred beams; only its blackened spire still stood. In what had been Derby Square, only the statue of Queen Victoria was untouched, that monarch surveying the destruction that surrounded her with characteristic grim disapproval on her granite features. Sophie felt her shoulders sag as bitter disappointment washed over her. Oh, they'd heard how badly Liverpool had suffered in the terrible, week-long blitz of May 1941. Even far away on the island they'd heard the dull roar of the explosions and they'd seen the night sky glowing eerily red from the thousands of burning buildings. But she'd never expected the reality to be as bad as *this*!

'Are we nearly there, Mam? I'm cold and I'm hungry.'

Sophie dragged her stunned gaze away from the ruined

city and looked down at Bella. Her daughter was so like her father Andrew that tears pricked her eyes. Wearily she brushed a strand of Bella's dark brown hair away from her cheek and with an effort forced herself to smile. 'Not long now. We'll soon be sitting in Aunty Lizzie's nice warm kitchen having our breakfast.'

'That's if Aunty Lizzie still has got a kitchen!' Maria said grimly, unable to conceal her feelings. She too was cold, tired, hungry and now utterly dispirited. The salty air was making her long dark hair curl frizzily. Her knitted red tam-o'-shanter did little to protect it from the dampness in the morning air. She always took great pride in her appearance, even though most of her clothes were either hand-me-downs or had been made by Sophie. She spent hours trying to tame her thick unruly hair, even though her mam told her it was her 'crowning glory' and she shouldn't complain about it so much. Sophie's hair was just as thick but it was poker straight, which she considered very unfair considering that they both took after Sarah, whose own hair had once been as dark and straight as Sophie's but was now grey and worn in a neat bun. Maria was missing her mother already for she'd never been away from home before. 'Aunty Lizzie may not have a roof over her head at all.'

'You could be right there, girl,' agreed a small, plump woman standing beside them. She wore a black coat and a grey felt hat jammed tightly over short salt and pepper hair, and from her accent Maria realised she was Liverpudlian.

She turned to the woman, frowning. 'Oh, don't say that!

Isn't it bad enough that we've come on this fool of a journey without having to find we now have nowhere to live?'

The woman bristled with indignation. 'You should 'ave been here during the Blitz, girl! There were thousands of people left without a 'ome, left with nothing but the clothes they stood up in but grateful they still 'ad their lives. *Youse* lot had it soft over there. I've been to see me sister-in-law so I know. *Youse* never 'ad bombs raining down on yer night after night while yer were packed like sardines in the public air-raid shelter and terrified out of yer wits. And there's still 'undreds without 'omes of their own, even though it's all over now.'

Sophie glared at the woman, her dark eyes filled with grief and anger. 'Don't you dare say we had it soft on the island, missus! My poor pa risked his life to keep fish on your tables and then he went down with the *Tynwald* off North Africa. And I'm a widow! A widow at twenty-four and with this child to bring up alone. My husband's boat was dragged by its nets to the bottom of the sea by a U-boat! The whole crew drowned!'

'And your government dumped all those foreigners on us. We had internment and POW camps!' Maria added, although there was a note of sadness in her voice.

Mollified, the woman nodded. 'I know and I'm sorry for yer loss, girl. Where is it you two're hoping to stay?'

Maria fished out the scrap of paper from her coat pocket. 'Sixteen Harebell Street,' she informed their travelling companion.

'That's near Stanley 'ospital, it's Bootle,' the woman informed them, then, pausing, she frowned. 'Bootle 'ad it bad but I don't think them "flower" streets were hit. Not bad 'ouses either from what I've 'eard.'

Both Maria and Sophie were very relieved to hear this.

'Is it far from the Landing Stage?' Sophie enquired. Bella was now shivering and clutching her old rag doll tightly to her.

'Well, it's too far to walk, I know that. You'll 'ave to get a tram from the Pier 'ead, it's the terminus so just ask one of the conductors or drivers which tram to get. Tell them where yer want to get off too.'

The deck was now crowded with people and Maria increased her grip on her small suitcase as the ship came alongside, shuddering as it hit the huge rubber tyres attached to the side of the stage that acted as fenders, throwing everyone off balance.

'We'll be crushed to death before we even get near the gangway at this rate!' she cried.

Sophie bit her lip, realising her sister was right and terrified that Bella would be separated from her. She might even fall and be trampled in the rush for the gangway. 'See if you can catch the eye of one of those deck hands and ask for help. I'll have to keep hold of Bella and our luggage.'

Bella was shivering with cold and fright, terrified by the unfamiliar noises and the press of people who all seemed to tower above her. She had never been away from Peel in her life before. 'Mam, don't leave me! I don't like it here,

I want to go home! I want to go back to Granny Sarah!' Her big blue eyes filled with tears and she hugged her doll to her as she clung to Sophie, burying her face in the folds of her mother's skirt.

Sophie drew her closer. 'Hush now, it's all right. Mam's not going to let anything happen to you and we'll soon be off this ship and in Aunty Lizzie's house.'

Maria had no trouble at all in attracting attention. She had been considered one of the prettiest girls in Peel. A good-looking young lad, wearing a thick woollen jumper emblazoned across the chest with the Three Legs of Man, pushed his way towards her, smiling broadly.

'Why did I never meet you strolling along the Lock Promenade in Douglas?' he asked, admiration evident in both his eyes and voice.

'Because I come from Peel and why would I be bothered going all the way to Douglas to walk along a promenade?' she quipped, smiling archly and fluttering her long dark lashes. 'Will you help us to get down the gangway in one piece, please? My sister has her luggage and my little niece to see to.'

Thus appealed to, and as they were both very attractive girls, he immediately took both Maria and Sophie's cases and began to shoulder his way through the crowd shouting 'Make way there, folks! Make way! Follow close behind me. Where are you going?' he shouted to Maria over his shoulder.

'Somewhere called "Bootle", we've to get a tram,' she informed him.

'Took a bit of a hammering did Bootle, so one of the shore lads told me, especially the dock areas. A lot of the houses have been pulled down as being unsafe.'

Maria raised her eyes skyward impatiently; she was grateful for his help but it was difficult trying to keep up a conversation in such a crowd. 'Our aunt lives in Harebell Street and a woman told us those houses were fine.'

'I hope she was right. Still, it's all over and we got our own back in the end. Sometimes I feel a bit sorry for them now, their whole country's destroyed, according to the newspapers.'

'And so is ours and they should 'ave thought of that before they started the flaming war!' The woman in the black coat had elbowed her way to their side and was ruthlessly pushing forward.

'I suppose you're right, missus. Let's get you all off now,' the deck hand called as they reached the top of the gangway. He turned to Sophie. 'Can you manage this case and I'll carry the little lass down on my shoulders so she won't get crushed?'

'Oh, that's so good of you! I was wondering how I was going to manage,' Sophie replied with relief as he effortlessly hoisted Bella on to his shoulder.

'Hold on tightly to this kind man, Bella. We'll soon be off and your mam and I will be right behind you,' Maria urged her obviously apprehensive niece.

It was a relief to be off the ship at last and at the bottom of the gangway they parted company with both the woman in the black coat and the young deck hand, Maria flashing him a genuine smile of gratitude. People were still milling around but they made their way towards the line of green and cream waiting trams. Sophie made some enquiries of a man in a uniform, whom she took to be some sort of official, and was directed towards a tram at the front of the line. They climbed aboard and Maria showed the conductor the piece of paper bearing her aunt's address.

'I'll give yer a shout when we get to the nearest stop, luv,' he promised and they settled thankfully on to the wooden slatted seat, Sophie with Bella on her lap and her suitcase at her feet.

'I just hope she's going to have a pot of tea ready for us, I'm worn out,' Maria commented, gazing out of the window.

Sophie smiled tiredly. 'I'm sure she will. She knows what time the ferry was due in. Mam put it all in the letter and she said she was a friendly enough soul and should make us very welcome.'

'How does she know that? We never got a reply and she only met her the once, years ago before the war, when they came over on a day trip,' Maria reminded her. She didn't know Uncle Jim Quine, her mother's brother, at all. He'd gone to Liverpool to work before she'd even been born. Sophie didn't either, she'd only been a small baby.

Sophie didn't reply, she was too tired, heartsore and filled with misgivings to enter into an argument with Maria.

The tram had filled up and when the conductor came for their fares Sophie held out the pennies.

He took them but gave her one back, grinning conspiratorially. 'It's supposed to be half-price for the little 'un, but what the 'ell! She's sitting on yer knee an' I reckon that penny is better in your pocket than the flaming Corporation's.'

She thanked him and put it back in her purse. She *would* need every penny she had until she got a job. She had sold everything to come here, even her precious wedding ring. She wore one made of brass now. She had to make all her hopes and dreams for a better future come true, for Bella's sake. She hugged the pale, weary child to her, fighting back the tears of exhaustion and sorrow. Oh, Andrew! I still miss you so much, she thought. He'd been dead three years yet each time she had passed the harbour, where what was left of the fishing fleet was anchored, it broke her heart. Mam had been right to urge her to leave Peel and its bittersweet memories behind, but to have to face the future without him was daunting in the extreme. In truth she would never forget him or the brief happy years they'd had together, and nor did she want to. What made her heart ache was the knowledge that she would never again feel his strong arms around her, never be able to confide her fears and worries to him, or see his blue eyes dancing with mirth, or hear his laughter. She would never again feel her heart skip a beat with joy and relief when he came home to their cottage in Charles Street, the narrow winding street that led from Orry Lane down to the harbour, as the fishing fleet returned and the *Girl Sophie* was tied up. The cottage was now gone – rented out to someone else – and so was the *Girl Sophie*. She lay at the bottom of the Irish Sea and so did her poor Andrew. And just what lay ahead of her now? More anxiety, hardship and

23

disappointment? Life had never been easy. 'Chasing the herring' as her father had done all his life had never brought in much money and even when she'd married Andrew it had been hard to make ends meet, but she hadn't minded that. They'd been happy.

She looked out of the window as the tram trundled its way down Chapel Street and Tithebarn Street, the trolley sparking as it crossed the junctions. The sight that met her eyes only deepened her fears. Whole streets of houses, shops, churches, schools and pubs were in ruins. Was there any work to be had here at all, she wondered? Had she made the worst decision of her life? Why had she left the green fields, the wooded glens, the moorland where sheep grazed in the shadow of Snaefell, the quiet little villages, the rugged, towering cliffs at Bradda and Niarbyl, all the beauty of her small island home for an uncertain future in a strange, war-battered, crowded and noisy city? Was this wasteland of ruined buildings all she could now offer her precious daughter as 'home'? She prayed silently for the courage to face the days and months ahead.

When they alighted from the tram they walked in the direction the conductor had pointed out. The roadway was wide and cobbled and a horse and cart slowly passed them, the clattering of the iron-shod hooves of the heavy, patient Shire muffled slightly by the dampness in the air. She shivered as they passed the bottom of a street in which there were huge gaps where houses had once stood.

'This street is called "Woodbine" so it can't be very far

now,' Maria surmised, looking up at the sign attached to the wall of the end house. 'Didn't that woman say they were called the "flower" streets? Not that there's anything remotely "flowery" about this place!' she added.

Sophie nodded, gazing across the road to where soot-blackened buildings and mounds of rubble obscured the view of the docks and the river beyond.

Maria followed her gaze and pursed her lips, thinking how different it was from the view from the harbour at home. There the ruined castle crowned the top of the grassy hill on St Patrick's Isle and the gulls swooped and dived overhead.

Holding Bella's hand tightly, Sophie turned into Harebell Street and was thankful to see that all the houses were still standing. She managed a smile. 'Here we are, Bella. This is Harebell Street where Aunty Lizzie and Uncle Jim live. Aren't they fine, big houses?'

The child nodded slowly, still confused and very apprehensive for everything was strange to her. The houses did seem big compared to her Granny's cottage and the street was so much wider than the little narrow lanes she was used to, but she was determined not to cry. 'Will I have other children to play with here, Mam?'

'Of course you will and you'll make lots of new friends at school too,' Sophie replied with forced cheerfulness, wondering how Bella would settle amongst strangers.

'All we have to do now is find number sixteen and let's hope there's something to eat and a warm fire waiting for us,' Maria added as she began to count off the houses. At least they all looked fairly well cared for, she thought. Most had cotton lace curtains at the window and the doorsteps had been scrubbed and whitened. Maybe it wouldn't be too bad living here after all.

Chapter Two

THE FRONT DOOR OF number sixteen was painted dark brown but the paint was peeling and was badly scuffed at the bottom. The brass knocker and letterbox were tarnished but the curtains at the window were clean. In reply to Sophie's knocking the door was eventually opened by a thin girl of about Maria's age with reddish-brown hair and grey eyes that regarded the little group on the doorstep with open suspicion.

'Is this where Mrs Quine lives, Mrs Lizzie Quine?' Sophie asked, while Maria took in the girl's hand-knitted, multi-coloured, striped jumper – obviously made up from odds and ends – and her brown, well-worn tweed skirt. Judging by her appearance the Quines were far from 'well set up', she thought, which was how her mam had described her brother's family.

'Who wants to know?' was the ungracious reply.

Before Sophie could answer the voice of an older woman came from somewhere at the back of the house.

'Katie, who's at the front door at this hour of the morning?'

'It's two girls with a kid, asking do you live here, Mam! They've got cases with them an' all,' Katie yelled back.

Maria raised her eyes skywards. A nice way to describe anyone, she thought, and bad mannered too. This Katie – who was obviously their cousin – hadn't even bothered to ask their names. Well, she could soon put that right.

'It's us, Aunty Lizzie. Maria, Sophie and little Bella – from the Isle of Man! Mam wrote to you about us!' Maria yelled down the dark, narrow hallway.

Katie stared at her but before she had time to comment a door opened and a small, stout woman with greying hair twisted tightly up in curling papers, wearing a rather grubby, wrap-over pinafore over a flowered blouse and black skirt, bustled towards them, her face wreathed in smiles.

'I've a memory like a sieve these days! Never been the same since the Blitz, I haven't! You're Sarah's girls! Come on in with you all, you must be worn out after that journey,' she cried, hugging them each in turn before turning to her daughter who was looking a bit mystified. 'Katie, luv, these are your cousins – I told you they were coming. Maria, Sophia and little Isabella – named after the big wheel at Laxey, so our Jim says, isn't that right?'

Sophie smiled with relief. 'That's right, Aunty Lizzie. The wheel is called the "Lady Isabella" and I always thought it was such a pretty name that I named this little one Isabella, but we call her Bella for short.'

Lizzie ushered them all down the lobby and into the kitchen which to Sophie seemed crammed full of furniture and was very untidy. The overmantel above the range was littered with bric-a-brac, while ash had fallen from the range into the hearth. The dresser held not only dishes but a great and varied collection of odds and ends, the lino on the floor had seen better days and the table, which seemed to take up most of the room, was covered with newspaper and dirty dishes. Suspended from the ceiling was a rack, operated by a pulley and cord system, which was festooned with damp clothes.

'Well, sit yourselves down, take your coats off and tell me all about the journey and how your mam is getting on. You'll find things a bit different here, after living in Peel. Pretty little place, I remember it well from the time we took that trip over. Katie, put the kettle on, luv, and give that pan of porridge a stir. Come here to your Aunty Lizzie, queen, and let me take your coat and hat off,' she instructed Bella.

The child eyed her uncertainly; she'd never been called 'queen' before. She'd been named for the 'Lady' Isabella but maybe this new aunt had got it mixed up. She knew there was a *real* queen, Queen Elizabeth, King George's wife, because she had seen pictures of her. She was totally unaware that it was a local term of affection, but as her mother pushed her gently forward, she assumed there was nothing odd about being called 'queen'.

'I hope we're not going to put you out too much, Aunty Lizzie,' Sophie said tentatively. She knew that as well as her aunt and uncle and Katie, there were two other cousins, John and Billy. There had been three boys but the oldest, Albert, had been killed in Italy. John had been in the Army too but had survived and had now been demobbed.

Lizzie was busying herself with the teapot and the kettle. 'Oh, we'll manage, luv. We're good at managing now, we've had plenty of practice these last six years. We were lucky, we've still got our house. Some poor folk were bombed out two and even three times and there are houses with three or more families living in them. And then there's the flaming rationing to contend with,' she added tartly. 'But we'll manage, we'll sort out the beds after you've had some breakfast. Katie, see if you can find some clean dishes on that dresser.'

Maria's head was beginning to spin as she wondered if her aunt ever stopped to draw breath, but she was very grateful for the bowl of porridge and the mug of tea that were finally placed in front of her.

'That early ferry leaves at an ungodly hour, doesn't it? Almost the middle of the night. Your Uncle Jim and our John have gone off to work. They're both on the docks which have been patched up and working flat out again with all those Yanks and Canadians going home. You'll see them both at teatime. Oh, Lord!' Lizzie exclaimed, suddenly getting to her feet and rushing to the kitchen door.

Both girls looked startled as their aunt yanked open the door and bellowed, 'Billy Quine, are you out of that bed yet, you lazy little hooligan!' in a voice that belied her short stature.

Katie grinned. 'That's me brother Billy, he hates getting up, especially for school.'

'Go up and drag him out, Katie, luv. If he's late again I'll have that Mr Thomas round here on the bounce and I'll be mortified, then that lad will get a hiding from your da,' Lizzie instructed, pouring herself another cup of tea.

The grin vanished from Katie's face. 'Ah, Mam! Do I have to? He won't take no notice of me.'

Sophie got to her feet. 'Then maybe he'll take some notice of me for he certainly won't be expecting a strange cousin to appear in his room.'

Lizzie laughed delightedly. 'That he won't, luv. Aye, that should certainly do the trick.'

Katie cast Sophie a grateful look and sat down beside Maria, enviously eyeing her cousin's neat black and white checked dress and her thick curly dark hair. 'How old are you, Maria,' she asked hesitantly.

'Eighteen.'

'I'm seventeen,' Katie informed her.

'Don't you have a job? Sophie and I will have to get some kind of work and as soon as we possibly can.' Maria had finished the porridge and was now eyeing her cousin with far less hostility. It certainly couldn't be easy living in this madhouse, she thought.

'I work in a shop, a sort of small department store. Not like the big ones in town, of course, those that are left after all the bombing. It's called Heaton's, they sell all kinds of things, but it's my day off today.' She paused. 'I like your frock,' she added a little shyly.

'Sophie made it. She makes nearly all our clothes, when we can get the material. It's much cheaper than buying them,' Maria replied chattily, proud of her sister's accomplishments.

'Did she? Well, if she can sew like that she shouldn't have any trouble getting taken on at Marsden's, they make overalls. They're back in business now,' Lizzie informed her. 'And what are you good at, Maria?' she probed, thinking that beside Katie, her niece looked what her son John would call a 'real stunner'.

Maria shrugged. 'I'm not bad at figures and my writing is neat. I'm good at baking too. Mam says I've the lightest touch with pastry she's ever seen.'

'I could ask if there are any vacancies where I work, if you like?' Katie offered generously, wondering if Sophie would perhaps make her something to wear. It was ages since she'd had anything new and smart.

Maria beamed at her. 'Would you? I wouldn't mind working in a big shop. The shops at home are all small, unless you go to Douglas, of course.'

'Not that there's much in any of the shops these days. Still, things are bound to get better soon. At least I flaming well hope so, I was only saying to Martha Ryan next door—'

Lizzie's flow of conversation was interrupted by the

sudden appearance of a tousle-headed lad, hastily dragging a grey woollen jumper over his creased, knee-length school trousers. 'Who's that girl, Mam? She come into me room and dragged the quilt off me! She said 'er name is Sophie an' that she's me cousin!'

Lizzie glared at her eight-year-old son. 'Would you just look at the cut of him? Tidy yourself up and comb your hair, meladdo. She *is* your cousin Sophie and this is your other cousin, Maria, and if you'd got up when I first called you, you'd have been introduced properly, like. And don't think you've got time for much breakfast because you haven't. A bit of bread and dripping will have to do and you can eat it on the way to school. And tomorrow morning, you'll be up the same time as your da and John because you'll be taking little Bella here to school with you, it's all arranged, and we can't have her being late on her first morning.'

Young Billy Quine looked horrified at his mother's words. No proper breakfast and then tomorrow he'd have to be up at the same time as his da, which was almost the middle of the night! For the first time he caught sight of the girl his mam had called 'Bella'. She was small, about four or five, with a mop of dark curly hair that fell to her shoulders and she was gazing at him with the biggest, bluest eyes he'd ever seen.

'Is she old enough to go to school?' he asked apprehensively.

Bella, who had so far not uttered a word, found her voice. 'I am so! I'm five.' She had listened in fascination to her Aunty Lizzie's remarks, to her strange accent and way of going on and had decided she quite liked her. Having had breakfast and warmed up, she had begun to feel happier and more secure. Some of her natural self-confidence and determination had returned.

'See! She's got a mind of her own, has this little one. Now, get off with you and don't go dawdling or kicking the toes out of those boots either or I swear to God you'll go barefoot. New boots don't grow on trees,' Lizzie instructed firmly, getting to her feet and propelling her youngest son bodily through the door into the scullery.

Maria looked at Katie and grinned. 'Is it always like this?'

Katie rolled her eyes and giggled. 'It's worse when me da and our John are in too. Me mam can certainly talk the hind leg off a donkey, can't she?'

'She can indeed,' Maria laughed as Sophie returned to the kitchen.

'I can see you two are getting on well,' Sophie commented. 'Right, let's give Aunty Lizzie a hand to clear away and get these dishes washed.'

'Oh, there's no rush to do that, half the time Mam doesn't bother to do them until after dinnertime,' Katie informed her.

'Really? Well, don't you think it would be easier for her if we did them now? She must have a lot of housework to do.' Sophie smiled, glancing quickly at Maria, whose eyebrows had shot up. They had been brought up to keep the house tidy and dirty dishes had always been washed, dried and put away immediately after a meal.

Katie shrugged as Sophie began to quickly stack the dishes and Maria gathered up the stained newspapers on the table top.

'Aunty Lizzie, you sit down. We'll clear away, it's the least we can do. Mam told us to be sure we made ourselves useful. We're not here to be waited on,' Sophie said as her aunt came back into the room. She had no wish to offend her but she couldn't sit back and leave the place in such a mess.

'Ah, that's good of you, luv. I'm not getting any younger and I can tell you it's not easy clearing up after my lot. It wouldn't enter our Katie's head to help.' She shot a sharp look at her daughter. 'No, it's her day off.'

'Mam, I work the rest of the week! I'm on me feet all day, running here, there and everywhere!' Katie retorted, annoyed that her mother had more or less said she was lazy, which put her in a bad light. 'Aren't I entitled to a day off?'

'And when do I ever get a day off, milady?' Lizzie shot back indignantly.

Seeing that things were degenerating into an argument Sophie quickly sought to intervene. 'I'm sure Katie works really hard, Aunty Lizzie, and now that we're here, we can share all the chores, so you can take things easier.'

Katie, mollified by her words, made an effort to sweep up the ashes as Maria pushed the screwed-up newspapers into the range.

Lizzie was amazed at how quickly the kitchen was tidied, even little Bella had been given a few simple tasks to do. These two girls certainly were not afraid of housework, she thought. Life for herself would indeed be easier with them around.

When they'd finished, Lizzie took them upstairs and showed them the room they would be sharing with Katie.

'You'll be a bit cramped but Jim and I have one room and our John and Billy have the other and it's smaller than this one. We got the double bed when we knew you were coming,' Lizzie informed them.

Maria looked around in dismay. Crammed into the room were a double bed and a single bed, a small wardrobe and a chest of drawers. Obviously Bella would have to share a bed with Sophie and she would have to share with Katie. Of course she'd shared a bed with Sophie until her sister had got married but that had been different, they'd always shared, and the room hadn't been as cluttered as this. There was barely room to move in here.

'Of course we'll manage, Aunty Lizzie,' Sophie said firmly, ignoring the look on Maria's face but feeling rather dismayed herself.

'Couldn't we sleep in the parlour?' Maria asked tentatively. There was one; she'd observed that as they'd stood on the doorstep.

'You could if it was empty but Mr Chatsworth rents it from me, he's been here four years now and I couldn't put him out. He's nowhere else to go and he's no bother at all. Nice, quiet man he is, keeps himself to himself and always pays on time. His few bob come in very handy too,' Lizzie informed them.

Sophie frowned. So there were now nine people living in this house; still, as her aunt had said earlier, there were many overcrowded houses in this devastated city. They'd just have to make the best of it.

When Lizzie had left them to unpack, Maria sat down on one of the beds. 'Everywhere is very run down and things are so *worn*, Sophie.'

As she began to unpack Sophie nodded. 'I know, but perhaps after going through all that bombing and with such terrible shortages, it's the best she can do. When we've put our stuff away we'll get a tram into town and see what we can get. There must be places where we can buy sheets and towels cheaply, and a tablecloth. I'll put it to her tactfully, that we want to help, brighten things up a bit.'

'I noticed there was a small shop on the corner of the next street, we should be able to get things like washing soda, soap and Jeyes Fluid there.'

Sophie nodded. Maria was right but it would all eat into the small amount of money she had. They'd have to find work soon.

Chapter Three

LIZZIE HAD TOLD THEM that the shop was called Dodd's and that they sold everything from bacon to Brasso. Maggie Dodd, who owned it, would give selected customers things 'on tick', providing she knew them well enough. Sophie decided they would call in on the way home and they'd then taken the tram into town.

'Don't be worrying if you can't get everything, we'll manage,' had been Lizzie's parting words and Maria thought that she was beginning to hate the phrase "we'll manage" as much as she'd come to hate "there's a war on" and all the other catch phrases that had been so popular during the past six years.

Later that day, laden down with parcels and bags, they got off the tram and headed for Harebell Street, exhausted but satisfied with their purchases. Few of the big shops in the town centre had survived the bombing, Lewis's, Blackler's and Frisby Dyke's were burnt-out shells but they'd managed to get some sheets and pillowcases in a small shop off Church Street. They had been described as 'bomb damaged' and so were cheap. Sophie had examined the scorch marks carefully and then declared she could turn the sheets "ends to middle" and you'd hardly notice. In the same shop they'd bought two blue and white checked tablecloths, four cotton tea towels and three towels. From a street vendor they'd bought a slightly chipped china milk jug and sugar basin; the rest of their purchases they would make at Dodd's.

The little shop was quite busy and as they stood patiently waiting to be served, both girls noticed the avidly curious glances of the other customers. Just like the shops at home in Peel, Sophie realised that it was a place where neighbours exchanged news and gossip and as two strangers their presence was proving to be of some interest.

At last Maggie Dodd turned to them, as one of her daughters carefully weighed out a small amount of sugar for another customer. 'Right, girls, what can I get you? I hope you've got your ration books.'

'We have,' Sophie replied, handing them over. 'But it's mainly cleaning stuff we need.'

The older woman's eyebrows rose as she nodded. 'You must be Lizzie Quine's nieces. We heard you were coming over, although why you would want to leave that lovely little island to come to this battered, benighted city I don't know.'

'To work, Mrs Dodd. There are very few jobs for us over there now. Maria was in the Land Army and I worked too when I could, but having Bella meant I couldn't do as much.'

The mention of her days working on the small farm with Hans made Maria feel depressed so she didn't add anything to Sophie's statement.

'I would have thought that now the war is over people will start going back there, on holiday, like. They used to go in droves every summer, so there'll be more chances of work,' the woman who had been buying the sugar interrupted. 'I'm Mrs Ryan – Martha. We live next door to Lizzie.'

Sophie smiled at her. 'I'm very pleased to meet you, Mrs Ryan. I suppose people will start to come over on holiday again but the tourists go mainly to Douglas or Port Erin or Port St Mary. Fishing is the main occupation in Peel. My pa was a fisherman and my ma still helps to auction off the catches.'

Maggie Dodd leaned on the counter, tucking a stray wisp of hair back into the bun at the nape of her neck and looking wistful. 'Oh, the kids loved Port Erin. I used to take them every year for a week when they were small. Give them a bucket and spade and they'd be happy for hours on end.'

Maria shifted the parcel she was holding impatiently to her other arm. They would be here for hours if everyone got started reminiscing about holidays they'd taken years ago. To her relief Maggie became brisk and businesslike again.

'So, what do you need? Going to give Lizzie a hand to do a "spring clean", then?'

41

Sophie nodded and reeled off the things she required, paid for them and after thanking Maggie they left, accompanied by Martha Ryan.

'Must be a huge change for you both, coming here,' Martha commented. 'But you'll soon settle in, Lizzie's a good-hearted soul, but she's had her fair share of worry and grief. Same as we all have. It can wear you down if you let it.' She looked closely at Sophie. 'She told me you were a widow, luv?'

Sophie nodded, not really wanting to have to explain all the details of Andrew's death. The woman was only being friendly but she was tired as she'd been up very early that morning, her feet were aching and she needed a cup of tea.

'I'm sorry. It was all a terrible waste of so many lives, young and not so young, but I was fortunate, our Frank came through it all without a scratch. He was in the Royal Navy.'

'Is he home now?' Sophie asked politely.

'Oh, aye, but he's not *home* with me. He's living across the road with *her*! The young fool got married before he joined up.' Martha's voice was harsh and full of scorn and bitterness.

Sophie thought it best not to press the matter, obviously Martha didn't approve of her daughter-in-law.

'All the lads are being demobbed now. Most of them that went from our street are home and the couple who were out in the Far East will be back in a couple of weeks, thank God. There's been some talk of having another street party – like the ones we had for VE and VJ Day – to welcome them back, like.'

Maria hadn't really been taking much notice of this conversation until now. 'Really? That sounds like a great idea.'

'Oh, we'd try and put on a good show, luv,' Martha replied, thinking that Maria particularly would cause quite a stir amongst the young men in not only Harebell Street but the whole neighbourhood. She was by far the most attractive girl she'd seen in a long time and they both seemed to be pleasant, well mannered and neatly turned out. And they were obviously going to give that house of Lizzie's a good clean, something that hadn't been done for months. She wouldn't have minded her Frank taking up with someone like Maria Kinnin at all, instead of that little trollop Nora Richards that he'd gone and tied himself to for life.

After a cup of tea Sophie felt much better as she showed her aunt her purchases and informed her of their cost and then began to set the table with the new cloth.

Lizzie had a pan of scouse simmering on the range. 'Jim and John are always famished when they get in from work,' she said, stirring the stew with a wooden spoon.

Suddenly Sophie realised that she had seen nothing of Bella, who had been persuaded to stay with Lizzie and Katie. 'Where's Bella?' she asked, a little alarmed.

'Oh, she's fine, luv. Our Billy took her out to play when he got in from school. She got bored just sitting here with us. He must have taken a shine to her, said he was going to take her to see those other hooligans he calls his mates.'

'And he usually hates girls,' Katie added.

'But it's nearly dark now,' Sophie protested, concerned about her daughter.

Lizzie was peering into the pan. 'Go and see if there's any sign of them in the back entry, luv. It's time they were in anyway.'

As Sophie opened the yard door she was confronted by a small group of lads that included young Billy, all of whom were extremely grubby and untidy. In the middle of the group was her equally grubby daughter.

'Bella Teare, look at the state of you! What have you been up to?' Sophie cried, taking in the smudges of dirt and blood on the child's face, her tangled curls and the rip in the sleeve of her coat, which was also stained and dusty.

'She can't half climb, Sophie! She's as good as all of us an' she never even cried when she fell off the top of the pile,' Billy announced, his voice and expression full of admiration. The others were all nodding their approval.

'Fell off what *pile*?' Sophie demanded, horrified.

'Bricks an' stones, we was playing on the bombsite round the corner,' Billy replied, unfazed by his cousin's tone of voice. They always played there, it was great.

'Bella! You could have hurt yourself badly, you could have broken an arm or a leg! Get inside and have a good wash! Oh, just look at the state of your shoes and socks – and you've ruined your coat.' Sophie was now more annoyed than shocked.

Bella looked mutinous. 'I didn't hurt myself, Mam, and they dared me to do it.' In fact she was quite pleased with

44

herself. She'd showed them she was as good as they were and even though when she'd fallen she'd banged her head quite hard and scratched her face and it had hurt, she hadn't cried.

'What's going on here then? What have you lot been up to now?'

The little group turned as Jim Quine and his son John appeared behind them, their caps pulled well down and their jacket collars turned up against the penetrating chill of the evening.

Sophie looked relieved. 'I'm just getting these two little devils in for their tea, they've been playing on a bombsite. I'm Sophie, you must be Uncle Jim.'

Jim Quine was a big man, over six feet tall and with broad shoulders, and he reminded her so forcefully of her mother that her eyes filled with tears as she was embraced in a bear-like hug.

'Little Sophie!' he laughed. 'But not so little now. Come on, let's all get inside, that's a great smell coming from the kitchen. This is your cousin John, and' – he bent down – 'this must be Isabella.'

'Hello, John, and this is indeed a very dirty and naughty Bella Teare. I've never seen her so grubby and untidy.'

Jim laughed. 'I don't suppose there's many bombsites on the island, Sophie, are there? And I bet I know who the instigator of this little escapade was! Still, the kids have to play somewhere and you might have noticed that there aren't many fields or beaches around here.'

Sophie nodded as they crossed the small yard. 'They've

only just taken the barbed wire away from the beaches at home, Uncle Jim, and the parks were commandeered for the internment camps.'

He nodded gravely. 'We'll all get back to normal soon enough and you're very welcome here – all of you.'

Lizzie exclaimed and tutted over the state of the two children as she dished out the evening meal, after instructing both her husband and son to leave their dirty boots in the scullery in future as she wasn't having her two nieces killing themselves scrubbing floors just so they could walk in the dust and dirt of the docks on to the clean lino. This was followed by the instruction to hang up their jackets and caps behind the door and get a wash before sitting down at the table.

Maria and Sophie exchanged glances, obviously their aunt had had a change of attitude and they noticed that their uncle had nodded his approval at the neatly set table with its clean cloth, milk jug and sugar basin before doing as he was bid.

Katie dished out the stew, sharply nudging her brother who she noticed hadn't said a single word and who was gazing at Maria as though he'd been confronted by an apparition. 'Close your mouth, you look like a codfish on a fishmonger's slab,' she hissed at him.

John Quine realised he was staring open-mouthed at Maria and hastily dropped his eyes and began to poke at his meal with his spoon. He hadn't been aware they were due to arrive today. His mam had said they were coming and told them Sophie was a widow with a little girl, and that both

Maria and her sister had lost their father in the war, but he'd not really thought about them much. His mam always referred to them as 'Sarah's poor girls', but now he was stunned. He'd never seen anyone as utterly *gorgeous* as Maria. She was like a film star – like Vivien Leigh, except that Maria had the most beautiful dark brown eyes, fringed with thick sooty lashes, that he'd ever seen. It was an effort not to stare and he couldn't think of a single thing to say to her.

Lizzie had noticed. 'What's up with you, John? Are you sickening for something, you usually wolf your food down.'

'I'm . . . I'm all right, Mam,' John managed to mutter.

'Where's your manners then? You haven't even said hello to your cousins.'

Sophie could see he was acutely embarrassed and she smiled kindly at him. Maria often had this effect on young men. 'It's all right, Aunty Lizzie, we met in the yard, so to speak, didn't we, John?'

He looked up and smiled shyly at her, nodding.

Maria smiled at him. 'I didn't meet him in the yard. Hello, John, I'm Maria.'

John managed to reply although he was never able to remember just what he'd said. Thankfully his mother started to relate the events of the day to her family.

'Mrs Ryan from next door told me that people were thinking of holding a street party when the last of the boys get home,' Sophie remarked when Lizzie finally paused for breath.

'Oh, we are, luv. It'll be great if we can manage to scrape

together enough stuff for sandwiches and things, though these two might be able to get a few tins off the Yanks, they certainly aren't short of anything. A couple of bottles of whisky wouldn't go amiss either. A party will be just the thing to cheer everyone up; day-to-day life is still a bit grey and depressing with all the shortages.'

'If we can get some material we could have new dresses for it,' Maria added, beginning to catch some of her aunt's enthusiasm.

'Can I have a party frock, too, Mam?' Bella asked, now scrubbed clean, her hair tied back and wearing a clean pinafore over her dress.

Sophie laughed. 'As long as you don't go playing on any more bombsites, you can. We should have enough coupons for material, we haven't used many. Aunty Lizzie, do you know if anyone in the street has a sewing machine?'

Lizzie frowned. 'I'll ask, luv, but I don't think so.'

'It will take ages to do them by hand, Sophie,' Maria reminded her.

'Hasn't Mrs Richards, Nora's mam, got an old treadle thing in their back yard?' Katie asked of her mother.

Lizzie frowned. 'If she has it'll be rusted to hell by now and anyway, how do you know?'

'I remember Nora saying she was fed up falling over it in the blackout,' Katie replied sullenly, knowing her mother's opinion of the Richards family and Nora in particular. She'd only mentioned it because she was hoping Sophie would make a frock for her too.

'It would save an awful lot of time,' Maria stated.

'Maybe Frank could do something with it, if you ask him, Sophie,' Jim suggested, seeing the looks of disappointment on the faces of both Bella and Katie and his nieces' expressions of concern.

Lizzie glared at him. 'I don't want these girls having anything to do with that Nora, Jim, and you know why.'

Katie frowned, wishing now she'd never mentioned the sewing machine.

'What's the matter with her, this Nora?' Maria asked curiously.

'She's no better than she ought to be and her a married woman!' Lizzie snapped. 'Now, can we finish our meal in peace without any more mention of that lot across the road?'

Seeing that nothing more was to be forthcoming about Nora Richards or Ryan or whatever her name was, Maria turned to her sister. 'I don't mind helping to cut out and do the tacking and you'll help too, Katie, won't you?'

Katie nodded, still unsure if she was to be included in the dressmaking venture. 'And I can have a look and see if they've got any nice materials when I go into work tomorrow, I know one of the girls in that department.'

Sophie smiled at her. 'Would you, Katie? That's very generous of you. Look for something suitable for us all, including yourself.'

Delighted, Katie beamed at Sophie and Maria. 'And I'll go and ask if there are any vacancies too, for Maria.'

'And once I've got Bella settled at school I'll look for work myself,' Sophie added.

As Lizzie got to her feet to begin to clear away the dishes, all three girls rose too.

'You sit down, Aunty Lizzie. You cooked the meal, we'll wash up and then if you really don't mind, I'll go and ask Mrs Ryan next door if she would ask Frank about that sewing machine, because without it I'll never get five dresses done in time,' Sophie said firmly.

Lizzie looked astonished. '*Five* dresses!'

Sophie nodded. 'Well, we can't leave you out, now can we, Aunty Lizzie?'

It was Lizzie's turn to look stunned. 'I haven't had a brand-new frock in years.'

Jim grinned. 'You'll be a sight for sore eyes, Lizzie, and won't that give the neighbours something to talk about?' He cast a grateful look at Sophie, thinking she was a generous, thoughtful girl not to leave either his wife or daughter out. If she wanted to ask Frank Ryan about that old sewing machine he wasn't going to raise any objections.

Chapter Four

MARTHA WAS SURPRISED BUT pleased to see Sophie when she opened the door. 'Come on in, Sophie. I was just telling Pat what nice girls you and your sister are. Mind you, luv, you don't want to let that little girl of yours go running around with Billy and our Robbie and that lot. They'll turn her into a right little tomboy.'

'I won't, Mrs Ryan. I've told her she won't have a new dress for this street party if she goes off climbing on bombsites again and it's that I've come to see you about. I've a favour to ask you.'

Martha ushered her into their kitchen, which Sophie noticed immediately was quite a lot neater, tidier and well cared for than Aunty Lizzie's. Pat Ryan got to his feet and shook her hand warmly. 'It's a pleasure to meet you, Sophie. Do sit down.'

'Now, what can I help you with?' Martha pressed, eager to be of help.

'I've rather rashly promised to make everyone a new dress for this street party as it's obviously going to be something of an occasion. I make most of our clothes, it's something I'm quite good at even though I say it myself, and it does save money.'

Martha looked very impressed, 'Lizzie never said you were a seamstress.'

Sophie smiled a little ruefully. 'I'm not. I would have liked to have served my time at it but I didn't have the chance. I had a teacher at school who taught me the basics and I sort of picked it up from there with the help of paper patterns.'

'You really must have a talent for it then.' Martha had never met anyone who had been blessed with a natural gift with the needle and Sophie Teare went up still further in her estimation.

'Katie is going to look for materials when she goes into work tomorrow and both she and Maria will help me cut out, pin and tack—'

'Katie Quine – pin and tack! Wonders will never cease! I didn't think she could even sew a button on,' Martha interrupted.

'Under my supervision, of course. It's not really hard. But if I have to do all the sewing by hand I doubt I'll get them finished in time.'

'*Five* frocks? Is Lizzie having one too?'

Sophie nodded. 'I couldn't leave her out, she's been kind enough to take us in and make us welcome.'

'That's very generous of you, Sophie,' Martha replied. 'So, how can I help?'

'I wanted to ask you if you could mention to your Frank about the old treadle sewing machine that's in the yard at . . . er . . . Nora's house. Katie said she's sure they have one although Aunty Lizzie said it would be rusted up, but if Frank could do something with it, it would be a huge help to me.'

Martha's expression changed. Her brows twitched together and her lips became set in a tight, thin line of disapproval. 'I'm sorry, Sophie, but I don't have anything to do with that Nora or her family. If you want to go over there and ask our Frank that's up to you, but I'd strongly advise against it.'

Sophie was taken aback. 'Why? What on earth is wrong with them?'

Martha glanced at her husband, who shrugged and gave a slight nod of his head. 'I don't imagine Lizzie has said anything about them?'

Sophie shook her head. 'Not really.'

Martha sighed heavily. 'Well, I suppose you'd better know and sooner rather than later; you are too nice a girl to be kept in the dark about *that lot*. Hardly anyone in this street has anything to do with them – decent folk that is. Bertie Richards is a work-shy, good-for-nothing, idle drunk and always has been! And Nellie isn't much better; if she were she would

53

have sorted their Nora out long ago. All the rest of them have left home. The Lord alone knows where they are now, but we did hear that one of the lads was in prison. As for that Nora!' Martha bit her lip, smarting with humiliation, but if she didn't tell Sophie then Lizzie would. 'Well, luv, it broke my heart when our Frank got mixed up with her. I pleaded with him, Pat tried to reason with him, but he was besotted with her and wouldn't listen. I could hardly hold my head up, for the shame. But then, after a while, he seemed to be going off her, and we thought he'd finally seen sense and saw her for what she really is.' Martha paused and shook her head. 'Then, doesn't he go and marry her! They *had* to get married, of course, I still can't get over the shame of it, and then he went off into the Navy with her flaunting her wedding ring and insisting on being called *Mrs Ryan*. Oh, when I think of him living over there in that . . . that *pigsty*! He wasn't used to having to live like that; he was brought up to be decent, honest and hard working. I don't know how he sticks it but he's made his bed and he'll just have to put up with it and *her*!'

Understanding had begun to dawn on Sophie. Obviously Nora had got pregnant and Frank had done the decent thing and married her, even though Martha had said his feelings for her had changed. 'I'm so sorry, Mrs Ryan. I didn't know. These things do happen.'

'Well, they shouldn't and that's why we don't have anything to do with them,' Martha replied sharply.

'But surely you see your grandchild?'

Martha uttered a bitter laugh. 'What grandchild? There never was one, it was all just a pack of lies that little slut told him and like a fool he believed her!'

Sophie looked shocked, feeling very sorry for both Martha and Frank and wondering how Nora could have done such a thing. Maybe she'd really loved him and had seen no other way of keeping him? It must be awful to be trapped in what was obviously a joyless marriage. 'That was a terrible thing for her to do to him, I'm sorry.'

Martha nodded slowly. 'So now you know.'

Sophie stood up, unsure what to do about the sewing machine. 'I'll just have to think of something else, I won't go over now. I don't think Aunty Lizzie would approve.' She smiled wryly. 'To use one of her favorite sayings, "we'll manage". I'm sorry for having brought the matter up.'

'You weren't to know, luv, but I think you've made the right decision.'

When she got back only Lizzie and Jim were in the kitchen and her aunt informed her that Bella had been so tired that she'd had little trouble getting her to bed. Billy had been sent to bed in disgrace for some misdemeanour and Katie and John had taken Maria down the road to introduce her to a few of their mutual friends.

'I don't know where Maria gets her energy from, I'm exhausted, it's been a very long day,' Sophie said, sinking down in an armchair.

'So, how did you get on?' Lizzie asked, bluntly.

'I'll have to do them by hand, after what Martha Ryan told

me I hadn't the heart to go and ask about that damned sewing machine.'

Lizzie shook her head sadly. 'We've been friends for years and my heart goes out to that poor woman. She brought their Frank and Joan up honest and decent and she's trying with their Robbie. Joan married well, she lives in New Brighton, and if that Nora hadn't got her claws into Frank I've no doubt he'd have married a nice, respectable girl. Shocking family, the Richardses are, a disgrace to the street and the talk of the neighbourhood. And as for that Nora – words fail me!'

'It was a terrible thing to do to tell him such a blatant lie, especially when he was going off to war,' Sophie agreed.

Jim lowered the newspaper he'd been reading. 'I agree but he must have been playing with fire or she couldn't have trapped him like that.'

'And that wasn't the end of it, as well you know, Jim.' Lizzie lowered her voice as she turned back to Sophie. 'The carry-on out of her while he was away too! Utterly disgraceful! I'd have killed our Katie with my own two hands if she'd behaved like that. Nellie should have put a stop to it but she didn't, too busy sitting with her cronies in the pub. Their Nora had fellers in and out of the place by the minutes and we all know they weren't there just for a cup of tea!'

Sophie was really taken aback. Nora had been sleeping with other men? But that meant she couldn't have loved Frank, as Sophie had first thought, not to do something like that while he was away risking his life. 'How awful, how utterly humiliating for him. I . . . I didn't know that.'

'Well, Martha would hardly tell you, would she? She was mortified and absolutely furious. Oh, she had many a blazing row with both Nellie and Nora over it – much good that did.'

'I don't know why Frank put up with it, he knew what was going on. He had plenty of grounds for divorce,' Jim said soberly. Divorce was something people seldom resorted to but in the light of Nora's conduct quite a few of the men in the street felt the lad would be more than justified.

'You know he'd never do that, Jim. Everything would come out in court and it would be in all the papers. It's bad enough that the entire street knows what kind of a girl she is, but can you imagine what it would be like for the whole damned *city* to know?'

Sophie sighed; Frank Ryan's life seemed to be such a terrible mess. 'I'll do the sewing by hand, maybe the girls will help.'

Lizzie looked thoughtful. 'If they take you on at Marsden's maybe they'd let you do a bit on one of their machines, in your break, like.'

Sophie brightened up. 'I could ask; they can only refuse. That's if they take me on.'

'And why wouldn't they? A fine girl like you and a dab hand at sewing?' Lizzie said firmly.

It was going to be a big day for Bella, starting a new school and hopefully making new friends. When Mam had woken her up she'd told her to get a good wash and get dressed and then she could have her breakfast, but everybody else seemed to be trying to do the same things and there was a lot of shouting and confusion, which she wasn't used to at all.

'It's like a three-ringed circus in here,' Maria hissed to Sophie as both their uncle and two older cousins rushed in and out between the kitchen and scullery, with Billy still half asleep getting in everyone's way. Lizzie was on top note, firing instructions at everyone, which for the main part were ignored.

'We'll have to sort out a better system than this once we get jobs ourselves,' Sophie muttered as she sat Bella at the table and spooned out porridge for the child.

It seemed a minor miracle that all four of them were ready to leave at half past eight. Sophie and Maria were going to walk both Bella and Billy to school and then Sophie intended to go along to Marsden's, while Maria said she would go and see just what kind of a place this Heaton's Department Store was.

Sophie was relieved to find that Miss O'Malley, who was to be Bella's teacher, seemed both kind and sensible.

'She'll be just fine, Mrs Teare. I'll keep my eye on her,' she said confidently, and then she took Bella's hand. 'I think we'll sit you next to Emily Taylor, Bella. She lives in Crocus Street, which is the next one to where you live and she's the same age as you.'

Sophie smiled encouragingly. 'There you are, Bella. I told you there would be other little girls to make friends with. Perhaps you and Emily can walk home together?'

Miss O'Malley smiled too. 'What a good idea. Now, let's go and find your desk.'

As she watched them walk away Sophie felt a little anxious, hoping this Emily would indeed befriend her daughter, for everything was still so unfamiliar to Bella.

'At least there were no tears or tantrums,' Maria commented as they walked towards the tram stop.

The girls parted company further along Stanley Road, full of enthusiasm for their plans, agreeing to meet up at this same tram stop when they'd completed their objectives.

Maria arrived first, feeling hopeful and relieved. The shop had surprised her for it was not as small as she'd at first imagined. She'd wandered around a few departments but had lingered longest in Haberdashery, making a mental note of what was in stock.

After fifteen minutes waiting she was beginning to get impatient and decidedly cold. At least her sister's absence was a good sign, she thought as she walked up and down to keep her feet from becoming numb. Obviously Sophie hadn't just been turned away with a curt refusal.

It was another five minutes before she caught sight of her sister hurrying towards her, a smile on her face.

'I'm sorry I was so long, Maria, but I had to wait to see Mr Phillips, he's the manager, and I had to do some sewing to prove I can use a machine, but I'm to start tomorrow morning.'

'Oh, Sophie, that's great!' Maria cried.

'He was actually very nice and praised my bit of work and

I assured him I'm diligent, neat and hard working. How did you get on?'

'I didn't see Katie but it's a much bigger shop than she led us to believe. I looked around some of the departments – Aunty Lizzie was right, there's not a lot of choice but I saw a couple of materials that might suit us and their selection of trimmings wasn't too bad.'

'Were they practical materials, Maria? There's no point in buying something we won't get much wear out of,' Sophie asked.

'I suppose so but I thought these were to be special dresses? Bella thinks she's going to have a party frock.'

Sophie sighed. 'Oh, we'll see.' She decided to change the subject. 'Who did you meet last night when you were out with Katie and John?'

'Two girls called Ivy and Daisy Caldwell – they live at number ten and they were very friendly – and then two lads, Matt and Ben Seddon at number twenty,' Maria informed her.

'What were they like?' Sophie probed.

Maria shrugged. 'All right, I suppose. They'd both been in the Army with John, but at least they had more to say for themselves than he did. Honestly, Sophie, all he does is stare at me.'

Sophie grinned. 'He's a bit . . . in awe of you. I hope he isn't falling for you, though,' she added more seriously.

Maria looked sceptical. 'He'd better not. For one thing he's my first cousin and for another, well . . .' She shrugged, looking wistful.

Sophie looked at her sister closely and then sighed. 'I thought you'd got over him? You told Mam you had.'

Maria's dark eyes filled with tears. 'I only said that to pacify Mam but I know I'll never get over Hans, Sophie. I really loved him. You should know how I feel, you loved Andrew.'

Sophie put her arm around her sister. 'He's gone, Maria. You know you'll never see him again. He had no choice; they made them all go back to their own countries. You *have* to forget him and think about the future. That's why we thought it best for you to come here to live. You're young, you'll meet someone else. There was no future for you with him, Maria. In most people's minds there is little difference between Germans and Austrians. Hitler was Austrian, don't forget.'

Maria nodded miserably, but she couldn't forget Hans. What Sophie had said about people thinking he was a Nazi sympathiser wasn't true. He'd fled with his family before the Nazis had taken over his country. Being from a farming background they'd settled in Kent but when war had broken out, they'd been sent to the island and interned in Peel. Oh, why couldn't he have stayed, she thought? Why had he been sent back with his parents and sister? If he'd been allowed to stay she was sure that in time people would have accepted him. Lots of people in Peel knew his family had left Austria before the war and had had no part in it at all. Hans Bonhoeffer and his father had hated Hitler and all he stood for.

Sophie tried to cheer her up. 'Here's the tram. Let's get

back to Aunty Lizzie's. We both need a hot cup of tea and at least we have some good news to tell her. Let's hope Katie has some good news for you when she gets home tonight.'

Maria dashed away her tears with the back of her hand. She knew Sophie was right but it didn't help when she felt so miserable and bereft.

Chapter Five

OCTOBER WAS PASSING SWIFTLY and it was becoming much colder, Sophie thought as she walked home from the tram stop. It was a journey she was used to now. At least Maria had settled well into her job at Heaton's. Her sister worked in their small millinery department, much to Katie's envy. Katie worked in Soft Furnishings, which didn't appeal to her a great deal. She complained that she had little interest in cushion covers, lampshades or curtains, while hats were entirely different. Everyone was interested in them, although there certainly wasn't the wide selection now that had been available before the war. In fact lots of people tried to make their own, copying them from magazine pictures or those on display in the windows of shops like Hendersons and the Bon Marche, both of which had survived the bombing, but whose prices were beyond most people's pockets.

She, too, was getting on well at Marsden's, although she couldn't say she enjoyed it; far from it, for it was a world of heat, noise and constant, frenetic activity. The room she worked in was huge. Rows of sewing machines, in banks of two facing each other, filled it completely and the motorised belt that drove them ran on wheels above their heads, its loud clacking noise adding to the general cacophony. Between the machines was a shallow wooden trough into which the finished garments were deposited. Every worker relied on all the others to keep the line going so she had soon learned to work very rapidly indeed.

Having spent the entire day hunched over her machine, forcing the material under the drumming head of the needle, the noise of which was replicated by every other machine in the room, she always came out with a headache and stiff, aching shoulders and back. The pace of work was so relentless that there were often accidents. One of the girls who had long hair, which she wore loose, had got it entangled and but for the quick action of one of the pressers, who cut her free, would have been seriously injured. After that Mr Phillips had insisted that everyone wore turbans, but nearly every day someone was injured, usually by the needle piercing a finger or a nail. Still, the pay was good even if the conditions were not.

She pulled the collar of her coat up around her ears and shifted the carefully wrapped parcel to her other arm, smiling to herself. Two days ago she'd plucked up courage to ask Albert Phillips if she could possibly use her machine for some personal sewing during her breaks and to her relief he had agreed. She'd explained about the dresses for the forth-coming party, which it had been decided would take place on 5 November, Bonfire Night, and he'd nodded thoughtfully.

'So, you can make a complete garment from scratch, Mrs Teare? That's quite unusual. Even though all the girls can use a machine very few of them can actually do that.'

She'd smiled at him. He was a rather quiet, middle-aged man with a reserved manner, although he was a stickler for punctuality and hard work and didn't suffer fools gladly. 'I would have liked to have been a seamstress or a tailoress but I just didn't get the opportunity.'

He'd nodded. 'Not many people do get what they want out of life. I'd have liked to have been a qualified engineer but I had to leave school as my mother needed the money. I'd like to see the finished garments, if you don't mind, and there won't be a problem about using the machine in your break,' he added. If they were good he would see about having her transferred to the cutting room. Conditions were better and so was the pay and he liked her. She was quieter than most of the girls, pleasant and a good worker.

'Of course. I'll be pleased to show you them,' she'd replied.

When Sophie reached Dodd's corner shop she didn't stop to chat, she just waved to Maggie who was sweeping the floor, the rush of the day now over. Thanks to Mr Phillips the dresses were coming along well. Maria had got the materials

– she'd even managed to get a bit of a discount too – and she and Katie had worked hard, pinning and tacking. Sophie had done the cutting out herself and after a few mishaps Katie had soon mastered the tacking.

Aunty Lizzie had been astonished by their expertise, especially by that of Katie who she declared had never threaded a needle in her life before, and she kept up a constant stream of conversation while they worked. Sophie smiled to herself. Maria said it would give you a headache listening to her, but Maria didn't have to work all day in the sewing room at Marsden's, that really *did* give you a headache.

Her reverie was interrupted by shouts and laughter and she caught sight of a group of children, who appeared to be dragging a large piece of wood towards the bombsite where she could dimly make out a growing pile of other rubbish. She frowned. If Billy and Bella and Emily Taylor were amongst them she'd certainly have something to say to all of them – and Aunty Lizzie as well. They shouldn't be still out at this time and they'd be filthy dirty too.

She turned off the pavement and quickened her steps, peering into the gloom, trying to see if Bella was with them, and so didn't see the small pile of blackened bricks until she tripped over them. She fell sprawling, dropping both her bag and the parcel and uttering a cry of pain.

'Oh, damn!' she exclaimed, realising she'd grazed both her shins and her hands.

'Are you all right? That was quite a fall. Here, let me help you up.'

Sophie looked up into a pair of brown eyes that were full of concern and then a strong arm was around her, helping her to her feet. 'Thank you. I'm fine, just a few grazes I think.'

He retrieved her bag and the parcel as she examined her ruined stockings and tried to brush some of the dirt from her coat.

'You're Frank Ryan, aren't you? Aunty Lizzie pointed you out to me.'

He nodded and smiled at her. 'That's me, the neighborhood pariah, and you're Sophie Teare. I've seen you a few times going in and out of Lizzie's. You're sure you aren't hurt?'

She smiled back at him. You couldn't help but like him, she thought. He was tall and quite well built with dark auburn hair, brown eyes and pleasant features. In fact she thought he was quite handsome. 'No, I'm just a bit shaken up. I saw those kids and wanted to see if Bella and her friend Emily Taylor were with them and I tripped over some bricks.'

'Lucky I was only a few steps behind you then.' He looked across to where the little group was now adding the wood to the pile. 'They're building a bonfire for Guy Fawkes' Night.'

'Is that what they're at,' she replied as they both walked back towards the road. He'd handed back her bag but he was carrying the parcel.

'We always had a big bonfire in our street and fireworks on November fifth, before the war. Us lads spent weeks begging and . . . er . . . "purloining" stuff to build it.' He smiled ruefully, remembering his carefree childhood. 'There haven't been either bonfires or fireworks for the past six years so the kids are enjoying themselves.'

'I expect there were quite enough "bonfires" and "fireworks" during that time in this city for most people to contend with.'

He nodded grimly. 'There were indeed.'

They walked for a little while in silence and then Sophie turned to him. 'I heard you were in the Royal Navy.'

'I was. I was with Johnny Walker's lot, God rest him. He was a fine captain.'

Sophie didn't miss the note of pride mingled with sadness in his voice. 'What happened to him?'

'Died of a heart attack, but he was a casualty of the war just the same. He was a young man but he never stopped to rest, never spared himself. We were known as the "hunter-killers" and German U-boat captains hated and feared us – with good cause.'

Sophie nodded, a pang of grief tugging at her heart. 'You sank submarines?'

'We did, scores of them, and took pride in doing it. They'd sent too many good ships and fine men to the bottom of the Atlantic.'

'They killed my husband too. He was a fisherman and the boat was dragged down by its nets. He went out one evening in June three years ago and . . . and never came back. The weather was fine, there was no wind, and U-boats had been spotted just north of where the *Girl Sophie* was last seen. There was no other explanation.'

'I'm sorry,' he said sincerely.

'Oh, there were some folk who said it could possibly have been an accident. That the U-boat's crew might not have realised the nets were caught in the rigging or on the conning tower . . .'

He shook his head. 'They'd have known. They had sonar and they'd done it before, off the Scottish coast.' He felt sorry for her. She was young to be left a widow with a child to bring up, but then there were thousands like her now. 'Was the boat named after you?' he asked to try to lighten the conversation. He certainly wasn't in any rush to get home. He hated having to return to *that* house every night.

'No. Andrew didn't own the boat. It was just coincidence. Mr Austin Quirk owned it and his wife was called Sophie too.'

'I thought most skippers owned their boats. I presume your husband was a skipper?'

She smiled and nodded. She instinctively felt he understood, having been in the Navy, and she felt a sort of gratitude that he'd been instrumental in the destruction of the U-boats. 'He was. He felt it was just as important to try to keep food on people's tables as to join up.'

'It was and just as dangerous, as sadly you both found out.' They'd reached the bottom of Harebell Street and he slowed his steps even further. He'd much sooner stay talking to her than face Nora and her slovenly mother. Bertie Richards would still be in the pub.

Despite the fact that she wanted to get home and bathe the cuts, which were now smarting painfully, and have a cup of tea to steady her, Sophie remembered that there would be no warm welcome or decent meal waiting for him. She sighed; he seemed so kind and patient. 'The Manx system is different to others, I think. The catch is divided into shares between the owner of the boat, the owner of the nets, the skipper and the hands. It's a fairer way of doing it because it means the skipper and the hands can earn more. Oh, the owners and net owners can make a fortune, they have shares in lots of boats, but it does mean that a good skipper is a real asset and is usually well treated. They all work together; it's in everyone's interest. The skippers always inform each other of the whereabouts of the herring shoals, no one would speak to them if they didn't.'

'Your Uncle Jim gave it up to come here to work, didn't he?'

Sophie nodded. 'Mam said he couldn't stand all the superstition that went with it.' She managed a little laugh. 'Manx people are very superstitious, especially fishermen.'

He smiled down at her. She was a very attractive young woman, he thought. Not as strikingly lovely as her younger sister but more what people called a 'classical' beauty.

'What do you do now, for a job?' Sophie asked. She'd noticed the overalls beneath his jacket.

'I'm a joiner. I'd just finished serving my time when war broke out.'

They had finally reached Lizzie's house and Sophie stopped. 'Here we are. Thank you, Frank, for helping me and . . . and I've enjoyed talking to you.'

'I've enjoyed your company too, Sophie.' He hesitated a little. 'I walk home from the tram each night about this time. Maybe I'll see you again?'

'Perhaps, Frank. Well, goodnight.'

Reluctantly he turned away and crossed the road, feeling more miserable and frustrated than ever. He liked Sophie Teare very much and he made up his mind to try to see her again as she walked home. He'd even wait by the tram stop for her.

'In the name of God, what happened to you?' Lizzie cried as Sophie came into the kitchen. Sophie was relieved to see that Bella and Emily were sitting at the table, heads bent over a book.

'I fell over some bricks on the bombsite. I saw some kids and thought these two were with them. They were building a bonfire for Guy Fawkes' Night.'

Lizzie tutted. 'Sit down while I find the Dettol. We'd better clean those grazes or they'll turn septic.'

Sophie nodded. 'I'd sooner have a cup of tea first, Aunty Lizzie.'

'You'll not get much sewing done tonight with those hands,' Maria commented, examining the palms of her sister's hands.

'I won't have to if you and Katie can finish tacking Bella's dress. I can get it machined in my break tomorrow. I managed to get most of Aunty Lizzie's and yours done today. Do you think you can manage the hems? These cuts should be much better by tomorrow.'

Maria nodded. 'We're well on the way to having them ready by Bonfire Night. I hope it won't be really freezing, I don't want to have to wear a cardigan or worse still a jacket over mine. I've seen a lovely pair of earrings at work that will set it off and they don't cost a small fortune.'

'Those glittery black ones we were looking at today?' Katie queried. They'd spent their lunch break searching for cheap but smart accessories. Maria's dress was of scarlet material (what kind neither of them was really sure), and hers was of emerald green and royal blue check. They were two colours that Maria said really suited her and she was delighted with it, even though it wasn't quite finished.

Maria nodded. 'I'll put my hair up, that way it might not go too frizzy.'

'It's never frizzy! It's always gorgeous,' Katie enthused, wishing her own hair curled like her cousin's. Maybe Maria would put her hair up for her; she had a way with things like that.

'Will the pair of you give poor Sophie a few minutes' peace, for heaven's sake! Maria, get her a cup of tea while I see to these cuts and Katie, you'd better start dishing out that scouse, your da and John will be in any minute now. Emily, luv, I think it's time you went home for your tea too. Your mam won't be very happy if she has to keep it warm for you,' Lizzie instructed as she bustled about with the Dettol and a pad of cotton wool.

Sophie sipped her tea thankfully and said no more. She had the distinct feeling that she shouldn't mention Frank Ryan or the fact that he'd helped her up and walked home with her.

Chapter Six

———◆———

OVER THE NEXT COUPLE of weeks Sophie walked home with Frank Ryan most nights. If she was a little later leaving work she found him waiting patiently in the cold for her to alight from the tram. He was pleasant and she found it easy to talk to him; her liking for him grew steadily.

They talked mainly about her. He asked her all about the island, her childhood, what life had been like before and during the war and in turn he told about growing up here in Harebell Street, his school friends and his time in the Navy, but the party was nearly upon them before she finally plucked up courage to ask him about Nora.

He frowned, thrusting his hands deeper into the pockets of his jacket. He'd known that sooner or later she would ask. Any other girl would have questioned him long before now, he thought, but that was not Sophie's way. She had more tact and sensitivity.

'I was young and stupid. I fell for her in a big way, even though I'd grown up with her and knew the kind of family she came from. One day I looked at her and she . . . she just seemed *different*. Oh, Mam was furious and so was Da, but I was pig-headed and stubborn, I wouldn't listen – at least, not at first. But then things . . . things started to change. I still don't know why I changed my mind about her but I did. I suddenly began to notice how . . . coarse and brassy she looked and how loud and bad mannered she was. She'd bleached her hair and wore too much make-up and she drowned herself in cheap scent.' He paused. It was painful and humiliating but no doubt she'd heard both his mother's and Lizzie's version of events. 'I wasn't even sure if she was being truthful when she swore she loved me and only me. There had been a couple of rumours but I'd refused to believe them. When war was declared, I joined the Navy. I thought that it would all sort of . . . fizzle out, but then I found it was too late. I had to pay for my mistakes. She said she was expecting so I did the decent thing and married her, even though I then found that . . .'

Sophie listened in silence to his words but she realised how much it was costing him to tell her all this. She laid a hand on his arm. 'Frank, you don't have to go on. Everything . . . else . . . is between you and Nora. I got the general idea of the whole terrible situation from Aunty Lizzie.'

He nodded, but he was determined to tell her everything.

'I bet you did, but you may not know that Nora told me a pack of lies to trap me into marrying her. She said she'd made a mistake; that she'd honestly believed she was and had panicked, and only discovered she wasn't pregnant after the wedding. I didn't believe her and after that things just got worse between us, and while I was away she—'

'I know all about that too and I'm so sorry,' she interrupted. 'Is there really nothing at all that you can do? Life must be—'

'Pure hell!' he cut in bitterly. 'I made a mistake, Sophie. A big mistake, but I'll just have to live with it.'

'I really am so sorry, Frank,' she said, and she meant it.

'I suppose you think I'm a fool?'

She shook her head vehemently. 'No. You did make a mistake, but no one goes through life without doing that. You were lied to, trapped into marriage, betrayed and . . . and haven't much of a future now, but I think it takes a great deal of courage to go on paying for that mistake to spare your parents more shame.'

He turned his head away so she wouldn't see the tears that sprang to his eyes. She was the first person who had tried to understand. She didn't condemn him or think any the worse of him; she'd even praised his courage – and it *did* take courage to go on day after day, month after month living a life that was so completely hateful to him. In that moment he knew that what he felt for Sophie Teare was the love and deep affection he'd thought he felt for Nora, and he was tied for ever to Nora. Nora who was everything Sophie Teare was not. He prayed that he could find the courage to live with the reality now.

*

It hadn't gone unnoticed that Sophie and Frank were becoming increasingly friendly. Lizzie had been informed of the fact that they walked home together each night by Mary Seddon when she had been in Maggie Dodd's shop and the news hadn't pleased her one bit. She'd passed the information on to Jim who had cautioned her not to say too much on the subject.

'It's for her own good, Jim. She'll get talked about, you know what people are like.'

'Sophie is no fool, Lizzie. She's fully aware that he's a married man.'

'And look what he's married *to*! I don't want her being associated in any way with that lot, she's a decent girl.'

Jim had sighed. 'I'll have a word with her, Lizzie, but we can't stop her just talking to him on the way home.'

'I wish you would, Jim, she might take notice of you and she's got to think of Maria's reputation too. We don't want people gossiping and speculating about either of them.'

Jim had pointed out to Sophie that people had begun to talk.

She had expected it; she'd seen the curtains twitching. 'But I just chat to him, Uncle Jim, I know full well he's married. He's lonely; everyone shuns him, even his own mother, and his life is far from easy.'

'I agree, Sophie, but the women around here do gossip,' he replied.

'Then it's a pity they haven't got more to occupy them

78

than to be criticising me for just being *friendly*! I think he's a nice, decent man who just made a mistake.'

He'd nodded. She'd hit the nail exactly on the head but her attitude wouldn't please either his wife or Martha Ryan.

Fortunately for Sophie both women were becoming fully occupied with the preparations for the forthcoming party and Sophie herself was desperately trying to finish the last new dress, which was her own, so the matter wasn't referred to again.

Despite the rationing, tins of corned beef, Spam, pears and even pineapple chunks materialised, which had been acquired either from the departing American troops or from a broken crate on the dockside. Such damaged goods had always been regarded as the dockers' 'perks' and the foremen and the dock police usually turned a blind eye, unless greed took over and the thefts became too large and too blatantly obvious to ignore.

The red, white and blue bunting was got out again and strung up, and the Caldwell girls, with the help of Katie and Maria, had made a huge banner with the words 'Welcome Home Our Brave Boys' in black letters, which was also hung across the street. All the younger children were terribly excited and ran up and down the road and in and out of everyone's houses until they were chased out by their mothers with dire threats of 'no cake or jelly unless you behave'.

Bella was particularly over-excited for not only had she never been to such a big party before but she had a new dress too, and Aunty Maria had bought her a length of red velvet ribbon for her hair. It matched her dress, which was by far the nicest she'd ever had. Mam had unpicked one of scarlet velvet that she'd bought in a second-hand shop; the frock was unsuitable but she'd said the material was perfect and of good quality and had made a dress for her from it. It had long sleeves with lacy cuffs so she wouldn't be cold, a white lace collar, a full skirt and a wide sash. Emily had said she'd never seen anything as grand in her life. Bella would look like a princess, she'd said enviously. Mam had polished her black shoes until they shone and the red ribbon matched the dress perfectly.

'Will you keep still, Bella, while I tie this bow,' Sophie instructed firmly as she struggled with her daughter's long curls, but she was pleased with the results of her efforts. Bella looked a picture. The dress was lovely and the colour suited her.

'I'd tie that ribbon really tight or she'll have lost it by the end of the night, Sophie,' Lizzie advised as she bustled about the kitchen, resplendent in the russet-brown dress trimmed with cream braid that Jim said made her look years younger. She, too, was delighted with the way the dress had turned out. She felt very smart and quite elegant, especially as Maria had lent her a pair of clip-on earrings and had done her hair in a very flattering style. 'Bella, if you're ready, queen, go up and see if our Billy's got his Sunday trousers and jumper on. I can never trust that lad to do as he's told and he's quite likely to wear some old thing that's lost its shape.' She paused as Bella went into the lobby and Katie came into the kitchen.

'Katie, luv, take this last plate of meat-paste sandwiches out and see if Mr Seddon has managed to get their piano out, the last I heard it was stuck in the doorway. If he hasn't, your da will have to go and give him a hand or we'll have no music.'

Katie frowned as the plate was thrust into her hands. 'Mam, my hair will get all messed up if I go running up and down the street and it's taken Maria ages to do!' For the first time in her life Katie felt she was attractive. Her dress fitted perfectly, it was stylish and brightened her appearance up no end. She had found a pair of emerald-green earrings to match and Maria had put her hair up in a cluster of loose curls, which made her appear older, and with the light dusting of face powder, a little rouge and lipstick she could hardly believe the transformation when she'd looked in the mirror. She was hoping that Matt Seddon would notice it too.

'I'm not asking you to go running up and down, just take the plate out and have a quick look. I've to make sure your da, our Billy and John are presentable,' Lizzie said firmly, propelling her towards the door. 'Sophie, luv, would you go and give Mr Chatsworth a knock, tell him we're all nearly ready now.'

Sophie smiled. She'd been introduced to the lodger the day after they'd arrived and usually saw him at least once during the evenings, en route to the scullery or the privy in the yard. He was a very quiet, inoffensive, middle-aged man who kept himself very much to himself. What he did seemed to be a mystery for he didn't go out to work. Lizzie had said he had 'independent' means, probably a small pension of some kind, and he spent a lot of his time out walking or reading in the public library, and in the evenings he listened to his wireless in the front room.

She caught sight of herself in the mirror in the hall and frowned. She wasn't at all sure that this dress suited her. Maria had persuaded her to buy the black brocade, which had cost more than she had intended to spend. Maria had said it was so rich looking, and would make her look elegant and sophisticated.

'It's just the sort of material expensive cocktail dresses are made of. I saw one made of something similar in the window of the Bon Marche,' her sister had urged.

Sophie frowned again, wondering whether it made her look old and washed out. Maria had put her hair up in a French pleat and had borrowed a pair of diamanté drop earrings from a girl she worked with for her sister to wear. Maria had assured her she looked like a model in one of those expensive fashion magazines but she wasn't at all sure.

In reply to her knock Mr Chatsworth opened the door, smartly dressed in a rather old-fashioned but well-pressed suit and a spotless shirt with a high winged collar. His dark hair, which was thinning and turning grey at the temples, was brushed back tidily and his eyes crinkled up in a smile. 'Sophie, don't you look elegant!'

She smiled back at him. 'Thank you. Aunty Lizzie told me to tell you we are almost ready to go out now.' She paused. 'You don't think this dress makes me look like a widow who is fast approaching middle age? Black never really suited me and I'm not comfortable wearing it. It has too many painful connections.'

He nodded; he'd heard of her loss from Lizzie. 'I'm sure it has but you certainly don't look middle-aged or matronly. Far from it. You look . . . sophisticated. I've been wondering if I should attend this party myself. It's not really the kind of thing I enjoy. Oh, they are good people and they've been through a lot but . . .'

'You'll have to come now, Aunty Lizzie will go mad if you don't,' she urged.

He sighed. 'Yes, it would be very churlish of me . . . downright rude in fact, to back out now. I'll just have a couple of drinks to toast the boys then I'll come back inside.'

She smiled at him and nodded her understanding. When they'd all had a few drinks and the singing and dancing got under way, it would probably turn into quite a raucous evening. 'I won't be staying out there all night myself, I'll have to try to get Bella to bed at some stage, although it will be a struggle – she's very excited.'

Politely he offered her his arm. 'Then shall we venture forth, Sophie?'

With a final pat to check that the pins in her hair were not coming loose, she slipped her arm through his and smiled at him, wondering why he chose to live here. Aunty Lizzie said he didn't seem to have any family or friends and try as she might, she'd not been able to get a word out of him about his past. He was obviously far better educated and of a higher class, socially, than her aunt and uncle so why he chose to live with them was a mystery, but she supposed rented rooms in this city were very hard to come by at the moment, especially a room for single occupancy.

A couple of hours later the party was in full swing with Fred Seddon thumping out all the old favourites on their piano, which they had managed to manhandle on to the pavement. People stood around it in groups or were dancing and Sophie smiled as she noticed that Matt Seddon seemed to have attached himself to Katie, looking rather bemused and as if he hadn't known her nearly all his life. John Quine had overcome his usual shyness and was chatting away to Maria as they danced; obviously a few pints of beer had loosened his tongue, she thought. Bella was happily sitting on the Seddons' front step with Emily and some other young children, all having stuffed themselves with such rare delicacies as tinned salmon sandwiches, cakes and jelly topped with evaporated milk, and Lizzie and Martha were leaning on the top of the piano happily joining in with 'We'll Meet Again' in a loud and very poor imitation of Vera Lynn.

Maria was laughing at some of John's odd sayings when Ben Seddon tapped her cousin on the shoulder.

'You don't mind if I cut in, mate, do you? Just because she's your cousin doesn't mean you can keep the prettiest girl here to yourself.'

John grinned good-naturedly and relinquished his dancing partner to his friend and wandered off in search of another glass of beer.

'Both you and Katie look gorgeous tonight. Our Matt thinks so too.'

'You are a terrible flatterer, Ben Seddon,' Maria replied, smiling. He was a nice enough lad, she thought.

'I'm not, it's the truth,' Ben replied with mock indignation. 'Are you settling in all right, Maria? I mean things must still seem a bit different to you.'

'I am, thanks. Things are still "different" but in a nice, friendly way. Mind you, it's taking me a bit of time to find my way around the city, it's so big.'

'I'll be made up to show you around, Maria, if you'd let me, and there's lots of places to go. Perhaps I could take you out one night, to the cinema or a dance?' He looked down at her hopefully. Apart from being quite breathtakingly beautiful, something she really didn't seem to be aware of, she appeared to be a really nice girl and he liked her.

Maria smiled at him again but she wasn't sure she was ready to agree to spend an evening with him just yet. 'Perhaps, Ben, when I've settled in a bit more.'

At least she hadn't turned him down flat, he thought. 'Well, it will soon be December and everyone will be gearing up for Christmas, so maybe I could take you to a dance? There are always plenty next month.'

She nodded. 'Nearer Christmas would be nice, something to look forward to,' she promised.

'You look very stylish tonight, Sophie. Are you having a good time?' Frank Ryan asked, coming to stand beside her and thinking she looked far lovelier and much better dressed than any of the other girls and women. He really hadn't wanted to join in the party but neither had he wanted to pass up the opportunity of talking and perhaps dancing with her. He was staying well clear of his in-laws, who had congregated near the top end of the street with the few people who did bother with them and thankfully he hadn't seen Nora for over an hour.

'I am, Frank, and so is Maria, judging by the number of times she's been asked up to dance, and Katie is looking very pleased with herself as Matt seems to have suddenly noticed that she is really a very attractive girl.'

'All three of you have been making heads turn, I've noticed all the admiring glances. Would you like another drink?' he asked, seeing that the glass she was holding was now empty.

'Thanks, but I think I've had enough. There only seems to be sherry or a shandy on offer and I'm not very fond of either. Anyway, I'm going to have to try to get Bella in for bed soon and that's going to be quite a tussle. It will quite likely end in tears and tantrums. She can be a little madam at times, she's so stubborn.'

'It's nothing short of miraculous the way all that food and drink suddenly appeared,' he remarked.

She laughed. 'I know!'

Their conversation was interrupted by the appearance of Bella, Emily, Billy and young Robbie Ryan.

'Mam! Mam, can we go and see the bonfire on the bombsite?' Bella cried, tugging at Sophie's skirt.

'We heard they've got potatoes and sausages and they're cooking them on it. It sounds great and we haven't had a bonfire for ages and ages!' Billy added.

'Haven't you all had enough to eat?' Frank asked, grinning at the lads.

'I don't think you should all be going off round there on your own, it's late. It's really time you were all in bed,' Sophie added.

'Ah, Sophie! Don't be a misery! It's supposed to be a cele . . . cele . . . something,' the irrepressible Billy complained loudly.

'How about if we walk you round there, just to watch for a bit, then walk you back?' Frank suggested. It would solve the problem and mean that he could spend some time away from this street with Sophie without them encountering disapproving glances.

The bonfire was burning well, so well in fact that it was rumoured that someone had sent for the Fire Brigade.

'I can't see that it can do much damage here,' Sophie remarked, watching the orange flames leaping into the sky, while the dry wood and rubbish hissed and crackled as it burned, filling the night air with its pungent smell. People were standing around in groups while some of the more foolhardy younger ones were attempting to cook potatoes and sausages in the embers near the base, holding the meat on long pointed sticks.

'It will do a lot of damage to those young idiots if a piece of it becomes dislodged and falls on them,' Frank said grimly.

'And, there are a lot of people for whom a fire like that brings back terrible memories and even nightmares.'

Sophie nodded, remembering the garish orange glow that had spread across the sky during the nights of the bombings. 'You're right, Frank.' She turned to the little group standing beside them. 'Well, you've seen it now and as we have no potatoes or sausages, I think it's time we went back.'

Before either Billy or Robbie could protest the loud clanging of a fire engine bell came clearly to their ears.

'Here come the fire bobbies, so that's the end of the entertainment here,' Frank commented, guiding his young brother and Billy away from the scene, followed by Sophie with Bella and Emily.

The engine swung around the corner and came to a halt. As the firemen began running out the hoses people began to walk away, leaving a few of the more rowdy element to protest, their arguments falling on deaf ears.

They'd almost reached the road when a girl detached herself from a nearby group and began shouting at them.

'Go on ahead and take the kids with you, Sophie,' Frank urged. He'd recognised Nora's harsh, angry tones instantly.

Sophie looked puzzled until she too recognised Nora. She'd seen her a couple of times in the street, but it was too late now to get away without breaking into a run and she had no intention of doing that. She stood beside Frank holding the hands of the two girls and stared calmly at his wife. Nora was not an attractive sight, she thought. Dark roots showed in her badly peroxided hair, she wore a short, tight-fitting dress of some cheap royal-blue material that was far too light for a November evening and from the way she tottered on her high-heeled shoes it was obvious she'd been drinking.

'Why don't you go home and sleep it off, Nora,' Frank said, trying to keep the anger and shame from his voice.

'Why don't yer mind your own bleeding business?' Nora spat back at him. Her sharp features were accentuated by the light from the bonfire.

Sophie felt Bella's hand tighten in her own. 'I'd thank you not to use language like that in front of my daughter, she's not used to hearing it,' she said quietly but firmly.

Nora laughed, a coarse, high-pitched sound, and turned to her female companion. 'Oh, get her! Proper high and mighty! But not too much of a lady to be making eyes at *my* husband are yer, now yer've lost yer own? I've heard all about the carry-on of you two.' Her lips, heavily accentuated by lipstick in a shade known as oxblood, parted in a sneer, revealing small uneven teeth.

'Shut up, Nora, and go home!' Frank shouted at her. People were stopping and staring at them.

Sophie stiffened. She'd determined not to get into an argument with Nora Ryan but at her words that resolution disappeared. 'There is no "carrying on", as you put it. We walk a few hundred yards home from the tram stop and talk, that's all, and if people want to make more of that than there is that's up to them. I couldn't care less what the gossips think or say. Frank and I are friends. I am well aware he is *your* husband and I am still grieving for mine. Andrew Teare was a fine man whom I loved very much and who loved me freely and dearly. I had no need to lie to him; he wanted to marry me. But he was cruelly taken from me three years ago. So, *Mrs* Ryan, you can think and say what you like for I have absolutely no interest in you at all.'

Purposefully Frank took her arm and led her away, ushering the children ahead of them.

Nora stared after her, anger, envy and jealousy welling up inside her. Sophie Teare hadn't even raised her voice but her words had cut deeply. She hadn't denied being friendly with Frank at all and her voice and manner had been full of open, icy contempt, which hurt far more than if she had shouted back angrily. And she'd pointedly reminded her that she'd lied to Frank and that he didn't love her. Nora tried to make the most of her appearance, to keep up with all the fashions, and it wasn't easy given the shortages, but she knew that beside Sophie Teare's dark, natural beauty and elegant and seemingly effortless style, she faded into insignificance, in Frank's eyes at least.

Frank apologised as they walked home. 'I can't say how sorry I am, Sophie.'

'It wasn't your fault; you didn't know she would be there or that she'd been drinking. I'm not upset, Frank. We are friends, that's all, and that's nothing to be ashamed of, but I wasn't going to stand there and let her upset Bella or use language like that in front of her.'

He nodded, feeling upset and disappointed and he silently cursed Nora to hell and back for ruining the evening.

Chapter Seven

SOPHIE SAID NOTHING TO either Lizzie or Maria about her encounter with Nora Ryan but she was determined that she would continue to walk home with Frank. Nora could think what she liked, Sophie knew everything was open and above board and that's all that mattered. Nor would she hurt and disappoint Frank by shunning him too.

As the weeks passed, however, she began to realise that what he felt for her was more than just friendship. She'd noticed the way he looked at her, the way he seemed more animated and confident in her company. It disturbed her for it made her contemplate more deeply her feelings for him. It was impossible to think of Frank as anything other than a friend, she told herself. She had loved Andrew so much that to even consider having feelings for someone else seemed like a betrayal, and Frank was irrevocably tied to Nora. But it was the conversation she'd had with Arthur Chatsworth the night of the party that had caused her to think about her position and she was becoming more and more confused as the cold November days led to the equally bitter ones of early December.

That night, after she'd got Bella and Billy to bed, she had been making herself a cup of tea and trying to put the episode with Nora out of her mind when he'd come into the kitchen. Everyone else was still outside at the party.

'Did you enjoy yourself, Sophie?' he'd asked. He'd left the revels hours ago.

'Yes,' she'd replied, stirring up the embers in the range.

He'd looked at her closely, having noted the slight hesitation. 'You don't sound too sure?'

She'd frowned, wondering whether to tell him about Nora or not, then she'd decided she would for he never gossiped with Lizzie or anyone else. 'Everything was fine, until . . .'

'Did someone upset you?' he'd asked, concerned. The noise level out in the street had risen considerably over the last hours.

'Oh, not really.' She'd sat down at the table, holding the mug of tea between her hands. 'Bella, Billy and a couple of the other children wanted to go and see the big bonfire burning on the bombsite around the corner, so Frank Ryan and I took them to make sure they didn't come to any harm. We weren't there long when the Fire Brigade arrived so we decided to come home and then . . . then . . . Well, there was a bit of a nasty scene with Frank's wife.'

He'd sat down opposite her, looking concerned. 'Ah, yes. I'm afraid Mrs Nora Ryan isn't blessed with either manners or tact,' he'd said quietly.

'She'd been drinking, which didn't help. She was angry because I have befriended Frank. Oh, it's nothing, we just walk home from the tram stop together, but . . .'

'But she accused you of something more?' he'd pressed.

She'd nodded slowly, biting her lip. 'He's very nice and I find him easy to get on with. I feel sorry for him, he's lonely and miserable. His family shuns him because of Nora and . . .'

'I know Frank's situation, Sophie. Mrs Quine enlightened me about the Richards family – and Nora in particular – when I first became a lodger here and I feel very sorry for Frank. He's in a hopeless position.'

'Surely it's not such a terrible thing, just to be friendly with someone? Oh, I know people are beginning to gossip, not that I care about that. While they're talking about me they're leaving someone else alone.'

'Of course it's not wrong, Sophie. I'm certain that he values your friendship, given his circumstances.'

'Besides, I haven't got over Andrew and I sometimes think I never will.'

He'd looked at her kindly. 'You will, Sophie, in time. You are still a young woman and you've many years ahead of you yet and it can be very lonely . . . being on your own, without someone who cares for you.'

She'd nodded. There was a note of understanding and regret in his voice. 'Then . . . then you think I should . . . ?'

'I'm not telling you what to think or do, Sophie, that would be intrusive and wrong. All I am saying is that you don't have to envisage a future alone. You don't have to spend a lifetime grieving for a young man who in all probability wouldn't want you to be on your own for ever. Who would be happy to see you secure and . . . loved.'

She knew he was right. Andrew wouldn't have wanted her to struggle on by herself for ever and with Bella to bring up. He would have wanted her to be happy.

'From what little I know of him, Frank Ryan seems to be a decent, hard-working young man trapped in an intolerable situation, but as far as Frank is concerned, that's just it, Sophie. He isn't free.'

'I know and isn't that why it would be foolish of me to look on him as anything more than a friend? It's all he can ever be.'

'Of course, but I just wanted you to stop thinking negatively. You can't bury your heart for ever, Sophie.'

She'd felt the sense of loss wash over her again. 'I can never bury my husband either, Mr Chatsworth. I have no grave to visit, I have no sense of things being over and finished . . . *final*, and I find that so hard to come to terms with.'

'Arthur, please call me Arthur, Sophie. I know what it is to lose someone you love and if you ever need to talk . . . well, you know anything you tell me will be kept in the strictest confidence.'

She'd managed a smile. 'I know and thank you . . . Arthur.'

Quite soon after she had confided in Maria, relaying her conversation with Arthur Chatsworth.

'What he said does make sense, Sophie.' Maria had paused. How could she tell her sister that she couldn't bury her heart for ever when she just couldn't forget Hans? 'Maybe . . . in time, you might be able to love someone else, but you might not. As you told him, you think of Frank as a friend, that's all. Just as I think of Ben Seddon as a friend.'

Sophie had nodded and smiled at her, knowing she was thinking of Hans Bonhoeffer. 'We make a right pair of fools, don't we?'

It was Bella who was instrumental in Sophie seeking Frank's help and therefore more of his company. As Christmas approached she suggested that Bella, Emily, Billy and Robbie Ryan write to Santa Claus requesting gifts.

'I tried that a couple of times, last year. I asked him for a proper casie but I never got one,' Billy said sceptically.

'Maybe that's because he knew the damage you'd do with it,' Lizzie put in grimly, shaking her head. A real leather football had been beyond her means and not only because of the cost, hugely inflated by the shortage of leather and skilled men, but the scarcity of the item itself. And then there would have been the added expense of replacing the panes of glass in the windows that would have been broken by Billy with his football and the ensuing arguments with the neighbours.

'Maybe he was a bit short of things last year, Billy. The war was still on, perhaps there weren't enough to go round,' Sophie reminded him. 'Try again.'

'I'd ask for something different this time,' Lizzie urged, looking pointedly at Sophie.

'I'm going to ask him for a dolls' house with curtains and rugs and proper furniture in it,' Bella announced.

Lizzie's eyebrows shot up. 'Really? That will cost him a pretty penny.'

Sophie nodded, wondering where on earth she would get one and all the furniture her daughter seemed to have set her heart on.

Emily said she'd be happy with a doll and Robbie said he was going to ask for a box of lead soldiers, which prompted Billy to announce he would like a fort, then they could share their toys in the evenings when it was too cold and dark to play outside.

When the notes had duly been written and poked up the chimney by Sophie and Maria, Emily and Robbie had gone home and Bella and Billy were in bed, Lizzie brought the subject up again.

'I wish you hadn't encouraged them, Sophie. It's been hard enough to get them anything decent at all these last years, I couldn't get him a casie because they were scarce and cost a small fortune. Where in the name of God am I going to get a fort?'

'Where am I going to get a dolls' house and all the stuff for inside it? I thought she'd just ask for a doll with some clothes for it. I'm sorry I opened my mouth now but I thought it would keep them quiet for an hour or two.'

Maria had been sewing some braid on the bottom of a skirt to brighten it up but she put it aside. 'Ask Frank Ryan, he's a joiner or carpenter, isn't he? I would think he'd be delighted to have something to occupy him in the evenings and odd bits of wood aren't hard to get. He probably wouldn't charge much. You can make the curtains and rugs for it, Sophie, from scraps of material. You can't disappoint the pair of them, especially after Billy not getting a football last year.'

Lizzie didn't look convinced. 'I don't know, Martha might take umbrage . . .'

'She barely speaks to him so why should she take umbrage?' Maria couldn't see why her aunt was taking this attitude. 'Ask him, Sophie. You'll see him tomorrow night.'

Sophie wasn't sure. On the one hand she didn't want to disappoint either Bella or Billy, but on the other, it might make matters worse. If he agreed he'd obviously want her opinion as his work progressed, which would mean either she would have to go over to the Richardses' house or he would have to come over here, neither of which would please Lizzie. 'I don't suppose it would hurt to just ask, he might not want to commit himself, especially as there are only three weeks to Christmas now.'

Maria tutted as she'd renewed her efforts with the skirt. 'I can't see what the fuss is about. Even if you could find one in the shops it would be too expensive.'

Lizzie said nothing more on the matter so Sophie decided that she would ask Frank's help.

She broached the subject as they walked home, heads bent against the icy blasts of wind coming down the Mersey estuary.

Frank was both pleased and touched. 'I'd be delighted to do it, Sophie. There are always offcuts and bits of wood lying around at work. People usually take them to get the fires going at home.'

'We wouldn't want anything very elaborate. I'll make the curtains and rugs and quilts for the beds. Perhaps I can buy some bits of furniture and Billy's only asking for the fort, nothing to go in it. Your Robbie wants lead soldiers so they'll be able to share.'

'How big do you think they should be?' Frank asked, already planning to scrounge some paint with which to embellish the finished items.

'Oh, nothing too big. Lizzie hasn't got the room for a big fort and a grand dolls' house in the kitchen.'

Frank nodded. It would fill the empty hours each evening. He'd keep them in the yard under some sacking until they were finished. 'I could probably manage a table and two chairs for the dolls' house, and perhaps a sideboard and a couple of stools too.'

'That's really good of you, Frank, and both Lizzie and I will pay you for your time and skill. We'd never be able to afford them otherwise.'

'There's no need for that, Sophie. I'm just delighted

98

you've asked me. I'll make a start on them right away; I'll bring the wood home tomorrow, then when I've nearly finished them I'll bring them over for you to see. When the kids are in bed, of course.'

'Do you think I could see the dolls' house a bit earlier, just so I'll know what size the windows are?'

'Of course, and I'll show you the bits of furniture too, but will Lizzie object to me calling over so often?'

Sophie frowned. 'Seeing as you are doing her a great favour I don't think she has any right to object and I certainly won't. If I had my way, Frank, you'd be most welcome.'

Frank felt his heart skip a beat. 'Do you really mean that, Sophie?'

'I do. I can't understand either Aunty Lizzie or your mam's attitude. You haven't done anything wrong, Frank. You're not some sort of criminal. You made a mistake, that's all, and it's about time they put that behind them. You'd never bring Nora or her family over to their houses and they know that, but why they stop you visiting I don't know, especially your mam.'

'She . . . she's ashamed of me,' Frank said bitterly.

'She shouldn't be. You fought in the war. You have a good job, you work hard, and you don't spend your money on drink or the horses or . . . other things. She's ashamed of Nora but she shouldn't tar you with the same brush.'

He sighed heavily. He just wished his mam took the same attitude as Sophie but he didn't hold out much hope of her changing her mind at this stage. Where Nora was concerned she was pretty implacable.

'What will you do on Christmas Day?' Sophie asked.

'Probably what I did last year. Walk down to the Pier Head and watch the shipping, that kills a good few hours, then call in somewhere on the way back for a pint or two. You'd be hard put to get any kind of a Christmas dinner out of Nellie. They all spend most of the day in the pub – Nora included.'

Sophie's heart went out to him. What a miserable way to spend Christmas Day – a day when families all tried to spend time together. Surely Martha could show some Christian spirit on that one day in the year and have her eldest son for dinner? It wouldn't hurt her. Maybe she'd mention it to Lizzie, who seemed to have a bit of influence with Martha. But she would say nothing to Frank, she thought, in case his mam refused to relent. That would only make matters worse.

Chapter Eight

———◆———

A S CHRISTMAS DREW NEARER the more excited both Billy and Bella became. They wrote more notes to Santa Claus and tried their best to improve their behaviour, which seemed infinitely harder for Billy than Bella, but Sophie had said firmly that Santa could see everything they did and made a note of it.

'I'm beginning to think these little letters are a good idea, Sophie. That lad isn't half the handful he usually is, he's even polished his own boots,' Lizzie had remarked after Frank had carried across the fort which was almost complete. You couldn't have got anything better in the shops and it hadn't cost her a penny so far, she'd thought. Jim had also admired it and had said later that he'd take Frank out for a drink as a sort of payment for he was flatly refusing to take any money for his time and work. It was a pleasure to do it, he'd said and she could see that he meant it.

When he'd brought over the dolls' house, in the first stages of its construction, Sophie had been delighted with it. 'It's going to be perfect, Frank. The size is just right; it will fit easily on top of the table so she can play with it to her heart's content after meals.' She'd examined the miniature table and chairs he'd made closely. 'You really are very clever with wood, Frank. Look, Aunty Lizzie, the chairs even have little stretchers holding the legs together.'

Frank had smiled, basking in the unaccustomed attention and the praise being heaped upon him. 'I can sit and do the little pieces in my break at work.'

'Sophie's found some lovely material for curtains and things and she's going to decorate them with bits of lace and ribbon. She should have been a proper seamstress, she's so good at sewing,' Lizzie had impressed upon him, not wishing her niece's talents to be ignored.

Martha had just tutted and raised her eyes when she'd first heard how Sophie had asked him to help out with the toys but now Lizzie gave her a running commentary on their progress. The fact that her son seemed to be welcome in Lizzie's house and was refusing any form of payment had initially annoyed Martha but lately she'd begun to take more notice of her friend when she said that it really was such a terrible shame that a pleasant, well-mannered, generous fellow like Frank should have to put up with the likes of the Richardses, working away in that kitchen until all hours and then having to keep the half-finished toys in the back yard and pray that Bertie wouldn't fall on them and smash them as he staggered to and from the privy. Lizzie had shuddered when she'd uttered the word. 'I just dread to think what *that place* is like!'

Both women were desperately trying to get together enough food to put a decent dinner on the table on Christmas Day but it was far from easy. Nearly all the ingredients for both the pudding and the mince pies were unobtainable for rationing hadn't been relaxed, let alone abolished.

'I'll be lucky if I can get a bit of meat – any kind of meat at all for the dinner,' Martha had complained after they'd stood for hours in the queue at the butcher's, only to learn there would be not the slightest chance of a turkey, goose, duck or even a very small chicken, unless you knew someone who lived in the country and kept them, the butcher had stated morosely. He was having to bear the brunt of his disgruntled customers' outraged disappointment.

'I ask you, Lizzie, who around here knows anyone who lives in the country? The man's a fool! You'll see, we'll finish up with a few pathetic sausages if we're lucky.'

'We'll have potatoes and veg, we'll manage, Martha. We always do,' Lizzie had replied, but without much conviction. They were both very disappointed; they'd thought now that the war was over this Christmas would be a big improvement on the last six.

She was bemoaning the fact later that evening to Jim and the girls, wondering if they could manage between them to save their rations of flour, margarine, sugar and eggs to make a plain Victoria sponge which could take the place of the traditional pudding. There would be no jam to go in it, of course.

Sophie had been hemming a pair of tiny red and white gingham curtains for the kitchen of the dolls' house but she pondered the dilemma as she rethreaded her needle. 'I wonder if we wrote to Mrs Sayle – she's the wife of the farmer Maria worked for when she was a Land Girl – and sent her the money, would she let us have a goose? They've always kept chickens and geese. If she parcelled it up well in straw and cardboard she could send it across on the steam packet and one of us could go down and pick it up,' she suggested.

Lizzie looked at her with astonishment before her face became wreathed in smiles. 'A goose! A whole goose! Lord above! We haven't had one for years and years. That would be the best Christmas present ever, Sophie! Do you think she would let us have one?'

'Who would let us have what?' Maria asked, catching the end of the conversation. She was going out to the cinema in town with Ben Seddon and looked very smart in her black and white tweed coat and the small green hat with the black feather that she'd saved up her coupons to purchase at Heaton's (although she'd added the black feather herself).

'Will you write to Mrs Sayle and beg her to let us have a goose for the Christmas dinner? We'll send her the money.

You know you always got on well with her and Aunty Lizzie is having a terrible time trying to get *anything* to make some sort of a festival meal.'

'Oh, please, Maria? It would be such a *treat*,' Lizzie pleaded.

Maria smiled. 'I'll write when I get in later tonight and then you can post it in the morning, Aunty Lizzie. We'll need something festive to cheer us up; it's our first Christmas away from the island. That will be Ben now, see you later.' Maria picked up her bag and went into the lobby. She liked Ben Seddon but that was all. She often went out with him, mainly to the cinema or a dance, but there was no romance in the offing. Not on her part anyway. She'd realised weeks ago that this Christmas would bring back very painful memories. It would be the first one away from the island and her mam, and without Hans, and writing to Maude Sayle would only make her think of the times she'd spent working beside him in the fields.

Sophie carried on with her tasks while Lizzie made a pot of tea and Jim was engrossed in his newspaper but an idea was taking shape in her mind. When Lizzie placed a mug of tea beside her, she put down the sewing.

'Aunty Lizzie, if she sends us a good size bird do you think we should share it with Mrs Ryan and her family? It seems a bit sort of selfish for us to keep it all for ourselves when things are so scarce.'

Lizzie frowned. 'You mean cut it in half?'

'No. What if we shared everything and had our Christmas

dinner together? Maria and I would be glad to help out with all the preparations and the washing up.'

This hadn't occurred to Lizzie. 'You mean ask Martha and Pat to come in here?'

Sophie nodded eagerly. 'And young Robbie and . . . Frank too, of course. And we can't leave Mr Chatsworth out either, not when it's going to be such a great meal.'

Lizzie stared at her hard. 'Martha hasn't had him for a meal – any meal – since he married *that* one.'

'I know, but he told me that last year he spent the day walking to and from the river, just stopping off for a pint on the way back. They were all in the pub so I don't think he even got any kind of dinner. Aunty Lizzie, that's a terrible way to have to spend Christmas Day and he's been so kind making the toys for us and not taking a penny for them. Surely it's the least we can do to include him? It will be a chance for us all to have a really great day,' she pleaded.

Put like that Lizzie could find no reason to refuse but she wondered how Martha would take it. Still, Sophie was right. If they managed to get a goose, with potatoes and vegetables, and if she and Martha scraped together enough ingredients for a cake, and if Jim could get something for them to drink, it would be a meal to remember. She smiled at her niece. 'You've got a kind heart, Sophie. You're right, it's no way for anyone to spend Christmas. We'll have a great day. The kids can make paper chains to decorate the kitchen, that will keep them quiet, and we should be able to get holly and a small tree. Yes, luv, we'll have the best Christmas we've had in years.'

Lizzie had worked out what she was going to say to her friend before she went to see her, after she'd posted the letter Maria had written. Martha was so taken with the thought of a communal Christmas dinner with the Quines, and with the possibility of a whole *goose* no less, that when Lizzie informed her that Sophie was insisting they invite Frank too, considering he'd made the toys, she felt she really couldn't object.

'Under normal circumstances, Lizzie, I wouldn't have him over the doorstep, but . . .'

'It's not your doorstep, Martha,' Lizzie succinctly reminded her.

'Oh, you know what I mean. But . . . but these are exceptional circumstances. Does she think this woman will actually send a goose over?'

'Maria said she told her in her letter how bad things still are over here, about how the city is still in ruins and there's hardly anything in the shops – the ones that are still standing – and that it's their first Christmas away . . .'

Martha nodded. 'It will seem like a miracle, Lizzie. We'll be the envy of the entire street!'

Lizzie beamed with satisfaction. 'We'll be the envy of the entire *neighbourhood*, Martha. Now, let's sit down and see about getting together the rest of the stuff and you can send your Robbie in after school and we'll get the kids started making the paper chains. The few I had were years old and all fell to bits when I took them down last year.'

To Lizzie's delight and Sophie's relief, Maude Sayle agreed to send the bird over, ready plucked and wrapped in straw and cardboard. One of the captains employed by the Steam Packet Company was a cousin and would see that the parcel arrived safely and Jim would collect it. Billy, Robbie and Bella spent hours making paper chains from newspaper which they'd painted red and green, and with the sprigs of holly and a small tree, festooned with some rather tarnished and tatty tinsel plus a variety of homemade decorations, Lizzie declared that she'd not seen the kitchen looking so bright and cheerful for years.

On Christmas Eve it took all Sophie's patience to get the two over-excited children to bed while Lizzie, whose patience had worn thin, warned them both vociferously that if there was any more nonsense out of them then they'd find that Santa hadn't left them anything at all when they woke in the morning.

'They'll settle down eventually, Aunty Lizzie,' Maria laughed. 'We used to be so excited that every little sound we heard, we thought Santa had arrived, didn't we, Sophie?'

'We were in and out of bed by the minutes, we drove Mam mad,' Sophie replied. She wished her mother could be with them for Christmas, but they'd sent gifts to her and she was going to spend the day with friends.

'Well, the last thing we want is for them still to be up when Frank brings the toys over to us, there's not enough room in this kitchen to hide them. He'll just have to put them in the yard. Martha will be in later with her dishes and things and Pat's going to bring their chairs in tomorrow morning. I did ask Mr Chatsworth if he would join us but he refused – something about not wanting to intrude – so I said I'd pass a plate in to him. It's just as well as it's going to be a terrible squeeze, but—'

'We'll manage!' Sophie and Maria interrupted together, laughing.

The following morning Lizzie declared the shrieks of delight from Bella and Billy must have been heard at the top end of the street. Sophie looked on with pride and affection as Bella examined and exclaimed over the curtains, the chairs and table – complete with a tablecloth – and the little beds with their lace-trimmed coverlets. The hours of work both she and Frank had put in had been well worth it, she thought, just to see the wonder and delight in Bella's blue eyes. Billy was so overcome that he informed Lizzie, rather rashly she thought, that he intended to be on his best behaviour for the next year so that Santa would bring him something just as fantastic next Christmas.

At length the toys were put aside as Pat and Jim man-oeuvred the table and chairs into place, Katie and Maria set the table with both Lizzie and Martha's dishes and cutlery and Sophie helped her aunt with the meal, the smell of which would drive you absolutely mad with anticipation, so John declared happily.

'That's a very flowery way of putting it, have you been reading a dictionary?' Katie quipped good-naturedly as she arranged the glasses.

But the smell of the goose cooking was certainly making everyone's mouth water, and there was a bottle of port for the women and some bottles of beer for the men to look forward to as well.

By the time Frank arrived, wearing his best suit, bearing a half-bottle of whisky and looking slightly apprehensive, Lizzie and Martha were dishing out the soup. Although it was a little on the thin side, Lizzie declared it was very appetising just the same. Sophie, Katie, Maria, John, Pat and Jim and the three children were all seated around the table where there was barely room to move their arms. Billy declared that was going to make eating difficult, earning him a black look from his father.

'Squeeze in beside our John, and a drop of this will go down a treat later on,' Jim urged Frank, taking the proffered bottle.

'After such a feast and a few drinks, we'll have trouble keeping our eyes open, Jim,' Pat added, thinking that it was years since he'd sat down to a Christmas meal with his eldest son but that maybe it was time to let bygones be bygones. Just as long as Nora and her family didn't think any future fraternising included them.

Frank said little during the meal but his lack of conversation was barely noticed; everyone else more than made up for his long silences. He knew it was Sophie who had instigated this unheard-of and totally unexpected invitation and he wished there was some way of telling her how full his heart was. He once again felt part of a generous, happy family, who had made such an effort to make this day truly special for everyone, not just the kids, instead of spending it in the pub drinking until oblivion took over. He had been included . . . welcomed . . . to share the food, the drink and the cheerful ambience of the occasion and it was all because of Sophie Teare. He thanked God that she'd come to Liverpool, even though he knew what he felt for her could never be reciprocated.

Chapter Nine

———◆———

'I T DID TURN OUT to be a great day, didn't it? God bless Mrs Sayle and the goose,' Sophie sighed as she sank wearily down in a chair beside the range. The kitchen was warm and the delicious odours of the meal still lingered. The tinsel and silver paper ornaments on the tree glowed in the dying light of the fire, adding to the sense of cosy peace, quiet and contentment.

The Ryans' furniture and dishes had been taken back next door, the toys reluctantly put away and the children – equally reluctantly – put to bed, the pans and dishes washed and the room restored to some semblance of order. The three girls had volunteered to finish clearing up when the neighbours had all departed, as Lizzie said she was fair worn out with it all. Both she and Jim had retired and when the last dish had been put away Katie too had gone up to bed.

'It went much better than I expected it would, although you have to admit this kitchen resembled a bear pit at times,' Maria summed up as she eased off her shoes, took the pins from her hair and ran her fingers through the long, thick curls. 'It's no wonder Mr Chatsworth stayed in his room for a bit of peace and quiet.'

'In a way I was sorry he didn't join us. It's a day for families and as far as we know we're all the "family" he's got,' Sophie mused.

Maria nodded. 'He's a very strange man, but nice enough. Frank certainly looked as though he was very happy to be included as family today.'

Sophie smiled, thinking she'd never seen Frank looking so content or happy as he'd chatted to his parents, but she had also caught the dull look that had come into his eyes when his parents and brother had departed. It was so obvious that he didn't want to return to the house across the road where little or no 'festive spirit' would be in evidence, apart from that which came out of a bottle.

'Do you think now that the ice has finally been broken, Martha will let him visit them?' Maria asked, thinking how much more at ease Pat Ryan had seemed with his son. Far more so than Martha.

'I hope so. I think Aunty Lizzie has been working on her but I didn't want to say anything to raise his hopes.'

Maria got to her feet and picked up the almost empty

bottle of port. 'Aunty Lizzie and Martha seem to have drunk most of this but shall we finish it off, as a nightcap?'

Sophie smiled at her. 'Why not, I'll get two glasses.'

When Maria had poured the remaining very small amount of port into the glasses, she raised hers. 'To our first Christmas in Liverpool.'

Sophie laughed. 'It's one neither Bella or I will forget and it was good of Mam to send us those little gifts.' She looked fondly at her sister. 'Has it really been happy for you, Maria?'

Maria looked wistful as she twisted the stem of her empty glass between her fingers. 'When I woke this morning I wondered how Mam was feeling, not having us there and then I . . . I began to wonder where Hans was and what he was doing. Was he back on their farm? Was it snowing, did they have enough to eat? Did he . . . did he think about me today and wonder if I was happy? Had he sent me a card? Then I remembered that he doesn't even know where I am. He doesn't know we've left the island.'

Sophie nodded. 'If he had Mam would have mentioned it in her note.'

There had been no word from Hans Bonhoeffer since he'd returned to Austria, but Maria hadn't given up hope of hearing from him and seemed hurt that even at this special time he hadn't thought enough of her to send a card, but maybe it was for the best. 'That was a lovely little brooch Ben gave you,' Sophie said quietly. 'He's a nice lad, I like him a great deal.'

Maria nodded, fingering the little gilt brooch in the shape

of a leaf that was pinned to her dress. 'He *is* nice, Sophie, and I do like him a lot but . . . but . . .'

'You could do worse, Maria. He's got a decent job, he's steady and generous and it's obvious he's very taken with you.'

Maria sighed heavily. 'Oh, I know all that, but . . . I just don't love him, Sophie.'

'Don't give up on him, you might change your mind . . . in time,' Sophie urged. She wanted her sister to be happy, not pining for a lost and unsuitable love.

'I don't think I will, Sophie,' Maria said quietly. Her eyes were full of sadness and longing as she twisted a strand of dark curly hair between her fingers, a habit from childhood that always re-emerged when she was upset. The silence from Hans had upset her deeply.

'Oh, Maria, don't waste your life wishing for something you can't have.' She could have her pick of the young men in this neighbourhood but at this present time she didn't want any of them.

Maria looked at her sister and smiled wryly. 'You're a fine one to give me advice, Sophie,' she said, not unkindly.

'Why?'

Maria put down the glass. They had always been close, always been able to share their feelings, and Sophie had known about her love for Hans almost from the start. 'Sophie, I know how you feel about Frank Ryan, even if you won't admit it, even if you can't come to terms with it yourself. The look on your face, the light in your eyes gave you away. Each

116

time you looked at him today, it was obvious. At least to me it was, whether anyone else noticed I don't know. And he loves you too, that was *blindingly* obvious. Even Martha noticed, I saw her shaking her head sadly. But he's tied to that Nora and there is nothing either of you can do about it.'

Sophie looked down and studied her hands, not wanting to meet her sister's eyes. She'd been so happy that he'd been included in everything today, happy to see him enjoying himself but . . . but that was all, wasn't it? 'I know that, Maria,' she said quietly, 'all I wanted was for him to have the kind of Christmas he used to enjoy before . . .'

Maria stood up and put her hand on Sophie's shoulder. 'So neither of us can have the man we really want.'

Sophie looked up at her. 'You might, one day. You might have a change of heart for Ben.'

Maria shook her head but bent and kissed her cheek. 'Goodnight, Sophie.'

When she had gone Sophie stared into the dying embers of the fire in the range and shivered. The room was becoming chilly – or was she feeling the coldness of a life without love? Andrew's love had gone and what she now felt for Frank could never be realised. Just when her initial liking had turned to friendship and then deepened into affection she didn't know, but it had. Maria had been right, each time she'd looked at him today she'd felt so happy. Happier than she'd been for years, she now sadly admitted to herself. She had known the passionate love of a man, Bella was the proof of that, and she wished with all her heart that she could tell

Frank of her feelings for him, but it was impossible. It would destroy them both.

She stood up, drawing her cardigan closer around her. Whatever the future held for her she must put her feelings for Frank aside, she must think of Bella now. She must put all her energy into securing that better future for herself and her daughter because there was no future for her with Frank Ryan.

In the following days Lizzie declared to her family and neighbours that there would be no point in having yet another party for New Year. Everyone was hard up and still facing a grim future of shortages and as they'd had three street parties during the year that was more than enough. It was time to tighten their belts.

'Won't it all be a bit flat and depressing, like? I mean it's the first proper year of peace, seems a shame not to celebrate it in some way,' Maggie Dodd argued when Lizzie had issued her comments to a shop full of customers.

'I'm not saying don't celebrate it at all, we'll just be having a quiet drink in the house. Then Jim can go out into the street just before midnight with his lump of coal and bit of bread and salt to let the New Year in, same as always. It's just that I don't think there should be another communal celebration, it's taking things a bit too far,' Lizzie replied firmly.

'It will end up like one just the same, Lizzie. You know that everyone likes to go out and wish friends and neighbours

"Happy New Year" and sing "Auld Lang Syne",' Martha said.

'And this year they'll ring all the church bells, which they haven't been able to do for six years in case people thought it was the signal we were being invaded,' Mary Seddon added.

'And we'll all be deafened by the noise of the ships' whistles coming from the river and docks,' Ada Caldwell reminded everyone.

'I bet those two nieces of yours and little Bella will never have heard the like before. Don't deprive them of it all, Lizzie. It would be a shame if you did,' Maggie urged.

Lizzie pursed her lips, thinking she was sorry she'd opened her mouth. She'd had no intention of depriving anyone of anything; she'd just thought they'd had enough parties for one year.

Bella was excited to hear from Billy that they'd both be allowed to stay up and to go out into the street with everyone else, and when the hands on the Liver clock got to midnight, join hands in a big circle and sing and be kissed and hugged and listen to the bells and the ships on the river, which was great – although he wasn't all that keen on the being kissed bit.

'Is he telling the truth, Mam? Can I stay up?' she asked Sophie.

Sophie laughed. 'Of course you can, but you might be so tired that you'll fall asleep before midnight,' she warned.

'I won't! Really I won't, Mam!' Bella exclaimed, thinking that life in Harebell Street seemed to be very exciting with all kinds of parties and celebrations going on.

She tried so hard to stay awake on New Year's Eve as they sat in the kitchen playing games. Aunty Lizzie handed round the drinks and some biscuits she'd saved for the occasion but by eleven o'clock Bella lost her battle and was fast asleep with her head on Sophie's lap, still clutching her blue tiddlywink. Billy was manfully still fighting to stay awake although Lizzie doubted he'd last another half hour.

'Take her up, Sophie, she's out like a light. She probably won't even stir come midnight, despite the noise,' Lizzie urged.

Gently prising the little blue disc from her daughter's hand, Sophie carried her gently upstairs, took off her shoes and put her into bed fully dressed. She bent and smoothed the dark curls from her cheeks and kissed her. Aunty Lizzie was probably right, Bella would sleep through the noise.

At five to midnight there was a knock on the scullery door and Pat Ryan poked his head round. 'Right then, Jim? Five minutes to go.'

Jim put on his jacket and wound his muffler around his neck, took the coal, bread and salt Lizzie handed him and followed Pat out.

'I'd get your coats on if I were you, it's freezing out there. Billy, stir yourself, lad, it's time.' Lizzie shook her small son who was on the point of dozing off while Maria and Sophie got their coats and scarves.

The street was full of people, some still holding glasses, a few looking as though they'd been celebrating a bit too much already, and Sophie caught sight of Ben and Matt Seddon determinedly making their way towards Maria and Katie. Martha Ryan was winding a very long knitted scarf around the neck of a rather pale and tired-looking Robbie and instructing him that as soon as the singing was over he was to go straight to bed.

'Bella didn't last then, Sophie,' she stated.

Sophie grinned. 'No, I'm afraid not and she'll be so cross that she missed it all in the morning. We'll have a tantrum, I know it.'

Martha turned to Lizzie and jerked her head towards the nearest streetlamp. 'Here comes our Frank but there will be no prizes for guessing where *that one* is.'

Lizzie nodded grimly. 'In the pub with the rest of them and probably been there all afternoon, I don't wonder.'

'Thank God if she is. At least she's not here tormenting us,' Martha replied cuttingly.

Sophie had heard it all for she'd stayed close to both women as Katie and Maria and the two boys had gone to join a group of youngsters further down. She didn't want Frank to think she was avoiding him but she didn't trust her emotions. Before Frank had time to say anything to her, however, the men suddenly and loudly started to count down the seconds, joined by everyone else, and she found herself laughingly counting too and then the night erupted with noise. Above them fireworks exploded and the sky was filled with coloured stars and flashes. The bells of Liverpool's hundreds of churches pealed out across the city, ringing in the first year for so many not blighted by the shadow of war. From the river and the docks came a cacophony of noise, from the deep full-blasted steam whistles of the big Cunard and Canadian Pacific liners to the less deafening but still noisy blasts of the ferries and cargo ships, and the easily recognisable 'whoop whoop' of the naval vessels. And then everyone was kissing and hugging everyone else, wishing them 'Happy New Year', and Sophie found herself in Frank's arms and he was kissing her. The madness of the night seemed to claim her and she clung to him, kissing him passionately while elation surged through her.

'Happy New Year, Sophie!' Frank said softly, gazing down at her, still holding her in his arms.

'Happy New Year, Frank,' she managed to stammer before she was dragged from his embrace by her Uncle Jim who hugged her and kissed her on the cheek and then everyone was forming a huge circle and she was separated from Frank by Jim and Lizzie and Martha Ryan, none of whom had failed to notice that passionate embrace.

She had begun to feel more in control of herself by the time the singing ended but she was still trembling a little. 'I'd better just go and check on Bella,' she said to Lizzie.

'I'd do that, luv,' Lizzie advised and watched her walk quickly back towards the house. Martha had been right, she thought. Her friend had said that she was sure Frank had fallen for Sophie and that didn't bode well for either of them.

To Sophie's relief Bella was still fast asleep. She bent over and tucked the quilt more tightly around her. 'Happy New Year, my beautiful Bella. Mam promises that this year she'll

work very hard so that it will be a very good year for you.'
When she reached the door she turned and looked at her
sleeping daughter. What had happened tonight she must put
out of her mind, for Bella's sake and for her own sanity. She
wouldn't go out into the street again now, but how she was to
avoid Frank in future without hurting him she didn't know.

The front door was open so she went and stood on the
step, glancing up and down before closing it over to keep
out the cold night air. She could see her aunt and uncle with
the Ryans and some other neighbours but thankfully there
was no sign of Frank. Perhaps Lizzie or Martha had said
something to him, she thought.

She was in the act of pulling the door shut when it was
wrenched out of her hands and she was confronted by a drunk
and obviously furious Nora. She'd obviously been crying for
her mascara had run, her hair was straggling in untidy strands
around her face, her bright red lipstick was smudged and
Sophie almost reeled at the stench of beer and cheap scent
that emanated from her.

'I saw yer, yer bitch! I saw the way you was kissing him!
You're a bloody whore for all yer prim an' proper ways! You
leave my Frank alone, yer bitch!' Nora was screaming at the
top of her voice and Sophie visibly shrank back from her
tirade.

Desperately trying to think of something to say that would
calm the girl down, Sophie raised her hands. Nora mistook
the gesture and lashed out, catching Sophie across the face,
and then, still screaming abuse, she caught her by her hair,

pushed her down the hallway and began to try to batter her head against the wall. Sophie too had begun to scream but in pain and fear as she tried desperately to defend herself. Then suddenly Nora was dragged bodily away from her and back down the lobby towards the front door.

'Get out of my house, you drunken little slut!' Jim Quine roared as he hurled Nora into the street where she fell and remained half sitting, half lying on the paving stones.

'I've a good mind to get the scuffers on to you, you little trollop! Attacking decent people in their own homes! Jail is all you're fit for, like your flaming brother!' Lizzie roared at the girl, who was now sobbing and trying to stagger to her feet.

'He's *my* husband an' she's trying to get him into 'er knickers! She's the tart! She's the bloody trollop, not me!' Nora yelled.

Lizzie was livid with rage. 'One more word out of you, you foul-mouthed little bitch, and I'll belt you myself! If your mam had given you a damned good hiding years ago you'd have kept your filthy little hands off Frank Ryan. Everyone knows what you are, Nora *Richards* – I won't insult Pat and Martha's name! You're a liar, a cheat, a dirty little tart and a drunk! You say one single word to Sophie in the future and you'll feel the back of my hand, I swear to God!'

Jim and Martha both pulled Nora away, leading her towards her house, leaving the neighbours standing in shocked silence, staring as Nellie finally came out and dragged her daughter back across the road.

Lizzie was shaking with the force of her anger. 'I'll swing for that one yet! Someone should see the council about the lot of them! They're not fit to live amongst decent folk, they should be evicted. God knows they're behind with the rent often enough.'

'I couldn't agree more, Lizzie, but come on inside now,' Martha urged, although she felt that Frank had had no small part in instigating this scene. His feelings for Sophie were now obvious to everyone, including Nora, which had provoked the girl's drunken outburst, and she intended to tell him so. This had to stop now, before it got completely out of hand and created a terrible scandal, particularly for Sophie. Poor Sophie, she thought as she steered Lizzie towards the kitchen where Sophie had obviously taken refuge, before her thoughts turned again bitterly to what a terrible mess her eldest son had made of his life.

Chapter Ten

———◆———

Sophie had collapsed into the chair by the side of the range, badly shaken by Nora's attack. She was shaking, her head was aching and the scratches on her face made by Nora's nails were beginning to sting. She could hear the raised voices outside in the street, mainly Lizzie's, but could not distinguish exactly what her aunt was shouting. Thankfully, Bella didn't appear to have been disturbed by the commotion, she thought fleetingly.

'Sophie! My dear girl, what has happened to you? Just what is going on out there? Mrs Quine is yelling like a fish-wife at someone and before that I heard Mr Quine apparently throwing someone bodily out of the house. Has there been some kind of . . . attack on you?'

Sophie looked up to see Arthur Chatsworth standing in the doorway, looking very perturbed. Slowly she nodded, fighting back tears of shock. 'It was Nora Ryan. She was drunk and I was just standing in the doorway watching the celebrations and . . .' Her words faltered as she realised that she had been about to tell him that Frank's wife had become enraged by the sight of Frank and herself in what could only be described as a passionate embrace, one to which she had responded eagerly. She shook her head, shame and guilt compounding her emotions.

'That's absolutely appalling! Sophie, someone must go for the police at once, she can't be allowed to get away with this! This is an assault.' Even though he was fully aware of the type of neighbourhood he resided in, this unprovoked physical attack on a quiet, well-mannered girl like Sophie both upset and angered him.

'No! No, there's no need for that, really. I . . . I'm just shocked, not really hurt . . .'

Before he could protest further Martha pushed a still furious Lizzie in through the door.

'Mrs Quine, I really do feel that the police should be sent for. Nora Ryan should be arrested,' Lizzie's lodger announced forcefully.

'I couldn't agree more that jail is where she belongs but there's no need for the scuffers to get involved, is there, Lizzie? They'll have enough to cope with tonight without what they'll consider to be just a "domestic",' Martha replied, just as forcefully. It wasn't the way they did things in this street and besides, the police might well decide that Nora had been seriously provoked because either the girl herself or Nellie would be bound to blurt out what Frank and Sophie had been doing.

Lizzie had begun to calm down a little, particularly seeing Sophie's tear-streaked face, scratched cheeks and untidy hair and the fear and guilt that now filled her niece's eyes. She was thinking along the same lines as her friend. 'No, there's no need to call the police, Mr Chatsworth. Jim threw that vicious little bitch out on to the cobbles and I've given her a damned good tongue-lashing, so there's an end to it. Now, Sophie, luv, let me see to those marks on your face and Martha will make us all a nice cup of hot sweet tea.' She turned to her lodger. 'You're more than welcome to a cup; it's all been very upsetting for everyone.'

He stood for a few seconds looking undecidedly at the three women and then shook his head. 'No, thank you. If you are sure you don't want to take this further, I'll go back to my room.'

Lizzie nodded and he turned away, but he was an observant man and hadn't failed to notice the guarded expressions of the older women and the suddenly fearful one that had come into young Sophie's eyes. There was something going on here that he didn't fully understand.

Lizzie sat down at the table and ran a hand across her forehead. 'Isn't this a great start to the New Year and with him getting on his high horse too, wanting to call the scuffers? Are you all right, Sophie, luv? She hasn't hurt you?'

Sophie shook her head. 'Not really. I'm just more . . . shocked . . . than anything.'

Martha handed her a cup of tea and then looked at Lizzie who mouthed the words, 'Thank God for that.'

Martha nodded. 'I lay all the blame for this on our Frank's shoulders! If he hadn't gone carrying on like . . . that . . . and in front of everyone . . .'

Sophie broke down. 'It . . . it wasn't entirely his fault, it . . . it was mine too!' she sobbed. One moment of pure madness and look what it had led to – and just when she'd hoped that Frank and Martha were becoming reconciled.

'Now stop that, Sophie! It's New Year's Eve and people do sometimes get carried away with the spirit of things. It will all be forgotten in a day or so. Calm down and drink your tea, luv,' Lizzie urged. 'And I hope that *that* one has the most almighty hangover in the morning,' she finished venomously.

Martha said nothing but as she sipped her tea she thought that, unlike Lizzie, she wasn't going to let the matter lie. Whatever Nora was, Frank was married to her and he had no right to carry on towards Sophie as though he was a single man. He had no right to ruin the girl's reputation or, what was worse, break her heart. It had already been broken once and in her opinion Sophie didn't deserve any more pain and grief.

After Lizzie had got Sophie to bed and Jim and Maria at last came in Lizzie quietly explained to Maria what had happened for the girl hadn't seen the incident, having been further down the street.

'So, don't go upsetting her even further by asking her about it,' Lizzie instructed firmly and Maria nodded.

'This will all end badly if Frank Ryan doesn't stay away from Sophie,' Jim said heavily after Maria had left the room.

'I know, and Martha is going to have it out with him, but I do feel sorry for the lad and for poor Sophie, Jim. I think she's started to fall in love with him.'

Jim Quine shook his head slowly as he unlaced his boots, wondering if it would do any good to write to his sister Sarah. Perhaps suggesting – for Sophie's own welfare and that of Bella – that they go home to Peel? It wouldn't do that child any good at all to have Sophie upset and pining for someone she could never have, nor would any more confrontations with Nora or any of the Richards family.

When Frank alighted from the tram the next evening he found his mother waiting for him, her coat clutched snugly to her against the cold wind and a warm headscarf tied tightly under her chin. He had hoped to have got off a bit earlier, there had been so many of them absent from work today, which was not a Bank Holiday, that very little work had been achieved at all. He'd hoped to be able to wait for Sophie, realising that she too would have been at work. And he wanted to apologise to her for he'd heard about what Nora had done from one of the neighbours. Despite his protests, after the singing he'd been dragged off down the street by the Seddon brothers to where the younger element had congregated.

He wanted to see that Sophie was not hurt. Of course she was bound to be upset and he was going to swear to her that he would make every effort to keep his jealous, vicious slut of a wife away from her. Of course Nora hadn't been in any fit state to go to work that morning, in fact he'd hardly been able to get any sense out of her at all, but he was going to have it out with her tonight.

'If you've got any thoughts about hanging on here, waiting for Sophie Teare, then you can just forget them, Frank!' Martha greeted him.

'I was hoping to apologise to her, Mam, for—'

'Forget it!' Martha interrupted. 'In fact forget Sophie altogether, Frank. I blame you for that fiasco last night.'

'Me? All I did was wish Sophie "Happy New Year".'

'And that was just it! None of us could help but see that it was far more than just a "friendly" kiss. Oh, no, it was far more than that. No wonder that trollop you married was so livid. She's no fool – far from it – drunk or sober.'

'And she *was* drunk – as usual!' Frank retorted bitterly. 'She stank like a brewery this morning and didn't go to work. Not that she ever spends much time at those rope works anyway. And yes, it was more than just a friendly kiss, Mam, but I love Sophie.'

Martha was taken aback at his admission but she wasn't to be deterred. 'You aren't *free* to love Sophie! I'm telling you, Frank, to stay away from that girl. This has got to stop!'

'I can't, Mam! She means everything to me,' he replied determinedly. Sophie was the only reason he could face each

132

dreary day, didn't his mother understand that? He couldn't stay away from her, couldn't forgo those precious minutes he spent with her each evening. He couldn't give her up, especially now he knew that she loved him too. The way she had kissed him and clung to him had made him realise that and the knowledge had filled him with such joy and a happiness he hadn't known for years.

Martha looked at him steadily in the pale light from the streetlamp and she swallowed hard. He was her son and she did care about him; she knew how utterly miserable his life was but there was no way out of it for him and she wouldn't stand by and let poor Sophie Teare's life be ruined too.

'Frank, if you really do care for her then don't encourage her to love you in return. You can't offer her a single thing, son. Not marriage or a home, not security or any kind of a future. You'll break her heart, Frank, and that girl has suffered enough. She came here trying to find a new life, a new beginning – don't spoil it all. Don't take it away from her or Bella, it would be cruel. Leave her alone, Frank. She'll get over it in time.'

Frank stared back at her, shaking his head. '*I* won't get over it, Mam. I'll never get over her. I'll just go on hoping and praying that one day . . .'

Martha laid a hand on his arm. 'I know, son. But promise me you'll leave her in peace? Don't hurt her, don't ruin her life?'

Frank didn't reply. He couldn't, he couldn't promise to do something that would take away his very reason for living. He turned away and began to walk down the street, leaving Martha staring bleakly after him.

He'd always been stubborn, even as a little lad, she thought bitterly. That stubbornness had been at the root of his so-called 'passion' for Nora, and now it looked as if it would be the cause of a great deal of pain and unhappiness for Sophie too. She turned away. She'd tried but he was a grown man; there was nothing more she could do.

Chapter Eleven

———◆———

SOPHIE HAD MADE THE effort to get ready for work on New Year's Day but when she had entered the kitchen that morning, Lizzie had taken one look at her and said that a day off would do her more good than the money she would earn.

'Aunty Lizzie, I won't be earning any, I'll be short in my wages this week if I don't go in. You know they dock us a day's pay for being off and more so today,' she'd protested.

'No one will starve because of it. Now, take yourself back up those stairs and rest. I've got a bit of shopping to do so I'll take Bella with me. All the rest of them will be at work and our Billy is going off with his mates to the park. One of them got a bit of a toy boat for Christmas and they're going to sail it on the lake and I'm not risking them taking Bella along too, she's coming with me. You won't be disturbed,' Lizzie had informed her firmly, thinking Sophie had enough to contend with without Billy and his mates probably half soaking the child with their antics.

It was with some relief that Sophie had gone back upstairs and lain down on the bed, still feeling upset and confused. She felt exhausted and drained too for she hadn't slept at all well.

For what seemed like most of the night she had tossed and turned, listening to the breathing of Katie, Maria and the child tucked in beside her. She knew she couldn't risk seeing Frank again; it just wasn't possible, not if she wanted to keep her sanity – and for Bella's sake she had to. Maybe she did love him, she'd thought, and then with brutal honesty she admitted that she had fallen in love with him. She hadn't meant to, she had thought she would never love again, but somehow it had happened. But at the same time she knew there could never be anything between them. He would never divorce Nora and she couldn't – *wouldn't* – ask him to, so there could be no future together for them. She'd felt utterly miserable at the thought and her head had started to ache again. She didn't want to spend the rest of her life alone; as Arthur Chatsworth had reminded her, she *was* still young.

It had been just as the first faint rays of the grey January dawn were filtering through the gap in the curtains that she'd made her decision. She and Bella would have to leave Lizzie's house. She had come here to start her own business and provide a better future for Bella and she wasn't going to jeopardise that now by pining for Frank Ryan. She had to make a clean break.

After that she had started to wonder just where she would go and if Maria would go with her, for she wouldn't force her sister to leave here if she didn't want to. And where in this city would she find decent lodgings at a price she could afford, and who would take care of Bella after school and in the holidays? Her mind had become so clogged with worries that sleep had been impossible. Then she'd realized, when first Katie and then Maria had stirred, that it was time to get up and try to face everything.

For half an hour after Lizzie had sent her back upstairs Sophie tried to relax, but she just couldn't sleep. She gave up and went slowly back downstairs, feeling no better. The kitchen was deserted and untidy; her aunt had obviously decided to leave clearing up until she got back. Sighing heavily and feeling depressed, she began to clear away the dirty breakfast dishes but she turned as the door opened.

'Sophie, I didn't realise it was you, I thought it was Mrs Quine. I just came in to refill my water jug,' Arthur Chatsworth said quietly.

'I . . . I didn't go to work, Aunty Lizzie told me to stay off and rest.'

He nodded. 'Very wise. How are you feeling this morning?'

She managed a weak smile. 'Better, thank you, Arthur, but I didn't get much sleep, I'm afraid.'

Again he had the feeling that there was something else, apart from Nora, on her mind. 'Sophie, is there something upsetting you, other than the events of last night? My dear, let me assure you again that anything you tell me will be kept in the strictest confidence. My conversations with the family are brief, as you know, and I just pass the time of day with the neighbours – it would be discourteous to utterly ignore them.'

Sophie sat down at the table, twisting her hands together. It would be a relief to unburden herself of her feelings; surely it wouldn't hurt to confide in Arthur? He was such a pleasant, quiet man and he *was* discreet; he wasn't family and they had talked about Frank before. 'That awful incident last night was partly my . . . my fault,' she began, trying to chose her words carefully.

He sat down opposite her and although he looked surprised he made no comment.

'You remember before Christmas we . . . we had that conversation about me being "friends" with Frank Ryan and . . . and about me spending the rest of my life . . . alone . . .' She was struggling.

Understanding was beginning to dawn on Arthur Chatsworth and he decided to try to make it easier for her. 'You and Frank have become more than just "friends", is that it, Sophie?'

She nodded, biting her lip. 'Last night . . . things . . . Frank kissed me and I . . .'

'And Nora saw you?'

Again she nodded. 'So you see it was partly my fault and now . . .'

He looked at her ruefully. 'I think I, too, may have to share some of the blame.'

'You, Arthur?'

'Yes. Maybe I encouraged you, during that little talk. I did tell you that you were still a young woman and that life can be very lonely on your own . . .'

'No, it wasn't anything to do with that, I promise. It . . . it just sort of happened, but you know as well as I do that there is nothing to be done. Frank isn't free to . . . love me, no matter how I feel about him. I've made a decision.'

He looked interested. 'What have you decided, Sophie?'

'That Bella and I will have to find somewhere else to live, away from this street, away from this neighbourhood. Away from Frank.'

He didn't blame her but it was a drastic measure for a young woman with a child to contemplate. 'Where will you go, Sophie? How will you manage on your own?'

'I don't know. I . . . I had planned to rent a house in a decent area and run a business from it, making clothes hopefully for an increasing number of private clients. That way I could take care of Bella and give her a good home and future. It was one of the reasons I came to Liverpool, but I haven't saved up nearly enough money yet and it doesn't look as though I will ever be able to do so.'

'Will Maria go with you?' he asked, although his mind was working quickly. The position she now found herself in was hopeless but she was desperately trying to find a way to alleviate it. He had to try to help her.

Sophie shrugged. 'I don't know. I won't force her to, she seems happy enough here and she's very friendly with Katie

139

and a couple of the girls from further down.'

He leaned forward. 'I can fully understand your dilemma, Sophie, and I will be happy to help, if you'll let me.'

'How? How can you, Arthur?'

'I have some savings. It costs me very little to live here, my needs are few. I would be quite willing to invest some money in your business. I assume you will need to purchase certain things? A sewing machine, patterns and items of haberdashery? And you will need to advertise too.'

She was taken aback. 'It's very generous of you to offer, but why? Why should you help me, Arthur? You barely know me.'

He smiled. 'I hear most of what goes on in this house – the walls are very thin – and I know enough to put my faith and trust in you, Sophie. You are honest, kind, generous and a good mother.' He steepled his fingers and looked down at them, as if concentrating hard on his fingertips. 'I . . . I never had a daughter. In fact I have no children. My . . . my wife . . . died young. I'm alone but I . . . I would like to help you, Sophie, because I would like to think of you as the daughter I never had.' It cost him dearly to tell her that and the loneliness was evident in his tone.

Despite her confused emotions Sophie heard it and she smiled sadly. So he too knew how it felt to be bereaved and alone. 'Thank you,' she said quietly.

'So, will you let me help?'

She nodded, feeling a surge of relief wash over her. 'I can't leave here until I've got myself established with enough money coming in to provide for myself and Bella, and until

I've found somewhere else, and that might present a problem with Maria and . . . Frank.'

He looked serious. 'I think you should confide in your sister. You appear to be very close and as for Frank, well, how would it be if I met you and escorted you home from the tram each evening? That would give him no opportunity to speak to you.'

Sophie nodded slowly. It would hurt and upset Frank, she knew, but there was little else she could do.

'Of course, the neighbours may start to gossip, reading more into our friendship than there is.'

Sophie smiled. 'Let them. It won't be for long.'

He smiled back affectionately. 'Right, then the first thing I think you should do is place an advertisement in the newspapers, both the *Bootle Times* and the *Liverpool Echo*.'

Sophie became flustered. 'I wouldn't know what to say . . .'

'I'll compose it for you, then when we're both happy with it I'll take it down to the offices in Old Hall Street. If I get there early enough it should make this evening's edition.'

'Then I'll have to tell Aunty Lizzie about it. Someone is bound to see it and mention it to her.'

'Why not just tell her that you are trying to start a business – tentatively – it's what you had planned and you'll just see how it goes before you give up your job?' he suggested.

'But if I do get any replies, where can I see people? You know how crowded we all are here and you have to admit it sometimes gets like a three-ring circus.'

'Either in their own homes or you could use the front

room – my room. I'd go out for an hour or two; that way at least you would have a bit of privacy.'

'I couldn't put you to all that inconvenience,' she protested.

'I'm sure it won't be for long, Sophie. Now, if we're to get this advertisement in on time, we'd better make a start.'

It was far better than anything she could have put together, she thought after he'd left. It sounded so professional. He'd used words like 'bespoke' and 'discreet, impeccable service at competitive prices' and she felt infinitely better about things than she had first thing that morning. Now all she had to do was tell her aunt and Maria.

Lizzie listened in silence but with a slightly worried and cautious look on her face as Sophie outlined the plan and when her aunt voiced her doubts about how she would manage to cut out and sew in these cramped conditions and was it wise to think about giving up a steady job, Sophie explained that if it was successful – and she prayed it would be – she would move, reminding her aunt that it would be better for her to remove herself from the vicinity of Frank and Nora and also give Lizzie and her family more much-needed room. Put like that Lizzie had to agree, although she told her niece not to get her hopes up too high. Suitable lodgings were almost impossible to find and there were many well-patronised dressmaking establishments already in the city.

She broached the subject with Maria when her sister returned from work. Maria was close enough to Sophie to know that she was upset about what had happened last night and thought this the reason for the tête-à-tête. In fact she had been upset that she had been with Ben and the others and hadn't been at her sister's side to help her fend off Nora Ryan.

'Is it something to do with Frank and . . . Nora and last night?' she asked as she brushed out her long, dark curls, which she wore confined tidily in a neat chignon for work.

Sophie sighed and nodded as she sat down on the end of the bed Maria shared with Katie. Their cousin had gone down to see her friend Ivy to borrow a pair of earrings as she was going out with Matt later. The room was chilly and Sophie tucked the quilt around her feet. 'You know what happened last night. Well, it's no use me telling you not to waste your life waiting for someone you love but can never have, if . . .'

Maria turned and sat down beside her. Thoughts of Hans had flooded her mind at Sophie's words, but she determinedly pushed them away. 'Sophie, I knew it was more than just affection . . .'

'Oh, Maria, it started that way but . . . but now it's more. I realised that last night. It's hopeless, I know it – we all know it. I have to put him out of my mind and my heart and think of a future for Bella now. There is no future for Frank and me and I can't stay here, not when there is the chance I will see him almost every day.'

Maria was startled. 'You're not thinking of going home, are you, Sophie?'

Sophie reached out and put her arm around her sister's shoulder. 'No. I'm going to start my business, with the help of Arthur Chatsworth. He's offered to invest some of his savings in it. In fact there is an advertisement in the *Echo* tonight and if all goes well, I'll try to find somewhere else to live and to work.'

Maria just stared at her blankly as Sophie relayed her conversation with Lizzie's lodger. Of course she could understand just how Sophie felt. She couldn't go on living here, bumping into Frank regularly as she was bound to do and having to confront Nora on occasions as well. Seeing Frank would only make it harder for her sister.

'So, Aunty Lizzie does know that we'll be moving – sooner or later?'

'Yes, but you don't have to come with me, Maria, if you don't want to. You've settled well here and you've got Katie, Ivy and Daisy Caldwell, and of course Ben.'

Maria smiled wryly. 'Don't start on about Ben again, Sophie, and I'd sooner not be sharing a bed with Katie, even though I like her well enough. Of course I'll come with you. You're my sister, I don't want to leave you or Bella. I'd like to have a bit more room and some privacy too; everyone always seems to be on top of each other here.'

Sophie did feel more relieved that Maria was happy to go to a new home with her – when they found one.

Maria stood up, pulling her sister up too. 'Let's go and have a look at your advertisement – if we can prise the paper off Uncle Jim. I wonder how soon you'll get any replies?'

'One would be a start,' Sophie replied, smoothing down the quilt and following her sister out of the cramped and rather dismal room.

Chapter Twelve

divider ornament

FOR THE NEXT FEW days Frank did try to avoid Sophie, although it took all his resolve to do so. He deliberately lingered at the end of the working day so he missed his usual tram, arriving later at his destination, knowing Sophie would then be safely home at Lizzie's house. One evening, however, it had started to snow heavily and his foreman told him to 'get a move on' or else the trams would have stopped running and he'd have a long, cold walk home.

The tram was packed. He didn't see her but then he had been shepherded up to the upper deck by the conductor, who was loudly informing everyone that there was no more room downstairs and that as soon as they reached the depot – if they did – that was it. He for one was going home; there would be no more trams tonight.

Crushed in beside a window on the lower deck Sophie gazed out at the silent and increasingly heavy white flakes that were transforming the city, obliterating the ugly scars left by the blitz with a mantle of pristine white. She had started to get used to the sight of Arthur Chatsworth waiting patiently in the cold a few feet away from the tram stop even though ever since she'd returned to work there had been no sign of Frank.

Tonight she thought that Arthur's patient vigil was rather above the call of duty, given the weather, and she was deliberating whether or not to tell him not to come out tomorrow evening, that's if there were any trams or buses running. If there weren't she would be walking to and from work and she was determined not to drag the poor man all the way to Marsden's to meet her. Everyone would be home late this evening and they'd all probably have to walk to work tomorrow for there was little sign of the snow stopping.

Frank had managed to get on to the platform of the tram before it reached the stop but there were a dozen or so people crowded behind him and he couldn't see her. After he had alighted, he stood aside to let the other passengers pass. He'd decided to wait for her. It would be hard walking in this weather and she might easily slip. That was all it was, he assured himself, concern for her welfare. Concern that she reached Lizzie's house safely. Surely no one could read more into that? Anyone with a smattering of manners would help a woman – young or old – in such conditions.

At last he caught sight of her as she stepped off and on to

the snow, which had already been compacted by the feet of other passengers, and his heart began to beat faster. He took a few steps forward but was suddenly confronted by Arthur Chatsworth, muffled up in a heavy overcoat and scarf and with a trilby hat pulled well down on his head.

'Excuse me, Frank, I've come to meet Sophie and escort her home. I meet her regularly now. It's a terrible night and you'd be wise to get off home yourself.'

Frank stared at him for a moment, and then nodded curtly. Sophie stepped in front of Arthur.

'Frank, I'm sorry. I . . . I really don't want to hurt you but I've made a decision. I'll be moving away from Lizzie's soon. I'm going to start my own business – dressmaking. Arthur is helping me . . . backing me and . . . and it was his idea to meet me off the tram. I . . . I really am sorry, Frank. You have to believe me. It's for the best.' She turned back to Arthur. She was tired, cold, hungry and now felt miserable but at least she had explained things to Frank. She had been almost certain he would have been on that tram, considering the weather, and if Arthur hadn't been there, she would have had no option but to walk home with Frank and then . . .

'I suspect that will be the last tram going this way tonight. You were lucky to catch it, Sophie.'

Sophie looked up at her companion. 'I know and thank you for meeting me. I feel awful dragging you out in this weather. I just couldn't ignore Frank. He looked so hurt.'

'It's no trouble to me and I'm just helping you to stick to your resolution. It's for the best. Now, let's not dwell on it further. There are two letters waiting for you, your aunt said they came in the midday post, before the snow started.'

It took them almost twice as long to get home but when they arrived Lizzie had the table set and a big pan of oxtail soup simmering on the range. Both Maria and Katie were in, as were Bella and Billy, but of the men there was no sign yet.

'I swear it's getting worse out there. You both look frozen. Get those wet things off and have a bowl of soup. You too, Mr Chatsworth.' Lizzie bustled about, ladling the soup into two bowls, and for once Arthur didn't refuse or protest.

'Open your letters first, Sophie. We're dying to know who has written in reply to your advert,' Maria urged and Katie nodded eagerly. Katie thought it all very exciting; she'd never known anyone as young as her cousin who had started their own business.

'Will you give the girl a chance to get her coat and hat off?' Lizzie scolded.

Sophie sat down beside her sister and tore open a pale blue envelope, which Arthur noted was of good quality paper.

She scanned the lines of neat copperplate writing and then smiled. 'It's from a Miss Henrietta Foster. She would like me to call to see her with a view to having what she calls "some afternoon dresses" made.'

'Sounds a bit old fashioned, where does she live, Sophie?' Lizzie asked, placing a bowl of soup in front of her niece and trying to scan the contents of the letter over Sophie's shoulder.

'Number five Laurel Road,' Sophie supplied, looking questioningly up at her aunt.

Lizzie frowned, trying to think.

'If I remember correctly, it's about twenty minutes or maybe half an hour away – walking, that is,' Arthur informed them. 'I'm not sure if it's still classed as Stanley Road or if it's off Hawthorne Road. It's a quiet area. It used to be quite affluent at one time, I believe. I walk a great deal when the weather is fine,' he added rather self-consciously.

'That's right, Mr Chatsworth. Quite big, rather posh houses they are, or used to be,' Lizzie added.

'That sounds very promising, Sophie,' Maria enthused. 'Does she say when she wants you to call?'

'Saturday afternoon, if it's convenient, at three.' Sophie bit her lip, thinking that even if the snow was a couple of feet thick she would have to get there somehow, she couldn't let down this, her first prospective customer. She opened the second letter and scanned the lines. 'This is from a Mrs Henderson of fourteen Walton Park; she would like me to call on Saturday too. I can't see me making it to see both of them – and where *is* Walton Park anyway?'

Everyone looked mystified, including Arthur Chatsworth.

'Maybe Jim will know. They shouldn't be long now, they're nearly an hour later than usual,' Lizzie stated, looking anxiously at the clock on the mantel.

Neither Jim nor John Quine could enlighten Sophie when they finally arrived home, cold, wet and tired, having had to walk most of the way.

'Don't worry about it, Uncle Jim, Arthur said if you didn't know he would look it up in a copy of Kelly's Street Directory, they have one at the library,' Sophie said.

Jim nodded wearily, wondering how she was going to get to either address if the weather didn't let up.

When Frank arrived home it was to find both Nellie and Nora in the kitchen, which was decidedly unusual, and the sight of them gave him no pleasure at all. Despite the fact that he was cold and hungry, the stuffy, dirty and malodorous room was far from welcoming. Nellie was stirring something in a pan and Nora was sitting at the table amidst a variety of dirty dishes, flicking through an old magazine. Of Bertie there was no sign and Frank realised he was probably propping up the bar of some pub – as usual, snow or no snow. He turned away, intending to try to find some peace and quiet in which to nurse his feelings in the room he shared with Nora when her derisive laughter stopped him.

'I heard they send that old feller down ter the tram stop ter meet her now. So that's put a stop to your little game, hasn't it?'

'Shurrup, Nora! You'd start a row in an empty 'ouse,' Nellie muttered, glaring at her.

Nora ignored her mother's instruction. 'Maybe now yer'll get it into yer thick head that she's not for you, an' remember just who you're married to! Although from the carry-on out of her the other night, she's far from "pure as the driven snow"!' Nora laughed cuttingly, thinking her remark very witty and apt considering the weather.

'There's not much chance of me forgetting, is there? And don't talk about her like that. You're not fit to wipe her boots and never will be!' Frank snapped back. The fact that Nora had heard that Arthur Chatsworth now met Sophie each evening made the fact somehow even harder to bear.

'Not fit ter wipe her boots, my arse! She's no better than me, hanging around your neck like that ...' Nora's jealousy had had plenty of time to grow and each time she remembered that little scene on New Year's Eve, albeit her recollection of it was somewhat hazy, her hatred for them both increased. He'd shown everyone that he loved Sophie Teare and cared nothing for her. She'd told herself firmly that she didn't care, that there were plenty of other men who were only too interested in her charms, happy to spend money on her and show her a good time. She was more than over her 'romance' with Frank Ryan. All those years ago she had thought she loved him; she had wanted to marry him so much that she'd lied to him. She'd wanted to be Mrs Ryan with a home of her own and, in time, children, but she'd soon found that wasn't going to happen. She swore to herself now that it hadn't been 'love' at all, just a stupid infatuation, and she didn't care if he had affairs too, not even with the likes of Sophie Teare, but she couldn't keep the jealousy at bay. Her mam said she was just being a dog in the manger about it all. She didn't want him, but she didn't want anyone else to have him either.

'Shurrup, Nora! I'm bloody sick of listening ter yer going

on about it, you're like a cracked bloody gramophone record,' Nellie yelled.

Frank turned and walked out, slamming the door behind him. He'd get no damned peace in this house at all; he knew Nora of old – she'd follow him and pursue the argument. Snow was still falling relentlessly and it was too cold to walk the streets or even take refuge in a pub, not that he felt like the company of those diehards such as his father-in-law.

He put his cap back on. Surely his mam wouldn't turn him away on such a night as this? But then he remembered that Martha had been angry with him over Sophie. Still, he had to try; he couldn't stay here and listen to Nora, he felt too miserable and humiliated. If he could just sit for an hour in his mam's clean, warm, comfortable kitchen and talk to her and his da he could get through tonight.

Chapter Thirteen

IT WAS PAT WHO opened the door. His brows rose in surprise at finding his eldest son standing on the doorstep with snow covering his cap and dusting the shoulders of his jacket.

'Da, can I come in for just an hour, please? I can't stay over there another minute, Nora's being her usual bloody-minded, foul-mouthed self and I can't walk the streets in this and . . . and I desperately need to talk to you,' Frank pleaded.

Pat nodded. 'Come on into the kitchen, you must be frozen.'

As soon as Martha saw him she frowned and started to get to her feet.

'Now, Martha, luv, we can't turn him away on a night like this and he wants to talk to us.'

'If it's about Sophie he can save his breath,' came the sharp reply.

'Sit down, lad, and take off those wet things,' Pat urged.

Seeing she was wasting her time and also privately concurring with her husband about the weather, Martha picked up her knitting again. 'I suppose you've realised that Mr Chatsworth now meets Sophie?'

Frank nodded, holding his hands out to the warmth of the fire. He hadn't needed reminding.

'And he's investing some money in the business she's starting up. Lizzie was telling me all about it today. If she makes a go of it, and I just know she will, then she'll be moving. She'll need proper sewing and fitting rooms – there's no room to swing a cat next door. Lizzie said there were two replies to her advert in the post today, so that's a good start.'

Frank hadn't known any of this and his spirits plummeted further at the news that Sophie intended to move. 'What am I going to do with my life now?' he muttered, half to himself.

Pat leaned forward, his hands on his knees, a frown of concentration etched on his face. He was worried about Frank, although he said little to Martha. He was afraid that the lad's despair would reach such proportions that he would do something stupid. 'I've been giving that a bit of thought lately, Frank. There's nothing you can do about either Nora or Sophie. You're in a right mess, there's no two ways about it, but things could be a bit easier for you—'

'How, Da?' Frank interrupted but without any real enthusiasm in his tone.

'What if you went back to sea? I don't mean the Royal Navy, but the Merchant Marine. There are enough shipping companies in Liverpool and you've a trade and experience. You'd be away from Nora, you wouldn't be bumping into Sophie—'

'And you wouldn't have to spend much time in that pigsty Nellie Richards calls a "home",' Martha interrupted, wondering why Pat hadn't mentioned this to her or why neither of them had thought of this before. If Frank was away at sea he would at least be decently fed, clothed and looked after and he'd have company. It would be a better life than he had now.

There was silence in the room, broken only by the crackling of the flames in the hearth as Pat and Martha looked anxiously at Frank, who was staring into the fire, thinking about his father's suggestion. It wouldn't solve the problem completely: he would still be tied to Nora and could never be with Sophie. Yet if he could go away for long trips – months at a time – it would certainly be better than living at Nellie's and everything it entailed and Sophie . . . well, if his mam was right, Sophie would be moving. He hadn't minded being at sea and he knew that there was a great camaraderie on merchant ships, just as there had been on HMS *Kestrel*. Then he frowned as a thought occurred to him.

'My trade won't be much use to me. They all carry engineers and some carry electricians, but hardly any carry joiners. I'd have to sail as a steward or a waiter, or maybe even a deck hand.'

Both his parents sighed with relief that at least he was considering it.

'Would that be so bad?' Martha queried. 'The tips can be quite good on the big liners.'

'Some of the smaller coasters carry a ship's carpenter,' Pat reminded him.

'Aye, just the one, and openings are few and far between. Blokes stay in those jobs for years. No, I'll have to take whatever I can get. As soon as the weather gets better I'll go down to the "Pool" and see what there is on offer.' Maybe he'd be lucky and he could get a ship going to South Africa or even Australia or New Zealand.

Martha laid aside the sleeve of the jumper she was knitting for Robbie. 'We'll have a cup of tea and I'll do you a couple of sausages, a fried egg and a slice of fried bread. I don't suppose you've had anything to eat?'

Frank smiled gratefully. 'Thanks, Mam.' He'd almost begun to feel as though there was some point to his life now.

By Friday the snow had almost disappeared, turning first to slush and then to dirty puddles of water, which Lizzie declared made more mess than the snow. Sophie was feeling a little nervous as she got ready to go to meet Miss Foster on Saturday afternoon. She had decided, after discussing the matter with Arthur Chatsworth, that she would write to Mrs Henderson, suggesting she call later in the afternoon than the time suggested as she had a full day of appointments. This was stretching the truth rather but they both agreed it sounded better than saying she couldn't be in two places at once. He had found out where Walton Park was and had also found out the best and quickest way for her to get there and back.

'If you go to see her after Miss Foster you can get home here more directly,' he'd advised.

She had dressed plainly but she hoped smartly in her navy and white checked dress trimmed with a white piqué collar and navy braid, her good dark blue coat and a small felt hat of emerald green, borrowed from Maria, who had insisted on pinning the leaf-shaped brooch that Ben had given her at Christmas to the lapel of the coat.

'It just finishes it off, without looking fussy,' she'd stated. 'And good luck, Sophie. I just *know* you'll get good orders, it's the start of a new career for you, and then we can both look forward to moving and having a home of our own.'

Sophie had put a sketch pad and two pencils, some paper patterns and her price list into the leather briefcase Arthur had insisted on lending her and which Lizzie declared made her look very "professional", and she gripped it tightly as she got off the tram and walked in the direction of Laurel Road. Her aunt had been right, she thought, as she looked around. Although it wasn't all that far from Harebell Street, it was a much quieter neighbourhood. The houses were what were termed Victorian "villas". Red-brick, four-storeyed terraced with bay windows, steps up to the front doors and neat little front gardens enclosed by a wall. Decorative brickwork and plasterwork embellished the tops of the bays and they all appeared well cared for.

Number five had thick, cream-coloured cotton lace curtains at the windows, she noticed as she opened the front gate. There was a little patch of lawn and a narrow border containing rose bushes, all bare now. She took a deep breath and pressed the bell, wondering what kind of afternoon this would turn out to be. Successful, she hoped.

The door was opened by a small, slim old lady who was obviously in her late seventies. She had silver hair that was cut short and waved in a style fashionable in the 1920s. Her clothes, too, reminded Sophie forcefully of that era.

'Miss Henrietta Foster?' she enquired, feeling a little dispirited.

'And you must be Mrs Teare. I didn't expect you to be so . . . young, but you are very punctual. Do come in.'

Sophie stepped into a wide hallway half covered in Anaglypta painted cream, above which was brown and cream patterned wallpaper. A runner of brown carpet covered the floor and prints of hunting scenes in heavy frames adorned the walls.

'Do follow me, Mrs Teare, I'm quite eager to see if you can be of assistance to me.'

The room Sophie was ushered into was what Lizzie would have termed the "back parlour". Again the décor was of brown and cream, the furniture old fashioned and heavy but highly polished. It seemed that every surface was covered with bric-a-brac – cut-glass vases and bowls, ornaments, figurines, artificial plants and flowers – which made it appear cluttered. She sat down on a brocade-covered sofa next to

Miss Foster, glancing quickly at the array of photographs on a side table, and opened the briefcase.

'You said in your letter that you required some "afternoon dresses",' she said tentatively.

The old lady smiled. 'I do indeed, the ones I have are really very shabby but it's almost impossible to get what I require these days. Firstly there was the war and so many establishments were destroyed in the Blitz, and now all the styles I see are just too modern for my taste.'

Sophie smiled. 'We might still have a problem with the shortages.'

'Oh, no, my dear, that's not a problem. I have the material, I've had it all for years. Ada, my sister, always believed in keeping a good stock of materials in. She bought them as remnants, end of roll or discontinued lines; she believed in getting a bargain.'

'And will your sister require anything?' Sophie asked hopefully.

'Sadly not. Poor Ada died, three years ago now, and our brother Harold died before the war broke out. Of course he was that much older than us.'

'I'm sorry. So you live here alone now?' It seemed a big house for just one small old lady.

'I do but I am friendly with some of the ladies from church, which is why I require some dresses. I feel so awful having to wear the ones I have over and over again when I'm asked out for tea or entertain here. We take it in turns, you see, once a fortnight.'

Sophie thought that despite the six years of war Miss Foster seemed to live in a different and rather old-fashioned world. She smiled. 'Perhaps if you could let me see the materials and the style of dress you'd like me to make, we could progress from there.'

She was quite astonished at the variety of material Miss Foster produced. There were lengths of tweed and gabardine, fine wool crêpes, floral cottons, brocade and velvet, crêpe de Chine and lawn, and it was all of excellent quality. Much better than anything you could buy in the shops now, even if you had the coupons. The style of dress the old lady produced wouldn't present her with any problems, she thought, as they discussed which materials would be suitable and Sophie suggested trimmings.

Reluctantly declining the offer of tea, bearing in mind that she had to get to Walton, Sophie made notes and took measurements and they agreed a price for two dresses. Miss Foster had wanted to order four but Sophie insisted that she make just two to start with.

'That way I can be sure you are completely satisfied with my work, Miss Foster,' she said firmly.

'Hetty. Do call me Hetty. I like you, Mrs Teare, and I'm sure everything will be excellent.'

Sophie smiled; she had taken a liking to the old lady too. 'I'll have them ready for the first fitting next Saturday. Now, I'm afraid I really must go, I have an appointment in Walton.'

'I look forward to seeing you next Saturday, Mrs Teare, and then perhaps you can tell me a little more about yourself.

You're not a Liverpudlian, I know that.'

'No, I'm Manx, and please do call me Sophie. I'll be here at three on the dot,' she promised.

It was almost six o'clock when she finally returned to Lizzie's. She hadn't liked Mrs Henderson. The woman had kept her waiting for twenty minutes and had then dithered over whether or not to order a skirt. She had, in the end, decided to go ahead, but Sophie had felt it wasn't really worth her travelling so far. Still, it was better than no order at all, she told herself. She had to be thankful for everything.

Both Maria and Katie were in from work and both were going out later that evening, although Maria said she didn't really feel like going to a dance as she'd been on her feet all day. In fact she was trying to avoid seeing Ben Seddon so much lately.

'I thought you'd have been back earlier . . . Oh, look at this: it's not going to go very far. I'm sick to death of this blasted rationing,' Lizzie said, contemplating without much pleasure the small amount of meat she had been able to purchase in the butcher's for the Sunday lunch.

'She kept me waiting and then I missed a tram and had to wait,' Sophie said, taking off her hat and placing it on the dresser and then stooping down gave Bella a hug. Her small daughter looked decidedly mutinous. 'Have you been a good girl while I've been out?'

Bella scowled at Billy who was immersed in a copy of the *Beano* he'd borrowed from one of his mates. 'Billy wouldn't let me go with him to Charlie Blackley's house.'

Behind the comic Billy raised his eyes to the ceiling. He liked Bella but sometimes the way she followed him around embarrassed him, particularly as Charlie, who was almost a year older, had teased him about it.

'I don't know why you even wanted to go, I don't like that Charlie. He's got too much to say for himself, too hard-faced by half. Where's Emily this afternoon, Bella?' Lizzie asked, glaring at her youngest son.

'Gone into town with her mam,' Bella replied, her expression changing as Sophie handed her a new length of ribbon for her hair, which she'd been keeping as a little surprise.

'So, how did you get on with the one who wanted the "afternoon frocks"?' Maria demanded, grinning.

'She was lovely and you were right, Aunty Lizzie. Those houses are big and it's a nice area. She has dozens of lengths of material – her sister seems to have been a bit of a hoarder. Her sister's dead now, as is her brother; she lives there on her own. I'm making her two to start with.' Sophie smiled a little ruefully. 'She seems to live in a different world to the rest of us. She goes out "for tea" to friends from the church and has probably never worked in her life.'

'Lucky her! Maybe these friends of hers will want you to make things for them too, Sophie,' Lizzie mused.

'I hope so. I need all the work I can get if I'm going to try to make a living from dressmaking.'

Chapter Fourteen

———◆———

SOPHIE HAD THE TWO dresses tacked and ready for fitting the following Saturday. She'd worked hard and it hadn't been easy for she'd had to wait until the evening meal was over before she could commandeer the use of the kitchen table. The new Singer treadle sewing machine that Arthur had ordered and paid for had been delivered on Friday afternoon and now stood in a corner of his room. She wasn't going to see Mrs Henderson until Sunday afternoon so she would have plenty of time to spend with Miss Foster or 'Hetty'.

To her surprise, when she arrived at the house in Laurel Road she found the old lady had a small table set with a starched white lace cloth and pretty flowered china. 'I thought a nice cup of tea and some scones would be welcome, it's so bitterly cold today. I do hope we are not in for more snow.'

'That's very kind of you but there was no need to go to all this trouble,' Sophie said as she unbuttoned her coat after first unwrapping the two dresses, which she'd carefully parcelled up, first in tissue and then brown paper.

'Nonsense, dear. You are not pressed for time, I hope?' Hetty Foster carefully poured the tea, indicating that Sophie sit down.

'No, not today.' She sipped the tea gratefully for it was a bitterly cold afternoon. 'Do you have any help in the house? I don't want to sound as if I'm prying but it is a big house.' And if this room was anything to go by there was an awful lot of dusting to start with, she thought.

'No, poor dear Ada always said that a bit of housework and cooking never hurt anyone and it was a pure waste of money to pay someone to do it,' Hetty Foster confided.

'Poor dear Ada' sounded as though she'd been a bit on the mean side, Sophie thought, although she just smiled.

'Of course now a lot of the rooms are closed off. I just use this room, the kitchen, a bedroom and of course the bathroom.'

The luxury of a proper bathroom, Sophie thought enviously. She'd never lived in a house that had a bathroom with an inside toilet, not even in Peel. The little fishermen's cottages had had a privy in the yard, just as Lizzie's house had.

'And now, Sophie, tell me about yourself. Does your

164

husband have work here in Liverpool, is that why you came over to live?' Hetty offered the plate of scones.

Sophie shook her head. 'I'm a widow. Andrew . . . my husband was a fisherman, he . . . he was drowned. I have a daughter, she's five. Her name is Isabella but we call her Bella. There is very little work on the island so we came here, to my aunt's house: myself, Bella and my sister Maria. My mother is a widow too, so I couldn't expect her to keep us all. I had to find work. I have a job as a machinist in a factory that makes overalls but . . . but I always wanted to work for myself. I love sewing and I'm good at it.' She sipped her tea thoughtfully, wondering if she should broach the subject of hopefully obtaining some custom from Hetty Foster's friends but decided against it. She didn't know the old lady well enough.

Hetty nodded. What a tragedy, she thought. Poor girl, so young to be left with a child to bring up. 'And does your aunt live nearby?'

'Not too far away, in Harebell Street.'

As she refilled Sophie's cup Hetty Foster frowned. Surely those houses were quite small? 'Does your aunt have a family?'

'Oh, yes. Her eldest son was killed in the war but John came through it without a scratch and there's Katie and young Billy and she has a lodger. A very nice, middle-aged gentleman, Mr Chatsworth.'

'Goodness, you must be very crowded.'

Sophie laughed. 'We are but we manage. That's one of

Aunty Lizzie's favourite sayings: "We'll manage".' She stood up. 'Now, I'll help you to tidy away and wash these dishes and then we'll get on with the fitting.'

'Oh, leave the dishes, Sophie. I have all evening to see to them. I'm very eager to see how my new dresses are coming along. It's so long since I had anything new at all.'

Sophie began to fold back the tissue paper. 'I think you'll be pleased with them and I'll have them finished by next week, so when you next go out to tea you will look very smart indeed.'

Frank hadn't mentioned to anyone else his plans to go back to sea, but the more he thought about it the more optimistic he felt. Mingled with the feelings of relief at being able to escape, at least temporarily, from Nora and the Richards family was sadness at the thought that he wouldn't see Sophie either for weeks, possibly even months. Even though he realised that any brief daily conversations with her were now out of the question, he determined that if and when he got a ship he would go and ask Lizzie if he could see her before he sailed.

The clerk at the Pool, which was basically an employment exchange for seamen, was not very optimistic. 'If you'd have been a sparks it would have been easier. Now everyone's been demobbed, there's a lot of competition for jobs as waiters and stewards on passenger ships.'

'I'm aware of that but I'm a time-served joiner, not an electrician, so I don't have much choice. I've my Royal Navy experience, but that was as a gunner.'

'Not much call for that now, mate,' the clerk answered morosely while leafing through a sheaf of papers.

Frank didn't reply but waited until at last the man pulled a sheet out from the pile. 'There's a vacancy with the Harrison Line but it's for a very junior deck officer, which basically means it's just a half a step up from a deck hand. Nothing at all for CP, Blue Funnel, Elder Dempster or Union Castle, and Cunard sail from Southampton now.'

'Where does the Harrison Line go to?' Frank asked. At least it was *something*.

'Down to the Canary Islands, then the coast of East Africa, then South Africa and back again. Away three months. Pay's not great but the weather will be.'

Three months! Three whole months away from Nora, Frank thought, but it was also three months away from Sophie. 'I'll take it.'

'Right, you'll have to provide your own uniform and get a Discharge Book. You still got your service record and demob papers?'

Frank nodded.

'Bring them down here and we'll get all the documentation sorted out.' The clerk was busy writing something down on the sheet of paper.

'When do they sail?' Frank asked.

'Tuesday of next week. It's the *City of Exeter*; she's berthed at the Canada dock. Are you married or single?'

'Married, unfortunately,' Frank replied bitterly.

'Like that is it, mate? Well, you have my sympathies

but you'll need to leave the missus an allotment, it's the law.'

Frank nodded with resignation. It would be worth it to be away from Nora even though he knew whatever he left would be spent on drink, cigarettes and cheap cosmetics.

As he left the building and crossed the cobbled expanse of Man Island, heading for a tram to Park Lane and Greenberg's, the naval outfitters, his step was lighter than it had been in months. This time next week he would be leaving Liverpool, heading for the warm waters and tropical climate of Africa. Nora could carry on as much as she liked, he couldn't care less, but he was determined to see Sophie before he left, if only to explain where he was going. There would be no need to explain *why* he was going. She'd know.

Lizzie had been expecting him for Martha had informed her of his decision to go back to sea, so when she opened the door late on Sunday evening she wasn't surprised to see him standing there. Martha had also told her that Frank had no intention of informing Nora until the day before he was due to sail; the new uniform was hanging up behind a bedroom door in Martha's house. At least there it would stay in pristine condition, she'd remarked, something that wasn't guaranteed in Nellie's house. Martha had said she was so relieved that Frank had taken this decision, it wouldn't solve things but it would certainly help and she was far happier now to see him looking to the future with a bit more hope.

'You'd better come in, Frank. She's busy with the sewing in the front room but I expect Mr Chatsworth won't mind the interruption on this occasion.'

Frank nodded, relieved she hadn't flatly refused to let him in but wondering how he and Sophie could have any privacy with Arthur Chatsworth in the room, or maybe that was Lizzie's intention. Still, at least he would get to see Sophie and Lizzie's house was so overcrowded there was seldom the luxury of privacy.

Arthur Chatsworth looked questioningly at Sophie when Lizzie knocked and told her that Frank wanted to see her. Sophie's machining didn't disturb his reading, in fact he found the dull humming noise quite restful and Sophie didn't chatter on while she worked; her task seemed to require all her concentration.

'Aunty Lizzie, I don't know if . . . if it's wise . . .' Sophie bit her lip.

'I think you should see him, Sophie, this time, for it will be a while before anyone sees him again,' Lizzie urged.

Arthur got to his feet, looking perplexed, wondering what the lad had done now. Was he going somewhere? Was he finally leaving Nora? 'I'll go for a walk around the block, give you a few minutes . . .'

'There's no need for you to go out, Mr Chatsworth, it's freezing. Come and sit in with us. What he's got to say won't take long,' Lizzie said firmly as she turned and opened the door and beckoned to Frank.

Frank stepped inside and glanced around. The room was neat and tidy although sparsely furnished but his heart began to beat faster as he looked at Sophie where she sat at the machine. A cloud of some kind of lavender material was spread over the top of the machine and cascaded down, half covering her skirt. She was wearing a jumper in a shade of rose pink that seemed to make her skin glow and her long dark hair fell loosely over her shoulders. He just stared at her for a few seconds, thinking he would carry this image of her with him in his mind for the next three months.

'What is it, Frank?' she asked quietly. She could see the longing in his eyes but knew there was something else. He must obviously have come to some kind of a decision for her aunt to let him in.

'I came to say goodbye, Sophie. I'm going back to sea. I sail early on Tuesday morning.'

She was taken aback. 'You've gone back in the Navy?'

He shook his head. 'Not the Royal Navy. I'm sailing on the *City of Exeter*. It's a cargo ship. I . . . I couldn't stand it any longer, Sophie. Not being able to even speak to you . . .'

Sophie pushed aside the lavender wool crêpe of Hetty's new dress and sighed. 'Oh, Frank, I . . . I thought it was for the best, for both our sakes, I really did. You know I don't want to hurt you but . . .'

He nodded. 'It probably is, Sophie, but I couldn't go on living just across the road, having to put up with Nora, and not—'

'So, where are you going to?' she asked, not wanting the conversation to become bogged down in the futility of their situation.

'Eventually to South Africa. I'll be away for about three months.'

'It's a long time,' she managed to reply, feeling suddenly miserable.

'I didn't want a short trip. Can I . . . can I write, Sophie? Just something short, a postcard or two? To let you know I'm safe and well.'

She desperately wanted to say 'yes', the seas and oceans of the world could be treacherous, as she knew well, but she shook her head sadly. 'I don't think it would be wise, Frank. I'll hear from your mam how you are getting on. I know you'll be writing to her now that you've patched up your differences.'

'Yes, I suppose I will.' He couldn't keep the hurt and disappointment from his voice. 'I . . . love you, Sophie, and I'll never give up hope that one day . . . one day . . .'

She felt the tears welling up in her eyes but she fought them back. 'I know, Frank, and I hope too that one day . . .' The words caught in her throat.

Instantly he was beside her and, heedless of the folds of lavender material, he pulled her to her feet and held her. 'Oh, Sophie! I don't want to leave you but I have to go . . .'

For a second she clung to him, and then with an effort she pulled away. 'Yes, you do, Frank. It's best this way but . . . but take care of yourself, promise?'

He smiled down at her ruefully. 'I promise.'

Chapter Fifteen

<hr>

As SOPHIE WALKED UP Laurel Road that early April day she thought that at times the last three months seemed to have passed quickly and then at others they had seemed interminably long. Frank was well; she heard via his mother that he was finding life far more bearable now. Martha had even shown her a small snapshot he'd sent of himself and two other crew members taken at the top of Table Mountain. He looked tanned and fit and the sun had lightened his hair. When she'd commented on it, Martha had smiled and said she felt so relieved. It was a weight off her mind, she'd added, that he'd lost that terrible air of dejection, despair and neglect that had seemed to cling to him before he'd sailed.

Sophie smiled ruefully to herself as she recalled Martha's comments on the way Nora had acted up on learning of her husband's imminent and totally unexpected departure. The girl had all but accused Martha of instigating what she chose to regard as Frank's desertion of her. Martha's reply had been cutting and to the point. Everyone knew Frank couldn't stand the sight of Nora so it was only natural that he'd wanted to put a couple of thousand miles of ocean between them, and he wasn't 'deserting' her. She should be very grateful that he was leaving her an allotment, for if she'd had her way Nora wouldn't have got a brass farthing to waste on drink, cigarettes and the cheap tat she wore. And Nora certainly didn't stay in pining for Frank. She was always going out, 'dolled up to the nines' like the cheap trollop she was, Martha had remarked cuttingly.

In the time he had been away Sophie herself had become very busy. Two of Hetty Foster's friends from the church had ordered dresses and Hetty herself had decided she needed a new coat and then a new costume for Easter. Arthur had urged her to place another advertisement, for, as he'd pointed out, she couldn't rely totally on Hetty Foster and her friends for business. As she'd expected, Mrs Henderson hadn't ordered anything further.

The response to her second advert had been very encouraging, probably due to the better weather, and the fact that not only was there still not much choice in the shops but Sophie's prices were very 'affordable', as Lizzie had remarked. She was in fact having difficulty in coping with the orders and had been forced to stay up well after midnight each night for the past two weeks. She had at last concurred with Arthur and Lizzie that it was time to give in her notice at Marsden's.

What was troubling her now was finding suitable lodgings for the amounts of material, trimmings and garments in various stages of completion that had taken over most of her aunt's house – so much so that Uncle Jim had been heard to comment that it was like living in a dress shop. She needed two bedrooms, a kitchen, a living room plus a room suitable for cutting out, sewing and fittings and so far she hadn't been able to find anything.

Hetty had the table set and the tea made. It was a ritual now and one the old lady looked forward to. Sophie was only bringing back a dress for which she'd made a new collar and cuffs, for Hetty felt she had enough new clothes to last her for years, but they had become friends and Sophie rarely missed her Saturday afternoon visit, even though at times it was very brief. On a couple of occasions Maria had accompanied her and once she had taken Bella as Hetty had asked to meet the child, declaring her to be the prettiest little thing she'd ever seen. Sophie had been on tenterhooks lest Bella, who was naturally curious, had broken something, but Bella had been on her best behaviour, most probably overawed by her surroundings.

'Is it to be a brief visit, Sophie? You look tired, you're working too hard, dear,' Hetty chided, noting the dark circles under Sophie's eyes.

'I have been staying up very late to get things finished on time, but I gave in my notice yesterday, so I'll have more time after next week.'

'I'm glad to hear it. You are so gifted that you deserve all your success,' Hetty beamed, passing over a china cup and saucer.

'I've almost paid Arthur back too. All I have to do now is find somewhere to live and work. I'm afraid I've turned Aunty Lizzie's house into something resembling a small clothing factory. Uncle Jim says it's like living in a dress shop.'

Hetty nodded, stirring her tea slowly. 'I've been thinking about that, Sophie. As you once mentioned, this is a big house for just one person – much too big. Would you consider coming to live here, with me? I'd love to have you, we get on so well.'

Sophie was lost for words; she hadn't expected this. 'But there's not just me, Hetty, there's Bella and Maria too. You wouldn't want us crowding in on top of you and Bella can be a bit of a handful sometimes.'

'Nonsense, she's a sweet child. We could turn the big room at the front of the house into your workroom; it gets a lot of sun so the light is good. Then there's the breakfast room, which isn't used, and the dining room – either of those could be used for fittings. Upstairs there are four large bedrooms and the bathroom and then there is the attic, Bella could have that as a playroom for there is only a yard at the back of the house, no garden, I'm afraid, and children need somewhere to play. We aren't far from either the tram or bus stops so your customers could come here instead of you having to traipse all over the city carrying bags and parcels.'

'You really mean it, don't you? You have it all worked out,'

176

Sophie cried. It would be ideal, providing Hetty could adjust to a decidedly more hectic lifestyle and the times when Bella was being far from 'sweet'.

'I've had plenty of time to think about it, Sophie. Oh, please do say yes. I'd love the company, it's so very quiet here – especially during the winter months. Some days I never see a single soul.'

Slowly Sophie nodded, thinking how very fortunate she was that she had found two people who were so willing to help make her ambitions come true. 'Providing I pay you what I would have been prepared to pay in rent.'

Hetty waved her gnarled hands in a gesture of dismissal. 'We can sort all that out later. Now, have you time to see all the rooms or would a visit tomorrow afternoon be more convenient?'

Sophie desperately wanted to see the rest of the house for she'd only ever been in this room and the kitchen, but knew she just didn't have the time. 'Could I come tomorrow, after lunch please? And would it be possible to bring Maria too?'

'Of course. Bring Bella and your aunt as well, I'm sure she'll want to see the type of home you're coming to live in. I know I would if you were part of my family.'

Sophie got up and put her arms around Hetty's slightly rounded shoulders. 'Thank you, Hetty. It's so very kind of you and I do appreciate it. We'll be here at about half past two.'

'I'll take the dust sheets off everything,' Hetty said happily, thinking that from now on there would be no more quiet, empty days and long, lonely evenings, and that after many – far too many – long years a child's laughter would again be heard in this house.

Lizzie was utterly lost for words when Sophie arrived home and told her the news. Both Bella and Billy were out playing with friends but Sophie intended to break the news to her daughter that evening.

'And she wants you to go with us tomorrow, so you can see for yourself what kind of a place it is,' Sophie finished.

'And I can actually have a bedroom all to myself?' Maria cried, delighted at this unheard-of luxury.

Sophie nodded. 'There are four bedrooms, so we can all have one each.' She turned to Katie, who was looking just as startled as her mother. 'And you can have your bedroom to yourself now, Katie.'

'Does this mean that all the dressmaking paraphernalia will be disappearing too?' Jim asked with a twinkle in his eye.

'Yes. You won't have to move scissors or bits of material pinned to a paper pattern or anything else when you want to sit down to read your paper,' Sophie laughed.

Lizzie had regained her composure; of course she'd known that Sophie was looking for somewhere to rent, but there was no denying she was going to miss her nieces and little Bella.

'Most of the rooms have been shut off, things covered up with dust sheets and we'll probably need to move some furniture around,' Sophie said. 'Maybe before we move, Uncle Jim, John and perhaps even Arthur could help us do that. Now I really should go in and tell Arthur the good news, after all it's thanks to him that I met Hetty in the first place,' she reminded them, leaving her aunt, her cousin and her sister excitedly discussing the news.

Arthur was listening to his wireless but seeing Sophie's flushed cheeks and sparkling eyes he switched it off. 'I can see you are excited about something, Sophie. Is it good news?'

She nodded. 'Hetty Foster has asked us to go and live with her. She is all alone in that big house so there's plenty of room for us and for my workrooms. She's asked us to go tomorrow to see around the place and we might have to move some pieces of furniture and if we do I was wondering if you could give Uncle Jim and John a hand? Oh, I have so much to thank you for, Arthur! If it hadn't been for you I never would have been able to leave Marsden's, never would have met Hetty . . .' It all came out in a rush.

Arthur smiled. He was delighted for her but he would miss her. He'd got used to her sitting in his room at her machine each evening. 'I'm delighted for you, Sophie, I really mean that, but I have to say I'll miss you. It just won't be the same in here.'

The following afternoon the little group got off the tram at the less built-up end of Hawthorne Road and Lizzie looked around with approval. Sophie was holding a rather subdued and apprehensive Bella tightly by the hand for the child wasn't at all sure that she wanted to leave her aunt's home and Katie and Billy to go and live in a big, strange house that

179

Lyn Andrews

she remembered being full of things that would break easily. She would have to leave her school and Miss O'Malley and Emily and her other friends but her mam had said she would soon make new ones and that there was a big room at the top of the house that she was to have as a playroom.

Maria was as excited as Sophie, thinking of a proper bathroom and a bedroom of her own – and she also had her own reasons for wanting to move away from Harebell Street.

When they turned into Laurel Road Lizzie noted that there wasn't a soul to be seen even though it was a fine sunny afternoon. No kids playing; no women standing on their doorsteps gossiping. It was very quiet – a bit too quiet for her, she thought, thankful that Billy hadn't wanted to come as well. Billy and his hooligan friends wouldn't be welcomed with open arms in this street.

Arthur had also noted the air of tranquillity and the neatly kept little gardens, and as they approached number five, he thought how pleasant it would be to tend to those rose bushes on a summer evening. Then he dismissed the thought.

'Well, what do you think, Aunty Lizzie?' Sophie asked as she rang the bell.

'I think I'll wait and see inside before I pass judgment,' Lizzie answered succinctly.

It was a big house, bigger than she had imagined it would be, and so different to Harebell Street. It was roomy, certainly, but would it be homely?

Chapter Sixteen

———◆———

AFTER THEY HAD ALL been introduced by Sophie the old lady took them on a tour of the house, and as they moved from room to room Lizzie realised that even though everything had been wrapped in dust sheets, the whole place was in need of a thorough clean. It must have been years since these rooms had seen a duster or a carpet sweeper, she surmised. Perhaps Martha would come to give them a hand?

Sophie had taken one look at the front parlour and decided that it would make an excellent workroom, but that a lot of the heavy, old-fashioned furniture would have to be moved elsewhere. Thick dark green chenille curtains and cream cotton lace ones shut out most of the light so the heavy drapes would have to come down to let in more light. The breakfast room seemed more suitable as a fitting room than the dining room for it was smaller, contained less furniture and would be easier to heat. Also now that there would be four of them sitting down to at least one meal a day together they would need to utilise the dining room.

Lizzie was astounded by the size of the bedrooms and the quality of the furniture, bedspreads and eiderdowns, even though they were a little faded. With a good dusting, some elbow grease applied to the walnut and mahogany furniture, and laundering of the curtains and linen the place would be fit for the gentry, she thought rather enviously. Sophie noted how neat and tidy Hetty's own bedroom was and that the faint perfume of lavender pervaded the air.

In the bathroom Maria gazed at the big enamelled bath with something akin to wonder. It stood on legs and had splendid taps that were brass, albeit in need of a polish. Oh, wouldn't it be heavenly to lie back and soak in a bath like that and have the privacy of this special room? She'd only ever been used to the tin bath that was kept in the yard of her mam's cottage, hung on a nail, which had been brought in and filled with kettles once a week. It was a ritual that was also carried out at Lizzie's. Here there was also a separate washbasin with brass taps, a mahogany stand on which hung big white towels and, wonder of wonders, a flush toilet with a mahogany seat. No more having to go down the yard in all weathers – such luxury!

When they reached the attic, even though Sophie and Hetty enthusiastically pointed out all the advantages of having such a big room to play in, Bella was still very dubious.

'It's dark, Mam, and there isn't much room because it's full of boxes,' she pointed out.

Hetty laughed. 'We'll sort through all the boxes and then put them in the cellar. And it's not dark – look, there's a big window and if you stand on tiptoe you can see right across the rooftops.'

Bella smiled politely and turned to her mother. 'But who will I have to play with, Mam?' she persisted stubbornly, still unable to see why her mam and the old lady thought this room was so great.

'Your new friends from school, of course, and I'm sure Emily would like to come to play sometimes and maybe even Billy and Robbie too, if Aunty Hetty doesn't mind.'

Lizzie raised her eyebrows in horror at the thoughts of the antics her son and Robbie Ryan could get up to up here. They would probably succeed in bringing down the ceiling of the rooms below. The attic too would need a good clean and a fresh coat of distemper to brighten it up.

When they returned to the living room, Hetty Foster announced they were all now going to have tea: Lizzie insisted on helping Sophie's benefactress to prepare it. The kitchen was well equipped, she noticed: there was a gas cooker and shelves covered with green and white checked oilcloth for the pans and dishes; also a sink of the type known as a 'butler's sink' with a wooden draining board, and two mesh-fronted food presses. There was a scullery off the kitchen and a pantry too, and the floor was of red quarry tiles which would only need mopping over to keep clean. Every other room in the house she'd noted was carpeted, a luxury neither she nor any of her neighbours had never experienced.

After tea, when the dishes had all been washed and put away, Sophie, Maria and their aunt asked to go round the house once more to get a better idea of just what needed to be done and what furniture was to be moved, leaving Bella and Arthur with the old lady. Sophie had wisely brought along a bobbin and some coloured wool for Bella's 'French knitting', which was currently the child's favourite occupation; she and Emily were engaged in a competition to see who could make theirs the longest.

Hetty was quite content to sit in an armchair by the fire watching Bella work the wool over the four little pegs, while Arthur studied the numerous leather-bound volumes on the shelves of the large bookcase, which took up most of one wall.

'You have a wonderful collection of literature, Miss Foster. Do you enjoy reading?' he asked, carefully extracting a book and admiring the gilt-edged pages and the gold-embossed lettering on the spine.

'I used to, Mr Chatsworth, but my eyesight isn't what it was, nor is my concentration. I'm rather afraid magazines are my limit these days. My brother Harold loved to read, he collected most of the books. You may borrow that one if you wish. I can see by the way you are handling it that you will take care of it.'

'That's most generous of you. I do use the public library but have to spend quite a lot of time there as many of the books I find of interest are not available to take out on loan.'

Hetty nodded. She liked him; he was obviously a cultured and well-educated man. His speech had no trace of a local accent, or indeed any accent, and his manners were impeccable, as was the way he was dressed. His suit had been pressed, his shirt and winged collar were spotless and his boots highly polished. She wondered why he lodged with Sophie's aunt. 'Do you have no family at all, Mr Chatsworth?'

He seated himself opposite her. 'Not any longer. I . . . I've been a widower for many years. My wife . . . died young and we had no children. I had an older brother but he was killed on the first day of the Somme and of course my parents are long dead. I have one cousin who lives in America, in Vermont. We correspond occasionally, mainly at Christmas.'

Hetty sighed; his was a lonely life too, or so it appeared. 'My brother fought in the Great War, he was at Ypres, but thank God he survived. My dear sister Ada passed away three years ago and I've been alone ever since.'

Arthur smiled at her. 'But not for much longer, Miss Foster. I have to say it's most generous of you to offer Sophie and her little family a home, I know she's been worrying about finding decent rooms. I'm very fond of her; she is a lovely girl who deserves a far better hand than fate has so far dealt her.'

Hetty smiled at him. 'I agree and you recognised her potential and invested in her talent, didn't you, Mr Chatsworth? She told me she could never have managed it without your generosity and your help in wording the advertisements.'

He nodded. 'Please do call me Arthur, and yes, I had a little money put by and wanted to help and she's paid me back – with interest, although I didn't expect or ask for that. I just wanted to give her a chance, a better life than slaving away in a factory all day and then helping her aunt to manage in that cramped, overcrowded house.'

Hetty frowned. 'Arthur . . . er . . . I hope you won't think me impertinent but I'm curious as to why you reside in Mrs Quine's house? It can't be . . . comfortable? You said yourself it's cramped and overcrowded, surely you could find more . . .' She paused, searching for the right word. Mrs Quine was a kind, good-hearted woman and Sophie's aunt and she had no wish to cast aspersions on either the woman or her home.

'The bombing in Liverpool was very extensive, Miss Foster, I'm sure you'll agree. So many families lost their homes that lodgings of any kind were – and still are – hard to find.'

She sighed. 'Yes indeed, we were very fortunate not to be bombed out although Ada and I spent many nights down in the cellar, terrified we wouldn't survive it all. But did you never have a "family" home?'

He looked discomforted. 'Once . . . once I did, but then I was . . . away from where I lived for many years, so I had to let it go.'

Hetty realised she was being discourteous and got up to put more coal on the fire but he was instantly on his feet.

'Let me do that, Miss Foster. That scuttle is much too heavy for you to lift.'

She watched as he expertly banked up the fire and tidied

the hearth, just as Harold had used to do, and she came to a decision. The idea had been forming in her mind as she'd been conversing with him and learning that, like herself, he had no family. But, unlike herself, he had no real home either, just one small, cramped room in an overcrowded house that had few of the basic amenities . . . and he'd been very good to Sophie. 'Arthur, would you . . . would you consider coming with Sophie? To live here, I mean? I . . . it . . . would feel so much *safer* having a man about the place. This area is still quiet but it's not as . . . affluent as it used to be.'

Arthur was astonished and for a few moments he just stared at her, trying to take in the fact that she was offering him a home too, and such a comfortable and pleasant one. 'Miss Foster, I don't know what to say. I never expected . . . I never dreamed . . . but . . . but I will be *delighted* to. You have such a fine, comfortable and spacious home and I'm sure there are numerous ways I can make myself useful. I'm temperate in my habits and I hope well mannered—'

Hetty smiled at him as she interrupted: 'Indeed you are, I wouldn't have asked you otherwise. "Manners maketh the man", poor Ada always used to say, and Sophie has spoken of you often and with affection. And please do stop calling me Miss Foster, it's Hetty and I think we'll get on famously. You put me in mind of Harold, God rest him.'

Lizzie relayed every single detail of the house in Laurel Road to Martha next morning and when she'd finished Martha agreed to go and help with the spring clean, as Lizzie was calling it, wanting to see for herself the luxury in which Sophie, Maria, Bella and, surprisingly, Arthur Chatsworth too would soon be living.

'When do they intend to move in then?' she asked, sipping her tea.

'The weekend after Sophie finishes at Marsden's.'

'Fancy her asking Mr Chatsworth to go too. Mind you, you'll miss his money, Lizzie.'

Lizzie nodded her agreement. 'I will, but we'll manage. I'll miss the help in the house those girls give me too. You can be sure our Katie will revert back to her idle self once they've gone, all she thinks about these days is getting dressed up and going out with Matt Seddon. But we will have more room. Mr Chatsworth's always kept himself to himself, so we may hardly notice he's not there. And I can't blame Sophie, she does need proper workrooms now, her business is going from strength to strength.'

Martha looked thoughtful. 'And at least she'll have moved before our Frank arrives home. I had a postcard from a place called Las Palmas, wherever that is, saying he should be back in Liverpool by the nineteenth, weather permitting.'

Lizzie sighed and nodded. 'Will he be home for long, Martha? Did he say?'

'A week, he thinks. Then he does a short trip before going off for three months again.'

'And I suppose he'll be stopping over there or will he stay with you?' Lizzie jerked her head in the direction of Nellie Richards's house.

Martha shook her head, frowning. Her relationship with Frank was so much better these days but she didn't feel it would be right if he moved back into his former home. 'He can leave his stuff in our house and have a few meals with us too but he'll have to stay over there. He *is* still married to Nora and we don't want any more trouble with her.'

Lizzie pursed her lips, thinking no doubt it wouldn't be much of a homecoming for him. Nora seemed to be out enjoying herself most nights and the Lord alone knew with whom. There were bound to be rows. 'You'll have to tell him Sophie's moved, Martha, but tell him not to be going down there trying to see her. I don't think Hetty Foster would approve, do you?'

'No, I don't, but I don't know if he'll take any notice of me, Lizzie. He hasn't done up to now.'

'Then he might take notice of me. Sophie's getting on with her life, making a success of things, and she doesn't need him upsetting the apple cart or giving flaming Nora any reason to start carrying on. In the name of God, Martha, can you just imagine what Hetty Foster would think if that trollop fetched up on the doorstep yelling abuse about Sophie and your Frank?'

Martha finished her tea, her lips set in a line of determination. 'Leave it to me, Lizzie, I'll do my utmost to keep him away from Laurel Road,' she promised.

The time had just seemed to fly by, Sophie thought as they arrived in Laurel Road with the last of their belongings two

189

weeks later. Her sewing machine and all her things had been transferred by her uncle and cousin John, with the aid of Arthur Chatsworth, during the week, and Lizzie and Katie had helped with their clothes and Bella's toys.

'It's that big you'd get lost,' Katie had muttered on her first visit.

Sophie knew that Frank was due home the day after they moved in, Martha had told her, and although she desperately wanted to see him – she had missed him, missed his smile, his quiet, patient manner and the way he made her feel – she hoped he wouldn't try to visit her here for she'd said nothing to Hetty about him and didn't want to have to try to explain. Hetty had never even been 'walking out' with a young man, as she'd put it, her parents had never allowed it, so how on earth could she expect her to understand how she had fallen in love with a married man? The old lady would be shocked and most probably horrified.

She had plenty to keep her busy and not only her sewing. She had to get Bella settled in her new school and perhaps even invite some of her classmates for tea one evening to break the ice. She had her fitting room to finish rearranging and sorting out for she had a customer coming the day after tomorrow. Arthur was going to put shelves up in an alcove in her workroom to hold her cards of trimmings, boxes of buttons, reels of cotton and paper patterns and she would need to advise him on where to place them. Hetty was insisting on doing all the cooking but Sophie had promised that she would do the shopping as Maria would be out at work all day while she would be working from home. At the weekends Maria had promised to help her with the house-work and the washing and ironing. Yes, there was enough to keep her occupied without having to worry about a visit from Frank or lie awake at night thinking about him. Somehow it had seemed easier to keep her feelings for him under control while he'd been away. Not entirely 'out of sight, out of mind', he could never be that, but the knowledge that thousands of miles of ocean separated them had helped her. But the day after tomorrow he would only be a tram ride away and although she wanted to see him, she just couldn't risk it. After an absence of three months could either of them trust themselves?

Chapter Seventeen

———◆———

THANKFULLY MARTHA PREVAILED, ALTHOUGH not without some strong words, and Sophie did not see Frank during his time at home, and then she heard from Lizzie that he'd sailed again for South Africa after a brief trip to Rotterdam and Hamburg. She also heard from her aunt that there had been frequent rows between Frank and his wife over where Nora went of an evening and with whom. It was not that Frank objected to her going out, he'd told Martha; he couldn't care less about that because it meant he saw little of her, but it was the fact that it was obviously with other men that was so humiliating for him.

'Martha told him not to leave her any money, she just wastes it anyway. Told him to let her "fancy fellas" cough up,' Lizzie had said.

'What did he say?' she'd asked, thinking it rather insensitive of his mother.

'That by law he had to leave an allotment and if he changed it so that it was left to Martha, there would be more rows.'

Sophie had said nothing to that; Frank's time at home seemed to be miserable enough without adding to it.

The weather was getting steadily warmer now that it was nearly May and the evenings were much lighter, she thought as she set the table for the evening meal. She had opened the window of the dining room and the late sunlight streamed in making the rich wood of the furniture glow and picking out the gold edges on the china. They ate in some style these days, she mused, compared to Lizzie's small, crowded kitchen with its deal table, plain gingham cloth and selection of mismatched crockery. Hetty had some beautiful table linen – lace-edged and intricately embroidered – and two complete dinner services of bone china. At first Sophie had had serious misgivings about using it, especially for every day and with Bella, but Hetty had insisted, stating it was much better to use it than have it packed away in boxes gathering dust. Despite the fact that most people thought china delicate, it was in fact very robust and thankfully so far there had been no accidents. Arthur had brought in the first blooms from the little front garden, and she'd arranged the rosebuds in a cut-glass bowl and placed it in the centre of the table.

She smiled to herself as she surveyed her handiwork. It was something of an occasion today. It was Maria's birthday, she was nineteen and Hetty had planned a special meal and had insisted on making a cake, although there hadn't been any sugar for the icing.

'I'm so sorry, Maria, about the icing sugar. I wanted it to be a really special cake.' Hetty had been so disappointed when she'd discussed it with Maria.

'Aunty Hetty, it won't matter to me that it's not covered in a layer of royal icing. It's the thought that counts,' Maria had smiled. 'And it's the first time for years that I've not made my own cake, so you see it will be very special indeed.'

'Oh, I do hope it will come up to your standard, Maria, Sophie has told me that your baking skills are quite exceptional,' Hetty had said anxiously, wondering now if she had done the right thing in suggesting she make a cake at all.

Maria had laughed, but not unkindly. 'I think Sophie has been exaggerating a little, Aunty Hetty. I like baking and my pastry is light and my cakes . . . passable but certainly not what you'd call "exceptional". And it's been quite a long time since I've had the time to bake.'

Hetty had been relieved. 'Did you never think of becoming a confectioner, Maria? Celebration cakes for weddings and christenings are always in demand and usually quite expensive.'

Maria had shaken her head. 'No, I don't honestly think I'd be good enough to do things like that and I don't think I'd have the patience either. All that trelliswork and flowers and bows must take hours and hours and of course icing sugar has been almost impossible to get since before the war.'

Hetty had nodded and smiled at her. 'Which takes us back to where this conversation started.'

Maria had smiled back. 'So, no more worrying about it, Aunty Hetty.'

Sophie had bought her sister a silver filigree bracelet to mark the occasion of this, the first birthday Maria had celebrated in Liverpool. It wasn't new. She'd bought it in a pawnbroker's shop; it was an unclaimed pledge but Arthur said she had chosen wisely for there was no tax on second-hand jewellery and therefore she'd got better value for her hard-earned money. Hetty had given her a little box to put it in and she'd wrapped it nicely. A card had arrived in the lunchtime post from Sarah and she had propped it up against the bowl of rosebuds. Both she and Maria missed their mother. They corresponded regularly but it wasn't the same, and she had promised herself that at some time in the next few months she would try to make the ferry trip home. She smiled to herself. She still had the 'island' mentality. People who lived outside Douglas would often consider the journey to the capital a long way to travel and when they moved across to the mainland they seldom visited their former homes frequently.

She knew that both Hetty and Arthur had bought Maria gifts too. Bella had made her a lovely card and had carefully written 'Happy Birthday Aunty Maria' on it, and she also had a pretty handkerchief to give her aunt. She wondered if Ben Seddon had bought her sister anything; he'd bought her that nice little brooch at Christmas.

Sophie turned as Arthur came into the room. He never came to the table in shirt sleeves and braces as her Uncle Jim did but always wearing a jacket and tie. In fact she'd never seen him looking anything but neat and tidy. She smiled at him, thinking how well they'd all settled in here, even Bella, who had quickly made friends at her new school and was often asked out for tea. Emily came once a fortnight on a Saturday to play and Billy too had been a couple of times, despite the fact that Lizzie had been decidedly apprehensive.

For a good part of the day she was in her workroom but she knew Arthur often sat with Hetty. They got on well and seemed to have quite a lot in common, although she'd noticed he would never be drawn on his background. He had once let it slip that he'd worked for a firm of chartered accountants but not in Liverpool.

'The table looks lovely, Sophie. I thought I'd put my gift to Maria beside her place setting, a little surprise,' he said rather bashfully.

'Thank you and it's very thoughtful of you, Arthur. I know she isn't expecting anything from either you or Hetty.'

'I know but . . . but I've come to look on you both and Bella, and of course Hetty, as . . . family.'

Sophie smiled at him, before tweaking a table napkin she judged to be a little misplaced. 'We do all get on well, don't we?'

He nodded. 'And now that the weather is improving I'm going to suggest that I take Hetty on a few outings. She doesn't get out as much as I'm sure she'd like to. Perhaps we'll go over to New Brighton on the ferry or on the train to Southport.'

'Or on a day trip if she feels up to it, to Llandudno or even Douglas. In fine weather it's a lovely sail and they have some very nice hotels along the promenade where you can get lunch or tea,' she informed him.

'Perhaps we could all go one day, Sophie. Do you never wish to go home – for a visit?'

'I have been thinking about it, Arthur, it would be nice for Bella to see her Granny Sarah again and for us to see Mam. We'll see but I won't mention it to Bella in case we don't get the time.'

Maria was quite overcome by the fuss that was made of her and was delighted with her gifts.

'Oh, Hetty, this is lovely!' she cried upon opening the old lady's gift of a pure silk scarf in three different shades of blue. She draped it tastefully around her neck. Arthur (at Hetty's suggestion) had bought her a pair of gloves and Maria carefully stroked the soft cream leather as she tried them on. 'I'll save them for "best", Arthur. I've never had a pair of real leather gloves before, thank you.'

Arthur smiled with satisfaction while Maria enthused over Bella's card and the lace-edged handkerchief.

'Oh, Sophie! This must have cost a pretty penny, it's silver,' Maria exclaimed as she took the bracelet from its box. She had no expensive jewellery, just a few pairs of cheap earrings and a couple of strands of equally cheap beads and of course the brooch Ben had given her. She held it out to her sister. 'Fasten it on, I'll wear it tonight.'

'Are you going out with Ben?' Sophie enquired for Maria didn't seem to see as much of him lately, although she knew Katie was out with his brother Matt two or three times a week. She hoped Maria wasn't giving up on Ben as there still hadn't been any word from Hans Bonhoeffer and she thought there never would be.

Maria frowned as she nodded. 'I told him my birthday wasn't anything special but he insisted. He's taking me to the cinema. I said I'd meet him in town to save him coming all the way here to pick me up.'

Sophie looked across at Hetty, who smiled and nodded. Ben had indeed called twice for Maria and the old lady had approved of him. Privately, Arthur had told her that someone with Maria's looks and manners could do better than Ben Seddon but she hadn't agreed, thinking Ben was far more suitable than a poor farmer whom most people would consider an enemy.

There were cards from their mother, their Aunt Lizzie and from Katie, all of which Maria read out, and then Hetty brought in the cake and Bella helped her aunt blow out the token nine candles, it having been completely impossible to procure nineteen. In fact the ones Sophie had managed to obtain were all of different colours and sizes.

Sophie insisted that tonight she would do the washing up, helped by Bella, for Hetty had prepared the meal. Maria was to concentrate on getting herself ready to go out.

Maria decided to wear the cream linen costume Sophie had made her for Easter. It was very smart and made her look very grown up, she thought. She had a cream short-sleeved jumper and she'd wear the lovely silk scarf around her neck, the blue would set it off, and of course she had her new leather gloves. It was a pity she didn't have a new handbag or shoes but her black ones would just have to do. You couldn't have everything, she told herself firmly. She was saving up for them. She fingered the bracelet; it was so good of Sophie to buy her such a lovely thing and she'd treasure it always.

She knew Ben would also have bought her something and she wished he hadn't. Ever since they'd moved here she'd tried to cool their relationship. She still couldn't forget Hans and she'd hoped against hope that she would hear from him, that he would remember it was her birthday. He knew when it was for she'd once told him and he'd said he would never forget it because it was his mother's birthday too. She pushed aside the feelings of disappointment and hurt; everyone else had been so kind and thoughtful.

Ben was waiting for her outside the cinema and she saw the admiration in his eyes as he caught sight of her.

'Happy Birthday, Maria,' he greeted her, kissing her on the cheek and taking her arm. 'You look really gorgeous,' he added.

She smiled at him, thinking he was a thoroughly nice boy and that it was such a pity she wasn't in love with him and never would be.

He paid for good seats and after they were shown to them

by the usherette and settled in them he handed her a small box. Her heart plummeted for it looked like a box that would contain a ring and she prayed it wasn't for she just couldn't accept it. Thankfully, when she opened it she found it contained a pair of silver earrings. 'These are lovely, Ben, but you really shouldn't have spent so much on me. You don't earn a fortune.'

He looked a little embarrassed. 'I . . . I've been saving up, Maria. I wanted to get you something special.'

She didn't have time to reply for at that moment the lights went down and silence descended as the evening's programme commenced with the Pathé News.

In the interval she put the earrings on and he admired them, thinking it had been well worth the small sacrifices he'd made to save up for them. His mam had remarked that he was mad spending so much money on her, it wasn't as if they were even courting steadily or engaged. He'd wanted to say he hoped that by Christmas they might be engaged for he intended to ask her tonight but he'd said nothing, his mam wasn't known for her tact. In fact he'd heard his da often say she had a mouth 'like a parish oven'.

'There's something I want to ask you, Maria, later . . .' he whispered as the lights dimmed.

His words had filled Maria with such apprehension that she didn't really take much notice of the film. She had a good idea what it was he was going to ask her and she was struggling to find words that would not disappoint him too much while at the same time not build up his hopes. She couldn't commit herself, she *couldn't*. Not while there was the slightest chance that she would hear from Hans.

They decided to walk to the terminus at the Pier Head as it was a fine evening and the film hadn't finished too late. It would give her time to try to explain, she thought miserably, for she really didn't want to hurt him.

'You know I really do . . . like you, Maria. Well, it's more than just "like" . . .' he started rather awkwardly.

'I know and I do like you too, Ben. I . . . I enjoy your company, you are thoughtful, generous and—'

'And I've got a steady job too, Maria,' he added quickly. It was something that counted for a lot in this city. 'What . . . what I really want to say is that I . . . I love you and I want to . . . to marry you – one day, when I've saved up enough. I wouldn't expect you to live with Mam, you'd want a place of your own . . . *our* own. If you say you will, we could get engaged at Christmas, Maria, with a ring and everything.' It all came out in a rush and not quite in the romantic way he'd wanted it to but he wasn't all that good with words, he knew that.

Maria stopped walking and turned to look at him, seeing a shy and rather tongue-tied boy who'd just offered her his heart. She bit her lip. How was she going to turn him down without breaking his heart? 'Oh, Ben, I don't know what to say! You know I like you, I like you very much but . . . but I don't love you.'

'Couldn't you . . . try, Maria?' he pleaded.

She shook her head sadly. 'It isn't that simple, Ben. I might

202

– in time – if . . . if . . . there wasn't someone I know who might one day come . . . back to me.'

'You never said there was anyone else,' he said, the pain evident in his voice.

'I . . . I didn't think you were so serious, Ben.'

'Who is he? Where is he?' he demanded, feeling increasingly upset and humiliated.

'Someone I met on the island. He went back . . . back to where he came from. It's a long way away and I . . . I haven't heard from him since. It's been a year now.'

'Then you might never hear from him again, Maria.'

'No, I might not.' It hurt her to say it; it hurt her to even think it.

'Then . . . then . . . why . . . ?' He didn't understand why she was turning him down. Couldn't she see she might be wasting her life waiting for this bloke, whoever he was, to come back from wherever it was he'd gone to? He might even now be married to someone else.

She just shook her head. She couldn't bring herself to say 'because I love him and will never love anyone else, no matter what'.

He took her hand. 'It doesn't change the way I feel about you, Maria. I love you and I'd still like to marry you. We could make a go of it, I know we could.'

She swallowed hard, fighting back the tears. She knew she should put a stop to this now, it wasn't being at all fair to him, but she just couldn't. The words she knew she should say were just too hard and cold, they would cause him too much pain. 'I can't promise anything, please don't push me to say things I'll regret. I don't want to hurt you, Ben, you must believe that. I never wanted to hurt you . . .'

He seized on her words. 'I won't push you, Maria, I promise. I'll wait, wait until you feel . . . until you're ready.'

She didn't reply but as they walked the rest of the way in silence she had the feeling that he really hadn't understood how she felt. But was she being foolish? Was Sophie right? Was she wrong to turn Ben down, waiting for some word from a man who had gone out of her life all those months ago and who might never return?

Chapter Eighteen

AUGUST THAT YEAR WAS very hot and even though Sophie had opened all the windows, the stifling heat seemed trapped in the very fabric of the house. She had been kept busy all summer as people wanted summer dresses and light jackets made and her list of clients kept increasing as her work was highly recommended. She had also made two special outfits for customers whose daughters were getting married but who had not been able to afford the prices charged by the high-class establishments in Liverpool and had despaired of finding anything 'special' enough with their coupons in the less expensive shops. Both women had been delighted and had promised to recommend her to friends with weddings in the offing.

Frank had returned home in July and on a visit to Lizzie's

Sophie had bumped into him as she'd turned the corner into Harebell Street. Her heart had turned over; he'd looked so handsome in his uniform, his skin tanned by days spent in the sun and by the warm salt breezes.

'Sophie!' he'd cried and before she could say a word he'd hugged her and kissed her.

She'd pulled quickly away from him although the feelings that embrace had evoked had made it so very hard. 'You look well, Frank. I'm glad to see you,' she'd stammered, trying to compose herself.

'Do you really mean that?'

'Of course I do. Your mam must be glad to have you back home too, is that where you are going?'

'For a bit of supper, although I wish I could move back there,' he'd said, falling into step beside her.

'I'm going to Lizzie's,' she'd informed him. She'd tried to keep the conversation light and brief but she could see he wanted to linger and in truth so did she. But then Nora had emerged from Nellie's house in a gaudy, flowered cotton dress, which made her quickly hasten towards her aunt's house where the front door stood open and brought the fleeting meeting to an abrupt end.

True to his word, Arthur had taken Hetty out. They'd taken the train to Southport and the ferry across to New Brighton, and they'd gone to concerts in the Tower Ballroom. They'd even ventured as far as Hoylake on the other side of the Wirral peninsula. Hetty really did seem to enjoy these outings, Sophie thought, although they tired her; but she had colour now in her cheeks, which hadn't been there before.

Today they'd gone down early to the Liverpool Landing Stage where the *St Tudno* was tied up, taking aboard passengers for a day trip to Llandudno. It was so warm that the sail up the Mersey and around the coast of North Wales would be a pleasant relief, Arthur had stated. They intended to have lunch at the Imperial Hotel followed by a gentle stroll along the sea front before returning to the little steamer for the return trip. Nothing too strenuous, he'd promised Sophie.

It was a blessing they were out for the day, she thought, for Billy was coming after lunch, mainly to give his long-suffering mother a bit of peace and quiet. The houses in Harebell Street were like ovens, Lizzie had declared, even though all the windows were open and she kept both front and back doors wide open all day and most of the evening. It was the range; it had to be kept in for cooking and hot water – Sophie should be very thankful that they had a gas cooker – and as it was the school holidays Billy was driving her to distraction with his antics. So Sophie had insisted that he come and spend Sunday afternoon in Laurel Road.

'You must be mad, Sophie, having to put up with those two in this weather,' Maria had declared as she got ready to go out too. She was taking a trip on the ferry with one of her friends from work; it was just too hot to go anywhere else and at least on the river there was a bit of a breeze. These days Katie was too involved with Matt to be much company and the last thing she wanted was for her cousin to suggest that they take the trip with Matt and Ben. She still saw Ben but far less frequently for she didn't want to raise his hopes, it just wasn't fair. In fact she regretted now that she hadn't been totally honest with him and told him she could never marry him, but she just hated hurting anyone.

Sophie had debated taking Bella and Billy to the seaside but, as Maria had pointed out, everywhere would be absolutely packed and knowing Billy, he'd probably go and get lost, so she'd decided against it. Besides, she wanted to have a meal ready for when Hetty and Arthur returned for they'd both be tired and hungry.

She had some hemming to do so she'd sent the two children upstairs to play with the promise that they could have some ice cream later on, providing they behaved. She had the beginnings of a headache but put it down to the oppressive heat.

At three o'clock she gave them the promised ice cream, having grown tired of Bella's trips up- and downstairs to beg for the treat. Her headache hadn't lifted and she'd had to lay aside her work so it was with some relief that she heard the first dull rumble of thunder. Thank heaven for that, a good storm might just clear the air, she thought before remembering that Maria and Arthur and Hetty were out. As she closed her eyes and rested her head against the back of the chair she hoped they would all be able to find shelter of some kind. Perhaps Hetty and Arthur might even miss it being in Llandudno until five o'clock.

*

Billy and Bella were bored. They had finished the ice cream and were tired of playing games and now it was raining heavily so there was no possibility of going out.

'There's not much to do around here, Bella, is there? I mean at home we used to play out in the street or on the bombsite,' Billy complained, gazing morosely out of the attic window at the rooftops down which a deluge was pouring.

'No one plays in the street here, Billy,' Bella stated.

'That's just what I mean – it's dead boring.'

Bella pursed her lips, thinking her cousin used to be more fun when they lived in Harebell Street; all he did now was complain.

Billy suddenly had an idea and brightened up. 'I know, Bella, we'll explore. I bet there's rooms in this house you've never been in; we might even find some treasure.'

Bella was doubtful. 'What kind of treasure, Billy?'

'I don't know, secret papers, code books – stuff like that.' Billy ran a hand through his hair, leaving it sticking up in tufts. 'Come on, there's nothing else to do.'

They decided to start in the cellar after first having ascertained that Sophie was busy in her workroom, although to their surprise they found her dozing in her chair and quietly tiptoed away. The cellar proved to be a big disappointment for all they found were boxes of dishes and ornaments that Hetty and Sophie had packed away.

'Where shall we try next?' Bella asked as they came back upstairs, their hands liberally coated with dust, some of which had also transmitted itself to Billy's face. 'There's just sewing stuff in Mam's room and I know there's no treasure in the living room or dining room and only pans and stuff in the kitchen. Aunty Maria and Aunty Hetty wouldn't have any code books or stuff and neither has Mam.'

'What about Mr Chatsworth's room? I bet he's got loads of secret papers. Mam said he would never say what he did for a job or even where he came from, I bet he was a secret agent or something during the war.' Billy was quite taken by the idea of the mysterious Arthur Chatsworth being some kind of spy.

Bella wasn't too sure. 'I don't think we should go looking in Uncle Arthur's room, it's private. Mam wouldn't like it.'

'Don't be a scaredy cat! Anyway, she won't know, she's asleep and we'll be very quiet,' Billy urged.

Bella had never been in Mr Chatsworth's bedroom before and looked around curiously as Billy quietly closed the door behind them. There was a bed, two wardrobes, a tall chest of drawers and an easy chair. There was a big plant in a pot on a stand, a small bookcase on top of which were some ornaments and in the bay window there was a desk, which she thought was an odd thing to have in a bedroom.

Billy too had noticed it. 'Why's he got a desk in his bedroom, Bella?' he whispered.

She shrugged, not really interested and feeling uneasy at being in here. 'I don't know, maybe he writes a lot of letters.'

'Who to? I bet he really is a secret agent.' Billy was convinced now and crossed to the desk. He began to open the drawers. 'I bet he's got a special box somewhere where he keeps his code books. He might even have a gun,' he said, rifling through the contents, which seemed to comprise mainly of notepads, envelopes and dictionaries.

Bella was losing interest; she didn't honestly believe that Uncle Arthur was any kind of agent, secret or otherwise.

Billy was still engrossed in his search for the elusive 'treasure' and had piled a sheaf of papers from one of the drawers on to the top of the desk. Also on the top of the desk was a heavy, old-fashioned brass stand that contained two inkpots and a sort of blotting pad with a handle. There were two pens as well, one shaped like a quill. It was pretty and as Bella reached to pick it up her arm caught a large coloured glass paperweight. It fell off the desk, crashing on to the wooden boards of the bay where the carpet didn't reach.

They both stiffened and Billy stared at his cousin in horror. 'What did you go and do that for?'

Bella's face crumpled. 'I told you we shouldn't come in here and go rooting through Uncle Arthur's things. Mam will kill us!'

Billy made a grab at the papers and was frantically trying to stuff them back into the drawer when Sophie appeared, looking very annoyed.

'What on earth are you two doing in here? Get down those stairs this instant and the pair of you can apologise to Uncle Arthur when he gets back. This is his room where he is entitled to keep all his private things. Bella Teare, I'm shocked and surprised at you, you know better than to do something like this. I am very cross with you both and so will Uncle Arthur be. Now go down at once!'

The two miscreants fled, leaving Sophie shaking her head in disbelief and wondering just how she was going to explain this escapade to Arthur, for he valued his privacy greatly.

She bent and picked up the paperweight and then started to retrieve some of the documents that had fallen on the floor when Billy had tried to stuff them back into the drawer. The black lettering of the heading on one caught her eye and despite herself she began to read it. As she read, the colour slowly drained from her cheeks, her hands began to shake and she collapsed to the floor, leaning back against the desk. It couldn't be true! It just *couldn't*! But it was, this document proved it. Arthur Chatsworth had been in prison for fifteen years. That was the sentence he'd served for the crime he'd been found guilty of: manslaughter. She sat staring at the words, which now seemed to blur together. It all fell into place now: why he valued his privacy; his reluctance to talk about his past life; the reason he'd not been in the forces, the Home Guard or Civil Defence during the war; the reason he'd been forced to lodge with Lizzie.

She let the document fall as she tried to remember the odd things he had told them about himself. He had no family, just a cousin in Vermont whom he only wrote to at Christmas. He had been a widower for many years, his wife having died young. He'd lived with Lizzie for four years and now lived here with herself, Maria, Bella and Hetty – and they'd not known that he'd *killed* someone.

She fought down the panic and tried to think more rationally. He was an educated man, hadn't he said he'd worked for a chartered accountant? As long as she'd known him he'd always been quiet, well mannered, generous and thoughtful. He'd even lent her the money to start her business. She gathered up the papers and put them back and closed the drawer. She realised that she would have to confront him; there was nothing else she could do. She had to find out what had happened and then . . . then what?

Chapter Nineteen

SOPHIE HAD TAKEN BILLY home later that afternoon, accompanied by a penitent and subdued Bella, and to Billy's profound relief nothing was said about the matter to Lizzie. If it had been Billy knew there would have followed a severe telling-off from his mam and possibly chastisement by his da. He'd never seen Sophie so annoyed, although when she'd come downstairs she was very quiet.

By the time Arthur and Hetty returned Sophie had sent Bella up to bed and had laid out corned beef, tomatoes, lettuce, cucumber and bread and butter in the dining room for, despite the storm, it was still sultry and the last thing she'd felt like doing was cooking.

Hetty, however, noticed that she was preoccupied and looked rather pale and enquired if anything was wrong.

'No, it's just that it has been a rather trying afternoon, so hot and then with the storm,' Sophie replied.

'Thank goodness we missed it; we were quite astonished when we got back to Liverpool to hear about it. We had fine weather all the way,' Hetty informed her.

Thankfully the old lady retired early, worn out by the exertions of the day. Maria only dashed in and – after hastily changing out of her wet clothes, having not been as fortunate as Hetty – went out again with her friend Mavis.

Summoning up her courage Sophie sat down in the chair opposite Arthur, who had stated he was going to read the newspaper for half an hour before retiring as he hadn't had chance so far today to catch up on current events.

'Arthur, there is something I . . . I have to speak to you about,' she began hesitantly, dreading these few next minutes.

He folded the paper and laid it on a side table. 'It must be important Sophie, you look rather troubled. What's wrong?'

She nodded. 'The children got rather bored this afternoon and . . . and I'm afraid they went into your room and when I found them . . .' She paused and took a deep breath. '. . . they'd taken some documents from one of the desk drawers and I couldn't help but . . .' She began to twist her hands together nervously, afraid to look at him.

She heard his sharp intake of breath and bit her lip, wondering if he would become angry and start shouting or . . . worse. The seconds seemed to stretch into eternity before he at last spoke.

'So, you found out, Sophie.'

She looked up, surprised by his quiet, regretful tone, which was devoid of any anger. 'I . . . I couldn't believe it. I still can't.'

He nodded sadly. 'I'm afraid it's true. Did . . . did the children . . . ?'

'No. No, they don't know. But what happened, Arthur?'

'I'd better tell you the whole sorry story, Sophie. I should have told you long before this but . . . but I was afraid to and I was so ashamed.'

She sat in total silence as he told her how as a young man he'd worked hard and had secured a good position with a reputable firm of accountants in Manchester, and of how he'd met and married Marjorie, his wife. She'd come from quite a well-off family and they'd had a lovely home in one of the quiet suburbs but Marjorie had liked a good time. She was what had been called in those days a 'bright young thing' and she hadn't seen any reason why marriage should alter that way of life; she hadn't been prepared to sit at home just being a housewife. She wore all the latest fashions, was very attractive and enjoyed going out to the theatre, supper parties and then on to fashionable nightclubs. She always insisted on staying out late and eventually both his work and his bank balance had started to suffer. Consequently there had even been some doubt about his continued employment with Asquith and Mason.

He'd tried to reason with her, pointing out that if he lost his job their lifestyle would suffer drastically, but she'd refused to listen and then heated arguments had followed.

Finally she had insisted on going out alone, saying she had plenty of friends who enjoyed her company and who would see her safely home. And indeed she did have a wide circle of friends and so she'd got her own way. His life had suddenly been turned upside down and had become more and more intolerable, but he'd been at a loss as to how to repair their increasingly deteriorating relationship.

Then he'd come home unexpectedly early one evening suffering from the sudden onset of a digestive upset. He'd told her that morning that he would be working late and he had found her with someone else: a man who had instantly fled and whom she had sworn that she barely knew; he was little more than an acquaintance. He had just called on her, there had been no assignation and in fact he'd forced himself on her, which was why he'd left so quickly. Arthur hadn't believed her. It was so obviously a pack of lies. There had been a terrible row. She had called him a dull, pen-pushing bore who didn't know the meaning of the word 'enjoyment' and had accused him of ruining her life. Then when he forbade her to go out to nightclubs alone in future she had just laughed at him and he'd lost his temper. He'd lashed out at her, something he had never thought himself capable of doing. She had recoiled, tripped over a footstool and fallen, fallen awkwardly, and hit her head on the corner of the fireplace. He'd been horrified, unable to believe that she wasn't breathing. He'd never meant to strike her; let alone *kill* her. It was a terrible, terrible accident but he'd struck her. He himself had gone for the police when he'd realised she was dead. It had been in all the newspapers and there had been an outcry for things like that just didn't happen in that quiet, respectable suburb, and then . . . well, she knew the rest.

'At least I was convicted of manslaughter, not murder. I would have been hanged for that, but it was proved that I never intended to kill her. So you see, Sophie, why I didn't want anyone to know. Why I had to lodge with your aunt when I was released. I couldn't go back to Manchester, I had no home, no job and no hope of employment, and I still live with the guilt and shame. I . . . I served my sentence in Walton Jail and those years are ones I have since tried to put out of my mind; they were a living hell. There were times during the bombing when I prayed the jail would receive a direct hit and I would be put out of my misery. I paid dearly for my crime, Sophie, and I still regret her death bitterly.'

Sophie nodded slowly. 'It must all have been terrible for you, Arthur.' She meant it, it was obviously so out of character for him to raise his hand against anyone. And to have to spend fifteen long years locked up with hardened criminals – it was a wonder he had survived it all. 'Was it hard when . . . when you came out?'

'The world had changed so much, Sophie. A terrible war had been fought; cities were in ruins; thousands of good men dead. And thousands more wounded and crippled. Old ways, manners and customs had gone. I felt lost, disorientated and very, very alone. Oh, I wasn't short of money, for my father had died just before I went to jail, which compounded my guilt and despair for I'm sure the shock and the shame hastened his death, but he had left me a small legacy which was invested and which continued to earn interest but . . . but with my background I knew it would be hard to find lodgings. Eventually I found Mrs Quine and I was grateful.' He smiled ruefully. 'She used to think it very odd of me to spend so much time just walking the city streets but it was a luxury for me to wander wherever it suited me. I could please myself after years of having my life regimented.'

Sophie nodded again, understanding what he meant. How could she even have thought – however fleetingly – that he was a violent criminal?

'And what now, Sophie? Will you tell Hetty? Will you both ask me to leave?'

'No, Arthur, I won't tell Hetty, it would upset her dreadfully. She thinks very highly of you. As you said, it was a terrible, tragic accident for which you've more than paid. You were provoked, your life had become unbearable and . . . and I have to say this, I think she was treating you very badly. This is your home now; I couldn't turn you out and I have so much to be grateful to you for.' She got up and went and put her arms around him. He would never harm any of them, she was certain of it. Look how he took care of Hetty, look how concerned he'd been for her own feelings and her future. 'This is your home and we are your family now, Arthur. It will never be mentioned again – ever.'

'Thank you, Sophie, and God bless you,' he whispered with a catch in his voice.

She smiled at him. 'Although you have to admit that we are something of a strange "family". A widow with a child, a young girl who doesn't really know what she wants, a lonely old lady . . .'

'And an ex-convict. A strange collection indeed, Sophie,' he finished, but the sheer relief that filled him made the fact that she'd included him in this odd family a blessing indeed, one he'd never expected or looked for.

Chapter Twenty

———◆———

IT WAS ALMOST IMPOSSIBLE to believe that over a year had passed since they'd come to Liverpool, Sophie thought as she walked back from seeing Bella to school that cold, blustery late November morning. So much had changed; so much had happened in that time. Thanks to Hetty Foster they now had a very comfortable home; her business was successful and steady and she had a small but growing amount in a Post Office Savings account, Bella was doing well at school and was popular with her peers. And yet some things hadn't changed at all.

She frowned, thinking about Maria, who was still eating her heart out for Hans Bonhoeffer from whom there had still been no word. She continued to urge her sister to forget him, to go out with other young men, if not Ben Seddon whom Maria was trying to keep at arm's length. Her sister did go out quite a lot, usually with her friend Mavis, and Sophie knew she was never short of partners at the dances she went to, but Maria stubbornly refused all offers to be taken out by her admirers.

The wind tore at Sophie's beret and she pulled it further down over her forehead and wrapped her scarf more securely around her neck. Winter had come with a vengeance; it was bitterly cold, she thought. She knew Frank was home and she wondered if, after months spent in the tropics, he felt the cold more keenly. That was something else that hadn't changed, she mused sadly. She still loved him, and even though she saw little of him she missed him. Yet she had to try to suppress those feelings and it was so hard. Only to Arthur did she confide how unhappy she was at times and how lonely. It was strange that even though she was surrounded by people there were times when she felt so alone and Arthur understood that. No mention had ever been made about his past since that August day.

Christmas was again approaching; December was almost upon them and she remembered how enjoyable last Christmas had been for them all, even Frank, thanks in part to Mrs Sayle's goose. She sighed, things were slowly getting better – very slowly – but no doubt she would have to prevail upon Maude Sayle's generosity again this year for she was planning a real 'family' meal, mindful of the many lonely and miserable Christmases Arthur and Hetty must have spent. She was determined that this year was definitely going to be very different for them both.

When she arrived home it was to find she had a visitor: her aunt was sitting with Hetty by the fire in the living room drinking tea.

'It's very early for a visit, Aunty Lizzie, is something wrong?' For a moment she thought that Lizzie had come to impart some news of Frank, hopefully nothing bad.

Lizzie beamed at her. 'I thought I'd come down first thing to tell you the news.'

Sophie looked interested. 'It's something good, judging by the look on your face.'

'Our Katie and Matt Seddon are going to get engaged at Christmas; he's been saving up for the ring. He came round last night to see Jim, asked him proper, like, for his permission to marry her, seeing as she's only eighteen.'

'Oh, I'm delighted for Katie,' Sophie cried. She was but she wondered how his brother Ben would take the news, since he had still not given up on Maria.

'So, we've decided to have a bit of a family get-together for them. Nothing fancy, mind, it being Christmas, and it's going to be as hard to get stuff this year as it was last. But we'd like you all to come on Christmas Night for a drink to celebrate.'

'Won't it be a bit crowded with Matt's family and yours without us as well?' Sophie asked as Hetty poured her a cup of tea. She was still thinking of Ben and Maria.

'And Martha and Pat and young Robbie – Frank won't be

home for Christmas this year so Martha told me – but we'll manage, Sophie. It will only be for a couple of hours. You will come, Miss Foster? And Mr Chatsworth too?'

Hetty smiled, although she looked a little dubious, while Sophie felt a pang of regret that Frank would be away. It would have been wonderful to have spent a couple of hours in his company even surrounded by family and friends. It was better than not seeing him at all before he sailed again.

'We'd be delighted to, Mrs Quine, just for an hour, and I'm sure I can speak for Arthur as well,' Hetty replied courteously.

'Where is Mr Chatsworth?' Lizzie asked.

'Gone out for his morning constitutional. He likes to take a brisk walk first thing and usually buys his newspaper on the way back,' Hetty informed her.

'He must be mad in this weather. There's a real "lazy" wind coming off the river this morning. It cuts right through you instead of going around you.' Lizzie shivered as she sipped her tea.

Hetty smiled again. 'You do have some quaint sayings, Mrs Quine.'

Lizzie nodded and then looked thoughtful. 'You remember last year, Sophie, how you got the kids to write to Santa?'

'I do, it kept them quiet for ages,' Sophie replied, thinking of the hours Frank had spent making the fort and the dolls' house.

'Well, our Billy was so delighted that he got what he asked for that he's already started writing again and this year he

226

wants a scooter no less! Where that lad gets these ideas from I don't know. Has Bella said what she wants?'

Sophie shook her head. 'Not yet but no doubt we'll hear soon enough. I'll keep my eyes and ears open for a second-hand scooter, Aunty Lizzie.'

'You're a good girl, Sophie,' Lizzie said, getting to her feet. 'Well, I'd better get back; those dishes won't wash themselves – more's the pity. Oh, I nearly forgot.' Lizzie delved into her pocket. 'This came to our house in the post yesterday. It's for Maria. It's got a Manx stamp on it but it can't be from your mam.'

Sophie took it from her, scanning the handwriting. It wasn't from Sarah and she wondered who on the island was writing to her sister. One of her friends perhaps?

As Sophie saw her aunt out Hetty thought how much she was looking forward to Christmas this year. Sophie had said they would have a big tree in the dining room for there was plenty of room for it in there and that she and Bella would make the decorations to go on it. She was going to try to get some tinsel too. It would look very good when they had their Christmas lunch. They would decorate the hall and this room as well; there was never a shortage of holly. Sophie had already started hoarding items of food for the occasion and she'd said that Bella's face on Christmas morning was well worth the very early start to the day. Yes, Christmas this year would be so different to the usual rather cheerless and lonely days she'd spent over the years, especially since Ada had died. She would have to start to think about gifts for everyone, something else that was a new experience for her, and of course there would have to be an engagement present for Katie Quine, propriety demanded it even if she didn't attend the 'get-together'. The invitation had been extended and the girl could not be slighted. She'd discuss it all with both Sophie and Arthur, she thought happily.

All day the letter intrigued Sophie. No one, apart from their mother, ever wrote to Maria and whoever it was didn't know that they'd been living in Laurel Road for months. Nor could they have got Lizzie's address from Sarah for her mam would have told them they'd moved. She'd examined it carefully but there was no clue in the handwriting. The envelope itself was a cheap one, the sort you could buy any-where, and it was postmarked 'Peel' two days ago. Eventually she'd sighed and told herself she would just have to wait until Maria got in from work to enlighten her.

Bella had come home from school saying she had a sore throat and indeed Sophie thought she also had a temperature and so all thoughts of Maria's letter disappeared in her concern for her child. It wasn't until she'd got Bella settled in bed after giving her half an aspirin, followed with a mug of honey dissolved in hot water, that she even gave the letter another thought.

'I wouldn't send her to school tomorrow, Sophie, if she's still feeling like this, it's so cold,' Hetty advised, looking concerned as Sophie came back downstairs.

'I won't. If she's no better I'll take her to the doctor.' Catching sight of the envelope propped up on the mantelpiece she picked it up and handed it to her sister. 'Oh, Maria, Aunty Lizzie brought this round this morning, it was delivered to their house.'

Maria looked puzzled. She hadn't noticed it and Hetty had been so full of the news of Katie's forthcoming engagement that she hadn't mentioned a letter. She opened it, noting the stamp and wondering who on earth it was from, and then she uttered a cry of delight. 'Sophie! Oh, Sophie, it's from Hans! I knew he'd write; I just *knew* he would!'

'*Hans!*' Sophie echoed, feeling stunned. 'But how . . . who did he get Aunty Lizzie's address from? Mam wouldn't have given it to him.'

Maria was quickly scanning the lines of small, cramped handwriting that covered the single page. 'From Mrs Sayle. He went to see her, to ask for work and to ask about me. She had the address because of the goose last year. He . . . he says he didn't go to see Mam because he knew she didn't approve and . . . oh, Sophie, he came back to the island to be with me and he . . . he says he's coming to Liverpool just as soon as he can save up the fare for the ferry. It took every penny he had to get back to the island and the journey took him three months, but Mrs Sayle has given him work and is letting him stay in one of the outbuildings . . .' Maria hugged the single sheet of paper to her and closed her eyes, sheer joy surging through her. She'd prayed so hard for this day. He hadn't forgotten her – far from it – he'd travelled for three long months across Europe to be with her and soon . . . 'I'll send him the ferry fare, Sophie!'

Sophie had gathered her wits. 'Wait, Maria. You have to think hard about this.'

'What is there to think about, Sophie?' Maria's eyes were shining and sadly Sophie realised she'd never seen her sister look so happy.

Both Hetty and Arthur were looking at Maria with avid curiosity; neither of them knew about Hans Bonhoeffer, and Sophie knew explanations were expected. She wondered how they would both react.

'Come into the workroom with me and we'll talk about this,' she urged and then turning to Arthur and the old lady she promised she would enlighten them later on.

'All I can think about is the fact that he came back for me, Sophie. *He came back for me*. And he's just a few hours' sail away!' Maria cried as Sophie pushed her gently down in a chair and took her hands.

'Maria, he was lucky Maude Sayle took him in and has given him work, but she *knows* him. She knows his background and that he was an internee. Who will employ him here in Liverpool? He's Austrian and who will believe he left before the war started? This city is still in ruins; so many innocent people were killed in the Blitz – no one will give him work. It could even be dangerous for him, Maria. People would blame him, they'd say he was German and where would he stay? He'd never find anyone who would give him lodgings.'

Tears had come into Maria's eyes; couldn't Sophie understand that she loved him and that he loved her? That he'd spent every penny he had and travelled the long miles through war-ravaged countries to be with her? 'Couldn't he stay here, with us? We know he isn't German, that he wasn't to blame for . . . for everything that's happened.'

'Maria, how could I ask Hetty to take him in? She and her sister spent hours down in the cellar, terrified they'd be blown to bits, and Arthur's only brother was killed in the Great War. People have long memories. People won't believe he isn't German. Oh, think, Maria, *think*!'

Maria was frantic. 'I . . . I can't write and tell him not to come across, Sophie. He's travelled so far and suffered the Lord alone knows what hardships and I want to be with him. I love him so much, Sophie, surely you can understand how I feel? I've never given up hope he'd come back.'

Sophie nodded; she did know how her sister felt: in her heart she wouldn't give up hope that one day she and Frank could be together. But Maria couldn't expect Hetty to take Hans in, and she had to make Maria see that he would be met with hostility and maybe even violence in this city.

'Write and tell him . . . tell him . . . you'll go over to see him, this weekend – weather permitting. You'll have to get Saturday off. I can't stop you from seeing him; it wouldn't be fair to either of you, but try to explain the situation to him, Maria. He can't come here,' Sophie urged. She'd write to her mother tonight and try to explain but she could see no future at all for her sister with Hans Bonhoeffer. He was a penniless exile who could offer her nothing, not even a decent roof over her head, and whose very appearance, speech and manners would attract hostility. There was no future for him in Liverpool and no work for Maria in Peel. She just hoped her mother could talk some sense into Maria – but she very much doubted it. And she must ask her not to mention the fact that she had written. In her present state of mind Maria would see it as a betrayal.

She left a still tearful Maria to write to him and went back into the living room, wondering how she was to break this news to Arthur and Hetty.

'Is everything all right, Sophie?' Arthur asked, noting her expression.

She shook her head. 'That letter was from someone I hoped Maria would never hear from again.'

'A young man? An *unsuitable* young man?' Hetty asked, looking anxious.

'Yes. Oh, he's not unsuitable in many ways. He's a hard worker, he isn't rough or ignorant, he's polite and well mannered, honest and he has few vices—'

'Then what on earth is wrong with him?' Arthur interrupted.

'He was an internee on the island during the war. His name is Hans Bonhoeffer,' Sophie replied.

'Oh, Lord above! He . . . he's *German*!' Hetty exclaimed, her hand going to her throat.

'No. No, he's Austrian. He left Austria with his family when the Nazis took over. They hated everything Hitler stood for; they were farmers and so they settled in Kent but were brought to the island when war broke out.'

Arthur said nothing; he was mulling it all over in his mind. 'And apart from his nationality, what do you think of him, Sophie?' he asked at length.

'On the occasions I met him I . . . I liked him. As I said, he was polite and well mannered and Mrs Sayle spoke well of him. He worked on the Sayles' farm during the day although he went back to Peveril Camp at night. That's where Maria met him; they worked together. She was in the Land Army. But there can be no future for them and I've told her that many times. Mam did too.'

'Your mother knew about their . . . relationship?' Hetty asked, still getting over the shock.

'Yes, but he never came to the house. Maria only saw him at work, he wasn't allowed the freedom to roam about at will, so to speak. But during the summer months and particularly at harvest they worked long hours together. At the end of the war he and his family were repatriated and we thought that would be the end of everything but he's made his way back to the island and is trying to save the ferry fare to come across.'

Arthur shook his head gravely. 'He'll be lynched, Sophie, if he does. It's too soon – far too soon for people to even try to forgive, even though he had no part in any of it.'

'I've told her that but I can't stop her from seeing him, so I've suggested she go over at the weekend. I'm going to write to Mam, explaining, and hope she can do something, say *something*, but . . .'

'Oh, I hope she can prevail, Sophie. It's all so . . . unfortunate and distressing,' Hetty said nervously, feeling that a dark cloud had suddenly appeared on the horizon, casting a shadow over their quiet life and the anticipation of a happy Christmas.

Sophie nodded. It was distressing indeed and particularly for Maria and Hans and she could see no solution at all, at least not one that wouldn't bring pain and heartbreak for them both.

Chapter Twenty-One

━━◆━━

A LL THE PASSENGERS ON the *Lady of Man* were very relieved when the ferry at last entered the harbour at Douglas that cold, grey, stormy morning. It had been a very rough and consequently slow crossing and there had been quite a few who had thought of the fate of the passengers and crew of the *Ellan Vannin*, the little Steam Packet ferry that had sunk in Liverpool Bay earlier in the century on just such a December crossing.

Maria had not been one of them. Although she hadn't been sick, she had felt wretched and had fretted at the slowness of the crossing. It meant that the time she would have to spend with Hans would be shorter for she had to return to Liverpool tomorrow – weather permitting, of course. If the wind didn't drop, or what was worse, got even stronger, then the ferry wouldn't sail, and she had to be in work on Monday morning.

She got the bus from the quayside. In her letter she had told him not to make the journey to Douglas to meet her, he had his work to do; nor could he afford to waste money on the fare. She had intended to go home first, to see her mother and tidy herself up and then she would walk up to Sayles' Farm, but now time was so precious that she resolved to go to Maude Sayle's first.

As the bus made its way slowly along the road to Peel her heart began to beat faster. It wouldn't be long now before she would once again be in his arms and she had waited so long for that moment, never giving up hope that it would one day happen. She had had plenty of time to think about everything Sophie had said and she had very reluctantly come to the conclusion that her sister was right. It hadn't been easy to admit to herself that there would be no work and no home for Hans in Liverpool, and there might even be the threat of violence, but how was she to tell him that after he'd travelled so far and sacrificed so much?

At last the bus topped the rise of the hill and the little fishing port was visible below them: the narrow streets and lanes with the rows of stone cottages and Michael Street with its shops, all running down to the harbour and the causeway to St Patrick's Isle with its ruined castle and church. Gone was the barbed wire from the beach and promenade; the houses along Peveril Road, which had been cordoned off and secured and had served as the internment camp, were now once more occupied by their pre-war residents. She was home and soon, oh, very soon she would be with him again.

She got off before the bus began its descent into the village and, drawing her coat closer to her, her head bent against the wind, she began to walk along the road, turning off into a narrow lane flanked by high hedges of old gorse bushes, that led to the farm. She had walked up this lane so many times in the past, she thought, and in all the seasons of the year, but never with as much love in her heart.

With her head still bent she was so engrossed in her thoughts she didn't see him at first. He was standing at the top of the lane, waiting: a tall, slim figure in an old army greatcoat that was too big for him and torn in places, the wind whipping his blond hair across his face. The anxious look disappeared from his face and his blue eyes lit up as he caught sight of the petite, dark-haired girl clutching a small case who rounded the bend in the lane.

'Maria! My Maria! I have been waiting for you!'

She looked up and stopped, joy flooded her face, she dropped her case and then she was running.

'Oh, Hans! Hans! I've waited so long for this moment!'

He gathered her into his arms and held her tightly and she could feel his heart beating, almost as fast as her own.

'All the night, I lay awake listening to the wind and I worried for you, Maria. I worried for the boat, that it would not come safely to the island and then this morning, you did not come . . .'

'I came as quickly as I could, Hans. I've missed you so

much—' His lips cut off her words and it was quite a while before they drew apart. She reached up and gently touched his right cheek. There was a scar running down it that hadn't been there last time she'd seen him. 'You've been hurt.'

He smiled down at her. 'It is well now. Everything is well now that I am here and you, too, are here.'

They walked back to retrieve her case and then they retraced their steps, his arm tightly around her shoulders.

'Mrs Sayle is good to me. She gives me work and food and a place to sleep and, best of all, she gives me your address.'

Maria smiled up at him. He was still the Hans she knew and loved but there were subtle changes. He was thinner, his skin was no longer the healthy tanned colour it had been, there were tiny lines of fatigue or anxiety at the corners of his eyes and there was the scar.

Maude Sayle was waiting at the door of the farmhouse as they walked into the yard.

'I told him you'd be later coming up here with the weather so bad, but he's fussed and fretted all morning just the same. Come on inside with you both, there's a pot of tea made.'

The kitchen was warm and as clean and tidy as it had always been, Maria thought as, thankfully, she sat at the table while Mrs Sayle poured the tea. She couldn't take her eyes off Hans as he hung the old coat up on a hook behind the door and then sat down beside her.

'I take it you've not been to see your mam yet, Maria?' the older woman said, nodding in the direction of Maria's case.

'No, the ferry was so late I came straight here. I'll go down after I've had the tea but I *had* to see Hans, you do understand?'

The woman nodded. 'I do,' she said flatly. 'Well now, I'll leave you for a while, there's eggs to collect,' she added tactfully. It was the least she could do, she thought. They'd both travelled so far to see each other again; she knew and liked them both and they had a lot of difficulties to overcome without her adding to them.

'I've missed you so much but I never gave up hope that you would write and then just a few days ago I got your letter.'

'I missed you, too, my Maria but I did write. I wrote many times before I left Austria, but sadly I think the letters were lost.'

'Was it really awful, the journey, Hans?' Maria asked, reaching out to take his hand.

He nodded as he held her small hand tightly in his. 'Everywhere there is ruin and poverty, such poverty, Maria. My country is . . . is . . . I have not the words to tell you, but when we returned it was not how we remembered. I could not stay, I tried, but I could not stay without you. There was nothing left in Austria for me. I had little money, so I tried to find work but there is such hardship . . .' He frowned, his eyes clouding at the memories of towns and cities in ruins; people displaced, wandering with their remaining possessions along roads and villages looking for work or their lost, scattered or deceased families. The lack of even basic foods, amenities and transportation. Europe was a devastated continent, its people demoralised and disorientated.

'Who hurt you, Hans?' Maria asked quietly, sensing the hardships he'd endured on the journey. It was more than she could bear to think of him trudging the long miles in all weathers without money or food or shelter.

'There is still much trouble, Maria, for anyone who looks and speaks German.' He looked down at her hand and his grip on it tightened. He would never tell her of the humiliations he'd suffered. Cursed, spat at, beaten and slashed with a knife. He had been lucky to escape with his life that time. It had been useless to try to explain that he'd had no part in it, that he'd been interned for six years on a tiny island off the coast of England, his native tongue was German. It was a journey he wanted to forget, a part of his life he wanted to put behind him.

Maria knew he had given her the opening she needed. 'That's why I came to the island to see you, Hans. If . . . if you come to Liverpool there will be more trouble for you. Oh, Hans, I'm so sorry, I really am. I want nothing more than for us to be together but . . . but no one will give you a job, or even somewhere to stay. We knew the city had suffered badly with the bombings, but until we got there we didn't know just *how* badly. Food and many other things are still rationed.'

He shook his head slowly. 'Then what are we to do, Maria? I came back because I love you, I want to marry you. I . . . I had hope we could start a new life together, put everything from our minds. The people of Peel do not hate me, do not blame me or curse me for what I am . . .'

His words were like a knife in her heart. She desperately wanted to marry him and start the new life he wanted but it wasn't possible in Liverpool, not yet, not for a long, long time.

'Hans, the people here know you; they know you and your family were here for the war years. They know it wasn't you but the Luftwaffe who dropped the bombs that killed innocent people, but the people of Liverpool don't.' She struggled to find the words to help him understand for she could see how hurt and disappointed he was. 'I love you and I want to marry you but there wouldn't be a job for me here on the island. But you have work and a home – of sorts – here. I . . . I'll come over as often as I can, until . . . until we can sort something out, I promise.'

He looked at her bleakly. It had been the dream of returning here to her, to a life together, that had kept him going throughout that terrible journey. 'But it will not be often, I think.'

She tried to smile. 'No, Hans, it will not be as often as we both would like, but it will be better than not seeing you at all.' Reluctantly she stood up as Maude Sayle bustled in carrying a large basket filled with straw and a dozen brown eggs.

'I'd better go down and see Mam, she'll be getting worried.' Maria turned to Hans. 'When you have finished your work will you come down to Mam's cottage? I want you to meet her. Come for your supper.'

Maude Sayle nodded her agreement. It was about time Sarah Kinnin met the lad for it was obvious to her that he was here on the island to stay and despite his straitened circumstances had hopes of Maria.

Sarah too had realised that with the weather the ferry would be late in and when there had been no sign of Maria she deduced that her daughter had gone straight to Maude Sayle's. She had read Sophie's letter three times and had given the matter a lot of thought; she concurred with her eldest daughter that there was no future for Maria with Hans Bonhoeffer. It had surprised her to learn that the lad had come back to the island; she hadn't heard, which was strange in a community as small and as close as this. It had also surprised her to realise that Maria had never given up hope of him returning. Indeed Sophie had said she loved him; Maria wouldn't even look at anyone else.

Sarah sat down after stoking up the fire and stared into the flames. Sophie had asked her to try to talk some sense into Maria, but what could she say that Sophie hadn't already said and obviously all to no avail?

A draught from the door caused the smoke from the fire to billow into the room and Sarah turned. 'Maria, you're home at last,' she said, getting to her feet.

Maria hugged her. 'I went up to the farm first, Mam. I'm sorry if you were worried about me.'

Sarah nodded, thinking Maria looked well. Cold and

windswept but well. 'I realised that's where you'd gone. And . . . and you saw him?'

'I did. Oh, Mam, he had a terrible journey and he's been hurt and I know there are things he isn't telling me or can't find the right words to tell me.'

Sarah sank down again in the old bentwood rocker. 'Oh, what am I going to do with you, girl? I want you to be happy, to have a good life . . .'

Maria knelt down beside her and took her hand. Her mam was looking older and tired, she thought. She'd had a difficult life; she still worked hard helping to auction the catches and keep a home going. 'I know you do, Mam, but I want to spend my life with Hans, is that so terrible? I love him, he wants to marry me and he's a good person. He works hard, he's kind and honest – ask Mrs Sayle.'

Sarah shook her head sadly. Maria was young; there was more to a good marriage than just being in love. 'Be practical, girl. He earns a labourer's wage, you'll have no wage at all and you can't start out living in one of Maude Sayle's barns and I . . . I can't afford to keep you both. It's hard enough making ends meet now.'

'I know that, Mam. Oh, I don't know what we'll do, I'll just have to hope that in time he can get something better. I've promised him I'll come over as often as I can but that it won't be easy. I have to work Saturdays and I only get a half-day on Wednesday, but he can't come to Liverpool. It's not safe for him and he'll not get work or lodgings. I . . . I've asked him to come down here, Mam, for his supper. I want you to meet him.'

Sarah looked at her steadily and sighed. Maria had inherited a stubborn streak from her pa and it was obvious that she'd dug her heels in over this Hans Bonhoeffer. Well, she hoped she was a fair woman; she would meet him and judge for herself. She nodded. 'I don't suppose it will do any harm to meet the lad.'

Maria smiled with relief. 'And can I ask you a big favour, Mam? I won't be able to get over for Christmas so . . . so can Hans come here on Christmas Day, please? I don't want him to spend the day in that old barn by himself, not after what he's been through. I couldn't stand it; it would break my heart.'

Sarah hadn't even thought about Christmas but obviously Maria had. It was all happening too quickly for her, she thought. Sophie's letter and the news that the lad was back. Maria's hasty visit and the dawning realisation that Maria wouldn't be turned from her determination to marry him. And now his impending visit. She hadn't even met him yet and she might not take to him at all, but could she leave him alone in the Sayles' barn on Christmas Day?

'I'll think about it, Maria. I . . . I'll think about it all,' she said and was rewarded by the smile of pure happiness and relief on her daughter's face.

Chapter Twenty-Two

———

ALL AFTERNOON SOPHIE'S MIND was not on either her work or Bella's increasingly urgent requests to write to Santa; her thoughts were with her sister wondering how she was getting on. Maria had been very quiet, thoughtful and a little tearful over the past few days and Sophie hoped she was finally coming to terms with the situation.

'Mam, you're not listening to me, are you?' Bella complained petulantly as she sat at the table with a sheet of paper and a pencil. Sophie was finishing hemming a skirt for a customer, which was to be collected early on Monday morning.

'I am, Bella. You're asking Santa to bring you a dolls' pram and a nice pram set to go with it. You'll have to be very good because that will be expensive,' Sophie replied, thinking she'd better start looking out for a second-hand pram as well as the scooter for young Billy Quine. She could easily make the pram set herself. She glanced at the clock on the mantelpiece; it was almost four o'clock. Was Maria still with Hans or was she now at home with Sarah? And was her mother's reasoning having the desired effect? All being well, her sister would be back late tomorrow afternoon.

'I'm always good, Aunty Hetty says so.' Bella chewed the end of the pencil and looked thoughtful. 'Will I get presents from Aunty Hetty and Uncle Arthur too?'

Sophie raised her eyebrows and tried to look shocked. 'Bella Teare, don't be greedy and don't you dare go asking them that! You are a very lucky little girl to get presents from Santa and Aunty Maria and me. Lots of children only get an apple and a new penny in their stockings.'

Bella shrugged but she hoped she would get something from them both this year; after all it was going to be better than last Christmas, her Mam said so. They were going to have a big tree and lots of decorations and a big lunch and she was to have a new dress too. She'd seen the material; it was royal blue velvet.

Sophie snapped off the thread and carefully folded the garment; it would need a final pressing but she'd do that later on. Bella was now absorbed in writing her note, Arthur was out in town at the library in William Brown Street and Hetty was dozing in her chair in front of the fire. She smiled as she looked affectionately at the old lady. The cold months affected Hetty's rheumatism badly; she moved more slowly, especially first thing in the morning, and some nights she didn't sleep well, so she often dozed in the afternoons. Sophie sighed, getting to her feet; Arthur would be in soon and would be in need of a hot cup of tea. It was still cold and blustery although the ferocity of the wind had lessened, and it was almost time to start preparing the evening meal. As she got up and made to go to the kitchen she wondered would Maria be helping Mam prepare *their* evening meal?

She was startled by the sound of the front-door bell. She had no appointments and Arthur had a key so it wasn't him, she thought as she went to open the door, pausing for a fraction of a second to smooth her hair in the mirror on the hallstand. Maybe it was a client calling on the off chance that she could see them.

Frank Ryan was standing on the step, muffled up against the cold and looking apprehensive. Sophie's hand went to her throat but her heart turned over at the sight of him. 'Frank!'

'Sophie, I . . . I had to come to see you before I leave. It's been so long since I last saw you, let alone had the chance of a few words . . . and I'll be away for Christmas,' he explained, praying she wouldn't turn him away. No one knew he'd come here. He purposely hadn't mentioned it to his mam for she wouldn't have approved and would have tried to stop him.

Sophie hesitated, not knowing what to do for the best. Should she invite him in and thereby put all her resolutions in jeopardy or should she turn him away? But what he'd said was true, it had been such a long time since they'd had a conversation and he would be away for Christmas. Her feelings got the better of her. 'Come inside, Frank. It's bitterly cold.'

He stepped into the hall and she closed the front door, hardly daring to look at him. 'I . . . I knew you would be away, Aunty Lizzie told me when she was here last. Katie and Matt are getting engaged at Christmas; we're all going up to Harebell Street for a bit of a get-together to celebrate.'

'I know, Mam told me. At least they've *got* something to celebrate,' he replied bitterly.

Sophie nodded, wondering what she should say next. She was having trouble keeping her emotions under control; she just wanted to throw her arms around him and hold him and tell him how much she loved him and missed him. 'So, when do you sail?' she finally asked.

'Early tomorrow morning. Winter will be almost over by the time I get back. Oh, Sophie, I wish . . .' He made to take her arm but she drew back.

'Please don't, Frank! You know how I feel about you but . . . but . . .'

'Just a kiss, Sophie, please?' he begged. 'A kiss for Christmas and to say goodbye?'

She shook her head, backing away from him. If he reached out, if he kissed her she'd be lost. 'Please, Frank! I can't . . . I daren't . . .'

He moved towards her but stopped and it was with lightheaded relief that she heard Arthur's key in the lock.

'Frank! Sophie?' Arthur looked at her with concern but she smiled.

'Frank just called to wish me a "Happy Christmas". He's sailing early in the morning.'

Frank nodded calmly at Arthur but inside he felt miserable and dejected. A few more seconds and he knew she would have capitulated. It was tearing him apart to be so close to her and yet be unable to hold her and kiss her.

'Then it's to be hoped the weather will have improved by then for you, Frank, and a calm crossing would certainly benefit Maria. She must have felt pretty awful on that ferry this morning.' Arthur took off his coat and hat and hung them on the hallstand but then made no move to leave Frank and Sophie alone again.

'She went home to Peel this morning; she had to go to see someone,' Sophie enlightened him.

Frank nodded slowly. 'I . . . I'd better go, Sophie. Mam is expecting me for a farewell meal and I've to pick up my uniform and stuff.'

Arthur opened the door. 'Well, goodbye and safe trip, Frank.'

'Take care of yourself, Frank and . . . and thank you for coming. I . . . we'll be thinking of you at Christmas,' Sophie added as with one last look of longing Frank turned and left.

'He . . . he just turned up on the doorstep, Arthur, and I hadn't the heart to turn him away, but I'm glad you arrived when you did,' Sophie said, feeling a little shaky.

'Sophie, you've no need to explain to me. I know you love him and I know how difficult that is for you to live with,' he said gently.

She nodded, thinking he was right: it was so hard. Frank was still irrevocably tied to Nora but was she right to urge Maria to give up Hans? To make her suffer as she, Sophie, was suffering? They did have a chance of happiness together, no matter how slight or how impossible it seemed at the moment.

The room was warm and looked cosy, Maria thought as she helped her mother to set the table, and the delicious aroma of Sarah's fish pie wafted from the oven in the range. The wind had virtually died and now a sea fret was drifting in over the village. She knew he would come, she didn't doubt it at all and she wanted her mother to like him. If they had Sarah on their side then perhaps *something* could be worked out.

'Put the kettle on, Maria. The lad will be chilled to the bone walking all the way down the hill in this mist,' Sarah instructed as she checked on the pie. She was happy to have Maria home, even though the visit was brief, and she wished there was something stronger to drink than tea but there wasn't. Her husband, John Kinnin, had been a member of the Temperance Society so there had never been alcohol in this house. Not that he objected to others taking a drink, but drink and 'chasing the herring' did not go well together, he'd always said; it was a dangerous occupation and you needed your wits about you.

'He'll take no harm from Manannán's cloak, Mam,' Maria said, smiling, feeling the joy bubbling up inside her. He'd be here in a few minutes.

Sarah laughed good naturedly. 'That he won't, but he'll still need something to warm him,' she replied. It was an old Manx belief that the Celtic sea god, Manannán mac Lir, protected the island from all dangers with his cloak of mist.

The tea was made and Maria left it to draw but before she had time to set out the cups she heard the greatly anticipated knock on the cottage door.

'Well, go and open the door, Maria,' Sarah instructed, wiping her hands on her apron.

Maria's smile of welcome lit up her face as she ushered Hans into the room. 'Mam, this is Hans.'

Sarah held out her hand in greeting, seeing a tall, fair young man whose thin features bore the mark of hardship and suffering. The old coat he wore was torn and stained but she could see he'd made an effort with his appearance. His collarless shirt was clean if unironed and his boots, although badly worn, had been buffed. The hand that gripped hers was rough and calloused from hard manual work. She liked him. 'You are welcome, Hans.'

He smiled shyly and held out a neatly tied bundle of kindling. 'I have much shame that this is all I have to bring you, Mrs Kinnin, but I chopped it and tied it myself.'

Her heart softened as she took it from him. 'It is a very useful gift, lad, and it is the thought that counts, not the value of the gift.'

Maria took his coat and hung it up behind the door while Sarah handed him the tea. 'It is cold out tonight but at least the wind has dropped. Come closer to the fire,' she urged.

'You have a very comfortable home,' he commented, gazing around the small room with its colourful rag rugs, the dresser now almost devoid of dishes, which were set out on the small table, the brass candlesticks on the mantel above the range and the picture of St Patrick's Isle that hung on the wall beside the door.

Sarah nodded, not missing the wistful note in his voice. 'Sit down, the pie is ready,' she instructed, bustling about and placing first a large dish of potatoes followed by the pie on the table. Nor did she miss the look of delight that crossed his face at the sight of the simple meal. He was starving, she thought, although she was sure Maude gave him at least one good meal a day.

'Mam's fish pie is the best in the whole parish,' Maria said, beaming happily at him. Oh, how she had longed to see him sitting down with them for a meal!

He nodded his agreement, his mouth full of flaky pastry and the rich sauce full of large pieces of tasty fish. 'It is very good,' he agreed when he could speak. 'Mrs Sayle, she is good, she gives me a hot dinner each day and bread and cheese for breakfast, but never have I had such a pie.' He was trying his best not to cram the food into his mouth and appear bad mannered.

Maria relaxed as she watched him eat. If only he could stay here with Mam and go up to the farm to work each day. She would feel far better knowing he was being looked after and had a warm, dry bed at night, but she couldn't ask her mother that. It was too soon and Sarah had said nothing further so far about Hans spending Christmas Day here.

She listened intently as her mother asked him about his home in Austria and his family. He spoke with affection of his parents and his sister Ingrid, whom she had known slightly. She learned of their home in the high pastures of the Tyrol, a wooden chalet farmhouse where the animals were kept in the basement during the long winter months. Of how deep the snow was during those months, so deep they were often cut off, and of how, when spring came, the pastures were carpeted with alpine flowers and of how hard life was now and of how much he had missed Maria.

'So, I came back to the island where I was happy and where I met my Maria,' he finished.

Sarah nodded. She could see by the way his eyes lit up each time he looked at her daughter that he loved her deeply. She got to her feet. 'Leave the dishes in the sink in the scullery, Maria; we'll do them in the morning. I'll make up the fire and then I'm away to my bed.'

Hans was instantly on his feet. 'I will attend to the fire, Mrs Kinnin. Please, it is such a small thing for me to do to help.'

Sarah nodded. Had the weather been better she would have suggested that they go for a walk either by the harbour or along the promenade but she hadn't the heart to send them out into the cold mist and they had so little time together: just a few hours tonight for tomorrow he had his work at the farm and Maria must take the bus to Douglas for the ferry. 'Thank you, Hans. Goodnight.'

Although relieved that her mother was allowing them

some time alone Maria was perturbed that Sarah had made no mention of any future visit. 'Goodnight, Mam,' she said, trying to hide her disappointment.

'Goodnight and thank you, Mrs Kinnin,' Hans added politely.

When she reached the foot of the narrow stone stairs set into the wall Sarah turned. 'You are welcome in this house, Hans, and I would like you to come each Sunday for your supper, and you must come for your meal on Christmas Day too. I could not call myself a Christian woman if I left you alone on that day although I'm sure Maude would see you had a hot meal. Maria will not be able to get home, she has to work on Christmas Eve and the ferry does not sail over the holiday, so there will be just you and me.'

Maria took his hand and smiled at her mother, her eyes shining. 'Thank you, Mam. Oh, thank you so much!'

Sarah nodded and turned again towards the stairs. The look in Maria's eyes reminded her forcibly of the way she had felt the day she had married John Kinnin.

Chapter Twenty-Three

———•>+•<———

THAT NIGHT, AFTER HANS left, Maria lay awake for hours trying to find some way to solve the problem of how they could be together. It had been a bittersweet parting and she'd had to fight back her tears. She had hated to let him go and they'd clung together, she promising to come back as soon as she could.

Next morning the mist still heavily shrouded the land and she had feared that the ferry would once again be late, but once they cleared the shores of the island Mannanán's cloak disappeared and the wintry sun made the crossing a little more bearable.

'I've tea and some scones ready. How did it all . . . go?' Sophie asked as soon as Maria arrived back from the ferry and sank thankfully into the chair by the fire. They were alone for Sophie had persuaded Hetty to go up and have a nap, Bella was at Emily's house for the afternoon and Arthur had tactfully gone to his room on the pretext of writing his annual letter to his cousin in Vermont.

Maria told her everything and upon hearing of her mother's change of heart Sophie nodded slowly. 'I *can* understand how hard it is for you, Maria. What will you do?'

'What can I do, Sophie? I've asked Mam to send me the newspapers in case a job is advertised.'

'You'll never earn as much as you do now, Maria,' Sophie reminded her.

'I know but if . . . if I could get *something*, to use Aunty Lizzie's favorite saying, "we'll manage".'

Sophie didn't look convinced. 'So, he's going to Mam on Christmas Day?'

Maria nodded. 'I'll try and get over before then but . . . but if I can't I'm going to buy him some decent clothes and send them over. Oh, Sophie, it broke my heart to see the terrible old coat he had. He has nothing . . . *nothing*.'

Sophie nodded and sighed. 'Well, if you do manage to get over you can bring back a goose. I'm going to write to Mrs Sayle. I'm determined that this Christmas is going to be the best Hetty and Arthur have had in their lives.'

'I wish I could say it will be the best I've had, Sophie, but I'll try to keep cheerful. At least I know Hans loves me and that he's not too far away, which is more than I did last year,' Maria said with a rueful little smile.

Sophie thought of Frank who loved her and who would be

thousands of miles away but she said nothing; there would be so much to do in the weeks ahead that her mind would be fully occupied.

The days just seemed to fly by as Christmas approached. Arthur had seen an advertisement in a shop window for a scooter and so she'd bought it and she'd also managed to obtain a second-hand dolls' pram, both of which Arthur kindly spent many hours renovating until she declared that they looked brand new. She had made the pram set from some white broderie anglaise and she'd also made some new clothes for Bella's treasured dolls. She had been busy with her dressmaking too for people wanted new outfits for Christmas, and she'd made up the blue velvet for Bella and a dress of a similar shade in taffeta for Katie, which was her engagement gift to her cousin.

She and Hetty spent many hours baking and Arthur had gone into town and had come home with a huge tree and some big bunches of holly. He'd had to walk most of the way for he'd said jovially that there wasn't a conductor who would let him on a tram with so much prickly greenery. They'd festooned the hall and living room with the holly and she, Bella and Maria had made all the little decorations that now adorned the tree. She had bought gifts for her sister and Hetty and Arthur, and for Lizzie and Jim, which she'd wrapped and placed under the tree. Maria's, Hetty's and Arthur's gifts were duly added to the pile and Bella's excitement was growing each day.

'And there's to be no poking at them or tearing little holes in the wrapping paper to see what's inside, Bella. Remember, Santa can see you,' she'd warned her daughter.

Arthur was going to accompany Hetty to church on Christmas morning – he got on well with her friends – and then they would have lunch, after which Sophie intended to persuade Hetty to take a nap and no doubt Arthur would be glad of a few hours' peace and quiet, perhaps to read the *Father Brown Stories*, which was her present to him. She and Maria would wash up while Bella could play with her new toys.

'Do you think Hetty and Arthur will come with us to Aunty Lizzie's?' Maria asked on Christmas Eve as they were setting out Hetty's best china and glass on the table in the dining room. The vegetables were all peeled and in bowls of cold water in the kitchen. The goose had arrived and was sitting on the marble slab in the pantry alongside the bowl of stuffing Hetty had made using her mother's recipe.

'I don't honestly know but I think Hetty might be too tired and Arthur . . . well, you know how uncomfortable he feels with crowds of people.'

Maria nodded; she couldn't see either of them really enjoying themselves packed into Lizzie's parlour with half the neighbourhood.

'You do realise that Ben Seddon will be there, Maria?'

'I do,' Maria replied, polishing a crystal wine glass.

'And . . . ?' Sophie probed.

'I'm going to have to tell him, Sophie, that Hans is back

and that we'll be getting married.' She was bitterly disappointed that she hadn't been able to get over to see him again but she'd written and she'd sent the gifts she'd bought. He'd written back, thanking her for the brown cord trousers, cream shirt and the brown and cream heavy knitted sweater but bitterly regretting that he had nothing to send to her except his love. That was all she'd cared about but she wished Mam had a telephone or knew someone who had one; she would dearly have loved to have spoken to him on Christmas Day and told him so.

'It's not going to be a very happy occasion for Ben then,' Sophie remarked sadly.

Bella's cries of delight woke the whole household at six o'clock on Christmas Morning and even Hetty and Arthur, clad in warm dressing gowns, joined Sophie and Maria in the living room where Sophie had suggested Bella hang up her stocking.

'Mam, oh, Mam, it's *beautiful*! It's so shiny and look at the lovely eiderdown and pillow and he left new clothes for all my dolls too!' Bella's blue eyes were dancing with excitement, her cheeks flushed pink and her dark curls tumbling over her shoulders.

'Aren't you a lucky little girl? Now, I think you'd better get some clothes on or you'll catch cold,' Sophie laughed, her own eyes sparkling with pleasure at the child's delight.

'Can I open my other presents, Mam? The ones under the tree?' Bella begged, still patting the pram lovingly and resolving to dress her dolls in their new outfits and put them all in it and take them for a walk as soon as breakfast was over.

Sophie shook her head. 'No, you can't. It's much too early. We'll open them all after breakfast. Now, off you go and get dressed while I make a cup of tea to warm us up.'

The child reluctantly did as she was told while Sophie and Maria made the tea.

'I'll never forget the look on her face, Sophie, as long as I live. It was *magical*!' Hetty said, clasping her gnarled hands together, her face wreathed in smiles.

'And it's going to be a "magical" day too, I promise,' Sophie replied determinedly, pushing all thoughts of Frank Ryan from her mind.

By half past four both Hetty and Arthur agreed that it had been the best Christmas they'd ever experienced. They'd had a wonderful breakfast followed by the opening of their gifts, more gifts than either of them had ever received before. Hetty was especially delighted with the soft lavender wool shawl Sophie had given her and the large bottle of Yardley's Lavender Water, which was her favourite, from Maria. Arthur's gift was a silver brooch set with garnets, which were her favourite gem stone, and from Bella there were three lace-edged handkerchiefs, embroidered rather lopsidedly with the letter 'H', which Bella had spent many laborious hours sewing under her mother's guidance. Arthur had received a copy of the *Father Brown Stories* from Sophie and also a copy of *The Adventures of Sherlock Holmes* from Maria. From Hetty there was a real cashmere jumper wrapped in tissue paper. It had belonged to her brother but had never been worn, she'd confided. From Bella he'd received a bookmark made of stiff cardboard that she'd painted bright red and on to which she'd stuck the letters 'AC', which she'd cut from a magazine. Arthur said he would cherish and take great care of it.

Lunch had been a truly magnificent meal, they'd all declared: homemade soup followed by the goose and all the trimmings and then the pudding, which Sophie remarked was a vast improvement on last year's Victoria sponge cake. Bella had been thrilled when she'd found a silver threepenny piece in her portion. As they'd sat sipping the port wine which Arthur had bought Maria wondered what kind of a day Hans and her mother had had. At least he had some decent clothes to wear for it, she thought, if not a presentable overcoat. Sarah would make him welcome and feed him well and if they couldn't be together, she thought wistfully, then at least sharing Christmas with her mother and in her old home was the next best thing. She smiled at Sophie, knowing her sister's thoughts would be with Frank Ryan spending his day on a ship somewhere in a climate that was far warmer than this.

It was after seven when they finally arrived at Lizzie's house in Harebell Street. Hetty had said she wished she had the energy to accompany them but that she was utterly exhausted by the excitement of the day and would have an early night. Arthur, as Sophie had anticipated, had also decided to stay at home. He felt that Hetty shouldn't be left alone and as Bella flatly refused to be parted from her new toys, even to go to a party which as she said was really for grown-ups, he would keep his eye on the child too.

'It's very kind of you to look after her. She should go to bed no later than half past eight, which is very late but this is a special day,' Sophie had said to him.

Lizzie's house seemed to be bursting at the seams with people, she thought as they pushed their way up the narrow lobby. Not only were the family and the Seddons there but also Pat and Martha Ryan and quite a few of the other neighbours too.

'Lord, what a crowd! I thought she said it was just a family do?' Maria said, taking off her coat and adding it to the pile that already covered Katie's bed.

'She did and I think it's a good thing that Hetty and Arthur didn't come,' Sophie added as they went downstairs and in search of the happy couple.

Sophie had to admit that Katie looked lovely. The blue dress fitted her perfectly and the colour suited her. 'Katie, congratulations, you look lovely, you really do.' Sophie kissed her cousin on the cheek as Katie shyly held out her left hand.

'Oh, that's beautiful!' Maria enthused, examining the tiny diamond on Katie's finger. 'Congratulations to you both,' she added, smiling at Matt, who was managing to look shy and proud at the same time.

'What's happened to Miss Foster and Mr Chatsworth?' Lizzie demanded, emerging from the kitchen.

'They both apologise, Aunty Lizzie, but Hetty is exhausted, Bella had us all up at six o'clock, and Arthur is keeping his eye on her and Bella. Wild horses wouldn't drag her away from her toys and her pram,' Sophie laughed.

Lizzie rolled her eyes expressively. 'You wouldn't believe the job I've had to get our Billy in from the street with that scooter; he's been out there most of the day. He's absolutely over the moon with it, Sophie, bless you.'

Sophie handed over the gifts she'd brought for Katie and Matt. 'These are for you, Katie, from Miss Foster and Mr Chatsworth. They're for your "bottom drawer".'

Delightedly Katie pulled off the wrapping paper to reveal a hand-embroidered, lace-edged tablecloth from Hetty and a pair of silver serving spoons from Arthur.

'God help us all, she'll be getting fancy ideas now with real *silver* spoons and *linen and lace* tablecloths,' Lizzie declared, although she was as delighted as Katie.

'She can always pawn them when she's hard up, Lizzie,' Katie's future mother-in-law added, admiring the delicate lacework on the edge of the cloth. Mary Seddon had never had anything so fine in all her married life.

'Oh, Mam! What a thing to say and haven't I got a steady job? I hope she'll never have to set foot in a pawnbroker's,' Matt cried, looking slightly embarrassed.

'And so do I,' Lizzie added emphatically. 'Now, let's get you girls something to drink.'

It wasn't long before Ben made his way to Maria's side and she sighed inwardly as she smiled at him. 'Hello, Ben. Don't they look happy,' she remarked, nodding in the direction of his brother and her cousin.

'I never thought our Matt would be the first to get engaged, Maria. I thought . . . I hoped it would be me.'

She nodded slowly, feeling her spirits sink, knowing she was about to completely ruin his evening. 'I know, Ben, and I'm so sorry. I . . . I went home to Peel a few weeks ago.' She paused, summoning up her courage. 'You remember I told you I loved someone who had gone . . . away?' She thought of Hans and the long, hazardous journey he'd made to be with her. 'He came back and he wants to marry me and . . . and we hope to get married . . . sometime next year.' She couldn't look at him. She felt terrible; she should never have given him a shred of hope to cling to. How would she have felt if Hans had never returned?

'Then . . . then there's no . . .' He was struggling with his emotions.

'No. I'm sorry, Ben. I never meant to hurt you but . . . but Hans—'

He gripped her arm tightly, causing her to cry out. '*Hans!* What kind of a name is that? HANS! *HANS!* It's a bloody German name!' he shouted.

Conversation around them died as Maria backed away from him. She knew he was hurt, but she'd never expected this. 'No! He's *not* German. He's Austrian and he had nothing to do with the war, he was interned on the island, that's where I met him.'

Ben's bitter hurt and disappointment had turned to furious

anger. 'It's the same bloody thing, Maria! Hitler was Austrian. You saw with your own eyes what *they* did to this city. *I* saw what they did to people all over Europe, shot, tortured and gassed them in their thousands. What do you think we fought the bloody war for, Maria? Me, Frank Ryan, your cousin John and all the other lads who fought and died. What do you think your cousin Albert *died* for?'

Maria was shaking and the tears poured unheeded down her cheeks. Never before had she experienced such vitriol – and she didn't deserve it, Hans didn't deserve it!

Sophie and Jim had both pushed their way to her side, Sophie looking as shocked as her sister, their uncle looking grim.

'She's telling the truth, Ben,' Sophie said clearly so everyone could hear. 'Hans Bonhoeffer fled his country with his family before Hitler took over Austria. They went to live in Kent and then spent the war years on the island. My father and my husband died in the war, Ben. Do you think that either my mam or I would encourage Maria if Hans had had any part in it?'

'It's true, Ben. The war left my sister and Sophie widows but now it's over. I think you'd better go home,' Jim said forcefully, although he was shocked himself to learn of Maria's involvement with an internee.

Ben turned away and shoved his way through the crowd of neighbours.

'I . . . I think we'd better go too, Uncle Jim. It's not fair on Katie and Matt, we don't want to ruin their night entirely.'

An obviously stunned Lizzie got their coats and after apologising again to her aunt, Sophie led her sister out of the house.

'I just didn't think . . . I didn't realise, Sophie,' Maria sobbed. 'I . . . I never thought that someone as . . . quiet and . . . ordinary as Ben could be so . . . so . . . bitter. He wouldn't listen; he just wouldn't listen to me! Hans had no part at all in those terrible things . . .'

Sophie put her arm around her. 'Neither did I, Maria, but now you understand why Hans can't come here.'

Maria nodded, wiping her eyes, still shocked to the core by Ben Seddon's outburst. Sophie hugged her, thinking that she would have to go and see Lizzie and Jim and explain.

Chapter Twenty-Four

———❖———

CHRISTMAS NOW SEEMED SO long ago, Sophie thought as she walked up Harebell Street towards Lizzie's house that blustery but fine March morning. The wind still had a chilly edge to it but at least the sun was shining, she thought as she turned her face towards its increasingly strong rays. The streets were busy with people going about their work and women shopping or stopping to gossip, trams and buses trundling by and still many horse-drawn carts too; and when she'd passed Maggie Dodd's shop she saw Mr Dodd out washing down the paintwork. It was as if the brighter weather had energised people, she mused.

After the New Year celebrations the weather had turned very cold with heavy frosts at night and snow, which made conditions underfoot treacherous, and that, combined with the post-Christmas austerity that seemed to have affected most of her customers, had had an effect on her business. People did not appear to want new clothes, they were making do with what they had or asking for new trimmings to be added; nor did they seem prepared to venture out in such inclement weather. She hoped things would pick up now that spring had arrived and Easter was not far away.

The extra amount of time she seemed to have to herself was the reason why she was calling on her aunt this morning for a chat and to take back the skirt she had been altering for Katie, who like everyone else was not buying new clothes. Sophie smiled to herself; Katie was saving hard to get married. In fact Lizzie had told her that the girl was making all kinds of small sacrifices to save money.

She found her aunt sitting at the kitchen table, studying her rent book. There was a mug of tea at her elbow.

'That feller said I was in arrears with the rent but I swore I wasn't and I've just been checking up and I'm right. So I'll be having a few choice words to say to him next time he calls, I can tell you, Sophie. The flaming cheek of him. Oh, I know what he's up to, thinks he can con me into coughing up more money which will go straight into his pocket, not the landlord's. Well, he picked the wrong one to try that trick on.'

Sophie smiled at her. Lizzie never changed; as Katie often remarked, her mam could talk the hind leg off a donkey. 'I've brought Katie's skirt back. I thought she might need it.'

Lizzie nodded her thanks and poured a mug of tea for her niece. 'How is Miss Foster doing now, luv?'

Sophie sipped her tea before she replied. 'She's much better, thank goodness, and since I've had more spare time I've taken over more of the chores and all the cooking.' Hetty had caused her some concern over the past months, having had a couple of what the old lady termed 'little turns'. The last time Sophie had insisted on calling in the doctor and Arthur had backed her up. Dr Franklin had informed them that she had had a very minor stroke and had instructed Hetty to rest more. 'I'm planning a little celebration for her birthday next month, she'll be eighty,' she added.

'Really? Bye, that's a good age, Sophie, there's not many reach eighty in this day and age,' Lizzie said with some admiration.

'Just the family – which includes Uncle Jim and yourself – for tea, and I'm going to make and ice a special cake.'

Lizzie looked pleased; that was something to look forward to. 'Have you heard from your mam?'

Sophie nodded; Sarah wrote regularly. 'She's well and so is Hans.' Then she frowned, thinking of Sarah's last couple of letters. After Christmas when the weather had turned so much colder and her mother had got to know Hans better she had insisted he stay with her at night. She couldn't have him lying shivering on straw in Maude Sayle's barn with just an old coat and a single blanket to cover him, she'd said, not when the frost was so severe that the water pipes were freezing up. So, when he finished his work at Sayles' he now walked down to Sarah's cottage for his supper and a warm, comfortable bed for the night. Of course Maria had been delighted at this news and in payment he brought Sarah firewood and eggs he bought from Maude.

'What's wrong, Sophie? Is she having trouble with that lad?' Lizzie asked. After that outburst from Ben Seddon Sophie had come to see them and told them Hans's story in full and both she and Jim had come to terms with Maria's choice. Sarah had also written to them saying that the more she saw of the lad the better she liked and respected him. Over the months, her sister-in-law had said, he had opened up to her about his hard decision to leave his family and return to the island and of the hardships and dangers of the journey.

She'd also learned what his life had been like before the family had fled Austria and how he had written many times to his parents but had no way of knowing if they ever received his letters. If he could be certain they had he would have tried to enclose some money, though he had little enough himself, he'd told her. Sarah had warned him against doing that until he heard from them, which up to now he hadn't.

Sophie sighed. 'He seems to be getting more and more determined to come across to Liverpool, even though Mam is trying her best to dissuade him. Oh, Aunty Lizzie, I can understand how he feels and Maria is always fretting that she's only been able to go over three times since Christmas because of the bad weather and work and she's often depressed about it all. But it will be pointless because . . . well, we know how most people would treat him. Mam's afraid he'll get so desperate that he'll just up and leave.'

Lizzie shook her head. 'That wouldn't help anyone and he might even lose the bit of a job he has and then what would he do? Nor do I suppose that Mrs Sayle would be very pleased if he left them in the lurch. Farming is a seven-day-a-week job and she's been good to him.'

'I know. All we can do is hope that Mam can try to calm him down and keep him there. Maria should be able to get over more frequently during the next months so that should help.'

Lizzie finished her tea and tucked the rent book into her apron pocket. 'Frank Ryan was home last week, he's gone again though. Off on one of the short trips this time.'

Sophie's feelings at this news were mixed. Regret that she hadn't known he was home mingled with relief that she hadn't bumped into him on one of her visits. Much as she longed to see him she knew it would only reinforce the hopelessness of their situation. 'How is he, did Mrs Ryan say?'

'She said he looks well but he told her he was getting tired of being away for so long and that he might try another shipping line, one that does shorter trips, now he's got more experience. Martha said she tried to talk him out of it but . . .' Lizzie shrugged. 'Of course, I don't suppose *that one* cares much how long he's away.'

Sophie said nothing; she didn't want to hear anything at all about Nora Ryan. 'When will Frank be home again, did his mam say?'

'Next Monday and due to sail to South Africa again the following Friday, unless he signs on with someone else.'

Sophie got to her feet. 'I'd better be getting back. I know Arthur is planning to go out later and since Hetty's "turns" we don't like to leave her alone.'

'Give her my regards, Sophie, and Mr Chatsworth too.' Lizzie reluctantly got up and looked without much pleasure around the still untidy kitchen. 'I still miss having you and Maria here, you were both such a help to me. Our Katie is useless even though I keep telling her she'd better make some sort of effort or she won't turn out to be much of a catch for Matt. Mary Seddon keeps that house like a little palace. And she'd better learn to cook as well; Matt's used to coming home to a decent meal.'

Sophie relented and helped her aunt to wash up and then she kissed her and left to catch the tram home.

As she turned into Laurel Road she stopped dead, unable to believe her eyes. Hans Bonhoeffer was walking towards her. He looked a little older and thinner than when she had last seen him, his hair was longer and his clothes creased and well worn, but she would recognise him anywhere.

'Sophie, I have been waiting for you. I called at the house and the gentleman said you were not at home.'

So, Arthur knew he was here, she thought, but had not invited him in, although he must have guessed who the tall, blond young man with the guttural accent was.

'Hans, you shouldn't have come. Didn't Mam explain it to you? Does she even know?' Sophie asked.

'Your mother did all she could, Sophie, but . . . but I could not be apart from my Maria any longer. Do you not know how much I love her?' he pleaded.

'I know, Hans, but does Mam know? If she doesn't she'll worry about you. I'll have to send her a telegram.'

'I left a note and one for Mrs Sayle, too. I only want to be with Maria and I have a place to stay. I have hope, too, that I will soon find work. There are many ships in the docks.'

Sophie was relieved and surprised. 'Where are you staying?'

'At a lodging house only for men near what the Liverpool people call the "Dock Road",' he informed her. 'It has the name of "Mulligan's Lodging House".'

She'd heard of it. It was little more than a doss house for drunks and vagrants and in a very tough area near the docks. Her heart sank. If he stayed there he'd be bound to have a rough time, but how could she ask Hetty to take him in, especially as the old lady had had two strokes and needed to rest and certainly not be put under any kind of stress or worry? Nor could she ask Lizzie to house him, for once Ben Seddon found out there would be trouble. 'Hans, you must try to find somewhere else, that place is . . . bad, very bad.'

He nodded and smiled wryly. 'It is not good, I know, but I tell them I am Dutch; that I come from Amsterdam. They say I can find work unloading the ships.'

At least he realised the position he was in, she thought, but she just didn't know what to do. She couldn't leave him to hang around in the road until Maria came home from work. Someone would be bound to notice him; he was a stranger to the neighbourhood and so obviously foreign. He might even be reported to the police as a vagrant or a 'suspicious character' and that was the last thing she needed to happen. Her mind was working quickly; if she could keep him away from the house until after lunch, then Hetty would go for her afternoon nap and she could install him in her workroom until Maria came home. She would explain to Arthur and thankfully Bella was going to her friend Anne's house after school. Bella was a curious child and would certainly demand to know who he was.

She delved into her bag and took out her purse. 'Hans, take this and go and get yourself something to eat, and then come back here – to the house – at two o'clock. Then you can wait with us until Maria comes home.' She handed him some coins.

He took them and nodded. 'Thank you, Sophie. I will come back at two o'clock.'

She watched him walk away and turn the corner before she resumed her journey, praying Arthur might be able to think of some solution to this problem, for she could see nothing but worry and trouble ahead.

Arthur agreed with her but could offer no solution except that the lad be persuaded to go back to Peel. 'Maybe he'll listen to Maria, if she can prevail upon him that it's for the best.'

Sophie shook her head. 'But will Maria *agree* it's for the

best? I don't know, I just don't know. He might convince her that now he's told everyone he's Dutch he will be fine staying in that doss house and trying to get work on the docks – and he might be Arthur, he just might. And then again he might not.'

Hans returned at two o'clock on the dot and she showed him into her workroom.

'You have a very fine . . . grand . . . house, Sophie,' he said, looking around the large room with admiration.

'It is not mine, Hans, it belongs to an old lady, Miss Foster. She is very kind and lets us live with her. Maria will not be home for many hours yet and I have chores to do, so I must leave you to wait,' she informed him.

'I do not mind that, Sophie. I am happy to wait here for Maria,' he said affably, sitting down on the chair she used at her sewing machine.

To her relief Arthur offered to go and sit with him for he was curious to meet this young man.

When it was nearly time for her sister to arrive home Sophie went into the hall to wait for her. Arthur was still sitting talking to Hans; she'd taken them tea an hour ago and they seemed to be getting on very well. She had also taken Hetty her tea in her room, saying it was warm and cosy there with the fire burning in the hearth and that the less Hetty climbed up and down the stairs the less tired she would feel. It was no trouble at all to bring it up on a tray and set it out on the little table by the fire. When Bella got home she would send her up to tell her all about her day, as usual.

Maria was tired for they had been stocktaking and it was not something she enjoyed, but thankfully it only occurred twice a year.

'Lord, Sophie, you gave me a fright! What on earth are you doing hiding behind the front door?'

'I'm not "hiding", I was waiting for you.'

'Why? Is something wrong? Is Hetty all right?'

'Hetty is fine; she's having her tea upstairs. I . . . I have something to tell you and I don't want you to go shrieking and upsetting Hetty. Hans is here. He's in my workroom with Arthur.'

The weariness instantly left Maria and her face lit up. 'Hans is *here*!' she cried, ignoring Sophie's warning.

'Hush! He left Mam and Maude Sayle a note; he was waiting for me at the bottom of the road when I got back from Lizzie's this morning. I gave him some money to get something to eat and he's been here all afternoon, but he can't stay, Maria. I . . . we can't risk upsetting Hetty.'

Slowly Maria nodded as reality began to dawn on her, dimming some of her delight. 'But where can he go, Sophie? You know how people will treat him. You can't have forgotten Ben Seddon.'

'He's already found himself lodgings although I wonder how safe he'll be there. He hopes to get work on the docks. He's told everyone he's met so far that he's Dutch, from Amsterdam.'

Hope surged through Maria. 'Oh, Sophie, that might just work! How many people will be able to tell the difference?

He . . . he could be a Dutch sailor who has jumped ship; he could say he's had enough of life at sea and wants to stay in Liverpool. I must tell him to say that. If people believe him he can stay here and I can see him every day. I must go to him, Sophie. I've missed him so much!' Maria pushed past her sister, flung open the door to Sophie's workroom and hurled herself into Hans's arms.

Arthur quietly closed the door behind him as he left them. 'Did you tell her everything, Sophie?'

She nodded. 'She knows he can't stay here, but she's so taken with the idea that he can pass himself off as a Dutchman that she's convinced everything will be all right.'

Arthur looked apprehensive. 'I've had a good talk to him, Sophie. He seems an honest, reliable and resourceful lad and he's been through a lot. He's also very determined to be with Maria.'

'As is she. She's going to tell him to say he's jumped ship,' Sophie added.

Arthur considered this. 'It might work, Sophie. There are a lot of foreign sailors in Liverpool; there always have been, with it being a port. I don't think there are many who work on the docks and especially who lodge at the likes of Mulligan's who would doubt him or know the difference between the Dutch and German languages.'

Sophie didn't look convinced. 'But we can't let Hetty know or even Bella, she'd be bound to let it slip.'

'No, I agree he can't come to the house. We can't risk upsetting Hetty. Maria will just have to meet him somewhere else. At least the weather is improving and the evenings are getting longer now,' he reminded her.

Sophie nodded. If the ruse worked and Hans were to stay then maybe . . . just maybe in time they could get married and find a place of their own.

Chapter Twenty-Five

——◆——

A T FIRST BOTH SOPHIE and Maria worried about Hans but as the days and then weeks passed they both began to be less concerned. He was still lodging at Mulligan's, something Maria particularly was far from happy about, but he kept very much to himself – and in fact was well able to look after himself too, although he always stayed clear of arguments and trouble.

The docks were busy with ships arriving from all over the Empire and beyond, bringing in the goods so desperately needed by a country trying to rebuild its infrastructure, restore its industries and solve the desperate rationing and housing situation. It was true that many men, having been demobbed, were seeking work, but also the many thousands of women who had done their jobs during the war had now returned to their positions in shops and offices or were back taking care of their homes and families. Hans was a hard and conscientious worker with a strength that belied his slim build and so there were not many days when he had no work.

He always met Maria at the bottom of Laurel Road. They would spend the evening together, usually walking in one of the parks or taking a trip across the river and back on the ferry, both of which cost little or nothing, and then he would escort her back to Laurel Road where they would say good-night. He was trying to save as much as he could, Maria had told Sophie, but he had to eat and pay for his lodgings. He kept just enough money with him to see him through each day, the rest he gave to Maria for safekeeping. It would have been quickly stolen had he left it at Mulligan's. She had persuaded him to buy himself some second-hand clothes to wear after work: nothing too good in case they too were stolen. She just hoped in time he would be able to find better lodgings; they couldn't spend so much time outdoors in the autumn and winter months. The situation was far from ideal but it was so much better than them being apart, she told herself.

Sophie was becoming increasingly busier both with her work and the preparations for Hetty's birthday tea. She had discussed it with Arthur and they had agreed that it would be somewhat rash to make it a surprise party, bearing in mind Hetty's increasing frailness. So, Sophie had allowed Bella to tell the old lady of their plans.

'Oh, Sophie, Bella has just told me what you are planning

for my birthday and I'm so *delighted*! I can't remember when I last had a party of any kind for my birthday. Why it must have been when I was a small child, and that's a very long time ago,' Hetty had confided.

'Did you not have one to celebrate your coming of age, at twenty-one?' Sophie had asked.

Hetty had shaken her head. 'Oh, no, dear. Our parents didn't believe that girls should be encouraged to think about things like that. You must remember that when I was a young girl, women who had no need to work stayed at home – I never went out to work in my life. Women had no rights at all, not even the right to vote. My father was dead by the time the suffrage movement came into being but he would have been shocked to the core by its formation. He would have considered it scandalous that women should even *want* to vote or become involved in politics at all.'

'Well, you will have a party to celebrate *this* birthday and we'll make it a very special day,' Sophie had promised. 'I know for a fact that Bella is already planning to help, she's excited too.'

Hetty had smiled. 'I am so lucky to have you all, Sophie. It's hard now to remember what my days were like before you came here. You, Bella, Maria and of course Arthur. He's such a considerate man, a true *gentleman*.'

Sophie had nodded her agreement. She never even thought about his past now. 'We're a family, Hetty. Not a conventional one, I have to say, but we all know we can rely on and help each other.'

Hetty had patted her hand affectionately. 'You're the best "family" I could wish for.'

On the following Friday evening Sophie was helping Bella to stick paper lace on the card the child was making for Hetty and they had just carefully placed it between two books so it would dry flat when Maria came in looking very anxious.

'You're home early, what's wrong? Don't you feel well?' Sophie asked, for Maria had only gone to meet Hans just over an hour ago.

Maria bit her lip and looked pointedly at Bella who was trying to decide what colour ribbon she should use for the bow that was to be added to the card next.

Sophie understood. 'Bella, why don't you go and ask Aunty Hetty what colour she would like?' she suggested.

'Mam, it's to be a surprise and if I ask her she'll know,' Bella replied indignantly.

'Then just ask her what her favourite colour is, then she won't guess.'

'We know what colour that is – lavender,' Bella said stubbornly, sensing she was being sent on a wild-goose chase.

'But she might have changed her mind, people do you know, and isn't it best to be safe than sorry? Wouldn't it be a shame if we put the wrong colour bow on it?' Sophie said seriously.

Bella considered this and decided her mother could be right. 'I'll just go and make sure.'

'Take the ribbons with you, then when you know you can cut a length off the right reel,' Sophie added.

'What's wrong, Maria?' she asked when the child had gone.

'I'm so worried, Sophie. He didn't turn up. I waited and I walked to the tram stop and back I don't know how many times. I didn't know whether to come back or not in case I missed him, but he's never late, not even by a few minutes. It's always me who's late; he's usually waiting for me. Something has happened to him, Sophie, I just *know* it has!' Maria was frantic with worry. 'What can we do? Should I go to that place – Mulligan's – and ask?'

'No! Neither of us is going anywhere near that place, not at this time in the evening,' Sophie said firmly, thinking of the numerous pubs in the dock area. Even this early there were always drunken brawls; you frequently read about them in the newspaper.

'Sophie, we have to do something! I have to know he's safe!' Maria pleaded.

'We'll wait a bit longer and then . . . then I'll ask Arthur if he would go and try to find out. There could be some simple explanation, Maria.'

'Like what, Sophie?' Maria twisted her hands together in desperation and began pacing up and down the room.

'He might have gone for a drink after he'd finished work and been delayed,' she suggested lamely.

'You know he never does that, he won't waste money and he dislikes the pubs around there,' Maria cried.

Sophie shrugged. She didn't know what else she could say; she was as worried as her sister.

'Oh, please, go and ask Arthur if he'll go now?' Maria begged.

Sophie nodded and got to her feet. There was little point in them sitting here worrying any longer.

Arthur agreed to go and make some enquiries, although he wasn't looking forward to either visiting Mulligan's or trawling the Dock Road in search of Hans Bonhoeffer, but he did realise the seriousness of the situation after Maria insisted that Hans had never failed to meet her before.

'Please, be careful, Arthur,' Sophie implored him as he left.

'I will,' he replied grimly.

Sophie tried to keep her mind on helping Bella tie and attach the lavender ribbon bow to Hetty's card but it was difficult, while Maria sat watching the hands on the clock on the wall move agonisingly slowly from numeral to numeral, praying that Arthur wouldn't be long and that he'd have news ... any news. 'Oh, please, please, God, don't let anything bad have happened to him,' she prayed.

Sophie had just got a reluctant Bella to bed and was coming down the stairs when she heard Arthur's key in the lock. She ran the few remaining steps to the door and pulled it open.

'Oh, dear God!' she cried, her eyes widening in shock and horror as she saw Arthur struggling to support Hans whose face was a mask of blood, his hair matted with it, his clothes torn. One arm was hanging limply at his side.

'Help me, Sophie, please. He's in a bad way, I found him lying in the alleyway a few streets away from the tram stop. He'd been trying to get here. I was on my way back, I'd had no luck at Mulligan's.'

Between them they got him into the hallway but before they could get any further Maria came rushing out of the sitting room and seeing him she screamed and rushed to him. '*Hans! Hans!* Oh, no! Oh, who did this to you?' she shrieked, her voice rising in panic.

'Maria, for God's sake pull yourself together and help us to get him on to the sofa. Take care, I think his arm is broken,' Sophie instructed curtly.

'He's badly hurt. He needs a doctor at least, if not an ambulance, Sophie,' Arthur advised gravely. The lad had taken a severe beating and he could have internal injuries.

Hans groaned in agony as they laid him on the sofa and Sophie put a cushion under his head.

'Maria, go and get some warm water and a cloth, we can at least bathe the blood from his poor face and, Arthur, could I ask you to fetch Doctor Franklin, please?'

'Are you sure I shouldn't call an ambulance and inform the police?'

'No, he can't go to hospital! They'll put him in a ward and won't let me be with him and I can't leave him, I can't, I *won't*!' Maria sobbed.

'And I think it would be a waste of time to inform the police, Arthur. They'll never find who did this to him; they won't even be very interested. He's just another foreigner involved in a brawl on the Dock Road,' Sophie added.

Arthur nodded. She was probably right and Maria was in such a state that if she was separated from the lad now she'd have a fit of hysterics. He left, heading again for the front door and wishing they had the luxury of a telephone. He was shaken himself. Even though he was no stranger to violence, he'd seen enough of it in jail, it still sickened him. In fact he abhorred it, and this mindless barbarity meted out to a lad whose only crime was to have been born in a country that had been part of the evil axis that had overrun Europe made him fume with both anger and impotence. The perpetrators would never be caught; there would be no justice or retribution for Hans Bonhoeffer.

Gently Sophie had bathed most of the congealed blood from his face, Maria was still quietly sobbing and her hands were shaking so much that she was of little use. Hans's nose was obviously broken, his lips split and puffy and his right eye was so swollen it was closed. He'd winced when she touched his cheekbone and she suspected it too was fractured. She was afraid to try to ascertain if he had broken ribs but she noticed that the knuckles on both his hands were skinned and bleeding. He'd obviously tried to defend himself.

'Hans, can you speak? What happened? Who did this?' she asked quietly.

'Oh, don't, Sophie. Can't you see how it hurts him to even try to breathe!' Maria whispered.

Sophie nodded. They would learn in time, she thought.

When he recovered . . . if he recovered – but she instantly pushed that thought away.

Both girls were so engrossed in tending to Hans that neither of them realised for some minutes that both Hetty and Bella were standing in the doorway watching them. Bella was clinging tightly to the old lady's hand, her blue eyes filled with trepidation. Hetty's face was drained of all colour but there was pity mixed with shock in her eyes.

'Mam, who is he and what's happened to him?' Bella asked.

Sophie turned, biting her lip. She had completely forgotten about both her daughter and Hetty in the confusion and sense of emergency. 'He's been hurt, Bella. Uncle Arthur has gone for the doctor.'

'But who is he, Mam? Why did he come here?'

'He . . . he's a friend of Aunty Maria's. A very good friend who came a . . . a long way to see her.'

Hetty's eyes widened and her hand went to the lace collar of her dress. 'Is . . . is he . . . the foreign young man?'

Sophie nodded. 'Yes, he's been in Liverpool for a few weeks now.' It was with relief that she heard Arthur returning. Perhaps when he'd seen to Hans Dr Franklin could make sure Hetty was all right, she looked very pale and shaken, but then they all were. 'Here's the doctor now. I think it would be best if you went back to bed, Bella. Aunty Hetty will take you up, if you don't mind, Hetty? I'll come and see you later, after Dr Franklin has gone,' she promised as Arthur ushered the doctor into the room, the man's expression serious and concerned.

Hetty gently pushed the child into the hallway and closed the door, her gnarled hands shaking. Nothing like this . . . this distressing thing had ever happened before and the sight of all that blood had made her feel queasy.

Dr Franklin carefully examined Hans while Maria clung to Sophie and Arthur watched grimly, all of them wincing when Hans groaned pitifully.

'Two of his ribs are broken and his arm and nose. The cuts will heal, although you will have to make sure they don't fester, and the bruising will fade in time. I can strap up his ribs but he should go to the hospital to have that arm set.'

'Oh, please don't send him to hospital! Can't you set his arm, doctor?' Maria pleaded. 'He's in so much pain and it would be worse if . . .'

'I don't wish to question your professional judgement, doctor, but would it be wise to move him? You'll agree he is in great pain and must be suffering from shock,' Arthur said quietly and with as much respect as he could impart into his tone. 'He will be well looked after here, it is quiet and he will be with Maria and Sophie, both of whom he knows well,' he added. The last thing Hans needed was to become disorientated and maybe even afraid in the emergency department of Stanley Hospital, which was the nearest.

Dr Franklin considered it and then nodded. He'd heard the full story from Arthur on the way to the house. 'I'll give him an injection and set both his arm and his nose, and put a couple of stitches in that cut above his eye, if you could assist me, please, Mr Chatsworth? Mrs Teare, I will need something to serve as a splint and plenty of thick bandages, if you have them. If not, perhaps we can improvise.'

'I'll cut up a sheet, if that will serve, doctor. It won't take me long, I have dressmaking shears,' Sophie replied, feeling much calmer now. She turned to her sister, who was still tearful. 'Maria, go up to the airing cupboard and find a single-size sheet and then you can help me,' she instructed. It would be better if Maria were out of the room when they set the broken bones.

An hour later Hans, with his arm splinted and heavily bandaged, was sleeping fitfully with a far more composed Maria sitting by his side. She was still very wan but Sophie had made them all a cup of strong, sweet tea, with a little brandy added, after the doctor had gone. He had gone up to see Hetty and had said that although she was rather shaken, she appeared none the worse and was resting. He'd left her something to help her sleep. To Sophie's relief, when she'd gone in to see Bella she'd found the child fast asleep so there was no need for any explanations tonight.

'Are you sure you want to sit up all night with him, Maria? I don't mind taking turns with you. You have work in the morning, don't forget.'

'I'm sure but thanks, Sophie, and I'm not going to work tomorrow, how can I leave him?'

Sophie nodded. 'By Monday I'm sure he will be feeling a little better, perhaps then he will be able to tell us more about what happened.'

Maria reached over and gently smoothed back a strand of

hair from his forehead. 'I've made a decision, Sophie. When he's well again, we're going home, both of us. He . . . he could have died. They could have killed him and if he goes back to that place or to the docks, it could happen again. They *know* him now, Sophie. I'm not going to let him risk his life for . . . for me. I don't know what we'll do for work, either of us, but we'll manage somehow.'

Sophie frowned. She could fully understand how her sister felt and everything Maria had said was true, but would Maude Sayle take him back? And what could Maria do there? Mam couldn't afford to keep them both. Oh, she would try but it just wasn't fair, Sarah's life was hard enough. Maybe when he recovered Hans could return to the island and then Maria could follow later? But Sophie had no intention of mentioning this to her sister now. It was too late and she was just too bone weary: exhausted by the events of the night.

Chapter Twenty-Six

———◆◆◆———

HANS SLOWLY RECOVERED AND they learned that on the day before he had been attacked he had had the misfortune to find himself working in the same gang as a man whose brother-in-law had indeed come from Amsterdam and who had picked up both a smattering of Dutch and a slight knowledge of the city. There had followed questions he could not answer and words he did not understand and it had been obvious that he had something to hide. Suspicion had immediately begun to mount against him. He'd heard the words 'Jerry' and 'Kraut' and 'Hun' muttered with curses but he'd tried to ignore the insults.

He'd said nothing to Maria that evening as he did not wish to upset or worry her but the following day the hostility was very much worse and at lunchtime the foreman had sought him out to inform him there was no work for him that afternoon nor would there be ever again. They did not employ Nazis. He'd known it was useless to try to explain so he'd returned to his cell-like room at Mulligan's for the rest of the afternoon, but when he'd left to meet Maria they'd been waiting for him in an alleyway. He'd fought like a tiger but there had been four of them and but for a couple of old women with bundles of washing on their heads, who had yelled at them to leave him alone and clear off or they'd call the scuffers, he feared they would have killed him.

They'd left him lying in the alley; where the old women had gone he didn't know but they hadn't stayed to help him. Maybe he had been calling out in German and they hadn't understood or wanted to become involved; he didn't know. He didn't remember much after that, except that he knew he must somehow get to Maria. He'd staggered through the streets for a very long time but then he had collapsed and the next thing he remembered was Arthur helping him up and bringing him here.

'Were they men you had worked with? Would you recognise them again, Hans?' Arthur had asked him.

'I think maybe two were but I'm not sure, and anyway, what can I do? It would be my word against that of them all and who would believe me?' He knew he had come very close to death and it had frightened him. He wanted no more trouble.

'He's right, Arthur. I know it's wrong, but I'm afraid it is true,' Sophie had said sadly.

'And he's not going to run the risk of getting beaten up

again,' Maria had added emphatically, taking his hand protectively, the one not encased in bandages, and more determined than ever that as soon as he was well enough, they were going back to Peel.

Hans recovered sufficiently to attend the birthday tea Sophie had planned for Hetty. Before she had mentioned it to Maria she had discussed it with Hetty for the last thing she wanted to do was upset the old lady.

'It's your birthday tomorrow, Hetty, and I was wondering how you would feel if we asked Hans to join us – for a little while? If you feel it would upset you or have any objections . . .' She left the rest unsaid.

Hetty thought about it and then nodded slowly. At first she had been very wary of him, even though she pitied him for the pain he was obviously suffering, but gradually she had come to realise that he posed no threat to either herself or those she considered her family. 'I wouldn't like to leave him out, Sophie. It wouldn't be the right thing to do at all. He seems a nice enough young man – for a foreigner – and he has suffered a great deal.'

Sophie nodded her agreement. 'He has. It was a great mistake for him to come to Liverpool, we all warned him but . . . but he loves Maria so much that the separation became unbearable. But as soon as he is well enough he will go back to Peel.' She didn't mention to Hetty that her sister was determined to go back to the island with Hans; she knew it would upset her.

Hetty smiled. 'Maria is very lucky, Sophie, to have someone who loves her so much.'

Sophie had smiled sadly as she nodded.

Maria was pleased that Hans was to be invited. 'I'm sure it will make him feel better, Sophie, to be included, but I'm still determined to take him home.'

'Well, don't go mentioning that to Hetty. I don't want her to get upset, not on her special day, and if she knows you're going too it will worry her.'

Maria promised she'd say nothing.

Everything was ready and the table looked lovely, Sophie thought with satisfaction. Maria had arranged spring flowers in one of the cut-glass vases and placed it in the centre of the table, beside the cake which Sophie thought looked very good. She had iced it carefully and had even managed to get the lettering fairly even. 'Happy 80th Birthday, Hetty' was what they had decided on and Sophie had tied a length of satin ribbon around the cake. Bella had wanted candles too but Sophie had said that it would be impossible to get eighty candles on the cake, even if she were lucky enough to find so many.

'But, Mam, blowing out the candles is the best part,' Bella had protested.

'Aunty Hetty is a very old lady, Bella, and it takes an awful lot of "blowing" to put out all those candles, it would exhaust her,' Sophie had said.

Bella had been persistent. 'But she won't be able to make a wish!'

'Of course she will,' Sophie had replied firmly.

Lizzie and Jim had arrived at ten to three, Lizzie bearing a fancy glass jar which contained coloured bath crystals.

'I just didn't know what to get her, Sophie, not that there's a great deal of choice. I mean what *do* you buy someone of her age? She's got so much already. Our Katie suggested these but I wasn't sure. What do you think?'

'I think she'll be delighted. She loves things like that,' Sophie reassured her aunt.

'How is the lad now?' Jim asked. They'd heard about the attack on Hans.

'Getting stronger each day. He's coming in to join us for half an hour.'

Lizzie raised her eyebrows but she was curious to meet this Hans Bonhoeffer. 'He was a fool to come here in the first place. I take it when he's got over it he'll be going back to Peel?'

Sophie nodded but not wishing to get into a discussion on Hans and Maria's future she urged her aunt to place the gift she'd brought on the table with the others before Hetty came down.

They had all bought Hetty a gift and these had been wrapped and were now set out on a side table, all except Bella's which Sophie had agreed the child could give to Hetty first.

Sophie had made the old lady a lovely bed jacket in lavender crêpe with a warm fleecy lining, trimmed with lace and ribbon. Maria had bought Hetty's favourite Yardley's

Old English Lavender soap, talcum powder and cologne and had added Hans's name to the gift card. From Arthur there was a silver-backed hairbrush in a box and he'd had 'Henrietta 80' engraved on the handle.

Bella was wearing her best dress, the royal blue velvet Sophie had made her for Christmas, and her hair was tied back neatly with a white satin ribbon. She was holding the card she had made, which Sophie had to admit had turned out very well; in fact she was beginning to realise that Bella was quite artistic.

At three o'clock Arthur escorted Hetty into the dining room and when she saw everyone eagerly waiting for her, her face lit up with pleasure.

'Happy Birthday, Aunty Hetty!' Bella cried, unable to contain herself any longer and thrusting the card into the old lady's hands. 'I made it for you for your special birthday!'

Hetty examined it carefully and then kissed the child on the cheek. 'It's *beautiful*! A true work of art. Thank you, Bella, you are a very clever girl and I will treasure it always,' she promised, her eyes suspiciously bright.

'Come and sit down and we'll have tea, or would you prefer to open your gifts first?' Sophie asked as Arthur settled Hetty in a comfortable carver at the head of the table.

Sensing Bella's excitement Hetty smiled. 'I think I'd like to open my presents first and Bella can help me.'

Carefully Bella brought each one from the table and placed it in front of Hetty, who exclaimed with pleasure and delight at each one she opened, thanking them all for their generosity. Then Sophie and Maria brought in the tea, the sandwiches and scones and finally Hetty was urged to cut the cake.

'You have to make a wish, Aunty Hetty!' Bella urged as Hetty prepared to make the first cut.

Hetty looked around her. 'There's nothing more I can wish for, Bella. I have absolutely everything a person could want.'

'But you *have* to, Aunty Hetty,' Bella insisted.

Hetty's gaze fell on Maria, who was sitting beside Hans and spreading jam on a scone for him. It was so obvious that they were very much in love. 'Then I wish that Maria and Hans have a long and very happy life together.'

Maria blushed and smiled. 'Thank you, Hetty. I hope we will and I hope that you . . . that everyone will come to our wedding, whenever and wherever it takes place.'

Hans smiled and nodded. 'You will all be most welcome, especially you, Miss Foster. It is a great occasion for me to help celebrate your birthday, I have much appreciation.'

Lizzie looked surreptitiously at Jim. You had to admit that the lad had good manners, and he seemed genuinely fond of Maria and pleased that he had been included in this little celebration. And if Sarah didn't object to the match then who were they to do so?

Lizzie and Jim had finally departed, Lizzie reluctantly for she greatly enjoyed the comfort and luxury of Hetty's house, to say nothing of the quiet peaceful atmosphere, something which was decidedly missing in Harebell Street. Billy usually made sure of that. But it was all a bit *too* quiet and refined, Jim remarked as they walked to the tram stop. He intended to go for a pint or two with Pat Ryan when they got back, Lizzie no doubt would quite happily sit and relay every detail to Martha.

Sophie and Maria cleared the dishes away while Arthur helped Hans up the stairs for Maria insisted he must rest now. He had been installed in Bella's room and the child was now sharing with Sophie. Hetty and Bella, too, had been persuaded to go up for Hetty was tired and Bella had school the next day.

'It all went very well, didn't it? Hans enjoyed it too,' Maria remarked contentedly.

Sophie nodded. 'Maria, I've been thinking about you going back . . .'

Maria stopped folding the tablecloth and looked closely at her sister. 'I'm not going to let him go on his own, Sophie. He won't be able to use that arm for quite a while yet and what if he fell and hurt his ribs even more?'

'I wasn't going to suggest he went on his own. I'm just worried about how Mam will manage with the two of you and if, when he's able, Maude Sayle will take him back. She might not; she might have taken someone else on now. Wouldn't it be better, Maria, if you stayed here for a while? You could save up a bit more, it would help until one of you managed to get work and Mam wouldn't have you both under her feet; you know how small the cottage is. If Hans was there on his own it wouldn't be too bad.'

Maria bit her lip. Everything Sophie had pointed out was true.

'Just, say, for a month and then—' Sophie urged.

'Am I interrupting?' Arthur asked as he came into the room.

'Of course not. I was just urging Maria to stay here for a month after Hans goes back, to save up a bit more money to help tide them over until he can work again—'

'Hans doesn't want to stay here for very much longer, he knows that when he's well again he won't be able to go out and says he feels cooped up, he's used to being outdoors. He's very, very grateful of course but he wants to get back as soon as he can. But I can't let him make that journey on his own,' Maria interrupted.

Arthur nodded slowly; he could see both points of view. 'Would it help if I were to accompany him? We could take the morning ferry and I could return the following day. Of course I wouldn't want to impose on your mother – is there an hotel or a bed-and-breakfast establishment where I could stay?'

Maria looked very relieved. It would help solve some of the immediate problems. 'Oh, that would be a huge help, Arthur, thank you. I'd feel much happier knowing you were with him.'

'I'll write to Mam and tell her and ask her to find you some suitable accommodation,' Sophie added.

'Then that's settled. As soon as he's well enough I'll go with him but I think we'd better ask the doctor when that will be,' Arthur advised.

It was three weeks later when Hans, accompanied by Arthur and Maria, went down to the Pier Head to get the ferry. Maria had agreed to stay on for another month, which would help increase her small amount of savings and also give Hetty time to get used to the idea that she was going home and in all probability would not be coming back. Sarah had written informing Sophie that she had booked Arthur into a small but clean and comfortable bed and breakfast on the edge of the village and had been up to see Maude Sayle, who had indeed taken on someone else to replace Hans. But, as summer approached and they became busier, Sarah wrote, he might well be employed for the harvest.

Maria was going straight to work after seeing Hans off so Sophie had taken the opportunity of giving the bedroom he'd used a thorough clean and had changed the bedding. Bella was moving back into her room that evening. After lunch Emily had arrived as it was her week for visiting Bella and the two children were playing quite happily upstairs in the playroom so Sophie took the opportunity to cut out two dresses that had been ordered. Hetty as usual was having a nap.

'They got off all right?' Sophie asked when Maria returned that evening and Sophie was preparing the meal.

'Yes, they'll be safely with Mam now.' She sighed. 'Oh, I miss him already, Sophie. I've got so used to being with him every day . . .'

'Mam will take good care of him, Maria, and the time will pass quickly enough.'

'I know but—'

'Go up and get changed and tell Bella and Emily that tea is almost ready,' Sophie instructed. She wanted to take her sister's mind off Hans. 'Would you tell Hetty too, please?'

Maria sighed again but nodded and left the room.

Sophie was pouring the boiling water from the kettle into the teapot when Maria ran into the kitchen.

'Sophie! Sophie, come quickly! There's something wrong with Hetty!'

Sophie's eyes widened and she put the kettle down. 'What is it? What's wrong with her, Maria?'

'I . . . I can't wake her, Sophie, I think . . . I think she's . . .'

'Oh, my God!' Sophie cried and rushed into the hall, followed by Maria, who was pale and shocked.

The old lady was still in bed. Her eyes were closed and the magazine she'd been leafing through had fallen to the floor. Sophie took her hand, feeling for a pulse.

'Hetty! Hetty, are you ill? Hetty, can you hear me?' she pleaded frantically. She could feel no pulse and as she looked closer she realised Hetty wasn't breathing. A sob caught in her throat. Hetty was dead, she knew she was, and she'd died up here . . . alone.

'Shall I go for the doctor, Sophie?' Maria asked, a note of panic in her voice.

Sophie nodded, the tears welling up in her eyes. 'Yes, but . . . but he won't be able to help her. She . . . she's dead, Maria. It must have been another stroke, but . . . but he'll know.'

'Oh, no! Oh, Sophie, she was fine this morning . . .' Maria

301

broke down and the two girls clung together. 'She was so good to us, Sophie,' Maria sobbed.

'I know and she . . . she was all alone when she . . . went, Maria. Oh, I wish I'd been with her, I *should* have been with her.' Sophie was trembling with shock and grief. She wished Arthur were here.

'What will we do, Sophie?' Maria asked tearfully.

Sophie realised she had to try to pull herself together. Bella and Emily were upstairs and Maria was looking to her for comfort. She wiped her eyes. 'You go for Dr Franklin and I . . . I'll go up to Bella. I'll have to find the words to tell her that her dear, kind, lovely Aunty Hetty has gone to heaven.'

The next hours seemed very unreal to Sophie, they reminded her of the way she'd felt when she'd learned that Andrew had disappeared, but this time she didn't have her mother to help her get through them. Dr Franklin had come and had confirmed that Hetty Foster had indeed had another stroke but assured both girls that she wouldn't have suffered, which was a blessing. Upon learning that Arthur Chatsworth was away, he had signed the death certificate and had suggested that Sophie contact the undertakers, gently assuring her that they would take care of everything. He also suggested that she go through Hetty's papers to see if she had left any instructions regarding which firm, if any, she had a preference for.

'We'll have to let Arthur know, Sophie. Will I send a telegram to Mam?' Maria had asked and she had agreed. It wasn't something that could be left until Arthur returned tomorrow. He had to know what awaited him.

Bella had been very upset and tearful but having Emily with her had helped, Sophie thought as she went through the papers in the drawer where Hetty had kept them. Oh, she hated doing this, she thought, but thankfully she had found a business card with the name, address and phone number of a firm of funeral directors. When Maria returned she would go to the local public telephone and call them. Her sister was going to call in to inform their aunt on her way back and she knew Lizzie would come as soon as she could and she'd be very grateful for her support. She felt so utterly confused, bereft and alone. If it hadn't been for Hetty Foster she wouldn't have been able to do so well with her business, she wouldn't have been able to give Bella such a comfortable home. Hetty had loved the child and Bella had looked on the old lady as a grandmother for she hadn't seen Sarah for a long time.

Maria returned with Lizzie, who then sent her niece out to phone the undertakers.

'It was so sudden, Aunty Lizzie,' Sophie confided as Lizzie made a pot of tea.

'But she didn't suffer, Sophie, and she was a good age, a very good age indeed,' Lizzie reminded her.

Sophie nodded.

'Things will be better in the morning, luv, once the undertakers have been and you've had some time to get over the shock and some sleep. I'll take Emily home and then

303

when Mr Chatsworth gets back tomorrow you can decide on the details of the funeral. I'm sure he'll see to all the formalities such as going to register the death. I'll come tomorrow afternoon to discuss everything with you.' Lizzie paused. 'Did she leave a will?'

Sophie looked at her blankly. 'I don't know.'

'Was there anything with her papers?'

'I didn't look. I . . . I felt terrible going through them. They were all her . . . private things.'

Lizzie patted her hand. There would be time enough for all that when Arthur Chatsworth got back. At least he was the kind of man you could rely on.

Chapter Twenty-Seven

‹————›

S OPHIE WAS VERY RELIEVED when after lunch the following
day Arthur arrived back. He was very shocked and upset,
he told her. He'd been unable to believe it at first, until Sarah
had given him the telegram to read. He told Maria that Hans
had told him to tell her that he was so very sorry he could not
be with her and that he had great respect for Miss Foster.

'Mr Coyne, the funeral director, suggested they should
take her to their chapel of rest where we could go to pay our
respects, but I . . . I couldn't send her away. This was her
home and she loved it,' Sophie informed him.

He'd nodded his agreement. 'You did the right thing,
Sophie. She was happy here – with us. How is Bella taking
it?'

'She cried a lot last night but she's much better now. I

305

took her in to see Hetty, they've laid her out in her bedroom, and Bella said she just looks as if she's asleep, which she does. That seemed to help Bella and she's put the card she made for her eightieth birthday in the coffin beside her.' Sophie wiped away a tear. 'She said she could show it to Jesus in heaven. She doesn't really understand that it's only Hetty's soul that will be heaven.'

Arthur swallowed hard, feeling the tears prick his own eyes. 'You can leave all the formalities to me, Sophie. First thing in the morning I'll go down to Brougham Terrace and register the death then I'll call in to Coyne's. We'll have to decide today on the details. I'll go along after Evensong to see the vicar, I presume she will want the service at her church and to be buried in the churchyard.'

Sophie nodded. 'Aunty Lizzie said she'd call this afternoon, to discuss what she called the "funeral tea" and what flowers we'd want.' She sighed heavily. 'Oh, there is so much to think about and I'm still so shocked and confused.'

He patted her hand. 'We all are, Sophie. We all owe her so much. At least she knew she was held in great affection and she derived so much pleasure from her last Christmas and the birthday party you organised for her. Her last days were happy ones. You must take comfort from that.'

It was a sentiment expressed by Lizzie too when she arrived later that afternoon with Martha Ryan, who had come to offer her condolences.

'You couldn't have done more, Sophie.'

'It was little enough, Aunty Lizzie, after everything she did for us.'

'Well now, have you sorted out the arrangements?' Lizzie was businesslike.

'It's to be on Friday morning at ten. The service is to be at Christ Church and she's to be buried in the churchyard,' Sophie informed her aunt.

'How many will there be coming back to the house afterwards?' Lizzie enquired.

'Just us and the ladies from the church.'

'And Jim and myself and our Katie, Miss Foster gave her that lovely tablecloth, remember, when she got engaged.'

'And Pat and I will come too and we'll go halves with Lizzie for a wreath,' Martha added, feeling it was little enough to support Sophie in her loss. If things had been different, Frank would have been here to do it, she thought sadly.

'That's very good of you, Mrs Ryan,' Sophie replied, thinking of Frank and wanting to ask about him but knowing this was neither the time nor the place.

Martha patted her hand. 'For heaven's sake, Sophie, call me Martha.'

'So, there will be twelve of us, including Bella, or are you going to send her to school?' Lizzie asked.

Sophie shook her head. Bella would be upset but she would never forgive her if she didn't let her say goodbye properly to her Aunty Hetty.

'We'll just have to see what we can get, Martha, in the way

of fillings for sandwiches,' Lizzie said gloomily, wondering if they would ever be able to purchase things without the blasted ration books or would they go to their graves with the flaming things. Hetty Foster hadn't lived long enough to see the end of rationing. 'But don't worry, Sophie, we'll manage.'

Martha raised her eyes to the ceiling, wondering if Lizzie would ever give up saying that. She doubted it.

'Did Mr Chatsworth have a look through her papers for anything "official", like?' Lizzie asked. Jim had said that Hetty Foster's 'estate', as these things were called officially, might have to go through probate as she had no next of kin, although he wasn't too clear on what exactly probate was. But he'd expressed some concern about Sophie being able to continue to live in this house; after all, she wasn't related to the old lady.

Sophie nodded, fully aware of what her aunt meant. 'He did and she has left a will, which he is going to take to Hetty's solicitor tomorrow. Then after the funeral is over, he will go with me for it to be read. He said he's . . . he's certain that she has left me . . . something. Not that I want anything, not that I expected anything. She gave me . . . us . . . so much.'

'Of course she did, luv, but you have to go through these legal . . . things,' Lizzie assured her. She sincerely hoped that Hetty Foster had indeed remembered Sophie in her will, otherwise she would have no alternative but to have her niece and her little family move back into Harebell Street and how they would manage with all Sophie's work stuff she didn't know.

*

Friday morning was overcast and dull and Sophie hoped it would not rain. She wore her black and white checked dress with a black jacket over it and a small black hat. Maria had a navy jacket over her dress and a navy hat and Bella wore her blue velvet dress, it being the only one of a suitably dark colour. Arthur wore his good dark grey Crombie overcoat although it really was too warm, and his dark suit and a black tie, which made his white shirt look brighter. His black bowler hat had been brushed and his boots were highly polished. They were all going in one car; Lizzie, Jim, Katie, Pat and Martha were going in the other. Even though she had no real family at least she was going to have a decent send-off, Sophie thought sadly as she went downstairs – stairs Hetty Foster would never descend again.

In the church there were many friends and acquaintances of Hetty's. In his sermon the vicar praised Hetty's virtues and said she would be sadly missed by both himself and his congregation.

Thankfully when they stood in the churchyard the sun at last broke through the clouds and Sophie felt it was a good omen, a sign that Hetty was happy and at peace. Bella had shed a few tears in church and was now clinging tightly to her hand but at least she wasn't sobbing heart-brokenly. Lizzie had remarked that in her experience children were remarkably resilient. That had surprised Sophie who hadn't heard her aunt utter anything so profound in all the time she'd known her, but she'd thought that possibly Lizzie was right.

The funeral tea had been a quiet affair with just Hetty's friends and themselves and before she took her leave Martha had informed her that Frank would be home in two weeks but that she would do everything in her power to prevent him from annoying Sophie.

'He doesn't annoy me, Martha, far from it,' Sophie answered sadly.

'Oh, you know what I mean, Sophie, but this is a difficult enough time for you as it is without our Frank making it harder. I wish . . . things were different, Sophie, believe me I really do,' Martha added, seeing the tears on Sophie's lashes and knowing they were not entirely for Hetty Foster.

'So do I, Martha, but . . .'

Martha squeezed her hand. 'Don't give up hope, luv.'

Sophie managed a smile. 'I won't, but it's not easy.'

Martha's expression changed. 'You never know, luv. *That one* might get run over by a bus one of these days although I doubt it. *Her* kind seems to survive and flourish – like weeds!'

Maria, who had been listening, frowned, thinking that Martha Ryan wasn't being particularly tactful and judging by the look on her Aunty Lizzie's face, she didn't think so either.

The following Monday morning Arthur accompanied Sophie to the offices of Grey, Corbett and Entwhistle in India Buildings. It was a very apt name for him, Sophie thought as Mr Grey ushered them into his office. His hair was grey, as was his suit, and his office also seemed to be decorated and furnished in similar shades.

'Mrs Teare, Mr Chatsworth, please do sit down,' he instructed formally, sorting through the papers on his desk and extracting the one he had been looking for. 'Ah, yes. "The Last Will and Testament of Miss Henrietta Sybil Foster", which she made on the sixteenth of August last year. Duly signed and witnessed, everything is in order.' He cleared his throat and began to read the contents aloud.

Sophie sat in stunned silence as she learned that Hetty had left Arthur a sum of five hundred pounds. That she had also left both Maria and Bella bequests of five hundred pounds each and that the rest of her estate, which comprised the house in Laurel Road, its contents and a sum of £1,250, was to go to herself. She hadn't expected anything like this. Maybe a piece of jewellery or a trinket as a keepsake but . . . over a *thousand pounds*! 'You are *sure*, Mr Grey?' she finally managed to stammer when he'd finished reading.

'Absolutely positive, Mrs Teare. It's all here in black and white and perfectly legal. I will have all the necessary paperwork drawn up concerning the transfer of the deeds of the house. You will all be able to draw upon the funds as you see fit, except the child of course. You, Mrs Teare, will be in charge of her legacy until she comes of age.'

Arthur, himself taken aback that she had left him such a generous amount, stood up. 'Thank you for your time, Mr Grey.' He extended his hand and the solicitor shook it.

'Good day to you, Mr Chatsworth, Mrs Teare . . .'

When they were outside the building Sophie burst into tears.

'Whatever is wrong, Sophie?' Arthur asked, full of concern.

'Oh, Arthur! I never expected her to leave *everything* to me. It's . . . it's just too much! Oh, bless you, Hetty! Bless you!'

He smiled, handing her his handkerchief. 'I knew she had, Sophie. She told me but swore me to secrecy. She said you had turned that house into a happy home for us all and she wanted you to have it. I honestly didn't think she had left me anything and I didn't want her to. She welcomed me into her home and I was content with that.'

Sophie nodded, feeling a bit calmer and suddenly realising that she was now quite well off. Her future was secure, she could provide a much easier life for her mother, and there was a nest egg for Bella too. And Maria. Maria now had five hundred pounds, which would ensure that she could marry Hans and not have to live in virtual poverty. 'Oh, Arthur, we are all so very, very lucky. This means that Maria can marry Hans; that Mam won't have to work any more and will be comfortable in her old age. That Bella's future is secure and that I . . .'

He smiled at her. 'That you are now quite a well-off young woman, Sophie.'

She took his arm as they walked toward the tram stop, still unable to take it all in. Oh, she had so much now and she had dear, kind, thoughtful, generous Hetty to thank for it all. If she could have had Frank at her side then her happiness would be complete, she thought, but then told herself that she was wishing for the moon and it was ungrateful to want more. There was nothing anyone – not even Hetty – could do to resolve that situation.

Maria could hardly believe it when she arrived home that evening. '*Five hundred pounds*! She's left me that much!' she cried when Sophie told her the news.

'She's been so very generous to us all, I'm still finding it difficult to realise that now this house belongs to me,' Sophie added.

Maria's hands were pressed against her cheeks. 'Oh, Sophie! I can go home now . . . home to Hans. We can get married; money won't be a problem.'

Sophie smiled at her but Arthur looked a little more serious.

'It won't last for ever, Maria. You should think about how best to use it,' he advised.

Maria sat down opposite him, more thoughtful herself. She and Hans did have a future but he was right and she trusted his judgement. 'Should I put most of it in a bank account or some kind of savings scheme? We won't need a great deal for the wedding and we'll rent somewhere to live, nothing grand.'

He considered this. 'You could, it would gain interest in time but would it not be better to put some of it into a . . . venture that would provide you both with an income to live on?'

Sophie too was interested in his advice, after all she herself had the money Hetty had left her. 'You mean some kind of business?'

'But Hans only knows about farming. Do you mean see if we can rent some land and keep animals and grow crops?' Maria didn't think this was very feasible. Manx farmers passed their lands down through the generations and, as she well knew, working on the land was far from easy. It was seven days a week, fifty-two weeks a year in all weathers.

'You'd be hard put to do that, Maria. Maybe you could buy shares in the fishing fleet and in the nets,' Sophie suggested.

'You know as well as I do, Sophie, that fishing isn't doing as well as it used to. The fleet is small now; there aren't nearly as many boats as there were when we were children. Mam says the days of the fishing fleet are numbered and she should know.'

Sophie nodded, biting her lip.

'But what I did notice on my very short visit and before we received the telegram was that there were quite a lot of people who were obviously on holiday or having a day out, the beach was quite crowded.' Arthur mused.

'Perhaps I could open a shop,' Maria wondered aloud. 'But selling what?'

'Things holidaymakers would want to buy,' Sophie suggested.

'They always want to have a cup of tea and something to eat, perhaps a café?' Suddenly Maria clapped her hands together. 'I know what I'll do! I'll open a tea shop, selling sandwiches, cakes, scones and maybe even ice cream. I've always been good at baking. I enjoy it.'

'You could do Afternoon Teas, that kind of thing,' Arthur suggested. 'On my walk around the harbour and along the quayside I didn't see any sign of such an establishment.'

'If I could find the right premises, somewhere with a nice view of the castle and St Patrick's Isle and near to the beach, I'm sure I would do well,' Maria enthused.

'Of course you would have to be open long hours and probably seven days a week, it would be hard work, and you would have to make enough money through the summer to see you through the winter months when there are few holidaymakers,' Arthur pointed out.

Maria nodded slowly. It would be hard work and what part could Hans play in this venture? 'I'll have to think about it carefully, Arthur, and discuss it with Hans, of course. It's his future too.'

Sophie smiled at her. 'So, when do you think you'll be leaving us?'

Maria smiled back. 'Just as soon as I can. In fact I think I'll go and write to Hans now, telling him the good news. That I'm coming home and that we can be married and that all our worries are over.'

Sophie got to her feet as Maria left the room and turned to Arthur. 'Shall I make some tea or would you prefer something stronger?'

'Tea will be fine, Sophie, thank you.'

'Do you really think a tea shop would be successful?'

'There isn't one in Peel and if she found the right premises, in the right spot . . .'

'I didn't give a thought to it being seasonal though,' Sophie said.

'It need not be. If they have a good reputation local people might come in through the colder months, especially if she then considered serving homemade soup and a bread roll as well.'

Sophie looked at him with admiration. 'You have some great ideas and you know you could be right, Arthur: things are getting better now on the island.'

He smiled but then looked serious. 'And what about . . . me, Sophie?'

She was puzzled. 'What about you?'

'Well, this is your house now. You might want to . . . change things and I might not . . . fit in.'

Understanding dawned and she crossed and put her arm around his shoulders. 'Arthur, this is your home and it always will be. It's what Hetty would have wanted, you know it is. How could you even think that I wouldn't want you here? What would I do without you?'

Arthur let his breath out slowly and with great relief. 'Thank you, Sophie. Thank you.'

Chapter Twenty-Eight

———◆◆◆———

IT WAS OVER A week later when Maria got off the bus in Peel to find Hans waiting for her, his face wreathed in smiles. He looked well, she thought. His shirt was clean, his jacket had been brushed and pressed, his boots polished and his hair had been cut. His bruises had disappeared and the cut above his eye had healed. It would, however, leave a scar and his nose would never be totally straight, although Dr Franklin had done a good job. But it didn't matter to her; every time she looked at him she knew those scars would remind her of what he had suffered to be with her.

'Maria! Is it all true? We can be married now?' he asked as she threw her arms around his neck, still careful of his arm and ribs, and he had kissed her.

'It is, Hans. Let's get to Mam's, I'm starving and I can tell you both everything then,' she urged. Sophie had persuaded her to work her week's notice, telling her she couldn't afford to waste money. She would need every penny for whatever venture she and Hans decided upon.

Sarah had the pot of tea ready and hot meat and potato pasties she'd baked that morning. 'It's good to have you home, Maria,' she greeted her younger daughter.

'Oh, Mam, it's good to *be* home.' She smiled at Hans who was deftly tending to the fire with his good hand.

'I still can't get over that Miss Foster leaving you all that money and her house to Sophie and neither of you any kin at all,' Sarah said, indicating that they both sit down at the table.

'It is wonderful to know that there is still kindness and goodness in the world,' Hans added.

Maria nodded sadly. 'She was lovely and she *was* kind and good. Do you remember, Hans, on her birthday she wished for us to have a long and happy life together? She knew then that she'd left me the money in her will, even if we didn't.'

'And what are you going to do with the money, girl?' Sarah asked. She'd never had as much money in her entire life.

'Use some of it to get married—' Maria replied.

'I hope you don't intend to waste it on a big fancy wedding?' Sarah interrupted.

'No, it will be quiet, unless you want something more . . . ?' Maria looked questioningly at Hans.

'I wish only for a quiet service, Maria. I have no family here, no friends,' he replied.

'You can ask Maude Sayle to come and perhaps her husband Edward could act as best man for you,' Sarah suggested, then, seeing the look of mystification in his eyes, she amended it 'to be your witness'.

'And I've had a wonderful idea. Arthur Chatsworth suggested that we go into business of some kind, Hans and me, and I think we should open a tea shop. There isn't one here and he noticed that there seemed to be more people on holiday these days who would patronise it,' Maria informed her mother and fiancé.

Sarah nodded. 'There are, people seem to like the beach here and St Patrick's Isle and I hear there is a shop opening soon to sell ice cream and sweets.'

This was certainly news to Maria. 'I think we should look for a place with a view and near to the beach and sell sandwiches, cakes, scones and "Afternoon Teas". It will be hard work and we'd have to make enough during the summer to keep us through the winter months.'

Hans was trying to look enthusiastic but was wondering what there would be for him to do in this tea shop? Would he be expected to wait on the tables with trays of tea and cakes? 'So, you have decided, Maria,' he said quietly.

'No, I wanted to discuss it with you. What do you think about it, Hans?'

'I think that it is good . . . for you, Maria, and I know how to make strudel, my mother taught Ingrid when she was a small girl and I watched,' he smiled. 'I have always a good appetite for strudel.'

Sarah nodded her understanding. He wasn't cut out to work in a tea shop, cooped inside all day waiting on tables or in the back, boiling kettles and washing dishes. 'It's not really the kind of thing you'd want to do, Hans, is it?'

He looked uncomfortable. He'd come back here with nothing and he still had very little to offer Maria and he didn't want to appear difficult or ungrateful.

'I couldn't manage a tea shop all on my own,' Maria said quietly. 'Perhaps we should think of doing something else.'

'We could run it together, Maria,' Sarah suggested. She would enjoy it, she wouldn't have to stand on the quay in all weathers trying to cajole the best price she could get for the catch out of reluctant and notoriously parsimonious buyers, who wanted the cod and whiting and herring at rock-bottom prices so they could make a handsome profit.

Both Maria and Hans looked at her hopefully and then Hans spoke. 'But what of me, what can I do? How can I make money for us? I have to help too. I cannot depend on Maria.'

Sarah smiled at him; it was understandable that the lad had his pride and he'd been humiliated enough without having it said he was living off his wife's inheritance. 'You'll think of something, Hans.'

He nodded. He'd worked on the land all his life. The one thing he knew best was farming. Slowly, a smile spread across his face. 'I have thought what it would be best for me to do. I will buy a tractor. There are not many tractors on the island – they are too expensive. I will hire myself and my tractor out to do ploughing, harrowing, sowing – anything that needs

320

doing. A tractor is much faster than a pair of horses: the work would be done in no time at all and people will have much pleasure.'

Sarah beamed at him. 'That's a wonderful idea, Hans. Why don't you go up and talk to Edward Sayle about it? And, the Commissioners might even be glad of you and your tractor when the lifeboat needs to be launched.'

Maria laughed delightedly. 'Oh, Hans, you're wonderful, you really are! I would never have thought of that and it will be perfect for you! And Mam and I will run the tea shop together. Now we can start to plan the wedding and look for suitable premises and a place to live when we're married.'

'And I will go to visit Mr Sayle and we will talk about tractors and which one is best and how much to pay,' Hans added, taking Maria's hand and smiling excitedly. Thanks to an old lady whom he hadn't even known very well their future now looked very bright indeed. It had been the right thing to do to come back to the island and he felt that all the hardships, sacrifices and beatings had not been in vain.

The house seemed very quiet now, Sophie thought, with Hetty gone and Maria and Hans back in Peel. Bella was at school for most of the day and so there were just her and Arthur and Arthur was often out too. He loved to walk and now that the weather was warmer and the days longer the time he spent away from the house had increased. Of course it gave her the much needed time to get on with her work, for as April had turned to May so the orders had increased. She was aware that now she really didn't need to work but as she'd said to Arthur, 'what else would I do with myself all day?'

Her thoughts turned to Frank as she made her way to Lizzie's that sunny afternoon. There had been a long letter from Maria in the lunchtime post, which was the reason she was on her way to see her aunt. She didn't know what Martha had said to Frank when he was last home but he hadn't come to see her, not even to offer his condolences. Even though she knew seeing him was pointless and would only have increased her dejection, she felt upset that he hadn't come. There were nights when she didn't sleep well and then, during those long hours, she had even begun to wonder if he still loved her or was he becoming so despondent, feeling everything was so hopeless, that he was wondering if it would be best if he tried to forget her. She couldn't blame him; sometimes it was so hard to cling to the hope that one day they could be together that she came close to despair herself. But then she would remind herself that she had once thought that Maria would never hear from Hans Bonhoeffer again and now they were full of plans for their future. Looking back she acknowledged that she'd been wrong to try to persuade her sister not to give up on Ben Seddon. Maria had never loved him, she'd given her heart to Hans.

Lizzie was standing on her front step talking to Martha. It was obvious from the cloth in her hand and the bucket at her feet that she had been attempting to clean the windows. Catching sight of Sophie she beamed and waved.

'Sophie, come on in and we'll have a cup of tea. I'm

wasting my time with these blasted windows; they'll be as bad as ever by tomorrow morning there's that much soot and muck in the air. Come in and join us, Martha,' she invited her neighbour.

'I bet you're finding that house very quiet, you must miss everyone, Sophie,' Lizzie stated as she filled the kettle.

'I do. I seem to spend a lot of time on my own now. I suppose it's one of the drawbacks of working from home.' She smiled: 'But the advantages do outweigh that.'

'And isn't it a grand "home" too? I still can't get over the old lady leaving everything to you, Sophie.'

'How is Maria getting on?' Martha asked, changing the subject. Hetty Foster's decision had provided Lizzie with hours of speculation.

'That's why I came. I had a letter today, four pages long, which is very unusual for Maria. She and Mam have been scouring Peel for suitable premises and she says she's finally found them. Right on the quay, opposite St Patrick's Isle and just across the road from the beach. It's part of an old stone storehouse but the big room downstairs will be great for the tea room, and upstairs there are three smaller rooms which will serve as living accommodation. The rent they're asking isn't too bad but she says Mam will "negotiate" with the owner as she's known him for years. It all needs doing up, of course, but Hans will do most of the heavy work himself.'

'And your mam is happy to help her run it?' Martha queried, although Lizzie had told her Sarah was delighted with the whole idea. Lizzie had added that it sounded like a lot of hard work to her: all that baking and waiting on tables and washing up.

'She is. Maria loves baking and Mam enjoys chatting to people – she'll make them feel welcome. Hans has ordered a tractor, a Fordson Major, which apparently is the latest thing, and hopes to have it delivered by the end of the month. But it's the wedding that took up most of the letter.'

'I thought it was only going to be a quiet affair?' Lizzie said, thinking that Katie would do well to follow Maria's example. Her daughter seemed to have plans that would cost a fortune – something she certainly didn't have.

'Oh, it is, but she'd like you and Uncle Jim to go over for it and if possible Katie and Matt. She'd like Uncle Jim to give her away, seeing as Pa's dead. I'll be going, of course, with Bella and Arthur. She's having Bella as a bridesmaid and I'm to be matron of honour. Mam's going to arrange all the accommodation and I'm making Bella's dress, my own and Mam's.'

'Where is Maria getting hers?' Martha enquired.

'Douglas, I think, and she's taking Hans there too for a decent suit.'

Lizzie was digesting all this. It was only natural for Maria to want Jim to give her away in place of her father John; Jim was Sarah's brother and Maria's closest male relative. It would be great to go for a brief visit too, she could do with a bit of a holiday. She hadn't had one in years. In fact she couldn't remember when she'd last had one at all, but it was the expense. Jim would lose at least two days' pay and they'd have to give Maria some sort of wedding present. There was the fare and accommodation, she'd have to have a good dress and a hat, particularly as Sarah was going to be dressed up – she didn't want to let anyone down. She doubted Katie would go, she was saving hard for her own home and wedding, nor would John, but she wondered would it be wise to leave Billy with his brother and sister. The Lord alone knew what that lad would get up to without Jim's restraining presence.

'What about Hans? He's no family to invite – well, he has but they couldn't possibly travel so far,' Martha commented.

'Mr Sayle is going to be best man and Maude will come too, but that's all. He says he doesn't mind, that it will be a very happy day for him even without his family there. Will I write back and tell her you'll be going over, Aunty Lizzie?' Sophie asked.

Lizzie hesitated. 'Well, I . . . I'll have to talk it over with Jim first.'

Sophie instantly understood. 'Aunty Lizzie, if you are worrying about the expense of it all – don't. I'll be happy to pay for the trip and I'll make you an outfit too, it's not for another month. I wouldn't want Maria to be disappointed and you were so good to us when we first came across. You gave us a home, don't forget.'

Lizzie nodded. 'Ah, what else could I have done, Sophie? You're family, but I'd be very grateful for help with the expenses, luv. I wouldn't want to disappoint Maria either but it would be a bit beyond me, I'm afraid.'

Sophie smiled. 'That's all settled then. I'll write and tell

Maria. And you must come down to me on Sunday afternoon and we'll decide on a colour and style for your outfit. I already know what I'm making for Mam so we can make sure we won't clash. It's much easier to choose things for a summer wedding, there are more colours that are suitable.'

'Are you sure about that, Sophie? I mean I know you're busy and you've got your outfits to make.' Lizzie felt that now she could possibly afford to buy a dress if necessary.

Sophie nodded firmly. 'I'm sure. I know my list of clients has increased over time, people seem to like my ideas, especially for weddings, but I send work out now, Aunty Lizzie: the tacking, plain sewing, hems and finishing off.' She turned to Martha. 'Did Frank get off all right? Did he sign on with another company?' She had to ask, she couldn't let the opportunity pass.

'No. The only other places available were on even longer trips. He wasn't very happy about it but it's better than being stuck here with *her*.'

Sophie didn't want to hear about Nora but from the scowl on Martha's face she realised that she was going to.

'You know who she's taken up with now? I was only telling Lizzie about it this morning.'

Sophie tried to look interested but didn't quite succeed.

Martha didn't notice. 'Only that Jake Harvey. *His* lot are as bad as the Richardses, father a drunk, brothers all in and out of jail. And that Jake is probably the worst of the lot. A real hard case, he is. It's a living disgrace, that's what it is. She's been seen out on the town with him regularly, all dressed up to the nines in stuff that no doubt *he's* paid for, or thieved more like.'

Lizzie shook her head. 'Well, you never know, Martha, he might just take her off your Frank's hands. If it's serious, that Jake might want to marry her. She might well ask your Frank for a divorce. *She* wouldn't care about having her name in all the papers and neither would Jake Harvey.'

'He might be a thief, a blackguard and a jailbird but he's not a fool, Lizzie. Who'd want to take her on? She's shop soiled. Damaged goods. Nothing more than a flaming little tart!' Martha retorted.

'You never know, Martha. He's certainly no angel himself so he might not care. They'd suit each other down to the ground,' Lizzie replied sagely.

Sophie felt her heart quicken. If what Martha and Lizzie had just said was true then . . . then there just might be a ray of hope for Frank and herself.

Chapter Twenty-Nine

———◆———

THE TIME SEEMED TO fly by for Sophie as she rushed to complete all her orders and the wedding outfits; she had little time to dwell on Frank and how, if at all, Nora's new liaison would affect the marriage. As the weeks progressed Bella was becoming more and more excited at the thought of being a bridesmaid and of going to see her Granny Sarah.

It had been decided that Billy would go too, as Lizzie felt it would be courting disaster to leave him behind, but Katie had regretfully declined to accompany her parents. Even though Sophie had offered to pay Matt had said he wouldn't feel at all comfortable about going after the way Maria had treated his brother and in the light of the bridegroom's nationality being somewhat suspect. Ben for one didn't believe a word that had been said about Hans Bonhoeffer. Lizzie hadn't told Sophie that, she'd just said that Katie was grateful but had decided that it was going to cost her cousin quite enough without herself and Matt adding to the expense.

Arthur had purchased a new suit for the occasion and had undertaken the booking of the ferry and the writing of the letters of confirmation to the various bed-and-breakfast accommodations Sarah had found for everyone. Lizzie was delighted with the pale green and cream floral dress and matching jacket Sophie had made for her and had treated herself to a pale green hat, trimmed with cream artificial flowers. They had both been carefully packed in tissue paper and were now in the case. Jim's suit had been cleaned and pressed; he had a new shirt and she'd got new trousers and a nice white shirt and a tie for Billy, who'd muttered that he hated being done up like a dog's dinner and was glad none of his mates would be there to skit him. For that he'd received a clip around the ear from Lizzie, who had added that he should be grateful he was being included at all and that none of his "mates" were lucky enough to be going on what she termed as a "bit of a holiday".

'I'll kill him with my own two hands if he makes a show of us, Sophie, I swear I will!' Lizzie had declared darkly.

'Oh, he'll be fine. Bella will show him everything of interest and if it's fine they can play on the beach,' Sophie had reassured her aunt.

*

It was with mixed feelings of relief, apprehension and excitement that Jim and Arthur shepherded the little party to their seats on the *Lady of Man* that June morning. The early mist that hung over the waters of the Mersey gave promise of a fine, hot day and Sophie remarked that it would be a lovely crossing. They'd brought sandwiches with them and Bella and Billy had been promised that they could have their 'picnic' on deck, providing they behaved and didn't run around and annoy everyone else.

'Is there a *real* beach, Bella? Not just a mucky bit of sand like there is at New Brighton? Mam said she thought there was but she couldn't remember,' Billy asked as they sat on the deck, watching the Mersey estuary fade in the distance.

'Of course there is, there are lots of beaches and there's a harbour with fishing boats and the lifeboat and the causeway across to the Isle. And there's a castle and a church there too.'

'Does anyone live there, in the castle?' Billy was beginning to feel that this was going to be quite an adventure and worth having to be 'dressed up' for.

'No, it's all falling down, but it's a great place to explore.' Bella too was looking forward to this visit.

'Is it much further now?' Billy had no concept of distance whatsoever and it already seemed ages since they'd left Liverpool.

'There's miles and miles to go yet, Billy,' Bella replied, remembering how the crossing had seemed interminable to her when she'd first come across and how everything had seemed so strange and frightening.

'Maybe we should ask Mam can we have the picnic now,' Billy wondered.

Bella raised her huge blue eyes to the sky. Boys seemed to think of nothing else but food!

Everyone was up on deck as the ferry steamed slowly into Douglas harbour.

'I have to say that this is going to be a much happier occasion than my last visit here turned out to be,' Arthur remarked to Sophie.

'And it's thanks to Hetty that we're all here today, bless her,' Sophie replied as she took Bella's hand.

Lizzie was hanging on firmly to Billy and Jim had the suitcase and was looking rather nostalgic. It was the first time in more years than he cared to remember that he'd been home, he thought, watching the hills behind Douglas drawing nearer. It was so long since he'd thought of this small island with its glens and mountains, quiet villages, tranquil harbours, steep cliffs and long stretches of sandy beach as 'home'.

They had caught the bus and Billy had been fascinated by the horse-drawn trams on the promenade and then as they'd left the town behind he had gazed around in delight at the passing scenery. He'd never realised that there could be so much open space; there seemed to be miles and miles of fields with sheep and cows in them and there were very few buildings. There were no rows and rows of houses and pubs and shops as there were in Liverpool and when the bus finally came over the brow of the hill and Bella pointed out the fishing village below with its little offshore island complete with castle and church, he decided that this was definitely worth all the travelling and fuss.

It was a while before they were all settled in the various houses and cottages around the village but Sarah had insisted that Sophie at least have a cup of tea and that the wedding finery be unpacked and hung up before Maria dragged her off to view what was destined to be the tea shop.

They left Bella with her Granny Sarah and walked the short distance down to the quayside.

'Oh, I remember this place. Didn't they used to store herring barrels here?' Sophie stood looking up at the old stone building. 'I hope the place doesn't still smell of fish,' she laughed.

'Of course it doesn't! We've had all the windows and doors open. Hans has cleared out the rubbish and has given everywhere a coat of whitewash, just to make it look clean and bright. Then we'll get it painted properly.' Maria let them in and Sophie nodded as she could see the potential.

Maria was full of enthusiasm and ideas. 'We're going to have a seaside theme, we think it's appropriate. White table-cloths, blue and white china, shells and things as ornaments and I think we could even drape a bit of fishing net across those beams up there. I'm going to go to the next auction and see what I can pick up in the way of old copper kettles and pans; they'd look nice as decorative pieces too.'

Sophie smiled at her. 'You'll do well, I know you will, and is Hans happy at not having to work here?'

'Oh, he's delighted and he can't wait for the tractor

to arrive. He's going to be in great demand at harvest time.'

'Have you decided on a name for it?'

'We have. "Castle View Tea Rooms".'

'And everything is in hand for the big day?'

Maria nodded, her eyes shining. 'I got a really lovely dress, Sophie, it's—'

'No! Don't tell me, I want it to be a surprise, but you'd look lovely in a sack, Maria.'

'And I wouldn't even have minded that, Sophie. Just as long as Hans and I could be married. I'll never ever forget how much we owe to Hetty and we've agreed that when we have our first baby it will be called either Henry or Henrietta,' Maria said firmly.

Sophie put her arm around her. 'She'd have liked that, Maria. I know she would.'

The morning of the wedding dawned sunny and warm. The thin mist that had covered the tops of the hills had been burned off by the sun; the sky was a cloudless azure blue and the sea a shade of deep aquamarine and rays of sunlight danced on the ripples and wavelets, making them sparkle.

'Oh, it's just perfect, Mam,' Sophie said thankfully.

Sarah smiled and nodded. 'This is one day when we can do without Manannán's cloak but we'll have to get a move on, we have to be in the chapel in just over an hour.'

'I hope Aunty Lizzie is a bit more organised than she usually is,' Sophie remarked as she took the long pale blue organdie dress with the wide white sash from its hanger and called Bella to come down quickly. Sophie's own dress was of hyacinth-blue crêpe de Chine with cape sleeves and a full skirt and she had attached a short veil to a blue headband which she thought more appropriate than artificial flowers.

'It suits you, Sophie,' Sarah commented as she adjusted the coffee-coloured hat that matched her coffee and cream crêpe de Chine dress and jacket. Sophie had bought it in Val Smith's, which she said was one of Liverpool's best millinery shops. Sarah felt very smart and, for once in her life, truly elegant. Sophie had wonderful taste and a way with fabric and colours.

Both Bella and Sarah were ready when Jim, Lizzie and Billy arrived, followed a few minutes later by Arthur, who looked very smart indeed in his new suit and new bowler hat.

'Is she ready?' Lizzie asked, thinking that she, Sarah and Sophie looked like society ladies instead of the working-class women they were and it was all thanks to Sophie's talents.

'She was just fixing her veil when I came down,' Sophie informed them. 'She looks absolutely *gorgeous*, doesn't she, Mam?'

Sarah nodded, a lump in her throat. Oh, Maria had always been considered one of the prettiest girls in Peel but today, well, she did indeed look gorgeous.

Lizzie exclaimed out loud as Maria came down the stairs, thinking that never in a million years could her poor Katie look as beautiful. Maria was slim and petite and the dress was perfect. It was very plain, made of white duchesse satin that seemed to have a sheen to it. As tradition demanded it had a high neck with a little stand-up collar edged with lace and the same lace bordered the cuffs of the long tight sleeves. At the back it spread into a fishtail-shaped train attached to the dress with a large bow. Maria's long dark hair fell in loose curls and her face was framed by clouds of tulle held in place with a band of white satin embroidered with silver bugle beads.

Sophie passed her the small bouquet of summer flowers and trailing green smilax. 'You'll be the loveliest bride Peel has ever seen.'

'Just as long as Hans thinks so,' Maria said, smiling a little shyly.

It wasn't far to the little chapel where both Sophie and Sarah had been married and so the wedding party walked, to be admired and even clapped by everyone they passed, locals and holidaymakers alike. Lizzie thought it was all so much better, more "personal" than going in carriages or cars, so she remarked to Sarah.

'You'd have a bit of a job to get a carriage or a car down some of these lanes,' Sarah replied, feeling very proud and pleased that Maria was marrying the man she loved, that they were both starting out in business and had the security of a few hundred pounds in the bank.

When Maria entered the chapel and Hans turned towards her there was no doubt in anyone's mind that this was the happiest day of both their lives. Both their smiles were radiant as Maria handed her bouquet to Sophie and Hans took her hand in his and murmured, 'I love you, my beautiful Maria.'

He was a good-looking lad, Lizzie thought. You had to

admit that. Tall and slim, his blond hair lightened by the sun and his skin tanned by both sun and wind. He looked much better than the last time she'd seen him at Hetty Foster's birthday tea. Today he was wearing a smart charcoal-grey suit, a sprig of heather from the hillside in his buttonhole. They looked so much in love and had conquered so many obstacles to be together that it was like a fairy tale; it brought tears to your eyes. She fumbled in her bag for a handkerchief as the service began.

'Mam, will it take long? Bella said there's going to be great things to eat afterwards. That Mrs Sayle sent down a huge piece of ham and I'm starving already,' Billy whispered loudly, tugging at Lizzie's skirt. He'd be glad when the 'serious' bit was over and the holiday could really begin. He could take off this soppy shirt and the much-hated tie. The beach looked great and there were so many things to explore.

'Shut up and stop making a show of me!' Lizzie hissed, raising her eyes to the chapel roof and hoping that no one had heard.

Bella looked up at her mother who was trying hard to suppress a grin.

'Boys!' Sophie whispered and Bella smiled too. Everyone would certainly enjoy themselves today.

Chapter Thirty

———◆◆◆———

Nora had heard that Lizzie and her family had gone off to a wedding. That niece of hers – the one who looked like Vivien Leigh – was marrying some foreigner over on the Isle of Man. She presumed that that Sophie had gone too. Hadn't she done well for herself, she thought spitefully. Conning some daft old woman into leaving her that big house and a small fortune, or so she'd heard. Well, she certainly wouldn't want to know Frank Ryan now. Not now that she'd come up in the world and had money. It would serve him right.

She applied another coat of scarlet lipstick and smiled at her reflection in the mirror. Her hair was bleached by a professional hairdresser now and she'd let it grow and wore it in the long pageboy style which half covered the left side of her face like Veronica Lake, the film star. She had 'come up in the world' herself – a bit. She had more clothes and jewellery and perfume now than she could afford to buy with the pittance of an allotment Frank left her, thanks to Jake Harvey.

She frowned, pursing her lips. She was still young and attractive and all she wanted out of life was a good time and a bit of excitement. Jake gave her that, certainly, but he didn't *own* her, she thought. Oh, no, she was far too wise to get caught like that now. That Maria Kinnin must be mad, tying herself down to one man for life and working her fingers to the bone to keep him happy, she'd soon lose her looks that way. Nora Ryan wasn't going down that road, thank you very much. What had she ever got out of marriage? Nothing that she could see. She'd had some bloody stupid ideas when she'd been young and had been desperate to marry Frank Ryan; she'd even lied through her teeth to get him. She'd thought she was in love then, she never looked at anyone else; she'd been sure that the future held only happiness. She'd very soon learned it didn't and now she was glad Frank spent so much time at sea. And what was 'love' anyway? Most men were only interested in one thing and it wasn't 'love and romance'. She knew Frank wouldn't divorce her and she didn't particularly care, things were going along quite nicely as they were. Anyway, while he was still married to her he couldn't marry Sophie Teare. Not that *she'd* want him now she had money.

She wasn't seeing Jake tonight, he was going somewhere

'important', which meant that he and his 'associates', as he called his mates, were up to no good again, but she didn't ask questions. She knew better than to do that. If he'd wanted her to know, he'd have told her, but she hoped that there might be something at the end of tonight's escapade for her. Both her mam and da were out – in the pub as usual – and so Harry Thomas was calling here. She'd met him a couple of weeks ago at a dance (Jake had been doing something 'important' that night, too) and he was *gorgeous*, there was no other word for it. The image of Clark Gable in *Gone With the Wind* and such nice manners and ways too. Of course she wasn't stupid enough to believe everything he said; he was a born flatterer – with looks like that he was bound to be. But it still felt good to be told she was the equal of any Hollywood star.

She'd tidied the room up a bit and was wearing her newest peach satin camiknickers, slip and matching bra under her cerise cotton dress. Harry had said he'd bring a bottle of gin and she had a small bottle of Rose's Lime Juice. Gin and lime was so much more 'sophisticated' than beer, Harry had told her. She was looking forward to an evening in with him; he was bound to have had a great deal of experience with women.

They had a couple of drinks and chatted amiably about the latest films and she was looking forward to the minute when he would take her in his arms. She smiled archly at him.

'Harry, are we going ter spend all night talking about what films we'd like ter see . . . ?' She began to undo the buttons that ran down the front of her dress.

He smiled back and put down his glass. She was quite attractive and very seductive although she seemed oblivious to the untidy, dirty room and its smell, which wasn't masked by the overpowering perfume she wore. Still, he could put up with that for a couple of hours.

'Of course not, Nora. I was just being polite.' He stood up and drew her to her feet.

'Yer don't have to be "polite" with me, Harry,' she said as he took her in his arms and began to kiss her passionately. This was *much* better, she thought, feeling a little light-headed but excited.

They had moved to the bed and things had progressed. Nora's dress lay in a crumpled heap on the floor along with her slip and bra and Harry was pouring them another drink when there came the sound of the back door being thrown open.

'Oh, bloody hell! Da must have been thrown out again,' Nora cursed, pulling the old blanket up to cover her naked breasts and hoping he wouldn't come barging in here. Of all the times for him to have been chucked out of the blasted pub.

Harry had grabbed his shirt and jacket and was hastily shoving his feet back into his shoes, cursing under his breath as the door was flung open.

Nora's eyes widened as she caught sight of Jake standing in the doorway. His face was red and he was panting heavily – he'd obviously been running – but his eyes narrowed as he caught sight of Harry Thomas.

'Who the 'ell is 'e?' he shouted at her.

Nora decided the best form of defence was attack. 'What the bloody hell are you doing here, Jake, and can't yer knock before barging in?' she yelled back.

Harry didn't like the look of this bloke at all. He was obviously a thug of the first order. He edged his way slowly towards the door as Jake advanced into the room.

'I said who the 'ell is he? As soon as me back's turned you're whoring with this feller!' Jake yelled, his face turning almost puce and the veins in his neck standing out as anger consumed him.

Nora held her ground although she was beginning to feel apprehensive; she'd never seen him this angry before. 'And I asked yer what the bloody hell you was doing here? You said you had something important to do – obviously more flaming "important" than me, so why should I sit at home on me own?'

Harry left as quickly and as quietly as he could, feeling he'd had a lucky escape for he'd finally realised who this was. He'd heard of Jake Harvey and his reputation.

'It went wrong, didn't it? That thicko Mick Gates got things mixed up, that's why I came 'ere, Nora. So youse could say I was with yer all night and I find yer effing well in bed with *that* feller!'

Nora was dragging on her dress. 'You don't own me, Jake Harvey. I do what I like, now clear off!'

He came towards her, fury filling him. 'But everything you've got I bloody well gave yer, Nora. You were 'appy enough to take all that stuff.'

She still held her ground and laughed cuttingly. 'Stuff you'd *nicked*! You never paid for any of it and you expect me to be grateful. Oh, thanks a lot, Jake! It's *so* generous of yer! And then you come barging in here, calling me a whore, and now you want me to lie for yer ter keep yer out of jail. Well, you can go ter hell, I'm saying nothing of the kind an' Harry will back me up. It will be *our* word against yours. You're going down – again, Jake!'

A red mist of rage danced before his eyes. She was an ungrateful, two-timing whore and now she was refusing to give him an alibi and he knew this time he'd serve five years with hard labour. The bitch! The bloody whoring *bitch*!

Nora screamed as he grabbed her by the throat but the sound was choked off. She began to fight with every ounce of strength she possessed but it wasn't long before that strength ebbed away and her arms fell to her side. Her knees buckled and at last she fell to the ground, her eyes filled with pure terror before her head rolled to one side and she lay still.

Jake prodded her with his foot; she didn't move. He looked down at her lifeless form and panic drove out the rage. He'd killed her. Oh, Christ! He'd swing for this! He could almost feel the rope around his neck – there'd be no five years' hard labour for this, he'd hang! He had to get away *now*, this minute! He'd have to get out of the city altogether, he'd have to go down to the docks as fast as he could before anyone found her and try to sneak aboard a ship. He wouldn't feel safe until he was out of the country.

He ran out of the house the way he'd come in, leaving the door wide open behind him. As he raced across the yard and into the back entry his heart was pounding and cold sweat ran unheeded down his face. At the bottom of the entry he almost knocked over two young lads who had been kicking an empty can along the pavement. He cursed and kept on running, his legs working like pistons.

'That feller's in a big hurry! He nearly flattened the pair of us,' Robbie Ryan said indignantly to his mate Charlie Blackley.

'Wonder what he's been up to now? Yer know who it was, don't yer?' Charlie replied.

'Who? I've never seen him round here before,' Robbie puzzled.

'Jake Harvey. He's a dead bad lot, me da says.'

Robbie looked impressed but Charlie had retrieved the can and had resumed kicking it along the road so Robbie forgot all about the incident and ran after his mate.

It was two hours later when Martha went out into the street wondering who was making such a terrible racket. Nellie Richards was standing in the road screaming hysterically and pointing towards her house. This was more than just a drunken outburst, Martha surmised as she reluctantly crossed towards her. Mary Seddon too was out, as was Flo Caldwell.

'For God's sake, what's wrong, Nellie?' Martha shouted, taking the distraught woman by the shoulders.

Nellie was incoherent.

'Shake her, Martha, she's hysterical!' Mary Seddon urged.

Martha shook her hard. 'Calm down, Nellie, and tell us what's wrong.'

Nellie began to sob. 'Nora! It . . . it's our Nora! She's . . . she's been . . . killed! She's dead! I cum 'ome an' . . .' Nellie again became incoherent.

The three women looked at each other.

'Mary, go and see if she's telling the truth. The girl might not be dead, just *dead* drunk. I'll stay with Nellie.' Martha had no intention of setting foot in *that* house.

Both Mary and Flo went into the house and came out looking pale and shocked. 'She's right, Martha. Nora's lying on the floor in the bedroom and . . . and it looks as if she's been murdered.'

'Oh, God Almighty! How . . . Are you sure?'

Flo nodded. 'We . . . we think she's been . . . strangled.' She half whispered the word, unable to believe it.

'What'll we do now? We'll get no sense out of Nellie and she can't go back in there yet,' Mary asked.

'We'd better get her into our house and I'll send Pat over to . . . to make sure.' Much as Martha disliked and despised Nellie Richards she couldn't leave the women out in the street in this state. And God knows what time Bertie would eventually stagger home.

Pat was informed of what had happened and while Martha sat Nellie down Mary Seddon put the kettle on.

Pat was back within minutes, looking shocked and grim.

He nodded curtly to his wife, and then turned to his neighbour. 'Mary, would you ask Fred if he could go and find Bertie Richards and get him home while I go for the police.'

'Tell our Ernie to go with him, Mary, he'll be in no fit state to take it all in,' Flo Caldwell instructed.

Nellie had calmed down a little by the time the police arrived and it soon seemed to Martha that they were completely taking over her home. There were four uniformed officers and three in plain clothes. They could get little out of Nellie except that she'd come home from the pub and found Nora. She had no idea if anyone else had been with her daughter; Nora was a married woman and did as she pleased.

'Where's the husband?' one of the grim-faced CID men asked bluntly.

Martha's patience had reached breaking point. 'Our Frank, my *son*, is away at sea and has been for the past three months. He's with the Harrison Line, so don't you dare to even *think* he had anything to do with ... all this,' she snapped.

He was unfazed by her outburst. 'It had to be asked,' he stated flatly before turning to one of the uniformed officers. 'Jones, get on to the Coroner's Officer, we'll need him down here, and Fingerprints, and get someone to cordon the place off. Hardcastle, you and the lads had better start door to door, see if anyone saw or heard anything.'

Martha was still trembling with shock and indignation at Frank's name being dragged into it as they all left.

'What are we going to do with *her* and *him* when they finally find Bertie Richards?' Mary muttered to Flo.

Flo shrugged and looked questioningly at Martha. Nora had been her daughter-in-law, after all. 'They won't let them back into that house yet.'

'Well, they'll flaming well have to because I'm not having them here all night!' Martha said flatly.

Mary nodded. 'We'll just have to tell the scuffers that they've got to let them back in, they've nowhere else to go. It's not as if they aren't familiar with them, they know the Richards family only too well,' she said. It was terrible what had happened to Nora but it didn't change the facts about that disgraceful lot.

The discussion was cut short by the appearance of young Robbie, who'd heard all the commotion and had come downstairs. He was astounded to see Nellie Richards in his mam's kitchen. 'Mam, what's going on out there, there's scuffers everywhere?'

'Nora's had an . . . accident,' Martha replied.

'What kind of accident?'

Nellie, who had been sitting in a silent daze, started to cry again. 'She's dead! Someone's *murdered* her!'

Robbie's eyes widened with shock. 'Mam, is . . . is . . .'

'Yes. I'm afraid it's true, now you get back up to bed. The police have got everything in hand, there's nothing for you to worry about,' Martha said firmly, pushing him towards the door.

Robbie was halfway down the lobby when he remembered

the man who'd come running out of the entry and nearly knocked him over. He turned around and went back into the kitchen. Jake Harvey; that was who Charlie had said it was and he'd been running as fast as he could away from Harebell Street. He must have murdered Nora.

Chapter Thirty-One

───◆───

THE REST OF THAT night and the following day seemed totally chaotic to Martha. It had been an hour and a half before Fred Seddon and Ernie Caldwell brought Bertie Richards back to Martha's house, a considerably more sober Bertie than when the two men had dragged him out of the Melrose Castle.

'The police want to take a statement from both you and Nellie and then you can go back into your house,' Martha had informed him. As soon as she'd found out that an ambulance had arrived to take Nora to the City Mortuary she'd gone over and told the CID officer who seemed to be in charge that she wasn't having Nellie and Bertie Richards staying the night. Hers was a decent, respectable home.

He'd nodded slowly. 'Understandable, Mrs Ryan,' he'd

said in a clipped tone. 'They're not the most praiseworthy citizens I've ever come across. Bertie's been in the Bridewell overnight on numerous occasions and so has she and I put one of their lads away in Walton myself. Oh, and we'll have to check with the Harrison Line on your son, it's standard procedure,' he'd added as an afterthought.

'You do what you like. The only thing our Frank ever did wrong in his life was to marry Nora Richards, and he's regretted it every day since,' Martha had said curtly.

'Well, he won't have to worry about that any more, will he? He'll be informed, of course,' had been the equally curt reply.

It hadn't been until she'd been lying in bed beside Pat, trying to get to sleep, that it suddenly hit her what he'd meant. Frank was now a free man. She'd reached out and shook Pat hard. 'Pat! Pat, our Frank!'

'What? What . . . about Frank?' Pat had muttered grumpily.

'Now that she – Nora – is dead, he's free! He's free to marry Sophie Teare!'

Pat had grunted and turned over. 'Suppose he is,' he'd muttered.

Martha had lain back, feeling relief wash over her. The nightmare was over for Frank: he could now spend the rest of his life with Sophie. And she, his mother would be able to hold her head up again. Oh, it would be uncharitable in the extreme to say that Nora had got what she deserved, but she'd certainly been no good . . . Martha stopped herself. No one deserved to die in such a terrible way. She'd finally fallen asleep wondering if she should send Lizzie a telegram telling her the news.

The next morning the police were still there making inquiries and so too were the reporters from the newspapers. Young Robbie and his mate Charlie Blackley had both been interviewed and their statements taken, although the superintendent had assured Martha and Mrs Blackley that it was very unlikely that lads of their age would be expected to go to court and give evidence in person. The reporters had wanted to interview the lads too but the superintendent was very firm with them in his refusal to allow that.

Martha, Mary and Flo were all asked to relate the events of the previous night but could give only a few sketchy details. Nellie was a different kettle of fish, however. She told them at great length how she'd come home and found her daughter lying dead and with each telling Nora's character grew more and more spotless. She hadn't been a bad girl, she'd worked hard. It wasn't a happy marriage and her husband had neglected her. He was away at sea for months on end; Nora was still young so wasn't it only natural that she would want to go out a bit, not sit at home night after night.

Martha was outraged when Mary Seddon had relayed this information. 'By the time she's finished that Nora will sound like a flaming saint! Whose fault was it the marriage wasn't happy? How dare she say our Frank "neglected" her! She didn't tell them Nora was in and out of bed with all and sundry, and that it had been going on for years – even when he was away in the Navy – did she?' she raged to Mary.

'Well then, Martha, it's up to you to put the record straight,' Mary stated.

'You'll say nothing, Martha,' Pat said very firmly indeed. 'Do you want our Frank to be a laughing stock in every pub in the city? They've got that Harvey feller, the superintendent told me the Dock Police caught him trying to sneak aboard a freighter and he put up a fight. It will all come out soon enough in court and then, hopefully, it will be forgotten and we can get on with our lives.'

'And has he admitted it?' Mary asked, this being news to her.

'He wouldn't at first, swore he didn't even know her, but after belting one of the constables who was arresting him, having no good explanation as to why he was trying to stow away and being told that he'd been seen and recognised he changed his tune. I don't think they told him the witnesses were only two young lads, and there may have been a bit of "persuasion" involved too, but with all that and his reputation . . .' Pat shrugged.

'He'll hang,' Martha stated.

'Serves him right and he'll be no loss to society,' Pat added. 'So don't get upset about what Nellie's saying, you can bet your life whoever defends Jake Harvey will make sure everyone knows just what she was like and hopefully our Frank will be away when he goes for trial.'

Martha nodded. 'Wait until Lizzie hears all this.'

'The only time she goes away she misses the most shocking thing that has happened around here since the Blitz. When's she back?' Mary asked.

'The day after tomorrow,' Martha replied, wondering if it would be best if Lizzie told Sophie about it, or whether she should do it herself.

Mary's thoughts were running along the same lines. 'Will the Harrison Line get word to Frank?'

Martha nodded. 'Yes, but I'm going to write to him myself and explain . . . everything. He's not due home for another three weeks and I don't think he'll be in any rush to get back for Nora's funeral, even if Harrison's make the offer to try to get him on a faster ship home.'

Lizzie couldn't believe it. Sophie, Bella and Arthur had gone straight to Laurel Road from the Pier Head and they'd come back to Harebell Street. She'd seen the big bold headline on the front of the *Daily Post* as the news vendor had waved a copy at them after they'd come off the ferry, but all it had said was 'WOMAN FOUND STRANGLED. MAN CHARGED'.

'In the name of God Almighty! Nora! Nora Ryan's been murdered!' she cried after Martha had told her.

'The street has been in uproar ever since, you can't go out the door without falling over reporters, police and gawpers. It's sickening that some people find it entertaining to come and stand and stare at Nellie's house.' Martha was full of disapproval. 'That Jake Harvey did it but they caught him down at the docks. We heard he came to the house and found her in bed with some other feller and just went berserk.'

Lizzie nodded slowly. 'I suppose in a way you can understand it, but . . . but . . . to *kill* the girl.'

'He'll probably try to claim it was manslaughter, that he was provoked and didn't mean to kill her,' Jim ventured, shocked by the news himself.

'Fat chance with his record for theft, extortion and violence. He's charged with Murder, Resisting Arrest, Assaulting a Police Officer and Grievous Bodily Harm. They've thrown the book at him,' Martha replied.

'When will they be . . . burying her?' Lizzie enquired.

Martha shrugged. 'Who knows? But I know one thing, Lizzie, I'll be damned if I'll be a hypocrite and go to the funeral. I never liked the girl, I *hated* the way she treated our Frank and I'm not very concerned about "not speaking ill of the dead"; she was no good and everyone knew it. There won't be many in this street who will be going to the funeral.'

'What about your Frank? Does he know?' Lizzie asked.

'The company are sending a wireless message out to the ship but I've written myself, care of the agents in the Canary Islands, giving him all the details. Lord knows what they'll have put in the message,' Martha replied.

'What a thing to come home to and after we'd all had such a good time.' Lizzie suddenly thought of Sophie. 'Martha, I'll have to go down and tell Sophie.'

Martha nodded. 'Do you want me to come with you? It

was quite a while before I realised just what Nora's . . . death means for our Frank and Sophie.'

Lizzie considered this but then decided it would be better if she went alone. There would be plenty of time for Martha to talk to Sophie and she admitted to herself that her friend wasn't always the most tactful of people. 'Thanks for the offer, Martha, but I'll go on my own.'

Sophie was startled to see her aunt again so soon. 'Aunty Lizzie, is something wrong?' she asked as she ushered her in. Arthur was upstairs unpacking and Bella had gone up to the playroom to make sure her family of dolls was all right, for she'd had to leave them behind.

'I think you'd better sit down, luv,' Lizzie urged.

Sophie paled visibly. 'Frank? Is . . . is it Frank?'

'No, luv, but it does affect him.' Briefly Lizzie relayed the details of Nora's death and Sophie's eyes widened with shock.

'Oh, Aunty Lizzie, that's . . . *terrible*!' she gasped.

'I suppose there's some that would say she had it coming, two-timing a feller like that Jake Harvey, but I'm not one of them. She didn't deserve to be murdered.'

Sophie nodded, feeling a surge of pity for Nora although she hadn't liked her. 'That poor unhappy girl. I . . . I feel so sorry for her, it's horrible, just *horrible*.'

Lizzie leaned across and took her hand. 'Harrison's have sent a message to Frank and Martha's written and . . . and well, you do realise what this means, Sophie? Now she's . . . dead, he's a free man.'

Sophie nodded slowly but her eyes were full of tears of pity for Nora Ryan. 'But never in a million years would he have wanted it to end like this, Aunty Lizzie. He had no time for her but he would never have harmed her like that . . . and he had more cause than . . . than Jake Harvey.'

'I know, Sophie, and that feller will dance at the end of a rope for what he's done, but when everything is . . . over, at least you and Frank will have a future together.'

Sophie should have been delighted that Frank was now free but she just couldn't think like that. The circumstances were too tragic.

'Will you write to him now, Sophie? He won't be home for another three weeks, Martha says,' Lizzie asked gently.

'I . . . I don't know.'

'Just to offer your condolences?'

'What could I say, Aunty Lizzie? He didn't love her, he won't miss her, and he hated even being in the same house as her.'

'He won't be home when she's buried,' Lizzie informed her.

Sophie shook her head. 'I think it will be best if I wait until he's home. There are some things it's better to talk about face to face, rather than try to put in a letter.'

'Well, maybe you're right, luv. I'll leave it up to you. I'll get back now, I haven't even unpacked yet and our Billy's going to be a right handful when he hears that Robbie Ryan saw Jake Harvey running away and has given a statement to the police.'

Sophie saw her out and after she closed the front door she leaned against it, wondering how Frank was feeling now. She couldn't write him a letter full of the usual platitudes, they just weren't appropriate in this instance. They would be lies. What was true, though, was how shocked and very sorry she was that Nora had met such a terrible fate.

Chapter Thirty-Two

———◆◆◆———

F RANK HAD BEEN VERY surprised when Captain Fletcher had sent for him and as he knocked on the wardroom door he'd begun to feel uneasy. As far as he knew he'd done nothing to merit this summons.

'You sent for me, sir,' he said respectfully, removing his cap.

The older man nodded, looking grave. It was never easy being the bearer of bad news and this was just about as bad as it could get. 'I've had a wireless message from company headquarters in Liverpool, Ryan.' He picked up a single sheet of paper. 'I think you'd better sit down.'

Frank felt his stomach turn over. His mam? His dad? Not Sophie, please God, not Sophie! he thought.

'It's concerning your wife. Mrs Nora Ryan. I'm not in

possession of all the facts, but . . . but I'm very sorry to have to tell you that she . . . she has been found dead. She'd been murdered.' He paused, wondering if the lad was going to pass out. He'd gone deathly pale. 'If it's any consolation to you, they've got the culprit and he's been charged.' He paused again. 'As we're on our return voyage it won't be feasible to try to transfer you to another ship until we reach Las Palmas, but then if you feel . . .'

Frank shook his head. He was still trying to take it in. Questions hurtled into mind but he didn't voice them. He couldn't. Slowly and a little unsteadily he stood up. 'Thank you, sir, if you don't mind . . .'

Captain Fletcher also got to his feet. 'Of course. You're excused duties for the rest of the day, Ryan. Go and find the bar steward and ask him for a tot of something, tell him I sent you. Is there anything else I can do? Anyone who needs to be contacted?'

Again Frank shook his head and Captain Fletcher escorted him to the door. It was a bad business, this, he thought. A very bad business indeed. Never in all his years at sea had he ever had to impart such news. Death, yes, but not violent death – not in peacetime.

Frank made his way across the deck, automatically avoiding the winches and their cables, and stood gripping the rail, staring out across the vast expanse of flat blue ocean. Nora was *dead*! Someone had *killed* her! Who? Why? When? Where? How? The questions swirled around in his mind. What about his mam, did she know? And . . . and Sophie . . .

He closed his eyes, beginning to tremble with shock. After a few minutes he decided he would go down and get himself a drink, maybe then he could try and take it in, try to make some sense of it.

Nora Ryan's funeral wasn't the small, quiet affair Martha had surmised it would be. The case had attracted so much media attention that many people who had never even known Nora had turned up and there was a piece in the *Echo* the following evening about it.

Few of the neighbours had attended but Lizzie had decided that they couldn't ignore it totally so she'd collected for a communal wreath and had written 'Rest in Peace, Nora, from the residents of Harebell Street', on the card.

Lizzie also heard that for once in his life Bertie Richards had remained sober, at least until later that evening, and that Nellie had been almost dignified. She'd been more smartly turned out than she'd ever been before, probably because she'd realised that the people from the newspapers would be there, so Mary Seddon had remarked. Two of Nora's brothers had also attended, although they hadn't stayed around long afterwards, but not the eldest, who was still in jail.

Sophie had come to see Lizzie the day before the funeral. 'I haven't sent a card to Mrs Richards. I discussed it with Arthur and he said there was no need.'

'He's right. You only lived here for a few months and she caused you enough trouble when she was alive, don't forget,' Lizzie had agreed.

'But I feel as if I should do something, Aunty Lizzie. I think Frank would want me to seeing as he's not here.'

'You can give me a few shillings towards the wreath; that will be enough, Sophie.'

'I didn't know whether to send a wreath from Maria and me?' Sophie had been thinking aloud.

'Definitely not, luv,' Lizzie had said firmly. 'If Nellie saw your name on it, well, it would be like a red rag to a bull. She'd cause a big song and dance and then you'd have those reporter fellers knocking on your door. Leave things be. Pat Ryan has organised a wreath from Frank, just as a token. No "Beloved wife of" or anything like that. Just "RIP Frank".'

'Has . . . has Martha heard anything from him?' Sophie had asked.

Lizzie had shaken her head. 'Frank won't get her letter until they arrive in the Canaries. I suppose he'll reply but it's more likely he'll be home before his letter. It's not like the mail going to America. That goes on Cunard's fast Royal Mail ships or even by plane these days. I don't know who brings it from places like that Las . . . Las something or other.'

'I wrote and told Maria but I haven't heard from her yet,' Sophie had informed her aunt.

'I suppose she's got more important things on her mind, Sophie, and she never had much liking for Nora either.'

Sophie had nodded. She still found it hard to believe that Nora was dead.

'Martha's heard that Jake Harvey's trial is set for the

beginning of next month. At the Crown Court in St George's Hall,' Lizzie had announced. 'It shouldn't take long.'

'Will Frank be home?' Sophie had asked, thinking it would be all over the newspapers again.

Lizzie had nodded grimly. 'Pat is going to see if he can persuade him to do one of those short trips they do in between the long ones. Of course now she's . . . gone . . . he won't have to stay at Nellie's any more; he can go home to Martha's. He won't need to go back to sea at all but Pat feels it would be best if he wasn't here.'

Sophie had nodded her agreement. She didn't want Frank to have to suffer all the questions, the pitying glances, the whispering. He had enough to contend with.

It had taken a few days for it to really sink in, Frank thought as they finally came alongside in Las Palmas and the shipping agent came aboard with, amongst other things, the mail. The sun beat down on his head and shoulders and the collar of his white tropical shirt felt uncomfortable as he stood watching the activity on the dockside. He had his duties, helping to supervise the unloading of cargo, and he was grateful he had something to occupy his mind.

The rest of the crew had been good when they'd heard, he mused. Sympathetic but not overdoing the condolences or asking too many questions. The two older men he shared a cabin with knew how things had stood between him and Nora and had advised him to try to put it all behind him.

He'd worked out that she must have been up to her usual

tricks but this time had taken up with someone who wasn't prepared to tolerate her goings on. If that were the case, he still thought she hadn't deserved to die for it. He'd have to face all that when he got home: her parents, the trial of whoever had killed her; but at least he wouldn't be there for the funeral and no one could cast aspersions or criticise him for it. It was beyond his control. He'd also realised that now at last he was free of her. Free to go back to work at his trade and live in his mam's house – to start with. Free to look with hope to the future, free to love and marry Sophie.

His mother's letter was waiting for him when he at last went below decks and he took it to the tiny room that was used by the crew as a lounge. Everyone who was not on watch was getting ready to go ashore. He opened it and scanned the lines, shaking his head. My God, Jake Harvey of all people! He was an out-and-out gangster; she'd certainly been scraping the barrel. But she hadn't been content with him and everything he'd showered on her and he'd caught her with this other fellow, so his mam wrote. Well, she had indeed picked a real bad one there and she'd paid dearly for her mistake. It had been his own brother, Robbie, who'd seen Harvey running away and the police had more than enough evidence to convict him. He'd hang. Frank sighed heavily; at least justice would be done. He supposed Nellie and Bertie could take some consolation from that.

Martha continued that thankfully Sophie had been away when it had happened. Maria had been married to the young Austrian lad and they'd all gone over to the island for the wedding. She added that when he finally docked in Liverpool he was to come straight home, he wasn't to go and see Nellie and she didn't think it would be wise to go to see Sophie straight away either. These days there seemed to be news-papermen everywhere and she didn't want either himself or Sophie hounded by them. Things were quite bad enough.

He folded the letter and put it back in the envelope. Nora had never really been happy or content, he thought, she had never seemed to know exactly what she wanted from life but it certainly hadn't been himself. If he was honest he had to admit that she hadn't stood much of a chance in life, not with parents like that. Still, he hoped that now at least she was at peace, wherever she was.

He got up and walked slowly across to the desk that was set against the far bulkhead. There was always writing paper and envelopes in one of the drawers. He'd write to both his mam and Sophie. They were in port for almost a week so he could give them to the agent and hopefully the letters would arrive in Liverpool before he did. It wasn't often they got bad weather at this time of year but they had to cross the Bay of Biscay so it wasn't automatically guaranteed. As he sat down and placed a sheet of paper with the company emblem and '*MV City of Exeter*' embossed on the top he felt his spirits lift for the first time since he'd been summoned by Captain Fletcher. He was going home and it was to a better life than he'd envisaged this time last week.

Chapter Thirty-Three

———◆———

ARTHUR HAD PICKED UP the post that morning but on seeing the foreign stamp he realised that it was from Frank and had just handed the letter to Sophie and excused himself.

Her hands shook a little as she opened it. She had wondered if he would write.

My dearest Sophie,

I hope you receive this letter before I get home as there are certain things I want you to know. Mam's letter has just arrived giving me all the details of Nora's tragic death. I had been informed earlier, of course, and so I have had a little time to try to come to terms with it. It was a terrible shock but now I know who she was mixed up with I can understand how it happened. I have to admit that my emotions are still very mixed and rather confused. Shock, revulsion, regret and pity, of course. I never wished her harm, you know that, despite everything. But I also feel a great sense of relief knowing that I am no longer tied to a woman I never loved and actively disliked. Relief that I can look forward to the future and happiness. I want nothing more than to see you, Sophie, the minute I get home, but Mam has advised against it. She says the newspapermen are everywhere as obviously the case has given rise to great public interest. I don't know if she is exaggerating – she often does – but I don't want you to become involved in all the publicity Jake Harvey's trial is bound to generate. I don't want you to be upset, hurt or humiliated in any way, so it might be as well if I leave coming to see you for a while, although it will be very hard to stay away. I wanted to explain this to you so you wouldn't think I don't love you or care about your feelings and reputation. You know, Sophie, how much I love you. Now that I'm free, I am counting the days until I can ask you to marry me.

With all my love,
Frank

She folded it and held it to her. She longed to be on the dockside waiting when his ship tied up but she knew it wasn't possible. How would it look if she was seen running into the arms of a man whose wife had just been murdered and who was hardly cold in her grave? The vilification that would be heaped on both Frank and her would be unbearable. He was right, it would be better if they didn't see each other for a while. As he'd said, it would be hard, very hard, when they had waited so long for this day. There had been times when she'd almost given up hope of that ever happening but now in the not-too-distant future it would, she must be patient for just a while longer, she told herself.

He hadn't said when he hoped to be home and she wondered had that been deliberate? She wondered had he also written to his mother? Very probably. Had he mentioned it to Martha? She got to her feet. She would go and see his mother and find out; it would help a little if she at least *knew* when he would be back in Liverpool.

As she went into the hall Arthur was coming down the stairs. He looked at her anxiously.

'Is everything all right, Sophie? I take it the letter was from Frank? How is he?'

'Yes, it was. He's shocked, of course, but he isn't glad she's dead. He feels nothing but pity for her, but he feels relieved too.'

Arthur nodded. 'That's only to be expected, Sophie. Does he say when he'll be home?'

'No, but I think he's written to his mother too so I'm going to see her. It will help if I at least know . . .'

He smiled at her. 'It will all blow over, Sophie. In a few weeks, when the trial is over, people will forget all about it. There will be some other sensation in the press that will grab their attention and in six months' time no one will even remember who Nora Ryan or Jake Harvey were. The general public has a very short memory, trust me. I know that from experience.'

'Of course you do, Arthur,' she replied sadly.

Martha had wondered if Sophie would come to see her. She'd had a letter in the post that morning and Frank had said he'd written to Sophie too.

She greeted her with a smile. 'Come in, Sophie. At least things have quietened down a bit in the street now the funeral is over.'

'I got a letter from Frank in the post this morning and I wondered if he'd written to you as well.'

Martha put the kettle on. 'He did. He seems to be taking it well enough; I suppose he's had time to get over the shock now.'

Sophie nodded. 'He said he doesn't think it wise if he comes to see me straight away and I think he's right. It wouldn't look . . . right. Not so soon after . . .'

'No, luv, I don't suppose it would.'

'Did he say when he does expect to be home? It's just that if I had some idea . . . ?'

'At the beginning of next week, that's in three days' time, unless they are held up by bad weather in the Bay of Biscay. Pat seems to think they might be – he's always listening to the shipping forecast – though I can't see that myself.'

Sophie pondered this as she sipped her tea. 'It will be hard for him, being just across the road to where . . .'

Martha nodded firmly. 'We'll try to make it as easy as possible for him. I'll go over and collect any of his things that are still at Nellie's. There will be no need for him to go there again. He'll not need to have anything more to do with them. He never got on with them anyway and hated living there. And I'm not having Nellie accusing him of neglecting Nora or anything else either. He was a saint to put up with her and *them* for all these years.' Martha refilled her cup. 'And Pat and I are going to persuade him not to sign off straight away with Harrison's but to do the next short trip over to Hamburg and Rotterdam, that way he won't be here for Jake Harvey's trial.'

'But he'll only be away a week, what if it lasts longer than that?'

Martha looked sceptical. 'It won't. It's a cut-and-dried case. He'll be found guilty and sentenced although I've no idea when they'll hang him. It won't be straight away though – more's the pity.'

Sophie shuddered. 'That will be something else we'll have to contend with.'

'At least it will be the end of it all and we can put it behind us and get on with our lives,' Martha stated briskly.

'So, I suppose it will be a few weeks yet before I can see Frank.' Sophie smiled ruefully. 'It will be very hard for us both.'

Martha reached across and patted her arm. 'I know it will, Sophie. He loves you a great deal, he told me so in the letter.'

Sophie sighed and nodded, trying to fight down the

feelings of impatience and disappointment that had risen in her at Martha's words. 'And I love him too. I . . . I never thought I would ever love anyone again after Andrew was drowned, but I fell in love with Frank although at times it all looked so hopeless. We've waited so long and he . . . he had to put up with so much . . .'

'I know, but it will all soon be over for you both and I'll welcome you as a daughter-in-law with open arms, Sophie.' Martha meant what she said and she thought that all this press interest was terribly unfair on them both. 'You know, luv, there's nothing to stop you paying a visit to Lizzie on Tuesday night, she *is* your aunt and you do often come to see her.'

Sophie looked a little puzzled.

Martha smiled conspiratorially. 'I'm sure it could be arranged for Frank to slip in to see Lizzie at the same time, using the back way in through the entry. Who would know except us and Lizzie's family and none of us are likely to mention it to anyone else.'

Sophie's eyes lit up and she took Martha's hand. 'Could you arrange it?'

'Of course I will. I'll go in to see Lizzie straight after you've gone and I know she'll be delighted. She can make sure that her lot are all out.'

Sophie took her leave feeling much happier than she'd done when she'd arrived. As she walked to the tram stop her step was light and her heart was beating faster. In two short days he would be home and she wouldn't have to wait weeks to see him, just a single day, and then for the first time since that fateful New Year's Eve he would hold her and kiss her and this time there would be no shocked and disapproving glances or justifiably jealous outbursts or attacks from Nora. The waiting would be over and they could plan their future together.

Lizzie was a little put out when Martha informed her that Sophie had been to see her. 'Well, she might have called in to see me as well, I *am* her aunt.'

'Just hold on a minute, Lizzie, will you. She wanted to know when Frank would be home.'

Lizzie frowned. 'I thought you said you'd advised him not to see her straight away. Well, of course he will *want* to but it wouldn't be the wisest thing to do, they wouldn't want the papers to get hold of it.'

'That's what I've come to tell you. I've sorted out a way round it. I had a letter this morning and he'll be home on Monday. No one can read anything into her paying you a visit on Tuesday evening, can they? She often comes to see you and, as you've just said, you're her aunt. So, what I suggested was that when she's here our Frank slips in the back way.'

As understanding dawned Lizzie began to smile. 'Now why didn't I think of that?'

'Do you think you can get rid of your lot for a few hours? Give them a bit of time alone? God knows they deserve it.'

Lizzie nodded enthusiastically. 'Jim and our John can go

for a couple of pints, Katie spends half her life down at Mary Seddon's anyway these days so I'll make sure she's with Matt that night . . .'

'And you and your Billy can come in to me. In fact Pat can go to the pub with Jim as well and the two lads do play well together. There's no need to tell those two what it's all about, Lizzie. The least our Robbie and your Billy know, the better. We can't trust them to keep their mouths shut,' Martha added.

'And Sophie can leave Bella with Arthur Chatsworth,' Lizzie mused. 'So, it's all sorted, Martha, and I'm glad. There will be another wedding in the offing before long, I'll bet. They've waited so long that I can't see them wanting to delay much.' She smiled broadly at her friend. 'Just think, then we'll be related, Martha. He's your son and she's my niece: I'm not quite sure what "relation" that makes us to each other but I think we'll have a cup of tea to celebrate just the same.'

Martha nodded happily. 'It looks as if things will be turning out for the best all round now, Lizzie. Maria already happily married; next it will be Sophie and Frank and then your Katie and Matt Seddon.'

Lizzie grinned at her again. 'It's like trams and buses, Martha. You wait for ages and none turn up and then three come altogether.'

Chapter Thirty-Four

———❖———

SOPHIE HADN'T BEEN ABLE to contain her sheer joy when she'd arrived home. Her sparkling eyes and flushed cheeks gave her away.

'I can see by your face that he'll be home soon, Sophie,' Arthur deduced.

'On Monday, so Martha says, and she is going to arrange with Aunty Lizzie for me to see him in Lizzie's house on Tuesday evening. Neither of us wanted to have to wait but . . . we felt if we were seen together as soon as he got home it would attract the wrong kind of interest and there would be a storm of criticism. So, to all intents and purposes I'll just be going to visit Aunty Lizzie and—'

Arthur smiled. 'Frank will just "happen" to be there too?'

'No, he'll slip in the back way. Oh, Arthur, I'm so happy! I can't believe that now everything is going to be . . .' She flung her arms around him and hugged him.

'You deserve to be happy, Sophie. You both deserve to be happy and I wish you a wonderful future together. When will you tell Bella?'

Sophie hadn't thought about that. In the past she had been so careful not to let the child know that there was anything between her and Frank but now she realised that she would have to break it to her daughter that soon she would have a new father.

'I'll tell her as soon as she comes in from school this afternoon.'

'The sooner the better, Sophie, and I'm sure she'll be happy about it although she might be a bit . . . apprehensive at first.'

Sophie nodded thoughtfully. At least she had a couple of hours to think about what she would say to Bella.

Arthur decided that it would be prudent if he went out and so he put on his jacket, picked up his hat from the hallstand and let himself out quietly half an hour before Bella was due home.

Sophie was waiting at the front gate when Bella at last turned into Laurel Road. Bella walked home with her friends these days, saying she was too old now to be met, but she walked the last few yards alone, having left the others on Hawthorne Road.

'Did you have a good day?' Sophie asked, taking the child's bag and cardigan from her.

'It was *all right*, I suppose, but I'm glad it's Saturday tomorrow. Can I go and play at Anne's house in the afternoon, Mam?'

Sophie nodded. 'Of course you can.'

'Where's Uncle Arthur?' Bella asked on entering the living room and finding it empty.

'I think he's gone out for a walk, he . . . he knew there was something I had to tell you, something important.' Sophie sat down and gently drew the child to her. 'Do you remember your pa, Bella?'

Bella nodded, gazing at her mother. 'I think I do, Mam. He's in heaven with Aunty Hetty, isn't he? Granny Sarah showed me the house where we all used to live, before he went to heaven and we came here.'

'He is.' Sophie paused, she hadn't realised it was going to be this hard and Bella's reaction depended so much on how she put this. 'When he . . . died, Bella, I was very sad. I cried a lot and I missed him and was very lonely even though I had you and I love you very much.'

The child regarded her seriously with her big blue eyes.

'But when we were living with Aunty Lizzie I . . . I became friends with Frank, who lived across the road.'

'Robbie's big brother. I remember him, he's nice. He took us to see that bonfire at the street party.'

Sophie hoped she didn't remember that Nora had also been there that night as well. 'Frank and I were very good friends, Bella, for a long time, and . . . and well, then we discovered that we'd fallen in love.'

'Wasn't he married to that Nora? The one who was killed,' Bella asked.

Sophie sighed. It had been impossible to keep it from the child; everyone in school had heard about it. 'He was married to her but . . . but he didn't love her, Bella. Sometimes that happens, you'll understand when you are grown up. And now that poor Nora is dead, Frank wants to marry me. I still get very lonely sometimes, Bella, and I do love him and I want to marry him. Then he'll be your new pa and he'll be a great pa to you, I promise.'

Bella frowned, trying to digest all this. 'Will you be happy if you marry him, Mam? You won't be lonely any more?' she asked at length.

Sophie nodded. 'I'll be happy. Will you be happy to have a new pa? I want you to be happy, Bella. It's very important to me that you are.'

It was a few seconds before the child nodded slowly. 'I'd like a new pa, Mam. I'm the only one in my class who hasn't got a pa and sometimes I feel . . . left out when all the others talk about theirs.'

Sophie hadn't known that and suddenly she felt the tears prick her eyes. She'd never realised that Bella felt like this. She was aware that Bella looked on Arthur as a grandfather but it wasn't the same. She put her arms around the child. 'Well, you'll have a pa now too, Bella, and he'll love you just as much as your pa in heaven does.'

Bella smiled. 'Can I be a bridesmaid again, Mam?'

Sophie hugged her with relief. 'Of course you can.'

*

Everything looked the same, Frank thought as he walked up Harebell Street towards his parents' house. It was late morning and was already very warm; the cobbles were dusty and little clouds of flies hovered over the rubbish in the gutter. Yes, everything looked the same but it didn't *feel* the same at all. As he drew nearer he glanced over at Nellie's house. As usual the front door stood open, revealing the scuffed, cracked lino, the curtains at the windows were grey with grime, the brasses dull and pitted. There was no sign of life and he felt a wave of relief wash over him. Nora would never taunt, torment or humiliate him again. He would never have to set foot in Nellie's house again either. At the top of the street a group of young lads were playing, swinging on a rope tied to one of the arms of the cast-iron lamppost; his brother was amongst them. He didn't shout or wave to him; he didn't want to call attention to himself. Robbie would be in soon enough for something to eat. Lads of that age always seemed to be hungry.

He paused for a second outside his mam's house. Her door too stood open but the lino was polished, the windows sparkling, the curtains pristine and the brasses well polished. Even the step had been scrubbed.

'Mam, I'm home!' he called as he dropped his kitbag in the lobby, and never had those words been uttered with such enthusiasm and cheerfulness.

Martha instantly appeared from the kitchen, wiping her hands on her apron, her face wreathed in smiles.

'Come on in, Frank, it's good to have you home, and I'm so sorry for the way I treated you in the past, when you were married to Nora.' She hugged him, silently giving thanks that all the trials and sorrows of the past were over at last. 'I've a real treat for you, lad. Homemade cottage pie and with a decent bit of minced beef too. And I've a surprise too! You'll be seeing Sophie tomorrow night.'

'But, Mam, I thought—'

'Don't worry, Lizzie and I have arranged it all. No one will be any the wiser. Now sit yourself down while I get the pie out of the oven.'

Frank digested her words and felt a surge of joy rush through him. 'I've never felt so happy for years, Mam. I know the circumstances are tragic and that things will still be a bit difficult, but as soon as I caught sight of the Three Graces at the Pier Head I felt I was home and that from now on life will be so much better for us all.'

Martha nodded and, putting down the pie, hugged him. 'They will, Frank. They will indeed.'

For Sophie the next four days had seemed unbearably long and when Tuesday at last arrived she knew it would be best if she kept herself busy all day, otherwise she would get herself into such a state of nervous excitement that she'd be fit for nothing. She intended to get to Lizzie's for about eight o'clock. It would of course still be light but at least there would be less activity in the street and fewer people about.

She wanted to take a great deal of care with her appearance

and had decided to wear a navy and white flowered dress with a white jacket over it. Smart but not too brightly coloured: she didn't want to attract attention to herself. She'd put her hair up and wore a small white straw hat with a narrow brim trimmed with navy ribbon.

She had very mixed emotions as she walked towards Harebell Street. Her heart was beating jerkily with happiness, excitement and some nervousness too. There had been times over the weekend when she'd had to pinch herself and tell herself that it really was happening.

As she passed Maggie Dodd's shop, Maggie was just drawing down the blinds.

'You look smart, Sophie. Paying Lizzie a visit?' Maggie asked pleasantly.

'Yes, I haven't been to see her since we got back from Maria's wedding, so I thought I'd pop along this evening for an hour,' Sophie answered, trying to keep her tone calm and matter of fact.

'You were wise, Sophie, what with all that's been going on. Shocking it's been.'

Sophie nodded, looking serious. 'It was a terrible tragedy, Mrs Dodd. We heard about it when we got back from the island. It was such a shock.'

Maggie picked up the tub that held a collection of brushes and brooms and prepared to take them inside. 'Well, it's all over now – bar the shouting as they say, thank God.'

Sophie moved away thankfully. 'Goodnight, Mrs Dodd.'

Maggie nodded and closed the shop door and Sophie

walked on. She was grateful Maggie hadn't mentioned Frank. Maybe she hadn't heard that he was home, although she doubted that. There wasn't much in this neighbourhood that Maggie didn't know about.

As usual Lizzie's front door was slightly ajar and she let herself in. 'Aunty Lizzie! It's me, Sophie,' she called as she went down the lobby. She was hoping Lizzie would let her see Frank in the parlour for there was never any privacy in the kitchen. She stopped dead as the kitchen door opened. Frank was standing in the doorway. Her heart seemed to leap into her throat and she couldn't utter a word. He looked so handsome and so well. It was as though all the anguish and anxiety had been lifted from him.

'Sophie! Oh, Sophie!' he cried, coming towards her.

Then he took her in his arms and she clung to him, still unable to speak. Her heart was so full.

He kissed her tenderly at first but then with increasing passion. 'Oh, Sophie, my darling, I never thought this moment would come.'

She drew away a little, thinking of Lizzie and her family. 'Aunty Lizzie?'

He smiled down at her. 'They're all out; we've the house to ourselves for a couple of hours.'

It was quite a while before they drew apart and Frank led her towards Lizzie's front room. 'Mam planned it all, so we could be alone,' he informed her.

'I'd hoped Lizzie would let us use the parlour as I thought they'd all be in. This . . . this is so much better. Oh, Frank, I can't believe it. I really can't. You're here at last and it . . . it's all over.'

He drew her down onto the sofa. 'There are times when I've thought that too. It's really *over*, Sophie. I'm free. We have a future now – or at least very soon we will.'

She leaned her head on his shoulder. 'There's still the trial, Frank.'

'I know but they've persuaded me to do a last short trip. I know it's only a week but hopefully things will have settled down when I get back. Sophie, I want to marry you as soon as possible – that's if you want to marry me?' he added hopefully.

'Oh, Frank, of course I do! And I don't want to wait for very long either. I've already told Bella.'

He nodded, looking a little anxious. 'How did she take it?'

'Very well.' She smiled up at him. 'She's looking forward to having a new pa and to being a bridesmaid.' She became serious again. 'How long do you think we should wait?'

'I've had plenty of time to think about that, my love. Would you be happy to get married in four weeks? The banns will have to be called, if you want a church wedding.'

'Yes, I'd like it to be in church, Frank, but a very quiet affair. Just us, Bella, Arthur, your parents and Uncle Jim and Aunty Lizzie.'

'Not Maria and her husband and your mother?'

She shook her head. She'd had her family around her the first time she'd been married and it wouldn't be fair to drag them across now. 'Mam is very busy helping Maria to get the tea shop they're opening up and running before the season is over and Hans already has half a dozen contracts for his new tractor. They'll understand, I know they will, and it's not as though it's the first time . . . for either of us.'

'I just wish it could be sooner, Sophie, I love you so much and I want you so much.' He held her tightly.

'I know, Frank, but it really isn't very long to wait and you will be away for a week too. We have a lot of things to talk about and decide on and I will have things to organise, including a dress for Bella. She'll want a new—' she replied before his lips cut off her words.

All too soon they heard Lizzie and Billy returning, Lizzie making rather a lot of noise as she closed the scullery door and loudly informing Billy he was to go straight up to bed as it was way past his bedtime.

Frank stood up, pulling Sophie up with him. 'I think that's the signal for me to go back to Mam's,' he whispered reluctantly.

Sophie smiled. 'She'll be in here any minute now.'

Lizzie's head appeared around the door. 'We're back, so you'd best go now, Frank. Our Billy's safely upstairs. Is everything sorted out?'

'More or less. We hope to get married in four weeks. Frank is going to go and see the vicar at Christ Church tomorrow, I'm going to meet him there,' Sophie informed her.

Lizzie beamed at them. 'I'm delighted and so will Martha be.' She cocked her head to one side, listening. 'That sounds like Jim and Pat coming back. Come into the kitchen, Sophie, and we'll have a cup of tea before you go home,' she instructed before bustling back into the lobby.

Frank kissed her again. 'At least I'll see you tomorrow for an hour, Sophie.'

She held him tightly. 'It won't be long now, Frank, before we never have to say goodbye again.'

Arthur was sitting reading when she arrived back but he looked up expectantly as she came into the sitting room. After Bella had gone to bed he'd had time to think about things, mainly his future.

'Are you relieved now you've seen him, Sophie?'

She took off her jacket and hat and sat down. 'Yes, and I'm so happy, Arthur. He looks so well; that dejected, hopeless air has gone. We're getting married in four weeks; we're going to see the vicar at Christ Church tomorrow. It will be very quiet, just family – which includes you.'

He nodded. He'd been certain she would include him. 'And have you discussed where you will live and what Frank will do?'

'Not in great detail. He hopes to go back to his trade and I suppose we'll live here.'

'I've been thinking about that, Sophie.'

'Arthur, it won't affect you. This is your home and always will be, you know that.'

'But you'll want some time together, alone as man and wife, Sophie.'

Lyn Andrews

'With Bella too. She'll need time to get used to Frank,' she reminded him.

'Of course, but you can do without me hanging around the place too. So I've decided to go and pay a visit to my cousin Edward in Vermont. He's asked me to go often enough and now I feel the time is right. I'm getting a bit long in the tooth and don't want to leave it much longer and I have the money Hetty left me. It's too far to go for a short visit, so I'll be away for a few months. I was thinking of returning in November, before the weather gets too bad.' He smiled at her. 'That will give all three of you time to get settled.'

Sophie nodded and then smiled. 'You are such a considerate man, Arthur, and I really do appreciate it.'

'There is no one more considerate or generous than you, Sophie. Why don't you bring Frank back here tomorrow after you've seen the vicar? I'd like to see him. I really didn't get to know him very well when I lived with your aunt and it's very quiet around here. No one will comment on his visit and you can spend some time together. After all, he might like to see what is to be his new home. The only time he ever came here, he only got as far as the hall.'

Sophie remembered that day. 'I know and it will be nice to have more time alone with him as, sadly, he'll be going away again at the weekend.'

Arthur looked serious. 'It's for the best, Sophie. The sooner this whole sorry business is over the better.'

Epilogue

———◆———

IT WAS EASY TO see that winter was on its way now, Sophie thought as she drew back the curtains that Sunday morning. The trees that lined the road were almost bare, as were the rose bushes in the tiny garden, and there was a dusting of frost on the pavements. She drew her dressing gown more closely to her as she went back to the bed and shook Frank gently.

'Time to get up, Frank. It's a special day today, remember, and I've already heard Bella up and about.'

Frank reluctantly opened his eyes. 'It's Sunday, Sophie. Don't we usually have a lie-in on a Sunday morning?'

Sophie smiled at him. They had been married for nearly four months and they were so happy. 'We do, but not this morning. Up you get, Mr Ryan.'

'Not until I get my morning kiss, Mrs Ryan,' Frank replied, reaching out and drawing her towards him. He loved her even more now than when they'd been married. Ever since that day his life had changed. He had a wife he adored and a very comfortable home. Bella was a delight; they got on so well and on Sunday afternoons he often took her on outings. He had a steady job working at the trade to which he'd served his time, that of a joiner, which he enjoyed. Sophie didn't do a great deal of sewing now; she didn't need to work at all but she insisted on making clothes for a few of the ladies who had patronised her since she'd first started her business. Sophie was content living in Liverpool, she and his mother got on well together and Martha often came to visit, as did Lizzie. Sarah wrote as often as she could, more frequently of late now that the summer visitors had mainly gone. The tea shop had proved to be very popular, as had Hans and his tractor, and they were very happy with their life. Frank planned to take Sophie and Bella for a holiday to that misty little island, next spring or summer. He didn't want Bella to lose touch with her grandmother and aunt or her heritage.

'You've forgotten that we've to be at Lime Street Station for half past eleven, haven't you?' Sophie chided him gently, sitting beside him on the bed. 'Arthur is coming home today. Oh, and I have a surprise for you too.'

Frank sat up. He had indeed forgotten that Arthur would be arriving on the train from London. The *Queen Mary* had docked late last night and Arthur was taking the boat train from Southampton to Euston very early this morning. 'I have to admit I had forgotten. What kind of surprise?'

Sophie smiled happily and bent and kissed him on the forehead. 'Next year you are going to be a father.'

Frank gasped in surprise and took her in his arms. 'You're sure, Sophie?'

'I'm sure and I wanted to tell you before Arthur gets home, so we can meet him as a real "family" now.'

'Oh, Sophie! I love you so much and I'm the happiest man alive today!'

'Now, will you get up and we'll go and tell Bella that she is going to have a brother or a sister.'

Frank got up instantly. 'First of all I'm going to make you a cup of tea, then I'll bring Bella in and we'll tell her together. You just stay here and rest, you'll have to take care of yourself now, Sophie.'

She laughed. 'Frank, I'm pregnant, I'm not ill. Don't forget I've been through this once before? But go bring Bella up and we'll tell her. Then we really will have to get our skates on.'

Bella was almost as delighted by the news as Frank. 'Can I have a baby sister, Mam, please?' she begged, bouncing up and down on the bed.

Sophie laughed. 'I'm afraid it doesn't quite work like that, Bella. We have to have what God gives us and I'm sure you'll love a baby brother just as much. We'll have to start thinking of names. You can help us choose, can't she, Frank?'

'We wouldn't dream of choosing a name without asking you, Bella,' Frank said seriously.

'We'll have to have two sets of names then, won't we, Pa?'

Frank nodded. 'We will indeed so you'd better put your thinking cap on,' he replied, smiling happily. There was nothing else in life he could wish for now.

The station concourse wasn't too crowded, it being Sunday, Sophie thought as they stood at the barrier. With clouds of steam and the hissing and clanking of brakes the train pulled slowly in and came to a standstill.

'Can you see Uncle Arthur, Mam?' Bella asked impatiently, hopping from foot to foot. He'd sent her lots of postcards and on the last one he said he'd brought her some souvenirs as gifts.

'Not yet, there are a lot of people getting off and he has to get a porter to help him with his luggage,' Sophie replied. Frank had his arm protectively around her and she smiled up at him. It had been good to have the house to themselves for the months Arthur had been away but she'd missed him too.

'There he is now,' Frank said, pointing out to Bella the smartly turned-out gentleman accompanied by a porter, his cases neatly stacked on a trolley.

'Uncle Arthur! We're over here and we've got a surprise for you! I'm getting a baby sister – or brother!' Bella cried out, waving madly, her cheeks flushed and her blue eyes shining with excitement.

Sophie looked up at Frank and shook her head, laughing. 'Oh, Bella Teare! What a way to tell Uncle Arthur!'

Arthur looked bemused as he hugged first Bella and then

Sophie, and shook Frank warmly by the hand. 'Did I hear that correctly? My ears are not deceiving me, are they?'

'No. We were going to tell you but not in quite such a public way,' Sophie answered. 'And welcome home, we've missed you,' she added.

Arthur smiled broadly at them. 'Congratulations! What wonderful news.'

Frank looked pleased and proud. 'We think so too.'

Arthur took Bella's hand. 'I couldn't have wished for a nicer surprise or a better homecoming. I've missed you too.'

Frank looked across to the taxi rank. He'd already decided that Arthur had so much luggage that it would be impossible to get the tram home and besides, he was going to take special care of Sophie, she was very precious and this *was* a special occasion. He smiled at Arthur and Bella. 'We'll get a taxi home. I have to take good care of my family from now on.'

Bella skipped along excitedly beside Arthur and Frank and Sophie followed. 'And we're a very happy and contented "family" too,' Sophie added, her eyes shining.

Now you can buy any of these other bestselling books
by **Lyn Andrews** from your bookshop
or *direct from her publisher*.

FREE P&P AND UK DELIVERY

(Overseas and Ireland £3.50 per book)

To Love and to Cherish	£6.99
A Secret in the Family	£6.99
A Daughter's Journey	£6.99
Days of Hope	£6.99
Far From Home	£6.99
Every Mother's Son	£6.99
Friends Forever	£6.99
A Mother's Love	£6.99
Across a Summer Sea	£6.99
When Daylight Comes	£6.99
A Wing and a Prayer	£6.99
Love and a Promise	£6.99
The House on Lonely Street	£6.99
My Sister's Child	£6.99
Take These Broken Wings	£6.99
The Ties That Bind	£6.99
Angels of Mercy	£6.99
When Tomorrow Dawns	£6.99
From This Day Forth	£6.99
Where the Mersey Flows	£6.99
Liverpool Songbird	£6.99
The Sisters O'Donnell	£6.99
The Leaving of Liverpool	£6.99
Ellan Vannin	£6.99
Mersey Blues	£6.99

TO ORDER SIMPLY CALL THIS NUMBER

01235 400 414

or visit our website: www.headline.co.uk

Prices and availability subject to change without notice

It is 1945 and the war is finally over. But for sisters Sophie
and Maria, who have no choice but to leave their beloved home
on the Isle of Man, the upheaval is just beginning.

Eighteen-year-old Maria is loath to leave the island, as it's
there she met Hans Bonhoeffer, a young Austrian interned
during the war. For widowed Sophie, however, Liverpool
offers exciting opportunities. As Maria longs for a reunion
with Hans, Sophie is drawn to Frank Ryan, a man who is not
free to be with her. Will the sisters ever find happiness?

Praise for Lyn Andrews' compelling novels:

'An outstanding storyteller' *Woman's Weekly*

'A vivid portrayal of life' *Best*

'A compelling read' *Woman's Own*

headline
Fiction

e also available in
ebook and audio

www.headline.co.uk
£8.99
ISBN 978-0-7553-7186-0

9 780755 371860

Cover: www.headdesign.co.uk; background
© Planet News/Science & Society Picture Library
Author photograph © Michael Trevillion